I Know an Old Lady

Margaret Standafer

I Know an Old Lady

By Margaret Standafer

Cover Art: Kristin Bryant, kristindesign100@gmail.com

For Abby,
Who in the midst of a global pandemic, watching her wedding dreams fall apart around her, displayed nothing but grace. Thank you for reminding us all it's about a lifetime, not a day, thank you for marrying my son, and welcome to our family. We're lucky to have you!

1

I know an old lady who swallowed a fly
I don't know why she swallowed a fly
I guess she'll die.

I know an old lady who swallowed a spider
That wriggled and jiggled and tickled inside her
She swallowed the spider to catch the fly
But I don't know why she swallowed the fly
I guess she'll die.

Billy mumbled the words to himself and pedaled with the rhythm as he made his way along the dusty gravel road to her house. It was hot, easily ninety degrees, and he cursed the heat, the dust coating his bare legs and making them itch, the rusty bicycle that made biking far more work than it should be, and the old lady he was on his way to see as he sweated and started making up his own words.

I know an old lady who swallowed a fly
I know damn well why she swallowed the fly
She's too mean to die.

I know an old lady who swallowed a spider
But it wasn't poisonous, and it didn't kill her
She swallowed the spider to catch the fly
I know damn well why she swallowed the fly
I'm not lucky enough for her to die.

The song always reminded him of his sister. With the real words, not his words. He and Tracy used to sing it, laughing at the silliness of it, when they'd run through their wheat fields. Back when they had wheat fields. Back when there were things to laugh about.

His eyes burned the way they always did when he thought about Tracy, about how much he missed her. Not that he'd ever admit it—the tears or the fact that he missed her—but he did. A lot. So he made himself stop thinking about her and instead focused on the ugly, weathered, grey house that grew closer far too quickly.

Under the blistering sun, Billy swore he could see the paint peeling and curling, falling right off the warped siding. She was going to make him paint it, he knew she was. She'd snapped something to that effect a couple of times during the past week. Billy hoped she'd forget about it, but knew she wouldn't. Her Swiss cheese memory was maddeningly hole-free when it came to the crappy stuff.

And he'd probably have to paint the fence too. The brand new fence that mocked him every time he passed it.

Billy turned off the road and into her yard, keeping his back to the stupid fence. He threw down his bike on the lawn that was more weeds than it was lawn. But those weeds were meticulously cut since Billy mowed them once a week. Twice the week before since she'd been in a particularly foul mood. It had been the first thing she'd told him when he'd knocked on her door for the first time two-and-a-half weeks ago.

'Mower's in the shed, boy. Get busy.'

No introductions, no instructions, nothing but barked orders followed by a door slammed in his face. Today, like most days since, a note was taped to the door telling him what she expected him to do. Not that he needed the note. The paint cans on the porch were notice enough.

"Damn, bullshit paint," Billy muttered as he kicked at a can and ripped the note from the door. He swiped his arm across his forehead. He'd soaked through his shirt on the ride over and the sweating didn't show any signs of letting up. Billy eyed the house, looked up to the sky, and tried to work out whether he'd be able to somehow keep himself in the shade while he painted. Maybe if he moved from one side of the house to another…

Those hopes were dashed when he looked at the note.

Start with the back. Don't skimp on the scraping.

Scraping? What the hell did that mean? He looked down again at the paint cans and spotted a couple of rusty-handled things that looked kind of like his mom's old kitchen tools. The things she'd used when she made pancakes.

Billy hadn't eaten a pancake in five years.

He kicked the paint can again, hard enough this time that the pain in his big toe was almost worse than the pain in his heart.

Next to the flat things was some kind of brush. He picked it up and ran his hand over the bristles. Metal. Hard and sharp. He turned it over in his hands, squinted at the house, then took a tentative swipe across the peeling paint. Dirty, grey flakes snowed down and covered his hand and wrist.

"Well, shit."

He looked up, down, and across the expanse of the wide house front. He let his eyes wander to the right and pictured the high, flat wall dotted with windows on that side of the house. To the left, more of the same. The back, the side that faced the barn, had another door, a lot more windows, and endless, endless siding.

The job would take him the rest of his life.

Billy threw down the brush and trudged to the side of the house in search of the hose. He twisted the faucet and after a rattle and a thump, water sputtered from the end of the mottled green hose that was coiled tightly enough and hidden well enough by the weeds it looked like a snake ready to strike. He kind of wished it would. He felt ready for a fight.

He waited, then flicked one finger through the stream. Still too hot. He'd learned his lesson the week before when ready to pass out from the heat, he'd staggered to the hose, turned it on, and stuck his mouth under the stream, gulping. The scalding water that filled his mouth and splashed on his face had led to a stream of a different kind. Billy had been rather proud of the inventive swear words he'd screamed at the top of his lungs, but they had gotten the old lady out of her house and had gotten Billy an additional hour of work that day.

So now, he waited. When the water finally cooled enough, Billy sucked down what felt like gallons, but he knew within the hour he'd feel like he hadn't had a drop in days.

Damn Kansas summer.

When he returned to the front door, she was waiting.

"You turn that hose off all the way? It was dripping the other day."

"It's off."

"Better be." She looked him up and down. "You know how to paint?"

"Dip the brush in the paint then rub it on the house? I think I can handle it."

She fisted her hands on her hips and scowled at him. "Don't get smart with me, boy. Did you read the note? There's scraping needs to be done."

"I read it."

"I want all that old paint off before the new goes on, you hear me?"

"I hear you."

"Show me."

"Huh?"

"Show me you know what you're doing. Start scraping."

4

Billy huffed out his breath and slanted his eyes at the woman who had stepped all the way out of the door to stand behind him and watch. He picked up the brush he'd used earlier and stretching his hand over his head, ran it down over the rough, wood siding. Like before, flecks of paint fluttered to the ground.

"No, no, no. I thought you said you knew what you were doing?"

"You told me to scrape. I scraped. What the hell do you want?"

Her eyes narrowed to slits. "What did I tell you about language?"

Billy grunted at her and waited for the lecture he was certain would follow. Instead, she bent over with a grunt of her own and picked up one of the flat, kitchen tool-like things.

"This way, or you'll damage the wood."

She slid the tool from right to left. Larger curls of paint fell and with a couple of swipes, she cleared most of the board. She held out her hand for the brush, then used it to sweep lightly over what she'd already scraped to finish the job.

"Use this first." She pushed the scraper toward him. "It will take off most of the paint. Clean it up with the brush. And go easy."

"Yes ma'am."

Billy took the tools back from her. He clamped his teeth down on his tongue to keep himself from asking her why the hell she didn't just do the job herself if she thought she was so damn good at it. He didn't want more extra hours.

"Got it?"

"Yeah."

"Get the back scraped then paint that side before you move to the next side. Work from the top, down. You'll need a ladder. It's in the barn."

Billy froze, still bent over and reaching for the paint can.

"The barn? But—"

"Go in, get the ladder, and get out. It's on the left side. Don't expect the lights to work."

He didn't say any more, didn't ask any more questions, just stood and walked toward the barn. He heard her follow him off the porch, around the side of the house. Her eyes bored holes in his back, but he kept his trained on the barn door, not giving her the satisfaction of turning to look at her.

The door stuck with his first pull, catching on the dirt that years of relentless winds had piled in front of it. Billy kicked at the dirt, smoothing the pile and lowering it enough that he figured the door would swing over it. He was rewarded with a loud creak as the rusty hinges protested the unwelcome interruption of their years-long slumber.

Old, rotting hay, the faint memory of the animals that once called the barn home, and the acrid tang of gasoline and diesel fuel all blanketed under years of dust assailed Billy's nose. He sneezed.

It was dark; the only bit of light coming from the sunlight able to sneak through the partially open door or through the cracked and rotting boards of the barn's walls. The only windows were up high and were too dirty to let in much light. Part of him wanted to explore, to search, to find what he knew—what everyone knew—had to be there, somewhere, but another part of him wanted to run, didn't want to find anything but a ladder.

He'd been told from day one to stay out of the barn, that there was no reason for him to go inside as everything he'd need he'd find in the shed. She must not have considered he'd need a ladder for painting. Or, she'd forgotten where the ladder was. Whatever the reason, he was inside for the first time.

He turned his head one way, then the other. It wasn't so bad. If his friends were there, if she wasn't standing on the side of the house watching and waiting, if he had a flashlight, he'd look around. Yeah, he told himself, he'd look around. He wasn't afraid. The stories were true, everyone knew they were true, but he wasn't afraid. He stood up straighter and puffed out his chest.

When the door slammed shut behind him with enough force

to shake the walls and block out most of what little light there was, he crouched and threw his arms over his head. But nearly as quickly, he jumped up and looked around, as embarrassed as if he'd had an audience.

"Damn wind," he muttered as he pushed the door back open to let in what light he could.

The ladder was on the left, as she'd said, about twenty feet from the door, propped against the wall between an old milk can and a couple of shovels. Billy shuffled through the dirt and bits of trampled hay to grab it and hoist it over his shoulder. When he turned to head back for the door, the end of the ladder knocked over the shovels and sent up a cloud of dust that engulfed him. Sneezing again and swearing between each sneeze, he stomped out the door, kicking it closed behind him.

He watched her eye him, nod to herself when the barn door closed, then turn back toward the house without a word. Fine by him.

After an hour, Billy decided there wasn't much worse than scraping paint off an old house. He had paint flecks in his hair, in his eyes, all over his arms, and because he couldn't stop himself from swearing about the stupid job, the rickety ladder, and the endless expanse of warped siding, in his mouth.

At that moment, he hated Old Lady Baxter more than he'd ever hated anyone. And that was saying something as he had a long list of people he hated. To pass the time while he scraped, he listed and ranked them in his head.

Number One: Old Lady Baxter. It was her fault he was spending his summer slaving away under the blazing sun instead of hanging out at the lake with his friends and watching Julie Tucker who he knew would fill out her bikini far better than she had the year before.

Number Two: Damn Judge O'Malley. Also to blame for how he was spending his summer. While Billy begrudgingly admitted to himself that even scraping paint was better than jail, he still hated Judge O'Malley. And he always would.

Number Three: Cancer. Okay, so cancer wasn't a person, but he could still hate it. Five years ago, it had taken away his mom as viciously as if it had been a real live person wielding a gun. He could certainly hate it.

Number Four: His dad. Four and a half years ago, his dad had stopped giving a damn and started drinking. If life hadn't already been shitty enough, it got really shitty then.

Number Five: His Aunt Cindy. Four years and five months ago, Aunt Cindy took Tracy to live with her. Any bullshit she'd tried to feed him about wanting to take him too, about how sorry she was she didn't have the room, about how she knew that he wouldn't want to leave his home and his friends anyway, was just that. Bullshit. She didn't want a pain-in-the-ass troublemaker. Billy was smart enough to figure that out.

Number Six: His friends. They got to spend the summer at the lake, or working for money instead of for free. And getting their driver's licenses.

Number Seven: Himself.

2

Billy sucked on the stub of his cigarette until it burned his fingers. It was his last, the last of the pack he'd had sitting, untouched, on his dresser since school let out. He'd thought about getting more, about smoking them behind Old Lady Baxter's house, then denying it when she smelled the smoke, but as much as he liked the idea of messing with her, he'd realized he didn't much like smoking. Mostly, it was just another thing to do that he wasn't supposed to do, and without his friends around, he'd stop seeing the point of it.

As he blew out the last stream of smoke, he flicked the butt to the ground and with his next step, crushed it with the toe of his beat-up sneaker. Beat-up and paint-splattered. As if he needed another reason to hate painting, now he'd have to wear crappy looking shoes since no amount of scrubbing had taken off all the blotches of yellow. Yeah, that had been a fun surprise. The old hag decided her house should be yellow. Probably to be sure the paint really stood out on his white Adidas. He'd also learned once he finally finished painting the whole damn house yellow, he'd have to go back and paint the doors and trim white. The doors and trim that were now black. He hadn't a doubt she'd chosen the colors that would be the biggest pain in the ass.

"Hey, man, thought you moved or something."

John, seated on the bench of a picnic table, his back to the table and his long legs stretched out toward the parking lot of the drive-in restaurant, laughed at himself. A mug of root beer and a basket of fries sat untouched on the table behind him.

Bugs swarmed around the overhead lights, buzzing and crackling when they made the fatal decision to kamikaze themselves into the irresistible glow. John waved a hand in front of his face when one got too close.

"What's up?" Billy asked. He sat next to John, mimicking John's posture and once he was settled, letting his eyes scan the cars filling all the available parking spots. He recognized most of them. Typical Friday night in Munroe.

"Hanging out, waiting to see if you'd show up."

"I'm here."

John turned his head and looked at Billy. "Where you been? Haven't seen you since school got out."

"You know where I've been."

"During the day, yeah, but at night? Didn't even see you last weekend. Tried calling. No answer at your house."

"Mr. Thompson's letting me work some nights. Stocking shelves and cleaning and stuff."

"I thought he was pissed that you had to back out of the bagging job."

"He was pissed, really pissed, but he gave me a few hours a week at night. Some weekend hours. I guess Isaac finally got himself a real job and told his dad he's done working at the store. Mr. Thompson was desperate."

"That loser got a job? Doing what? He's the dumbest excuse for a human I've ever known."

Billy snorted. "Dumb as hell. Mr. Thompson said the elevator gave him a job in the office."

"He'll screw it up and be back at the grocery store by the end of the summer. I still don't know how he graduated from high school. Teacher's probably got so sick of him they finally just gave him a diploma."

"What about you? What've you been doing?"

"Working. Hanging out. Going to the lake when I'm not working."

"Yeah?"

"Been there a few times."

"How's that?"

"It's good."

"Lots of people there?"

"Bunch of moms with little kids."

"You know what I mean."

"Yeah, I know what you mean. She's been there. Got herself a new bikini. It's pink."

"Man..."

Billy let his imagination run with visions of Julie in a pink bikini, but the roar of a souped-up Firebird interrupted his thoughts. The car crawled past the drive-in, its driver revving the engine every few seconds while he smirked out the open window at everyone who turned to look.

"God, Randy is such a jackass," John said.

"He been around the lake? Him and Terrence?"

"Yeah. Terrence follows Julie around like a puppy, always waving his money around, buying her ice cream or a Coke or something."

"And Julie?"

"She's too nice to tell him to bug off, but everyone knows she can't stand him. Everyone except Terrence."

Billy wasn't sure that was true, but he appreciated John saying so. "He get a car yet?"

"Not yet. He says he's waiting for the seventy-threes to come out. Camaro, blue with white stripes. I'd say he's full of shit, but his dad's probably stupid enough to buy it for him."

"Probably, but Terrence is definitely stupid enough to crash it within a week. We've got that to look forward to."

"What a sweet car, though."

"Yeah, it is a sweet car."

Billy and John were both lost in car fantasies when Steve and Joel joined them. Steve dipped his hand in the basket of fries, pulled out a handful, and shoved them in his mouth.

"Help yourself," John said.

"Don't mind if I do."

"What's going on?" Joel asked. "Nice to finally see you, Billy."

"Same stuff, same people, same town, same everything," John said. "Nothing ever happens here, you know that."

"A guy can hope," Joel said.

"You guys have to order something if you're going to sit here. Boss is in tonight. Sorry about that."

Billy looked up at Linda who gave him a smile. Linda was a year ahead of them in school, had been working at the drive-in for two years, and would likely be working there for the next forty. Linda didn't set her sights very high. Everyone knew she'd marry Bud, everyone knew Bud would treat her like shit, but everyone, including Bud, knew she'd put up with it. Just like her mother put up with it from her father. But Linda was nice, always snuck them extra food when she could, and didn't harass them all that much about sitting there and not ordering.

"I'll take a root beer," Billy said.

"Me too, and some onion rings," Joel said.

Steve paused and cocked his head at Linda. "Me three, and since I got my first check today, burgers are on me. Bring us four."

Linda blinked in surprise. That was more food than the four of them ordered all last summer. "You got it. Being a working man looks good on you, Steve."

"Wow, big spender. They must pay you well at the gas station," John said.

"Well enough." Steve glanced around the parking lot then lowered his voice and said, "Well enough that I got us this." He unrolled the jacket he had bundled under his arm and gave them a peek at the bottle of whiskey hidden inside.

"Now things are looking up." John rubbed his hands together.

"How'd you get it?"

"Talked my sister into buying it for me. Cost me an extra two bucks, but what the hell."

"She won't tell your mom?" Joel asked.

"Nah. She tells Mom about the whiskey, I'll tell Mom she's running around with Fitch again. Mom'll skin her alive."

"Fitch? Your sister could get any guy in town. What does she want with that creep?" John asked. "Tell her I'll date her."

"I'll be sure to tell her. I'm sure now that Carrie's twenty-one, she's hoping a sixteen-year-old will ask her out."

Linda delivered their burgers and they dug in. Billy was starving. Like usual, there'd been nothing at home but some stale bread and a couple slices of bologna. He'd made a sandwich, finishing the little bit of bologna, and taken it with him to Old Lady Baxter's for lunch. He'd hear about it later, he was sure.

Mr. Thompson had told him he'd get a discount now at the grocery store so as soon as he got his first check, he'd buy some food. He'd just have to get stuff he could keep in his room and away from his dad. His dad had no problem eating, just had a problem remembering to buy food instead of booze.

"Tell me more about Old Lady Baxter's," Steve said. "What's she making you do?"

"More?" John asked. "When did he tell you any?"

"Saw him the other night when he was going into the grocery store. I was leaving the gas station. We had a minute to talk."

Billy swallowed his bite of burger. "Any kind of crap she can come up with. Mowing, weeding her garden, washing her car, replacing some boards on the old chicken coop, and now painting. Painting the whole damn house."

John choked on his burger. "The whole house? It's huge!"

"You're telling me. I've been painting all week, and you can hardly tell. I've got sunburn on top of sunburn. Not sure there's actually any skin left on my back."

"Do you have to talk to her?" Steve asked.

"Not much. Most of the time she leaves a note telling me what to do."

Steve scrunched up his face. "What do you do when you have to go to the bathroom? Do you go in her house?"

"God, no. There's an old outhouse. It's full of cobwebs and mosquitoes, but it's better than asking if I can go inside."

"Okay, hold on," Joel said. "I have some questions." He took a gulp of root beer, then held up a hand and proceeded to tick off items on his fingers. "An outhouse? It still works? Disgusting." He raised a second finger. "Chicken coop? She doesn't have any chickens, at least she didn't the last time I was there. You should have told her fixing it is stupid. Her car? She still drives? Isn't she about a hundred? And most importantly, have you found any bones?"

John shook his head at Joel and scoffed. "How does an outhouse quit working? It's a hole in the ground."

With an eye roll at Joel, Billy started answering questions. "Yeah, the outhouse is disgusting, but I figure it's better than her house." His friends nodded their agreement. "She's getting some chickens, at least that's what she said, so I had to fix the coop. Probably just bullshit, though. Yes, she still drives. I had to ride with her yesterday when she went to buy more paint. And chicken feed. She needed me to lift it. I was pretty sure I was going to die in that car. And no bones."

Billy paused and looked around at his friends. Joel looked disappointed. Out of all of them, he'd always been the most fascinated with the stories about Old Lady Baxter, always wanting to sneak onto her property and snoop. He twisted his mouth in a frown and leaned a freckle-covered cheek into his hand. Under the yellow lights of the drive-in, those freckles stood out like oranges in a bushel of apples.

Steve looked sympathetic, his blue eyes landing on Billy's and, Billy thought, somehow with just a look, speaking volumes. Steve understood best what Billy's life had been like for the past five years. Understood how eager Billy had been to start his first real job, to make some money, to further the break from his father. How hard it had been when Billy'd been handed his sentence. Steve's dad died when Steve was just a little kid, and he'd grown up with only a mom. So, Steve understood, but only some of it because Steve's mom was nice and she tried. A mom was way better than a dad, in Billy's opinion.

John looked bored. His shaggy, brown hair flopped over his eyes and he pushed it away as he'd been doing since Billy sat down. John craved excitement, needed it like most people needed air, and excitement was hard to come by in Munroe, Kansas.

"I did get inside the barn the other day, though."

"Old Lady Baxter's barn? You were in the barn?" John sat up straighter and his eyes lit up.

"Yeah, but just for a minute to get a ladder. Haven't been back inside."

"What did it look like?" Joel asked. "Did you find any evidence? Dried blood? Ripped clothes? Anything?"

"It looked like any old barn. I didn't have time to look around much cuz she was standing there waiting for me. There was nothing much to see but some rusty old junk."

"Right, right," Joel said. "It wouldn't be in plain sight. Probably buried or inside an old crate or something. You'll have to look around more next time."

"I don't know that there'll be a next time. That was one of her first rules, that I had to stay away from the barn, that I couldn't go inside under any circumstances. Guess she forgot I'd need the ladder to paint."

"See? She's worried," Joel said, leaning back with a satisfied nod. "She's hiding something, for sure."

"It's been thirty years," Billy said. "Seems like enough time that she would have gotten rid of whatever there was to get rid of."

"Maybe not. Maybe she kept stuff. Like souvenirs," Joel argued.

"Maybe we find out for ourselves," John said.

"What do you mean?" Billy asked.

"Let's go. Now. Let's go look," John said.

Joel threw his hands up in the air. "I've been telling you that for years!"

"We never had someone who knew their way around her property before. Who knows what's in the barn." John's eyes landed on Billy.

"I told you, I've only been in the barn for a few minutes. About all I know is that when I opened the door, it screamed louder than Mr. Kramer did when you started a fire in chemistry lab. No way you're gonna get in there quietly."

"Now that was funny. I wonder if all Lisa Stemen's hair has grown back?" John said. His eyes looked skyward and he grinned at the memory. But then he looked back at Billy. "Don't distract me. Let's go check it out. We'll open the door nice and slow. It won't make any noise."

"We can't. I can't. I'm in enough trouble. If she catches me hanging around there at night, I'll be working for her until I'm dead."

"She won't catch you," Joel said.

"I can probably get my mom's car," Steve said.

"What?" All three voices roared at once.

"She's out somewhere with friends from work, said she wouldn't be home until eleven, or so. My sister's out. They both got picked up so the car's there."

"Why didn't you say something earlier? We've been sitting here like idiots when we could have been driving around like idiots instead?" John said.

"She told me not to take it, keeps saying I haven't had enough practice since getting my license and I can't drive at night, but what the hell? I'll be careful and I'll have it back long before she gets home."

John slapped Steve on the back. "Now you're talking." He stood and reached for his root beer, gulping down what remained in his mug, then raised a hand in Linda's direction. "Thanks, Linda." He dropped a dollar on the table, giving Linda the first tip she'd ever gotten from the four of them.

They headed away from the glow of the drive-in lights.

"I've got my bike over by the school," Billy said. "We need to walk that way."

"Shit," John grumbled. "That's the opposite direction of Steve's house."

"It's not far out of the way. Quit complaining," Joel said. "Walking will give us time to plan. Do you think we should bring along some flashlights and shovels and stuff?"

"We're not going inside. I already told you that," Billy said.

"No," John corrected. "You said *you're* not going inside."

Once they were a couple of blocks away from the drive-in and on a mostly deserted street, Steve twisted the cap off the bottle of whiskey he'd kept hidden under his jacket. He took a swig, then winced and tried to cover his cough. He passed the bottle to Joel.

"Here's how I see it," John said. "We drive to Billy's house, then walk to Old Lady Baxter's from there to be sure she won't hear the car. If something happens and we need to hide, we can hide in the fields. Does she have any dogs around, Billy?"

"No," Billy said on a sigh.

They were at the school, so Billy grabbed his bike from the rack. He pedaled slowly, weaving in and out of the other three as they continued down the street.

"Good. We don't have to worry about barking alerting her that we're there." It was John's turn to take a swig from the bottle. He paused and gulped. Then he coughed and some sprayed from his mouth. "Shit, Steve, what kind of swill is this?"

"The cheap kind. You don't like it, you get some."

"I think it burned a hole in my throat," John complained.

"That means it's good," Steve said.

"So, we leave the car at Billy's, we walk to her house…does she still have a fence all the way around?" Joel asked.

"Yeah, same fence, with a nice new section," Billy answered.

"I'll probably have to paint that too."

"Not if she's in jail," Joel said. "That should be reason enough for you to want to get in that barn and find something."

Billy pulled one hand off the handlebars of his bike to take the bottle from John. He took a swig of the whiskey. It burned all the way to his belly. He had to agree with John. It was horrible, but he swallowed it without flinching.

"I'll be the one in jail if I get caught," Billy answered. "No way I'm going in front of that damn Judge O'Malley again and watch him grin while he tells me all about Leavenworth."

"He's full of shit. They don't send sixteen-year-olds to Leavenworth just for starting a fire in some old lady's field," John said.

Billy figured John was probably right, but also figured he wasn't taking any chances. The bottle made another round and Billy took another swig. It wasn't quite as awful the second time around.

"Maybe they'll send *her* to Leavenworth," Joel said. "Murder's a big deal."

"They don't send ladies to Leavenworth, you jackass," John said.

"Well, then they'll send her to some lady prison. Who cares where she goes. We find the evidence, we'll be heroes, and Billy won't have to paint her damn house."

They were on Steve's street, his house only a few houses away, when Steve told them, "You guys wait here. I want to make sure no one's around. The neighbors won't pay any attention to me, but they might notice four of us and say something to my mom. I'll be right back."

While he continued down the street, the rest of them waited. Billy leaned his bicycle against the corner street sign and sat down on the curb. "I can't go in that barn, you guys. No way. Maybe I can look around one day next week using the excuse I need some tool or something, but I can't go in there at night when I'm not supposed to be there."

"You're probably right," John conceded. "You can wait outside and be the lookout."

Billy breathed a little easier but was saved from answering when Steve pulled up in his mom's car.

John jumped in the front seat when Steve got out to open the trunk for Billy. They wedged his bike in as best they could, then Steve got back behind the wheel and Billy joined Joel in the back seat.

Billy had never ridden in a car with one of his friends before. It was a strange feeling. He felt grown up, free, like the whole world was suddenly open to him, but at the same time, he couldn't quite quash the feeling, the fear, that they'd get in trouble, that he'd somehow be blamed, that there was no way the night would end well.

But his friends were whooping and hollering, celebrating their newfound freedom, and Billy decided to hold on to that feeling and ignore the rest.

"Can I park at your house, Billy?" Steve asked. "Is your dad around?"

They all knew to avoid his dad. On a good day, he'd ignore them, maybe tell them all how stupid they were, but mostly just ignore them. On a bad day, it was anyone's guess. He'd taken a swing at John, he'd thrown a beer can at Joel, and he'd told Steve his mom was a whore. More than once. Mostly, Billy's friends didn't come around much.

"I haven't seen him for a couple days," Billy answered. "He usually comes home sometime before morning but he's never awake when I leave for Old Lady Baxter's. By the time I get home, he's gone again. It's Friday night. I doubt he's home, but turn off the lights and drive slow. His truck will be out front if he's there."

The truck wasn't there. Still, Billy went in first, checked out the living room and his dad's bedroom, before the others joined him.

"Love what you've done with the place," John said.

Billy looked around at the mess. The empty beer cans, the crumpled wrappers, the old newspapers, the dirty dishes. Living with it every day, he'd stopped seeing it. Pointed out to him, it was disgusting. His mom had insisted on a tidy house. He and Tracy had to keep their toys picked up and were expected to help with chores.

He remembered how he'd complained.

He wished, with every bit of him that could wish, to hear his mom tell him to pick up his erector set.

Billy bit down on the inside of his cheek until he tasted blood, until the pain distracted him enough that he could answer John.

"My dad's a slob. Every couple weeks he gets in a mood and starts hollering at me to clean the place up." Billy shrugged. "Guess he hasn't seen me enough lately to do any hollering."

Billy picked up the newspapers that littered the couch and shoved some beer cans out of the way to clear the coffee table. His friends dropped into seats. Steve passed the bottle to John.

"What, no more for you?" Joel asked.

"If my mom figures out I took the car, that's bad enough. If she smells booze on my breath, she'll beat the piss out of me. After she takes away my driver's license. Shit, Billy will be driving before I will."

John laughed and choked on his slug of whisky. "My eight-year-old-sister will be driving before Billy. And that's crap, Steve, your mom has never done more than pretend to swat at you with a wooden spoon."

"Maybe, but she tells me at least once a day about all the stuff she's gonna do if I get in trouble with the car or with booze."

"It's Friday night. If my parents smell booze in the morning, they'll just assume they're smelling themselves," John said. "Cheers!" He tipped the bottle and took another gulp.

"Okay. We need a plan," Joel said. "Billy, do you have any flashlights?"

"This is a bad idea," Billy said.

"It's the best idea we've had in a long time," Joel said. "We know the barn door is unlocked, we know we have to open it slowly, we know Old Lady Baxter doesn't have dogs around any more, the wheat is tall enough that it will hide us if we need to hide…it's like it was meant to be."

"Joel's right. Let's get moving. Steve has to have the car home before eleven. It'll be plenty dark by the time we get there," John said. He was back on his feet. Billy could almost see the excitement emanating from him.

"Flashlights, Billy?" Joel said.

Billy sighed and pushed to his feet. "Yeah. No idea if the batteries work, though."

Billy went to the kitchen and pulled open the drawer that held everything from unpaid bills to brittle rubber bands. He pushed aside old receipts and dried up pens, found a pack of Juicy Fruit and tucked it in his pocket. When he moved aside a sheet of paper to grab the flashlight he spotted beneath it, his eyes landed on a picture of his mother. From one of the funeral cards handed out like trading cards at the church where Billy was told he needed to say goodbye, she smiled at him.

Billy's breath caught and his heart pounded. For one moment, he laid a finger on his mom's face, remembering the happy, blue eyes, the light brown hair she rolled up in prickly curlers and covered with a hairnet, the faint line of freckles across her nose that she tried to cover with the powder that came from the case with a mirror she always had in her purse.

Before tears flooded his eyes, eyes that matched exactly those in the picture he'd just looked at, Billy grabbed the flashlight and slammed the drawer shut. He blinked as he walked back to the living room, making sure his friends wouldn't be able to spot any trace of tears in his blue eyes.

"Found one," he said when he rejoined them. He pushed the button and was surprised when a beam of light shone across the ragged carpet.

"Got any more?" Joel asked.

"How do I know? One's enough."

21

Billy walked toward the door, desperate to get away from the house and away from the memories.

"So, we're doing this?" Steve asked when they stood in Billy's back yard and looked across acres of wheat in the direction of Old Lady Baxter's house.

"Oh, we're doing this. It's going to go down as the best night of our lives. Generations from now, people will talk about us and how we solved the mystery no cop has been able to solve for thirty years, right Joel?" John said. "Come on."

John led the way with Joel on his heels. Steve glanced at Billy, but Billy just shrugged and trudged after them.

Billy's friends may not have grown up on farms, but like everyone in Munroe, heck, Billy thought, probably everyone in Kansas, they knew enough to skirt the wheat fields. Old Lady Baxter would seem like a pussycat compared to a pissed off farmer discovering his fields flattened by a bunch of kids. So, instead of a direct line, they followed the dusty road.

"How close do you reckon we can get before she can see us?" Joel asked.

"I don't know," Billy said. "Depends if she's still up. Her living room faces the front, her bedroom is in the back."

John stopped walking and turned back to face Billy. "Gross! Why do you know where her bedroom is?"

"I told you," Billy hissed through gritted teeth, "I have to paint the house. The curtains were open, I could see inside."

"Does she have a broomstick in the corner?" Joel asked, barely able to talk over his laughter. "There's still a Wicked Witch of the South that's unaccounted for, I hear."

Billy laughed along with him. Things seemed funnier than they had earlier in the evening. "Didn't see it, but she probably hides it during the day. Maybe we need to watch the sky rather than the windows."

The bottle made another round. Billy took another gulp. He tried to remember just how many gulps he'd had, but his thoughts were a little fuzzy.

"And watch for her flying monkeys," John said, laughing and stumbling over his feet. "Boo monkeys with little jackets."

Joel threw back his head and his laughter boomed. "You said 'boo monkeys.'"

"I did not. I said boo...blue monkeys."

"Shut up, you guys, we're almost there," Steve said.

Billy turned his grin, a grin he couldn't seem to wipe from his face, toward Old Lady Baxter's house. There it was, in all its hideous glory. Damn, it was big, he thought as he let his eyes wander from the ground to the pointed roof where two attic windows reflected the glare from her yard light and glowed like the eyes of a jack-o'-lantern.

They stopped far enough away that the darkness provided cover. One after the other, they dropped to lean their elbows on the split-rail fence that circled her yard.

"Can't see any lights on inside," Joel whispered.

"Remember, Billy said her bedroom's in back." John tried to whisper, but it turned into a burp. He clapped his hand over his mouth to stifle the laugh that followed.

"Gimme the flashlight, Billy," Joel said. "I think we should go around this side," he pointed to the left, "that way we'll be hidden by the garage for a while. When we get past the garage, we'll have to run to the barn."

"You can't use the flashlight," Billy said, "she might see the light."

"We're not going to use it until we get inside. Duh. We're not stupid," Joel said.

"Besides," John said, "we're faster than she is. If she sees us, all we have to do is run. There's no way she'll catch us."

"Yeah!" That seemed like an excellent idea to Billy and he wondered why he hadn't thought of it. The old lady could hardly walk; she certainly couldn't chase them. Maybe he should go along. It didn't seem that scary now that they were there. If there were no lights on at the front of the house, that meant she was sleeping, or at least upstairs. It would take her about an hour to get downstairs. They'd be long gone.

"Unless she comes on her broomstick," Steve said.

This time, they all had to smack their hands over their mouths to quiet their laughs. Then they stood for a few minutes, in the still silence that was a steamy, June night, and stared at the house.

"Hey, maybe I *should* come along," Billy said. "Like you said, I'm the only one who's been inside—"

"Shh!" Steve hissed and smacked Billy on the arm. "Listen."

At first, Billy heard nothing but the far-off chirp of a cricket. Then he heard it too. Footsteps. Coming fast.

"What the hell?" John whispered. "Is it her?"

"It's coming from down the road. Someone's running. Does someone know we're here?" Joel's whisper quavered as his bravado dissolved in a puddle of fear.

"Hide!" Steve commanded as he put a hand on the fence rail and flung his legs over.

Billy followed Steve, John and Joel right behind him. They ran, as fast as their legs would churn, the fifty yards to the edge of the wheat field. Once there, they dove with the precision of a team of synchronized swimmers, head first into the field. Muffled 'oofs' sounded as the ground knocked the breath from their heaving chests.

Billy turned, the three-foot-high, golden stalks providing cover, and peered toward the road. If someone was after them, if they needed to run, he wanted to have as much a head start as possible.

With the moon only about half-full, there wasn't much light. The footsteps still sounded, but Billy didn't see anyone coming toward them. His stomach roiled, the mixture of fear and crappy whiskey inching up his throat. He swallowed and prayed everything would stay down.

"Who is it?" Steve whispered. "Can anyone see anything?"

"There!" Joel said, too loudly, and earned himself an elbow in the ribs from John.

The white shorts stood out in the pale moonlight, as did the white shoes. The shirt was darker. The figure ran along the road, hugging the fence line where just a few moments before Billy and his friends had rested, but that figure never slowed, never turned its head.

"It's a guy," John said. "Where is he going? Do you think he saw us and is going to tell Old Lady Baxter?"

They waited, but he ran past the house and kept going.

Billy blew out a breath, then started to laugh and his stomach started to feel better. "It's just Skelly. Little Skelly. He runs."

"What do you mean, he runs? Runs where?" Steve asked.

"Just runs. I see him once in a while."

"What the hell for? Does he think he's in the Olympics or something?" John asked.

"I heard Big Skelly talking to my dad a while back. Said when Little Skelly came home from college he brought some fancy ideas with him. Fancy ideas about how to run the farm, fancy ideas about healthy food, healthy lifestyle, all kinds of shit. Big Skelly's words. I guess running around like a moron is part of it."

"That's the craziest damn thing I've ever heard," Joel said. "Unless one of them flying monkeys is after me, I'm not running anywhere I can walk."

They got to their feet and started back toward the fence.

"Does Skelly work these fields?" Steve asked.

"Yeah. He's been trying to buy the land from Old Lady Baxter ever since he bought our land, but she won't sell, will only lease it to him."

"Of course, she won't sell. Probably full of graves," Joel said.

They were back at the road. John looked in the direction Little Skelly had run. "Will he come back this way?"

Billy shrugged. "I don't know. Probably. Has to get back home sooner or later."

"Then we should probably get out of here," John said. "We don't have time to wait around until after he decides to go home."

Billy saw John dig his fist into his stomach and figured John felt about as lousy as he felt.

"Yeah, I've gotta get the car home," Steve said.

They started walking, retracing their steps back to Billy's house.

"Got a cigarette, Billy?" John asked. "I hear smoking in the middle of a bunch of wheat is a good idea."

"Funny, man, funny," Billy said.

They walked in silence for a while. Billy listened for the sound of footsteps and kept an eye out for his dad's truck. He wasn't sure which he dreaded more.

After a while, Joel broke the silence. "I still don't get it. He just runs?"

3

Monday morning came all too soon. Billy scowled as Old Lady Baxter's house loomed in front of him, looking bigger than ever. Maybe if he could see some yellow instead of nothing but dirty white, he'd feel a little better. But no. From the road, none of his work of the last week showed. All that told Billy was that he had a hell of a lot of painting left to do. And scraping. Can't forget the stupid scraping.

He'd even dreamt about it. The endless back and forth over the rough boards, the paint flecks raining down on him, the countless trips up and down the ladder. In his dream, he'd finished one side of the house, picked up the ladder to go to the next side, and found it stretched as far as he could see. Old Lady Baxter shouted at him to get moving, said he couldn't leave until he finished the job. A stupid dream maybe, but when he looked at the house, it didn't seem that far-fetched.

And he was tired before he even started. He'd spent his Sunday cleaning up his house. His dad hadn't been around enough to get to the hollering, but after Friday night, after his friends had commented on the mess, he'd decided he needed to do something about it. So, he'd hauled out trash, washed dishes, wiped up spilled drinks and food, vacuumed and swept, and even tried to clean up the bathroom. Never quite sure what cleaning stuff to use where, he'd just thrown some of the powder in the yellow container on everything and scrubbed it with a rag.

Billy remembered his mom using that stuff. She'd always called it cleanser and to a much younger Billy, the word had sounded an awful lot like cleaner, so in his mind, that was what to use for cleaning just about anything that needed cleaning.

For a while after his mom died, some of the ladies who lived nearby or who had been friends with his mom had come over and cleaned, washed clothes, cooked. That stopped a few years ago, though, and he and his dad had been on their own ever since. While Billy had always hated when those ladies came and did the stuff his mom should have been doing—and looked at him with pitying glances all the while they did it—he wished they'd come back. His dad wasn't any good at most of the house stuff and lately he'd pretty much given up even trying. Once in a while Billy would find some clean clothes in his room or find something to eat other than crap that came out of a can, but not often.

Even though cleaning the whole house had been hard, and even though he'd had to bike to town and mop floors and straighten shelves for four hours at Mr. Thompson's grocery store after he'd finished cleaning at his own house, it had felt good to wake up that morning to a clean house.

But that didn't change the fact that he was tired. As he dropped his bike in front of Old Lady Baxter's house, he knew it was only going to get worse. Sighing, he walked to the porch, grabbed the paint cans and all the painting and scraping tools he'd left there on Friday, and since there was no note telling him differently, started around to the back of the house.

His mood got worse when he tipped his head back and looked up. He remembered finishing more of the high part. He kicked at the dirt and swore. He'd be spending most of the day on the ladder again and he was plenty sick of the ladder, the up and down, the moving it a foot at a time to reach another section. Such a waste of time. As he grabbed the ladder and slammed it into position, inspiration struck.

The barn was full of old crap. There had to be another ladder or two in there, some old boards. He could rig up some sort of platform, some sort of scaffolding. Instead of dozens of trips up and down, he could walk across the platform.

Proud of himself, he almost smiled until he realized he'd have to ask Old Lady Baxter if he could go back inside the barn. Part of him wanted to just go search and deal with the consequences if and when he had to, but the other part of him, the logical part that overruled the gutsy part, was afraid. Not of her, exactly, but of what she might tell Judge O'Malley. Taking the chance that Judge O'Malley would increase his sentence, or change it to something even worse, wasn't worth it.

Resigning himself to facing her, Billy stomped back to the porch and with a deep breath, knocked on her door. He tapped his foot and fanned himself with his faded Royals ball cap for what seemed like hours before he finally heard her shuffling across the floor. It took another two minutes for her to unlock the door and open it.

She was nearly a foot shorter than Billy's six feet, so he had to look down. Her pink scalp showed through the thin grey hair that, like always, was pulled back into a bun. Billy briefly wondered how long that hair was and why she didn't just cut it off. The face that looked up at him was so deeply wrinkled it looked like someone had taken a knife and carved grooves in her cheeks. Not realizing he was doing it, Billy rubbed a hand over his own smooth cheek.

"Mornin', Mrs. Baxter. I was wondering if you might have another ladder or two in the barn and if I could use them?"

"What happened to the ladder you were using last week? Did you break it, boy?"

Billy gritted his teeth and bit back his smart-ass reply. "No, ma'am. I just thought if there's another, and maybe some old boards, I could rig up some kind of platform so I wouldn't have to go up and down the ladder all the time. It'd make the painting job go faster."

The old lady's cloudy eyes bored into him from behind thick glasses. Billy knew she was trying to spot signs he was lying. Maybe she'd seen them by her fence on Friday night. It wouldn't have been hard to figure out what they were doing there, she'd been chasing kids off her property for decades, and now here he was, asking her to let him in the barn.

Just when Billy was ready to tell her to forget it and get out from under her scrutiny, she waved a hand in the direction of the barn.

"There's probably something in there you can use. Be careful you don't hurt yourself."

"Oh. I will be. Thanks."

Billy turned to leave, eager to get away from those eyes he'd started to think could see right through him. Before he made it off the porch, he heard her again.

"Clever idea, boy. You might be smarter than I thought."

Since she didn't ask him a question, Billy saw no reason to respond. Or turn around. He walked toward the barn and played her last words over in his mind. Was there some sort of insult hidden in there somewhere? It hadn't sounded like it, but he couldn't be sure. An actual compliment, though, seemed unlikely. Was she messing with his mind? Trying to get him to let down his guard?

"Nuh uh," Billy muttered as he pulled open the creaky barn door. "Not falling for…"

Billy lost his train of thought when he stepped inside the barn. He realized he could take a little more time, look around a little more than the last time. This time, he had an excuse. Wanting as much light as possible, Billy propped open the door with an old bucket. He wished for a flashlight…and for his friends there beside him. He chuckled when he imagined Joel inside the barn, his lifelong dream come true. The closest they'd ever gotten to achieving that dream happened a couple years earlier when they'd snuck into Old Lady Baxter's yard and actually made it all the way to the barn. They'd tried to peer through a crack in one of the boards, but hadn't been able to see anything. As they'd been whispering about what they should do next, whether they dared try the door, the outside lights came on. Every one of them had nearly wet their pants. The lights had turned off just as quickly, as if she'd just flipped the wrong switch, but it had been enough to send them running. Even Joel hadn't wanted to go back for a while.

And now Billy was inside and without Old Lady Baxter watching and waiting. First, he just looked. His eyes travelled along the wall where he'd found the first ladder and he saw shovels, rakes, a broom, the kind of stuff he'd expect to see in any barn. Along the other wall, where the remains of some stalls stood, what he could see looked to be more of the same. The floor in front of him was littered with buckets, engine parts, gas cans, a couple of old wheelbarrows, some galvanized steel tubs. Again, no surprises. Also, no ladders.

Not sure what he'd expected to find, Billy walked toward the back wall. For years, Joel had been telling him there'd be graves dug in the floor of the barn. Or there'd be crates or something that could hold the bodies. Billy hadn't ever believed it, not entirely anyway, but now, creeping through the barn that had been the source of so much curiosity for so many years, he felt the icy fingers of fear march up his back and tickle his neck.

Telling himself he was being stupid, he scratched at the back of his neck and kept going. It got darker the farther he went, so he didn't notice the tarps right away.

Old, holey, and oil-stained, at least four of them were draped over something in the back corner. Something big. Those icy fingers were back, and this time they were doing more than marching. Billy shivered.

He walked slowly, his eyes darting from left to right. He realized he should have asked if the lights in the barn were broken or if they just needed new light bulbs. If he could have screwed in a couple of light bulbs, if he could see what he was doing, he'd feel a lot better about things.

Boards were piled on top of the tarps to keep them in place. The boards were just what he needed, so taking them off of whatever the tarps covered was justified. Billy grabbed the first one and lifted it, letting it come to rest on his shoulder. In case Old Lady Baxter was keeping an eye on the barn, Billy decided he should haul a couple of the boards outside to make it seem like he was doing what he was supposed to be doing.

When the first one hit the ground in a cloud of dust, Billy risked a glance toward the house. He didn't see her, but that didn't mean she wasn't watching. The house had about a hundred windows. Deciding she probably was watching, Billy made quick work of getting two more boards out in front of the barn. On his fourth trip back inside, Billy paused in front of whatever it was the tarps were covering. Telling himself to stop being a chicken, he lifted the corner, slowly at first, but once he caught a glimpse, he yanked the tarp away with a gasp.

A car. A really old, really cool car, the likes of which he'd only seen in movies. It was black, kind of boxy looking, with skinny wheels, a huge front grill, and a hood ornament that looked to be some kind of bird. A spare tire was fitted between the driver's door and the driver's side front fender. The headlights sat up high, big and round. Billy pulled off the remaining tarps and studied the car more closely. Running boards, something Billy had only ever seen on trucks but even wider, were situated beneath both the driver and the passenger doors.

He wanted to climb up to get a better look inside, but was afraid of damaging the car, so settled for what he could see by craning his neck. The steering wheel jutted out and looked kind of funny without anything around it. Same with the gear shift. It stuck up out of the floor and hung there, looking like it belonged in a tractor rather than a car. There were some gauges and dials, some chrome switches that he figured maybe controlled the lights, a glove compartment, and seats that seemed to be leather and in good shape.

Why a car like that was sitting in an old barn that likely couldn't withstand a good storm, was a mystery. Unless he thought like Joel and it was hiding something. Maybe a hole in the floor beneath the car? Billy dropped down to his knees but in the dim light, couldn't see anything out of the ordinary. Maybe evidence, like blood, in the car itself? Again, without better light, he had no way of knowing.

More than likely, it was there because it had been there for years and Old Lady Baxter didn't know what to do with it. Still, it seemed suspicious. Not quite ready to give up because he knew his friends would never let him hear the end of it if he did, he inched his hand toward the handle on the driver's door, lifted it, and eased open the door. With a deep breath, he slipped inside.

Getting a better look, Billy realized the car looked hardly used. He couldn't spot a mark or a tear anywhere on the seats, there were no scratches, dents, or dings on the dashboard, and even the floors looked clean. Gaining confidence, Billy popped open the glove compartment but found nothing inside except for a couple of old Diamond Motor Oil road maps, one of Kansas and one of Missouri. He squinted and tried to read the dates. It looked like 1933 on both of them.

He peeked into the back seat, but found nothing. The car was empty, as far as he could tell. While he wasn't sure what he'd expected to find, finding nothing was disappointing. It would be even more disappointing for Joel.

Billy decided he'd wasted enough time and needed to get busy finding a ladder. With a last look around the inside of the car, and being careful not to scratch or mark anything, he climbed out and closed the door. He grabbed one of the tarps and tossed it over the roof of the car. When it slid all the way over and landed on the opposite side, Billy cursed and circled around. The car was parked at an odd angle, sort of sideways in the barn. It was even darker in the corner blocked by the car, but when Billy went to get the tarp, he noticed what he hadn't noticed in his excitement at discovering the car.

Pushed back into the corner were a half dozen fifty-five-gallon drums. Billy knocked on the side of one and was rewarded with a dead-sounding thud, not the hollow ring of an empty drum. Curious, he knocked on the rest. Same thing. He yanked on the top of one to see if it came loose, but found it securely closed, as were the other five.

Steel drums were nothing unusual on a farm, there were a bunch littering his own yard and barn, but not full ones. He knew what Joel would say. *Plenty big enough to hold a kid.* Billy found himself agreeing.

Even though chances were good Old Lady Baxter hadn't been inside the barn in years and probably wouldn't be making a trip there anytime soon, Billy knew there was no way he could risk opening one. Besides, he'd need tools. Maybe another day, on another trip inside the barn. Billy thought about it. Maybe a trip she didn't know about, and a trip with someone else there beside him. Depending what he found, Billy wasn't sure he wanted to find it alone. With a last glance over his shoulder, Billy got the tarps back in place as fast as he could, then got away from the barrels as fast as he could.

He was more than ready to get out of the barn, but hadn't found a ladder. He walked by the stalls, peering into each as he did so. More junk was piled in every one. How did one person have so much junk? Billy knew his barn didn't have nearly the amount of crap hers did, but then, his dad had sold a lot of their stuff when he'd sold off their land. Maybe since his dad wasn't as old, he just hadn't had as many years to accumulate crap.

Then a thought stopped him in his tracks and had him turning in a circle to take in all of it at once. What if she told him once he finished painting, he had to clean out the barn? It was definitely a crappy enough job that she'd probably love to make him do it. Assuming she wasn't hiding anything in those drums. Billy looked around at the mountains of junk. It might be worse than painting.

Worried he'd already been in the barn too long, he decided he'd think about that later. He needed ladders, so he continued his walk along the row of stalls. Sometimes, he had to go inside and push aside junk to see what was behind it. His efforts were rewarded when, in the fifth stall, he found a stepladder—rickety-looking but better than nothing—propped up against the back wall. He lugged it outside and dropped it next to the boards.

Billy studied the pile on the ground. With the extension ladder he'd been using, the stepladder he'd just found, and the boards, he still needed a third ladder to make his plan work. Ideally, another step ladder to work with the first one so he could run a board or two between them. He trudged back inside.

His search of the remaining stalls turned up nothing useful. The only place left to look was up. There was a ladder to the hayloft, a tall one which was good, but just an old, wooden, straight ladder that wouldn't work for his plan unless he could figure out a way to brace it. That would have to be a last resort.

He climbed to the hayloft and was met with more junk. And hay, some loose, some baled, but scattered all over the place. More tools, hay forks, a stack of wood, old chain…it seemed the amount of junk was endless. Then, in the corner, he spotted another ladder, standing open and leading to another small platform at the back of the hayloft. Billy stood at the bottom of the ladder and looked up. With a few windows on this level of the barn, there was a little more light. It didn't look like there was anything on that platform, just a scattering of hay, and Billy decided he was done exploring for the day, anyway. He grabbed the ladder, folded it, and hauled it to the opening down to the main floor. He maneuvered it into position so he could lie down on his stomach and slide the ladder down as far as he could reach, then drop it to the ground. It looked as rickety as the others he'd found, but it survived the drop.

Having lost a half hour in the barn, the sun was higher in the sky and hotter than when he'd arrived. Even with his cap on, Billy had to wipe sweat out of his eyes twice before he managed to rig up a platform of sorts between the two ladders. With the straight ladder still against the house and the other two with the boards between them positioned in front of the straight ladder, the contraption showed promise.

Once he finished, Billy stood back to study it. He gave it a shake. Unsteady at best. Deadly at worst. What the hell, he figured, maybe crashing to his death would be better than painting. Or, maybe he'd break an arm or leg. No way she could expect him to paint a house with a broken leg. At least, he didn't think so.

Tucking the brushes and tools into the pockets of his cutoff jeans and grabbing hold of a paint can, Billy climbed the ladder. He squeezed his way between the house and the platform, then turned and clambered onto his makeshift scaffolding. When it didn't immediately crash down around him, Billy let out the breath he'd been holding. Carefully, he unloaded his pockets, set down the paint can, and took a couple of tentative steps. Gaining confidence with each successful step, Billy decided the old lady had been right. He was smarter than she'd thought.

Through trial and error, Billy learned he couldn't walk too far to either side before the boards tilted under his weight. A trip back to the barn yielded a couple of clamps which he used to secure the boards to the steps of the ladder and solve that problem.

Since the highest part of the house was done, and since Billy was nearly six feet tall, he was pleased to find he could stretch high enough to reach the topmost boards from his platform. The best part came when he worked his way down a few feet and could sit while he painted. The job didn't seem nearly as bad when he was sitting.

But the brutal midday sun baking his arms and the back of his neck threatened to take away even that bit of relief. Billy looked around him. There wasn't a cloud to be seen in the blue sky and not the slightest ripple in the endless acres of golden wheat that normally danced and swayed to the rhythm of the wind.

When he couldn't take it any longer, and deciding it was close enough to lunchtime that he'd eat the candy bar he'd brought with him, Billy climbed down from his perch and headed for the corner of the porch where he'd left the chocolate out of the sunlight.

As he rounded the corner and stepped onto the porch, he stopped short. On the rusty little table that sat between two metal, clamshell-backed lawn chairs, was what looked like a glass of lemonade and a plate with a sandwich.

Billy turned and looked over his shoulder, wondering if Old Lady Baxter was nearby and getting ready to eat her lunch on the porch, but he didn't see any sign of her. Not wanting to run into her but also not wanting to give up the shade the porch provided, Billy stayed on the far end, just out of the sun, and ate his candy bar, watching the door for any sign she was on her way out.

When she didn't appear, Billy inched closer to the table and found he'd been right. It was, in fact, a tall glass of lemonade, the ice cubes not yet melted, and a plate holding a sandwich. Billy's mouth watered. He stayed a few feet away from the table, but leaned forward when what he thought was a napkin tucked under the plate looked, as he got closer, to be a note.

Keeping his eyes moving between the door and the front windows, Billy walked to the table and picked up the piece of paper.

Eat some lunch and take a few minutes out of the sun.

Shocked, Billy's head whipped from side to side, certain it was some sort of trick. His first thought was his friends, that they'd been bored and decided to mess with him. They were probably hiding, watching and waiting to see what he'd do.

But when he looked again at the paper, it didn't look like one of his friends had written the note. It looked like shaky, old lady writing.

Maybe it was from her, and maybe it was poisoned. Billy considered that for a moment, but deemed it unlikely. First of all, she'd probably have a hard time explaining a dead kid and a half-eaten sandwich on her porch. Besides, much like falling off the scaffolding, dead Billy wouldn't be able to paint.

Billy reached for the lemonade and when the cool glass met his sweaty hand, his knees almost buckled. At that moment, he decided he didn't care where the lemonade and sandwich had come from, they were ending up in his stomach.

He took a few greedy gulps of the lemonade, then held the glass to his forehead, to the back of his neck. That was almost better than drinking it.

He didn't sit, just grabbed the sandwich with his other hand and took a huge bite, chomping on it with his mouth wide open. He was starving. A sandwich and a candy bar would be the most he'd eaten for lunch since his last school lunch a few weeks ago. Even though school lunches were always crappy, at least it was food to put in his stomach.

The sandwich was gone in less than two minutes, the lemonade a few seconds after that. Billy took his time with the ice cubes that remained, holding them in his mouth and letting them numb his tongue and cheeks. He took one in his hand and ran it over his neck until it melted. Then he wondered what he was supposed to do next.

Ring the doorbell and return the dishes? Leave the stuff on the porch? Write her a note thanking her? He considered. He didn't have a pencil so he couldn't write a note. He didn't want to have to talk to her, so didn't want to ring the doorbell. Just leaving the plate and glass where he'd found them seemed like the best option, so he set the glass on top of the plate and jogged off the porch before he had to face her. He paused at the corner of the porch and peeked back toward the front door. There was no sign of her. Billy shrugged, then circled around to the side of the house and finished off his lunch with a long drink from the hose. He decided to sit, for just a minute, in the sliver of shade alongside the house. He leaned back and pulled his cap over his eyes.

He hadn't intended on falling asleep, but when he woke with a start, he knew he was in trouble. The sun was lower in the sky —not too much, but enough that he knew he'd been sleeping long enough that she'd have plenty reason to yell at him.

Billy jumped to his feet and jogged back to the scaffolding. As fast as he could manage, he climbed up, gave the paint a stir, and started painting, watching out of the corner of his eye for any sign of Old Lady Baxter.

When she didn't show up and when enough time had passed that he'd managed to make up for lost time, he relaxed and let his mind wander back to what he'd seen in the barn and what he'd tell his friends. The car was interesting, they'd like hearing about that, but he knew they'd be far more interested in the drums and what might be inside them. In his mind, Billy listed his guesses.

Number One: Dead kids. That was for sure the most likely. Although, she'd probably had to put acid or something in there with them to get rid of their bodies, which accounted for the drums sounding so full.

Number Two: All the evidence like the clothes the kids had been wearing, the guns or knives she'd used to kill them, rope she'd used to tie them up. All that kind of stuff probably took up a lot of room. And maybe she'd packed it all in concrete so it couldn't be seen if the drums were opened.

Number Three: Money. Everyone said Old Lady Baxter was rich but never spent any of her money. Sealed drums would be a good place to hide all that money.

Billy scoffed but had to add another item to his list.

Number Four: Oil or grease for the farm equipment, or whatever originally came in the drums.

4

The next day, Billy woke to pouring rain. He could barely hear a staticky Neil Diamond crooning *Song Sung Blue* over the beat of raindrops on the roof. A fist to the clock radio perched on the nightstand next to his bed quieted the static, but it did nothing to quiet the rain.

Billy stared at the ceiling as he took stock of his aches and pains. A gentle pat on the bandage over his left elbow caused him to wince and suck in his breath. He drew his left knee up toward his chest and grunted. It was stiff and when he reached down, it stung with his touch. At least when he rotated the ankle on the other leg he was met with only a dull ache.

That hadn't been the case the day before when he'd had to bike home after a day of painting with a bloody and sore knee and elbow, and an ankle that hardly supported his weight. In his haste to finish the back of the house, he'd gotten careless and had leaned too far on his makeshift scaffolding. He'd stretched to reach a corner and had wound up on the ground, most of the scaffolding on top of him. The only fortunate part was that the paint can he'd been using had been nearly empty, so he hadn't needed to explain why he was out of paint so soon.

Groaning, Billy swung his legs over the side of the bed and pushed himself to sitting when all he wanted to do was bury his face in his pillow and sleep away the day. He rubbed both hands over his face then up and through his hair, his fingers getting tangled in the too-long, sandy brown curls. He needed a haircut, which meant he needed to ask his dad for some money, which meant either he'd have to endure his dad complaining about how much money Billy cost him or he'd have to endure another of his dad's haircuts. Maybe he should break the old hair clipper once and for all so there'd be no more danger of a "Tupper Special." His mom used to cut his hair—and his dad's hair—but she knew what she was doing and Billy had never minded. His dad just ran the clipper over Billy's head for a while, then pronounced it finished. Billy ended up looking like a fool every time. During the school year, Billy had been able to talk his dad out of home haircuts, but he feared with summer vacation upon them, his dad would say it didn't matter what he looked like and if he didn't like it, wear a hat.

Billy stood and looked out his bedroom window. The sky was black for as far as he could see. No way he'd be doing any painting in that weather, which led him to wonder what he would be doing. It was the first day since he'd started that it had done more than drizzle during the day, so the first day that outdoor work wasn't likely to happen. The farmers were celebrating, Billy was sure, but he wasn't. Something in her house or something in the barn, Billy figured. Both options left him feeling queasy.

His search of the kitchen turned up some corn flakes and milk, so he sat down with a bowl of cereal to ponder his fate. Try as he might, he couldn't come up with a scenario that wasn't horrible, even worse than painting.

Just as he finished eating, his father shuffled into the kitchen. He said nothing to Billy, just filled the coffee pot and poured himself a bowl of corn flakes. Since Billy hadn't seen his dad any of the other mornings before leaving for Old Lady Baxter's, he was leery and kept one narrowed eye on his dad while cleaning up his cereal bowl and spoon.

"You gotta go to Mrs. Baxter's this mornin'?"

"Yeah. Gotta go every day." Billy wanted to add that his dad should know that, that since he hadn't come to Billy's defense when Billy had to go in front of the judge, he'd be going to Mrs. Baxter's every morning, but he wisely kept those thoughts to himself.

"You hang on while I eat my breakfast and drink my coffee, I'll give you a ride."

Billy didn't think he'd heard right, but his dad nodded at him before digging into his own corn flakes.

"Uh, okay," Billy answered.

"Throw your bike in the back of the truck. Rain'll probably be done later. You can bike home."

"Okay."

His dad lowered his head and focused on his bowl of cereal, ending the ten second conversation. It was the longest one they'd had in days.

Not knowing what to make of the fact that first, his dad was up and out of bed, and second, that he'd offered to give him a ride, Billy was curious, but cautious. He wanted the ride, so he kept his mouth shut and backed out of the kitchen, trying his hardest not to limp.

Fifteen minutes later, his dad hadn't changed his mind, so they were in his truck, headed for Old Lady Baxter's.

"What's she got you doin' over there?"

"Been painting."

Billy's dad leaned over the steering wheel and looked through the windshield up at the sky. "Doesn't look much like paintin' weather today."

"No."

"Been doin' a good job?"

"I think so."

"See that you do," his dad said as they pulled up to her house.

"Okay. Thanks for the ride."

Billy grabbed his bike from the back, then watched his dad

pull out and head toward town. Billy just shook his head and mumbled, "Weird," as he sloshed through the puddles to the porch.

The door opened before he could knock.

"Didn't think you'd show up today."

"I didn't know not showing up was a choice."

"It's not, but you never know." She looked Billy up and down. "Come on, rain's getting in. Wipe your feet."

She turned and shuffled away from the door, leaving Billy standing there and staring after her. In? In her house? Billy wanted to run the opposite direction. Faced with the prospect of spending the day inside her house, he decided the barn was definitely the better option. But he wiped his feet and followed her. Then he looked around.

The inside of the house surprised him. It was clean, really clean, and for some reason, he'd expected a mess. Probably since the shed and the barn were so full of junk, he'd expected the same inside. There was a lot of stuff, more stuff than he'd ever seen, but he couldn't call it junk. It was house stuff.

Every surface was covered with little statues or candles or books or fake plants, and everything sat on top of weird, lacy things. The furniture looked old-fashioned, but the light blue couches and chairs seemed hardly used. More lacy things, bigger ones, hung over the backs of those couches and chairs. There were lamps everywhere, most with shades that had fringes or beads hanging from them, and all turned on so the room was bright, even with the dark gloom outside the windows.

The wood floor creaked a little as he walked across it and made him think of a haunted house. He half expected a bloody hand to reach for him from one of the lampshades. When Billy got closer to the far wall, he slowed and studied the wooden cabinet that held an ancient-looking TV, a radio, and a record player. The TV was for sure older than the crappy black and white at his house, and he wondered if any of the stuff actually worked.

How did it happen? Billy wondered. Did old people just decide one day that they don't need any new stuff? That they'd just keep all the old crap until either it conked out or they did? He stopped and looked at the rest of her stuff. Nothing he spotted looked like it had been purchased within the last twenty years. If she really had all that money, why didn't she spend it on a color TV? If he had the money, that would be one of the first things he'd buy. Their fuzzy old TV barely got a picture at all and Billy was dying to see Laurie Partridge and Cher in color. Most of the time, Cher barely wore any clothes and what she did wear was just glitter and feathers. Fuzzy black and white didn't do it justice.

Billy shook his head at the ancient TV and followed the sound of footsteps to what turned out to be the kitchen. Like the living room, it looked like something out of a history book with its outdated appliances and furniture.

Everywhere he looked, it was white. White stove, white refrigerator, white cabinets, white table. The only color came from the light blue counter tops and the light blue cushions on the chairs. The refrigerator had just one door like the old one that sat rusting in the barn at home. Billy knew that inside the big door, there'd be a smaller door for a freezer and that if it looked anything like his had until it had finally quit and his dad had been forced to buy a new one, it was so frosted over that you could hardly shove anything inside and what was in there, was probably frozen in place.

The stove was odd looking with four gas burners spread far apart on the top and two big doors above two drawers on the front. An oven behind one of the doors, he guessed, but he didn't know what the other door and the drawers were for. The thing was so big it took up half the wall.

But like the living room, everything was neat and clean. Billy didn't spot a spoon or a towel where it shouldn't be and didn't see a single crumb on any surface, even in front of the toaster. Billy frowned. On Sunday, he'd spent over an hour on the kitchen alone and it hadn't looked nearly this clean. Maybe she had someone come to help her clean, Billy thought. She seemed way too old to be able to do all that work herself.

Before he could decide whether that seemed a likely answer, she was talking to him.

"Before you head up to the attic, I need you to get a few things down from those high cupboards over there."

She pointed to a set of cupboards over the sink but Billy hardly noticed. The attic? He hadn't been paying much attention, but he was almost sure she'd said attic. His skin crawled with the thought of what she'd make him do up there. And what he might find.

"Boy, are you listening? There." She pointed again. "If you can't reach, there's a step stool in the closet."

Billy huffed out his breath. "I can reach."

"There should be some cake platters, a few serving dishes, sterling flatware. Get it all."

Billy didn't know what any of that stuff was, so he just grabbed what was there and set it on the counter. Some of it was heavy. He bobbled and nearly dropped a pink glass thing when he went to grab it with one hand and found it to be heavier than he expected. It tottered on the shelf and he just caught it before it could crash down onto the counter and onto all the other stuff he'd already piled there. He didn't dare turn around to see if she'd noticed.

Slower and more carefully, he continued until he'd emptied the cupboard of all sorts of strange looking colored glass things, some clunky and badly tarnished silverware, and the only things he recognized...some white bowls with blue flowers he knew were CorningWare because they had the same ones at his house.

"Oh, would you look at that," she said when she picked up a pink bowl with a cover. Her eyes had a faraway look, and much to Billy's horror, a creaky, twisted smile started spreading across her face. "My mother kept butterscotch candy in that until the day she died. For years, I did the same. I wondered where—"

As if she realized she was being almost friendly and caught herself, she set down the bowl with a snap and narrowed her eyes. Any trace of a smile disappeared and was replaced with the hard line of her thin lips.

"Follow me."

Behind her back, Billy rolled his eyes, but did as he was told. She left the kitchen the same way they'd come in, but she turned down a hallway that he could see led to a dining room. Before they got there, she stopped at a door in the hallway and opened it to a flight of stairs.

She went up first and following her was almost more than Billy could stand. He stomped his way up behind her, lifting each foot in slow motion and dropping it with an exaggerated thud. Never in his life had he seen anyone move so slowly. He wanted to push her, to jump in front of her and drag her, to do something—anything—to get her moving.

Finally, they reached another door at the top of the stairs and she pushed it open. It led to another hallway. A long rug extended the entire length and covered most of the width of the wood floor. Billy counted five doors that he assumed led to bedrooms, probably a bathroom, until they got to the end of the hall and the final door.

She turned the knob and pulled. Despite its creaking and moaning, it opened and stayed that way when she pushed it flat against the wall. For the first time, Billy spotted some cobwebs, a coating of dust, and smelled the musty, stale attic smell that whooshed down yet another flight of stairs hidden behind that door.

"There are six or seven boxes stacked along the wall on this side." She motioned with her hand. "Bring them down. Much of it is fragile, so be careful." She turned to face him. "Not like you were in the kitchen."

Billy ground his teeth together and didn't respond, just waited for more instructions he figured were coming.

"Bring them down to the kitchen. There should be a few

empty boxes underneath the windows. Bring those too."

She turned to leave, and Billy peered up the dark stairwell.

"Is there a light?"

She slowed and looked back at him. "A string at the top of the stairs. The bulb should work."

"*Should* work. Great," Billy muttered as he stuck his head into the dark and noted the crumbling plaster walls and the rickety wooden steps that seemed to just sort of hang there, not really attached to anything. He put his foot on the first step. When it didn't give out under him, he was surprised, but it wasn't enough to instill any confidence the same would be the case with the rest of the steps so he held his hands out to the side attempting to balance himself, and tested each step before putting all his weight on it.

He made it to the top without falling through the steps, then swung his hand over his head feeling for the light string. When his hand brushed against what he hoped was the string and not some kind of giant cobweb, he pulled. The light came on, surprising him again, but when he looked around, he sighed. The fact that crap was piled from floor to ceiling was no surprise whatsoever.

Wooden crates, old trunks, dusty suitcases, bags, and boxes were stacked and jumbled in every corner, along every wall. A dresser, a few chairs, a cracked mirror in a fancy, gold frame, a mattress, and a huge, impossibly heavy looking table were crowded into the middle of the room. How anyone had ever gotten the table up there, Billy had no idea. Every flat surface had more crap piled on it.

"For God's sake," Billy said as he turned in a circle. "No way I'm hauling all this shit out of here." He kept muttering as he pushed and kicked his way past stacks of old newspapers bundled and tied with twine. "Who's this stupid? Bunch of old newspapers."

On the wall she'd indicated, Billy found a stack of sagging cardboard boxes. He counted eight. Since she hadn't told him what was inside other than that some of it was fragile, there was no point in looking inside them. He'd have to lug them all downstairs.

He picked up the first one and felt the bottom drop. Panicked, he slid his hands underneath to support it. The underside of the box felt damp and Billy twisted his hands, wanting to get away from whatever it was making it feel that way. Telling himself it was only old cardboard, sitting around in a damp attic for years and not some bodily fluid, Billy fought the urge to gag and started down the steps for his first of many trips.

When he reached the first floor and made his way into the kitchen, she wasn't there. All the better, he thought, as he dropped the box on the table with a thud and started back upstairs.

Some boxes were a little heavier, some a little lighter, but he didn't dare try to balance more than one at a time while navigating the rickety attic stairway, so it took eight trips. He was sweating, and given the dampness of the still, humid air, his T-shirt clung to his clammy skin and left him feeling itchy from head to toe.

Like she had some sort of radar, Old Lady Baxter showed up just as Billy dropped the eighth box onto the table.

"What's all this?" she said.

"The boxes you wanted." He said it slowly, enunciating every word as if he were talking to a small child.

Her mouth moved silently as she counted with bobs of her head. "It's too many."

Billy lifted his arms high above his shoulders and let them drop back down to his thighs. This time, he didn't bother speaking slowly. His words came out in an angry rush.

"You told me to get the boxes along the wall. I did. That's how many there were." He jabbed a finger at the pile of boxes. "How was I supposed to know which ones you wanted?"

She frowned, her thin, bluish lips almost disappearing, and the lines around her mouth deepening. "I don't remember this many...no, not this many." she said, more to herself than to Billy.

Billy lifted his T-shirt and used it to wipe the sweat off his forehead while he waited. And watched. She looked confused; he'd seen her that way before. Billy didn't know if it was just because she was old or if she was losing her mind or something, but a few times before when she'd been talking to him, she'd acted like she forgot what she was doing or what she was saying. If she decided now she'd asked him for the wrong pile of boxes, if she expected him to haul them all back up to the attic and haul another pile down...

She pulled a strip of brittle tape off a box and opened it, taking out a plate. Apparently satisfied, she nodded and moved on to the next box. She opened three more with the same result. When she opened the next, though, she stiffened and Billy heard her sharp intake of breath. He couldn't see what was inside the box before she slapped it shut and pushed it aside.

After quick glances in the remaining boxes, she turned in her slow, stiff way and looked around the kitchen.

"Where are the empty boxes I asked for?"

Crap. He'd forgotten about those.

"Didn't get them yet," he muttered as he turned to head back to the attic.

"Just a minute." Painstakingly, she folded the flaps of the box that had seemed to cause her so much upset. When she finally finished, she stepped away from it. "Take this one back up there."

Billy grunted in reply and picked up the box.

"And bring some newspaper down with you," she called after him. "A couple of bundles should do it."

Billy swore to himself all the way up. When he got back to the stifling attic, he shoved the box he'd carried into a corner and went in search of the empty ones. Under the windows, he thought she'd said. Well, there was a mountain of boxes under the windows. Figuring they weren't all empty, he lifted the corners of a few on top and found them light enough that he figured they were probably empty, but not wanting to give her something else to complain about, he checked. The first four he checked were empty, and he decided that would be enough, at least for one trip since he had to carry newspapers too.

He set the empty boxes by the steps and went to grab a couple bundles of newspaper, but before he picked them up, the box he'd carried back upstairs caught his eye and curiosity got the better of him. Tiptoeing over some Christmas lights, he made his way back to the mysterious box. He didn't recall one being a lot heavier or a lot lighter than the others, or making a different sort of noise. For the most part, they'd all been about the same size, close to the same weight, and seemed like they probably all held the same sort of stuff.

It took him only a second to pop open the flaps it had taken her minutes to fold closed. When the box fell open, all he saw was a pile of old clothes. Some brown pants, a few pairs of socks, the peek of what looked to be a white dress shirt.

It didn't make much sense to him why she'd seemed so bothered by a bunch of clothes. Disappointed it wasn't something more exciting, he folded the flaps closed again. Maybe because he was so angry, maybe because he was careless, but whatever the reason, he shoved the flap too hard and the box tipped, spilling some of the contents to the floor. Mixed in with all the brown and white, a flash of red caught his eye.

It was a mitten. A small mitten to fit a small hand.

Billy sat back on his heels and picked through the clothing more carefully. He'd assumed it was old stuff that used to be her husband's, but everything was small. The kind of things a kid would wear.

Joel's warnings about looking for stuff belonging to her victims came rushing back. It would make sense, seeing how fast she'd closed the box once she'd seen what was inside. She hadn't wanted him to get a look at it.

Billy emptied the box. It looked like all boy clothes, but he was almost certain at least one of the missing kids had been a girl.

Maybe more. He tried to remember how many kids there had been but wasn't sure. There'd been so many stories over the years, he wasn't sure what was true and what wasn't. After thirty or forty years, he didn't know if anyone remembered the whole truth.

Now that the clothes were piled in front of him, he didn't want to touch them. What if some kid had been wearing them when he'd died? It would almost be like touching a dead body.

Disgusted by the idea, Billy tilted the box on its side and used his foot to push the pile of clothes back in. Once everything was inside, he used his foot again to squish the clothes down enough that he could fold the box flaps tight and keep everything out of sight and, he hoped, out of mind. As quick as he could, he shoved the box back against the wall. Jumping back over the string of Christmas lights, he barely slowed as he snagged a bundle of newspaper in each hand and hustled for the door, kicking the empty boxes down the stairs in front of him. Once he hit the second floor landing, he slammed the attic door shut.

Really hoping it was the last he'd see of the attic, he fit the empty boxes inside one another as best he could, juggled the bundles of newspaper, and headed back down the next flight of stairs.

When he got to the kitchen, she was waiting with her bony hands fisted on her hips.

"It sounded like there was an elephant up there. What were you doing, boy? Snooping?"

Billy was plenty sick of being called 'boy.' Seemed to him if she wanted to yell at him, the least she could do was use his name. It worked just fine for his dad. He wondered how she'd like it if he called her 'old lady.' Forcing himself to keep his cool, he settled for an eye roll he hoped she couldn't see from the other side of the room.

"Putting the box back, getting the newspaper and the empty boxes. It was a lot to carry."

Billy turned his back and set the newspaper bundles on the

floor with the empty boxes piled on top. He heard her grunt and grumble but kept his back to her, choosing to stare out the window at the driving rain rather than face her. His eyes wandered to the wall where a light blue clock hung. Ten o'clock. He never would have dreamed it possible, but the day was crawling by slower than a school day. When algebra and geography didn't seem that bad, he knew he was in the middle of a really crappy day.

"Well, get busy. The things you took out of the cupboards need to be wrapped in newspaper and packed in the empty boxes."

He didn't attempt to hide his sigh. Shoulders sagging and feet dragging, Billy plucked an empty box from the pile, shoved aside the rest, and grabbed a bundle of newspaper. He dropped both on the floor in front of the counter where he'd stacked the junk he'd moved from the high cabinets. When he pulled on the twine bundling the newspaper, it held tight. No amount of pulling loosened it. He looked around to see if he could spot a knife or scissors, but aside from the stuff he'd piled on the counter, the surfaces were frustratingly bare.

"Do you have a knife or scissors or something?"

"In the drawer in front of you."

Billy yanked open the drawer and found a tray holding a selection of kitchen knives, all neatly in a row, from small ones like his mom used to call her grapefruit knife to some that looked big enough to butcher a pig. He chose one of the smaller ones. When it sliced through the twine like a hot knife through butter, Billy couldn't help but steal a glance out of the corner of his eye and wonder what in the world she used all those knives for.

It took hours to package all the stuff to her satisfaction. Billy wrapped and rewrapped, packed and repacked, and she still found reasons to complain. *That bowl is delicate. Use more newspaper.* *Put that heavy platter on the bottom of the box, not on the top.* It seemed everything he did was wrong.

The seven boxes he'd carried down from the attic were all full of old dishes, tablecloths, sheets, blankets, all kinds of crap. He had to open every box, take out every item, unwrap it if it had been wrapped, then rewrap it while she painstakingly recorded every single item along with what Billy thought was a ridiculously long description in a spiral notebook. He wanted to ask why—it was so tempting, and he was so curious—but he wouldn't give her the satisfaction of knowing he cared even a little.

He hoped that she was getting ready to move. It seemed the most likely. She'd have to clear out the house, and it made sense to start with the stuff she never used. How she'd ever get through all of it, he had no idea, but he prayed that would happen sometime after the end of summer and would be someone else's problem.

"Whew!" Mrs. Baxter fell into one of the kitchen chairs and dabbed at her face with a handkerchief. "I didn't realize that would be so much work."

Billy glared at her back. So much work? She hadn't done anything but write.

She turned to look at him. "I'm going to have some lunch before we continue. Did you bring anything to eat?"

Billy felt his cheeks burn and though he fought it, his eyes dropped to the floor. "No," he mumbled. "Didn't have time."

When he forced his eyes to look at her, she was nodding, her mouth set in a hard, grim line. "Figured as much. I have beef roast."

Without another word, she rose and shuffled to the refrigerator. Billy watched as she pulled out foil-covered plates, a plastic bowl with what looked like cut-up cantaloupe, and a pitcher of lemonade. She reached into a cupboard for a loaf of bread. Not knowing if he was supposed to help, and growing increasingly uncomfortable, Billy stayed rooted to his spot. After a few minutes, she turned and held out a plate.

"Here you go. Glasses are over there." She nodded her head in the direction of the cabinets over the sink. "Get two glasses. There are ice cubes in the freezer if you want them."

Two glasses sounded ominous. They were going to eat lunch together? Billy wanted to tell her he'd rather go hungry. But he looked at the thick sandwich on the plate she handed him, saw the condensation already beading and running down the sides of the lemonade pitcher, and his mouth watered. He was starving, he was hot, and he'd figure out a way to sit at the table with her and not throw up.

After depositing his plate at the very end of the table, he went to the cabinet and pulled out two glasses. The offer of ice was too good to pass up, so he inched his way toward the refrigerator taking care not to get too close to the fleshy, white arms that moved with surprising speed when slicing meat and buttering bread.

The ice cube tray was an old metal one with a handle that, when pulled up, released the ice cubes. Memories bombarded him and Billy smiled before he caught himself and plastered the much more comfortable scowl back on his face. He remembered the trips to his grandparents' house when he'd been just a little kid. They'd had those kind of ice cube trays and he'd always wanted to be the one to pull the lever and hear the satisfying crack. His grandmother had never tired of telling the story of how proud Billy'd been the first time he'd been able to pull the lever hard enough to release the ice cubes.

Billy dropped a few ice cubes in each glass then poured lemonade over them, concentrating on the snapping and popping when the liquid hit the ice instead of the memories of all the people who'd died on him.

Hoping she'd take the hint, Billy put her glass at the far opposite end of the table from where he'd put his plate. He sat down and scooped up his sandwich, intending to eat as fast as possible and then find a reason to get out of the kitchen. He'd even go out in the rain to use the old outhouse just to put some distance between them for a while.

Billy was shoving cantaloupe into his mouth when she walked to the table. She cast her eyes to the glass at the far end, gave him a long look under raised brows, but took the far seat without commenting. Billy bent lower over his plate and hoped she'd stay quiet. She didn't.

"In this house, we say grace and we use manners."

Billy's hand froze halfway between the plate and his mouth, and his jaw stilled. Ever so slowly, he chewed what was in his mouth, swallowed, then set down his sandwich and with his head still bent over his plate, raised only his eyes and met hers. There'd been no saying grace, no manners, no nothing but eating to survive at his house for five long years. He hoped she wouldn't ask him to say something because he was pretty sure he didn't remember how.

It was a relief when she spoke and an even bigger relief when she kept it short. "For this food we are about to eat, we thank You. Amen."

"Amen," Billy whispered.

She seemed satisfied and picked up her sandwich. Billy did the same, but made himself take a smaller bite and give it more than two chomps before swallowing. It wasn't that he cared what she thought, he told himself, it was just that he didn't want to listen to a lecture. If it meant she'd keep her mouth shut, he'd do what she asked.

It was quiet for a few minutes before she said, "There are some empty boxes in the attic. We'll need those to pack up the things from the cupboard."

Billy huffed. "Another cupboard? I thought—"

His stomach did a weird flipping thing when he caught the blank look in her eyes and he realized she was talking about the empty boxes he'd already carried down and about the cupboard he'd already emptied. She'd forgotten they'd done it. Completely, totally forgotten.

Sweat sheathed him from head to toe as he watched her look to the cabinet, look at the boxes, then remove her glasses and rub her cloudy eyes. Her lips moved and she gestured with her hands as if she was carrying on a conversation. Maybe with herself, maybe with someone she thought was in the room.

Billy watched and waited. He didn't know if he should remind her they'd done it, pretend to do it again, or just ignore what she'd said and hope she'd snap out of whatever sort of fit she was having.

This was the worst of her odd episodes. Before, she'd repeated herself a couple of times or acted like she forgot what she'd been saying, but she'd never gone quite this crazy. What if one day she started to cook something and forgot about it? Or what if she started driving and forgot where she was going? Billy reminded himself he didn't care about her, that she was an evil witch who deserved whatever was happening to her, but it was still pretty horrible sitting there watching her.

Billy was still trying to figure out what to do when she jumped up from her chair and took her half-eaten lunch to the sink. She dumped what was left on her plate in the garbage, dumped her lemonade down the drain, and put her plate in the sink.

"Well then, we should see about getting these boxes to the church. I don't care much for driving in the rain. You know how to drive, don't you, boy?"

"Huh?" It was all Billy could come up with. She was acting like nothing had happened and he couldn't figure out if she really thought nothing had happened or if she was trying to ignore it and cover up her weird behavior. Either way, he had no idea what she meant about the church and he was almost certain it was because she hadn't mentioned it, not because he hadn't been paying attention.

"Oh, for heaven's sake. Please speak properly." Her voice cracked like a whip, her shoulders squared, and her eyes were clear when they drilled into him, almost daring him to challenge her.

Billy could only stare, wondering if she would start acting

crazy again or if she would keep her wits about her for a while.

"Do you know how to drive?" she asked again.

"Drive? Uh, yeah. I know how to drive."

Now he was just plain angry. Of course, he knew how to drive. And she knew he could drive. It had been the thing he'd fought stupid Judge O'Malley hardest over. Billy had known how to drive for years. A kid didn't grow up on a farm and not know how to drive by the time he was a teenager unless that kid was an idiot. Billy should have taken his test and gotten his license months ago, but now all the jackasses he went to school with who could barely maneuver their cars into a parking spot at the drive-in were getting their licenses while he rode his damn bike. His dad hadn't let him get behind the wheel of the truck for ages. And it was all her fault. He imagined himself throwing a box at her and getting the hell out of her house. The urge to really do it was overwhelming.

"Good, then you can drive. Let's get these things loaded."

She picked up a small box, one Billy knew held some tablecloths and wasn't heavy, and marched out of the kitchen.

He wanted to shout after her, to tell her what she could do with her stupid boxes and with her stupid car, but he didn't. Instead, he forced open his clenched fists, gulped the last of his lemonade, picked up two boxes, and, despite his anger, grinned on his way out of the house.

He was finally going to drive.

Listing the people he'd like to run over while he was driving made that grin bigger.

Number One: Judge O'Malley. It would be the best form of payback, Billy figured, after the stupid jackass had told Billy no driver's license for a year, if Billy could sit behind the wheel of a car and run over the scrawny little jerk.

Number Two: Terrence. The perfect way to keep him away from Julie.

Number Three: Old Lady Baxter. Driving her car for an hour didn't come close to making up for having to spend his whole summer doing crappy jobs for her.

Number Four: Billy debated with himself, but decided number four was his dad. If his dad wasn't around, Billy would probably have to go live with Aunt Cindy. She'd make his life miserable, he was sure of that, but at least he'd be with Tracy.

5

"You went to church with her?"

Joel's eyebrows nearly twisted in a knot the way they always did when, because he was confused, he wrinkled his forehead and squinted his eyes. Joel was confused a lot, Billy thought, as he started his story again and fought not to sigh.

"We went to *the* church, not *to* church. We went to drop off a bunch of her old crap for the rummage sale they're having."

"Oh, yeah, my mom took some stuff over there too. Clothes that don't fit us anymore." Joel nodded as if everything now made sense. "It's a benefit for Vietnam families. The ones who are having a rough time."

Billy hadn't known that. Old Lady Baxter hadn't said what the stuff was for. He held his breath and watched Joel closely, but Joel didn't hunch over like a turtle pulling its head into its shell. After a minute Billy figured it was safe to continue and said, "Yeah, well she had boxes of old stuff that I had to haul down from the attic and more stuff in her cupboards that I had to box up. It was a pain in the ass, I'll tell you that."

This time Joel's eyebrows shot up so high they disappeared under his red-orange bangs. "You were in the attic? Why didn't you tell me that first? What did you find? You must have found something and that's why you wanted to come over tonight, right?"

Billy had first called John, but there'd been no answer. Then he'd tried Steve only to find out Steve was working. Joel had been a last resort. With the way Joel got so excited about anything and everything to do with Old Lady Baxter, Billy wasn't sure Joel would be much help. Or any help. But Billy needed someone to help him unravel the puzzle, so he sat on his bike in Joel's driveway and chose his words carefully.

"I found some stuff. I don't know that it means anything, but it got me curious."

"What? What?"

"Some kid clothes. Boy stuff, and small, like it was for a little kid."

"Yep. That makes sense." Joel nodded. "She had to hide the clothes after she killed them. That's what I've always said. Was she up there with you? Does she know you found them?"

"No, she didn't go up to the attic." Billy explained how he'd carried down the boxes, how she'd seemed upset when she'd opened one of them, and how he'd looked inside later after carrying it back up to the attic.

Joel lifted his arms away from his sides with his palms facing upward. He waved them dramatically. "See? She didn't want you to get a look at what was inside." Joel paused and scratched his head. "Seems like she wouldn't have told you to take it back up to the attic, though. Seems like she would have put it in her bedroom or somewhere out of sight. Pretty easy for you to look inside when you're up in the attic all by yourself." Joel looked disappointed with his conclusion.

"That's what I thought. But there's something else."

"You found something else?"

"No, I mean there's something else to consider. She forgets things. It's weird. She'll be talking to me and in the middle of a sentence it's like she forgets what she's talking about. Today, while we were eating lunch, all of a sudden she told me to get empty boxes from the attic and pack up the stuff from the cupboards. I'd already done that. And there have been other times too."

Joel's jaw dropped open and for a moment, Billy thought maybe he knew something about what was wrong with her, maybe he'd heard something about her being sick or would have some ideas, but it was Billy's turn to be disappointed.

"You ate lunch with her?" Joel doubled over laughing and could barely get his next words out. "You went on a date with Old Lady Baxter!"

Billy sneered at him. "Shut up. That's not the point. The point is, she could have known the clothes bothered her, but could have forgotten why. Maybe she didn't realize having me carry the box back upstairs was a bad idea. Maybe her screwed up brain doesn't know what to think."

Slowly, Joel got himself under control, but he couldn't quite wipe the grin from his face. "I guess, but maybe she didn't realize you noticed her get upset about that one box. Maybe she didn't think there'd be any reason for you to open it."

Billy hadn't considered that possibility. She hadn't been facing him, she hadn't looked at him after she'd opened the box, so it made sense that she didn't know he'd seen her reaction. Still...

"Whatever the reason, do you really believe it was clothes from the kids who disappeared? And I mean *really* believe. Not what you want to believe, but what you think is the truth. If she did it, would she really keep stuff?"

Joel paced in a circle around the yard, his eyes down, and at least appearing to take some time to consider. Billy gave him the time. When Joel quit walking and stopped in front of Billy, some of the excitement, the eagerness, that Billy was used to seeing whenever the subject of Old Lady Baxter and the missing kids came up had vanished from Joel's eyes.

"I don't know if it was stuff from the kids who disappeared. It makes sense that she wouldn't have kept the stuff. All those years, she probably would have gotten rid of it. It's just always been fun to think she did keep stuff and that someday someone would find it. Now, with you working there and actually finding stuff, stuff that we can twist into seeming like it has to be evidence, it's even more fun. But if I'm being one hundred percent honest, I don't think she'd have a box of clothes that belonged to the missing kids sitting around in her attic."

Billy was speechless. First, because that was more words than he'd ever heard Joel string together at one time. Second, because they were words that made sense. Usually stupid questions, bad attempts at jokes, and second-hand rumors made up most of what Joel had to say. Third, Billy never thought he'd hear Joel admit that something didn't point right at Old Lady Baxter being a murderer.

"Really? As long as I've known you, you've been saying she's got to have evidence somewhere in her house. What made you change your mind now?"

"Oh, I still think there's evidence there, but a box of clothes doesn't much seem like evidence. A girl disappeared too. Where are the girl clothes? And keeping the stuff they were wearing seems kind of stupid. If you're going to kill them and get rid of the bodies, why bother taking off their clothes? Remember, a sock or shoe or something was found out by the old mine entrance. If she hid the body in the mine, maybe hid all of them in the mine, they must have been dressed in their own clothes when she did it so she wouldn't have their stuff boxed up in her attic."

Joel was making sense. Billy decided maybe it wasn't so bad Joel'd been the only one home that evening.

"How much do you know about what really happened? How many kids disappeared, where they were last seen, what sort of evidence the cops found, all that kind of stuff."

"Quite a bit. My grandma used to like to talk about it even though my mom would tell her not to. I think when I was younger, I'd get scared by my grandma's stories, but when I got older, I asked my grandma questions whenever my mom wasn't around."

Billy couldn't remember his grandparents ever talking about it. He figured that by the time he was old enough to pay attention to what the grown-ups were talking about, enough time had passed with nothing more happening that the topic wasn't a popular one any longer.

"Why was your grandma so interested in it?"

"She knew one of the families that lost a kid."

"What? You never told me that before."

"I told you. A long time ago, but I told you. You didn't believe me."

Billy didn't know if that was true, but guessed it could have been. A lot of what Joel used to say—a lot of what he still said— was bullshit.

"Well, I don't remember." Billy realized he didn't remember, or more accurately, didn't know, a lot of stuff. A lot of details. It was probably time to get the facts straight. "Maybe you should tell me everything you know. If I'm supposed to look around for evidence, I should know what I'm looking for."

Joel's face lit up like fireworks on the Fourth of July, and he jumped around like a firecracker ready to blow. The kid was weird.

"Okay! I know all kinds of stuff."

Billy dropped his bike on the skimpy patch of lawn in front of Joel's house then sat down, pulling a fat blade of crabgrass and positioning it between his thumbs. He blew and was rewarded with a loud honk. Billy played around with the grass for a minute, moving his hands and blasting tones that ranged from a shriek high-pitched enough to get the neighbor's dog howling, to a lower pitch that reminded him of the feeble attempts Steve had made with his trombone when his mom had made him take lessons at school.

Billy let himself remember sitting on the fence at home, his dad leaning against it alongside him, and teaching Billy how to position the blade of grass, how to hold his thumbs. 'Hold it tight, Billy Boy. If it slides around, it's not gonna make any sound.' Billy almost smiled, but instead threw down the grass and scowled. That was a long time ago, back when his dad used to do stuff with him. Back when Billy cared if he did.

Joel stopped jumping and dropped down next to Billy. "What do you want to know?"

"Tell me everything."

Billy lay back on the grass, clasping his hands behind his head and looking up at the sky that was starting to turn pink and orange with the approaching sunset. Did his dad ever wonder any more where Billy was? When he was coming home? If he was coming home? Did he know Billy biked into town and biked home long after dark? Probably not.

"When the first kid disappeared, it was winter and I guess the parents couldn't get to town to report him missing for a few days. The whole town searched for him, some people tried to use dogs to track the kid, but no one ever found him. He was just gone. Some figured he was kidnapped, but no one knew why. Kids got kidnapped when the parents had money to pay a ransom. This kid's parents didn't have two nickels to rub together. Of course, it was during the depression so no one had much money, but these people were really poor. Others figured he got lost in the blizzard, maybe got hurt and couldn't walk any more, then the coyotes got him."

"But there was never any sign of him or of an attack?"

"No, but a little kid like that? Coyotes could have dragged him off anywhere."

"Maybe." Billy remembered the time he'd been jolted awake by a gunshot. It was spring, back when they had cows, and some coyotes got into the barn. They'd gone after one of the calves, but the cows, sensing danger, had started to bellow. His dad got there in time to scare off the coyotes before they killed the calf, but not before they'd done some damage. Billy's mom had spent the next few days sitting in the barn, nursing that calf back to health. Billy recalled his dad saying it was no use, that it was a waste of time, that the calf wouldn't recover, but his mom had insisted that with a little time and a lot of love, the calf would be fine. She'd been right. If coyotes went after a hundred-and-fifty-pound calf, a scrawny kid wouldn't be much of a challenge. "Maybe," Billy repeated.

"Anyway, with one kid, people were sad, upset, all that stuff, but there were other things to worry about and after a while, life went back to normal, my grandma said. About a year later, another kid disappeared. Again, no one had seen anything strange, and there was no trace of him anywhere."

"So two kids just vanished. Why was Old Lady Baxter a suspect? Out of all the people around, why her?"

"I don't think she was. Not at first. I remember my grandma telling me that the kids who disappeared didn't have much in common except that they were both little boys and both from Munroe. One lived on a farm, the other closer to town. The farm family went to church, the other didn't. There was more, but I don't remember all of what she said. But then, a couple of years later, another kid disappeared. This one was old enough for school. Old Lady Baxter worked at the school."

The more Billy heard, the more he realized he didn't know. For as long as he could remember, he'd heard rumors about Old Lady Baxter, but they were stories like a bunch of other stories he'd grown up hearing: Stay out of the old, crumbling barn out on 53, it's haunted. If you swallow a watermelon seed, a watermelon will grow in your stomach. Don't cross your eyes, they'll stay that way. And Old Lady Baxter stole kids and killed them. He really needed to know the truth.

"What happened when the cops talked to Old Lady Baxter? Why did they think she did it and why couldn't they prove it?"

"Well, she worked at the school so it would have been easy for her to grab a kid. They—"

"Hang on. So she worked there. That doesn't mean she could just grab a kid on her way out the door and no one would notice. That seems pretty stupid."

Joel shrugged. "I don't know, my grandma just said that since she worked at the school, she was a suspect. I guess I'd always known she did it, so I didn't ask a lot of questions about why and how."

Wish as he might, Billy couldn't expect Joel to have all the answers. Even so, he was Billy's best source of information.

"Three kids over, what, four years or so? That's a lot of kids to disappear from a town the size of Munroe. Seems to me like the cops would do some serious investigating. Seems to me people would have demanded it."

Joel shrugged again. "Times were different, you know? So many people out of work, people losing their homes, going hungry. I'm sure people were concerned, probably watched out for their own kids a little more, but with all the other problems... it sounds horrible, but maybe they didn't have the time and energy to care as much as people would today."

It was starting to bug Billy a little that Joel was making sense, but maybe it was to be expected since Joel had spent a lot more time thinking about it than Billy ever had.

"Okay, but back to Old Lady Baxter. Did your grandma think she did it?"

"Oh, yeah, you better believe she did. She always warned me to stay far away from the Baxter place. She even tried to tell my mom that I shouldn't be friends with you because you lived so close to Old Lady Baxter's house."

Billy grinned at Joel. "Did you ever tell your grandma that you used to sneak over to Old Lady Baxter's house? That you tried to talk me into sneaking into her barn?"

The color drained from Joel's face. "No way. She would've killed me."

"After all her warnings, why did you always want to go over there?"

Joel shrugged. "Probably because of all her warnings. That's what kids do, isn't it? Things they're not supposed to do."

Billy nodded. Again, Joel sounded like the smart one and it left Billy wondering what was going on with his friend.

"What else? Was there ever any evidence other than the fact that she worked at the school that made the cops suspect Mrs. Baxter?"

"*Mrs.* Baxter? I've never heard you call her that."

The heat crept up Billy's neck to his cheeks and he was grateful for the waning light. "I have to call her that when I talk to her. Guess I'm getting used to it."

"Huh." Joel studied him for a long minute before answering. "I don't know. There was some talk that since she'd lost her kid, she wanted to get back at those who still had theirs. There could be something to that, I suppose."

Billy sat up. "Her kid? She had a kid? Why haven't you mentioned that before? Seems like an important piece of information."

It was Joel's turn to sigh. "I've mentioned it. I even remember the day. You and me and John rode our bikes past her house to get a look. There was an old kid's wagon sitting outside the garage with a bunch of stuff piled in it. I said it was probably left over from her kid, wondered how much other stuff was still around after all those years…wait a minute! The clothes in the attic could have been her kid's stuff."

Billy had gotten there a couple of minutes before Joel, but they were on the same page. "Yeah. Maybe it wasn't so much scared and nervous she was feeling when she opened the box as it was sad."

Billy felt a little tug at his heart he didn't understand. Sure, he knew what it was like to lose someone, the someone you loved the most, but equating those feelings with Old Lady Baxter didn't quite make sense in his head. And feeling anything like sympathy for the person who had doomed him to the most miserable summer in the history of summers *really* didn't make sense.

"Then we're back at square one?" Joel asked. "We don't have any actual evidence?"

Rubbing his hands over his eyes and up to press on his

forehead and temples gave Billy a little relief from the dull headache that was always lurking, just waiting, it seemed, to explode.

"I guess not," Billy answered. "Maybe she's just an old, forgetful lady who's had a hard life. Maybe she was an easy target when there weren't any other targets."

Joel's jaw dropped and he stared at Billy. "You think she's innocent? What'd she do to you, man? Put some kind of voodoo spell on you?"

"I don't know what to think, okay? She's a crazy, senile hag, but that doesn't make her a child killer. I'm not saying she's innocent, but I can't say she's guilty, either."

A growl not unlike that from a dog guarding its bone sounded from deep in Joel's throat. "I never thought you'd let her get to you."

Billy jumped to his feet, his hands flying up over his head. He had to fight to keep them from balling into fists. "She's not *getting to me*! Listen for once, damn it. You said yourself we don't have any evidence. I thought maybe the clothes...well, I thought maybe there was something there, but it's probably just crap that belonged to her kid. Nothing I've seen or heard gives me more reason than I had before my first day there to think she killed those kids." Billy yanked his bike from the grass. "Thanks for the info."

"Wait, wait," Joel called when Billy pushed off and headed down the driveway.

Billy let out a growl of his own, but braked and dropped his feet to the cracked concrete driveway. He twisted on his seat to look back at Joel.

"You're right. About all of it. But I hope you don't stop looking. Noticing. Just because you haven't found it yet, doesn't mean there's not something to find. As far as I know, you're the only one who's been inside her house, inside her barn, for years. You could be the one to finally get an answer to the question that everyone in Munroe has been asking for a long, long time."

Billy closed his eyes and shook his head. "I won't stop looking. And noticing. My whole life, I've thought she killed those kids. That doesn't change over night. It just seems like the more I find out, the more I realize I don't know. I wish we could talk to someone who knows what really happened back then."

"Most people are too young to remember anything but the rumors. Those who are old enough either don't like to talk about it or are as forgetful as Old Lady Baxter."

"Yeah, I guess so." Billy turned his bike and used his feet to push back up Joel's driveway. "I guess I got too hung up on all this. I let what you said get in my head, that if I find something to prove she's guilty, she'll go to jail and I'll be off the hook for the rest of the summer. Not likely to happen."

"We could go to the library," Joel said.

"What?"

"The library. That's where we could go to get some answers."

"What are you talking about? The library? That's like going to school in the summer. You want to spend your summer reading some stupid books, go right ahead. No way in hell I'm going to."

There was a glint in Joel's eye, visible even in the faint light. "Not books. Newspapers. Old newspapers. I think they keep old newspapers at the library. We could look back at papers from the times when those kids disappeared. That would be the way to get the real information, not just rumors and stories twisted around over the last thirty or forty years. You said you wanted answers."

Billy turned the idea over in his head. The thought of the library at any time of the year was enough to make him break out in a sweat, but during the summer, when he didn't have to go there, made him sick to his stomach. Normal people didn't go to the library if they didn't have to. But, he reluctantly admitted to himself, if Joel was right and if there were newspapers there, it was probably the only way he would get the whole story.

"I have to be at Old Lady Baxter's every day. Maybe you could go, maybe—"

"It's open Saturday morning."

Shit. With a gargantuan effort, Billy replied, "Fine. Saturday morning."

Joel grinned and did the weird bouncing thing he did when he got really excited. "Great! I'll see if Steve and John can go. If there are four of us, we'll get through the papers a lot faster."

"Sure, see if they can go," Billy said, unable to muster much enthusiasm.

6

The morning dawned crisp and cloudless, the kind of day Billy's mom used to call 'Hang-out-the-laundry day.' But no one hung out the laundry at Billy's house anymore, so all it meant to him was another day of painting.

There was no sign of his dad when Billy trudged to the kitchen that morning. There was also no sign of any corn flakes or any milk. Billy found some stale crackers and a mostly empty jar of peanut butter and called it breakfast. He looked for some bread thinking he'd make himself a sandwich to take with him, but there was also no sign of any bread. He was scheduled to work a few hours for Mr. Thompson that evening, and Mr. Thompson had promised him his first paycheck. He made a list in his head of the things he'd buy: bread, peanut butter, potato chips, candy bars, and cereal. All stuff he could stash in his closet. He'd get some milk too, even though he'd have to put that in the refrigerator. If his dad didn't find any cereal, he'd probably leave the milk alone. He drank his coffee black as tar and strong enough to stand a spoon up in the mug.

That decided, Billy threw on his old painting clothes, pulled his cap over the hair that, he reminded himself, needed to be cut, and headed out to the garage and his bike. As he'd guessed, his dad hadn't been around when Billy'd come home the night before. It'd been pitch dark, the three-mile ride from town without a light on his bike the crap shoot it always was, and no one at home to care.

So Billy didn't care either. At least that's what he kept telling himself. Steve's mom tried to monitor every minute of Steve's life. John's parents too. Maybe not quite as nuts about it as Steve's mom, but they asked questions and expected answers. Joel's parents were harder to figure. Ever since the notice had come that Joel's brother, Jeff, wouldn't be coming home from Vietnam, his parents alternated between controlling every move Joel made and rarely letting him leave the house to practically ignoring him and giving him free rein to do whatever he wanted. All Billy and his friends could figure when they'd talked about it was that Joel's parents were afraid to let Joel out of their sight for fear something would happen to him too, but were even more afraid to care too much.

It was a messed-up world.

And he had to paint it. The house loomed in front of him, taunting him with nothing but faded, ugly white siding. All the hours he'd worked, and when he looked from the road, not a speck of yellow paint was visible. Might as well be painting the whole damn world for as long as it was going to take him.

He threw down his bike harder than he'd intended and was rewarded with it bouncing back and knocking him in the shin.

"Shit!" Billy hopped on one foot and held the throbbing, bleeding leg. "Shit, shit, shit."

The blood was already seeping through his fingers. He didn't have a bandage, didn't even have a rag to tie around his leg. He'd either have to take his chances searching the barn for something he could use to stop the bleeding or knock on the door.

Billy remembered when he'd been about six and he'd stepped on an old, rusty nail. He'd been running barefoot, and the nail had gone deep into his foot. His mom had taken him to the hospital even though his dad had wanted to pull the nail out himself. At the hospital the doctor had removed the nail, cleaned his foot, bandaged it, and then given him a shot that Billy remembered as hurting more than the nail in his foot. Billy didn't remember what it was called, but the doctor said it would prevent an infection from the dirty nail. Since there was no way he was going to the doctor for another shot, and since he figured anything he'd find in the barn would be filthy, he growled and hobbled to Old Lady Baxter's door and pounded on it.

To try to slow the bleeding, he sat in one of the chairs and propped up his leg while he waited for her to open the door. It took forever and just when he was ready to take off his shirt and tie it around his leg, the door finally opened a crack.

"Who's there?"

She sounded scared, and for a minute Billy forgot his bleeding leg. Didn't she remember he was there every morning?

"Over here. It's me. Billy."

The door opened a little wider. First he saw her fingers as she grasped the side of the door, then her head as she leaned to peek around the door.

"Is that you, Tommy?"

Now it sounded like she was almost crying and Billy wished with everything he had that he could just disappear.

She looked right at Billy and repeated, "Tommy?"

"Mrs. Baxter, it's Billy. I was ready to start painting, but I cut my leg. I wondered if you might have a bandage? It's bleeding a lot."

She blinked once, then again, and her eyes seemed to clear. "You're bleeding."

"Yeah, I am. I think I need a bandage."

"I'd say you need a darn sight more than just a bandage. Stay where you are. I don't want you bleeding all over the house."

She shuffled away and Billy could only stare. Her episodes made him nervous. She seemed like she could keel over any second when she got all weird like that, and he didn't want to be around to see it happen. What if he had to help her? Touch her, or something? The idea made his skin crawl.

The bleeding seemed to be slowing some with his leg up. He was tempted to leave before she returned, willing to gamble that it would stop altogether, but he heard the floor creak and she was back on the porch before he could make up his mind.

She sat in the chair next to him, scooting it closer to his leg. "What did you do?" she demanded as she pulled his hand away from the gash.

"Did it on my bike."

"Be more careful, boy."

She dabbed at the blood with a cool washcloth. As disgusting as it was to have her helping him, to have her putting her hands on his leg, a part of him was grateful. It didn't matter that he'd seen his share of blood in his life, from farm injuries to butchered animals, it still made him queasy close-up, so he turned away and let her deal with it.

"Well, it's not deep enough that you'll need stitches. Have you had a tetanus shot lately?"

Tetanus. That was the word the doctor in the emergency room had used. "Few years ago." More like ten, he guessed, but he wasn't about to tell her that.

She dumped something on the cut that made him jump and turn back toward her and his bloody leg. "Shit! What the hell was that?"

"You want my help, you don't use that kind of language."

"Sorry," Billy mumbled even though he wasn't. "What did you put on my leg?"

"Antiseptic, since I'm certain you have no idea when your last tetanus shot was. Ask your father and if it's been a while, get one. This will do for now."

She squirted more stuff on his leg and Billy turned his head again, but this time held steady. He didn't look again until the bandage was in place.

"Maybe you shouldn't be up on a ladder today." She looked away and her forehead creased. When she spoke, her voice had that far-away sound to it again. "I could have you box up some things that need to go to the church, I suppose. Work inside today."

"Ah, no, that's okay. I'll be fine on the ladder. It's a nice day. Painting needs to get done."

"Maybe you're right. We'll save the inside work for a rainy day. That leg feel all right?"

"Fine. Thanks for bandaging it."

Billy got up. In his haste to get away from her, he stumbled and only just caught himself to prevent a headfirst tumble down the three steps.

"Slow down, boy. You cut yourself up again, you bandage yourself."

"Yeah."

"If you want some lunch, take a break around noon and knock on the door. I've got ham."

God, she was nuts. Up, then down; nice, then mean; sane—at least kind of sane, then completely crazy. As much as he hated school, Billy couldn't wait for the summer to be over.

The rain had washed away some of the heat and humidity, so painting wasn't all that bad. Sure, it was hard, and sure, it would probably never be finished, but Billy decided he didn't care how long it took if it kept him out of her house. If he did somehow finish before summer ended, he'd gladly start over rather than spend another day inside with her.

So, he painted and as he did, wondered what, if anything, they'd find if they got a look at some old newspapers. How much would have been reported? Would the paper mention other suspects? Had there been any other than Old Lady Baxter? Billy realized he didn't know the dates of the disappearances. How would they know where to look? They'd be there all day if they had to search through one paper after another. Hell of a way to spend a Saturday, especially if it turned out to be a nice Saturday. Maybe if they went early, they could head to the lake later. Maybe Julie would be there. Maybe he'd work up the nerve to talk to her. Maybe...

"You listening to me, boy? I've been calling you. Your lunch is ready."

Billy looked down from his perch on the scaffolding. She tried to look up at him, but her rounded shoulders seemed to make lifting her head difficult, and left her looking like some sort of hunchback. Her awkward stance gave him a bird's-eye view of her pink scalp and strings of whitish grey hair.

"Didn't hear you. And you didn't have to make me lunch."

"I know I didn't have to, but I did. I told you, I've got a ham. I can't eat it all myself, can I?"

Billy wanted to ask why the hell she made a ham if she couldn't eat it, but his stomach growled and he knew there was no way he was going to be able to refuse a ham sandwich. He climbed down and stood in front of her. "Thanks."

She looked at him, then at the ladders and boards Billy had fashioned into makeshift scaffolding. Her eyes moved from one end to the other, then up as far as she could manage in her stiff, awkward way.

"Is this safe?" She took hold of one of the ladders and gave it a shake.

Billy cringed, hoping everything would hold steady. "Yeah."

"I told you before to be careful."

"I'm being careful." Billy swiped the back of his hand across his sweaty forehead. He hadn't been thinking about lunch before she'd shown up, but now it was all he could think about and he was starving. If she asked more questions, if she decided they needed to stand there and talk...

"Hmph." She looked up once more, then turned. "Lunch is on the porch."

Billy jerked his head in a nod, then turned for the house. He took a few steps before he realized she was headed in the opposite direction. So much the better, he thought. No chance she'd join him for lunch. He turned back toward the house, took another step, then stopped and sighed mightily. What if she didn't know where she was going? What if she thought she was headed for the house and just kept walking? Damn.

"Mrs. Baxter?" he called to her back. "Do you need something from the barn?"

She stopped and shuffled her feet a little, turning one direction then the other. "I need to check on something."

Billy's stomach rumbled at him, but he ignored it and fought the building annoyance. "Do you need some help?"

"I think I can check on my own property in my own barn, thank you very much," she snapped at him.

Why the hell had he even tried? "Fine." But he remembered the mess on the floor, the heavy, rusty equipment scattered about, the fact that it was dark. Rolling his eyes, he said, "It's awfully dark in there. Are you sure you don't want me to help you?"

They were a few feet apart so he may not have been seeing clearly, but it looked like her face softened, like she almost smiled. And she seemed alert, not the foggy-headed scatterbrain he was becoming accustomed to seeing.

She reached into her apron pocket, pulled out a flashlight, and waved it at him. "I can manage." She paused, seemed to consider. "But thank you," she added.

Her steps seemed a bit quicker, her back a bit straighter as she made her way across the yard to the barn. Billy watched until she opened the door and disappeared inside.

"Whatever," he muttered with a shrug, then turned for the house and his lunch. He hoped there was lemonade again. Yesterday he'd spotted a cookie jar on the counter. Maybe even a cookie or two?

After an evening spent at Mr. Thompson's store where Billy had dusted, straightened, and restocked shelves then cleaned the bathroom and mopped the floors, he'd gotten his first real paycheck. He'd stared at it, his name neatly typed on the line titled 'Pay to the order of' and once he'd memorized how it looked, asked Mr. Thompson to cash it. Of the twenty-three dollars and eighty-seven cents he'd earned, he'd spent just over four dollars on some food, then pocketed the rest. While it had been thrilling to get that paycheck, he'd had a hard time not thinking about how much more the check could have been if he'd been able to work full time for Mr. Thompson as he'd planned.

The rest of the week passed in a blur of lawn mowing, painting, and sweating. The temperature rose as the week went on and except for a few showers overnight, the sky was cloudless and the sun relentless.

Billy used his stash of food to eat breakfast before heading to Mrs. Baxter's, but he seemed to have reached an unspoken agreement with her that she'd provide his lunch so he didn't bother making a sandwich to take with him. The deal suited him fine since she left lunch on the porch, he ate it alone, and for the most part, they kept their distance from one another.

On Friday afternoon, that ended. Billy was up on the scaffolding, stretching to reach a high point on the east side of the house, when she yelled at him through a window and nearly sent him tumbling to the ground.

"What did you do with it? Tell me now, or I'll call the police!"

Once he regained his balance and set down the paint can and brush, he squinted at her silhouette in the window a few feet away from him.

"What did I do with what?"

"Don't give me that. You know darn well what I'm talking about. You have one minute, boy, until I make a phone call." She coughed and it sort of went on and on, sounding like the horn on the train when it pulled into Munroe on its way to the elevator.

Billy threw his arms in the air. "I don't. I don't know what you're talking about." He fought to keep his tone reasonable, calming even, but he was angry. More than that, he was afraid.

He hadn't taken anything, he had no idea what she was talking about, and he figured within a few minutes she'd snap out of whatever sort of fit she was having, but if she called the cops before that happened, he'd have to answer their questions and the Munroe cops didn't look kindly on Billy Tupper.

"My flashlight, you insolent thief, you. Where is it?"

She stuck her arm out the window to shake a finger at Billy and when she did so, coughed again. Billy wanted to tell her to stop yelling before she choked to death.

"Don't think you can fool me. I know you've been sneaking around in my barn so I'm going to check on things, see what you've stolen, and I want my flashlight."

Oh, God. All that for a flashlight? Billy wanted to laugh but knew that would be a really bad idea. He didn't know what insolent meant, but seeing how mad she was, figured it wasn't anything good. He needed to settle her down, wait out her episode, and hope he could avoid a chat with the cops.

"I think you had it the other day when you went..." Billy decided to avoid mentioning the fact that she'd been in the barn a couple of days ago. "I think you had it in your apron pocket. Did you check there? Or maybe you dropped it. I could look around."

"It's not in my apron pocket. Don't you think I looked there?"

Her voice was rising, and she was angrier than Billy had ever seen her. "I'll take a look around. I'll be right back," he said.

Before she could answer one way or the other, Billy shimmied down the scaffolding and hurried around the house. Thankfully, the barn was out of sight of the window where she stood. If he hurried, she might not see him go inside.

So he ran. Dust kicked up behind his dirty, paint-splattered sneakers when he skidded to a halt in front of the door. Remembering how it squeaked, Billy didn't dare do more than ease it open inch by agonizing inch. Once he could sneak inside, he shoved a rake between the doors to hold them open, then scanned the area, willing his eyes to hurry and adjust to the dim light.

It took only a minute. The flashlight was right there, on an old milk can, about two feet from the door. She must have set it down before opening the door and once she was out in the daylight, forgotten about it.

Billy breathed a sigh of relief, but at the same time wondered how she'd react to him finding the stupid flashlight. If she decided he returned it just because she'd accused him of stealing it, he didn't know how he'd defend himself. He told himself the police weren't going to care about a missing flashlight but couldn't stop the twinge of worry that she'd accuse him of stealing other stuff too.

Seemed like figuring out how to finish painting her house should be his biggest worry, not figuring out how to keep his butt out of jail for stealing a damn flashlight he didn't even steal.

Back on the porch, he pounded on the screen door and kicked at the dried leaves wedged under the doorframe while he waited. And waited. He pounded again and leaned closer to the door to peer inside. While she'd lose a race to a turtle any day, she'd had plenty of time to get to the door. He wanted to set the flashlight on the table and go back to his painting, but couldn't get the idea out of his head that she was calling the police while he stood there.

"Ah, shit." He pulled on the screen door and didn't know whether to be relieved or disappointed when it opened.

He stuck his head inside and called, "Mrs. Baxter?" When there was no answer, he took a deep breath, and hoping he wasn't making a huge mistake, went inside.

"Mrs. Baxter? I found your flashlight. I can leave it on the table if you want."

Billy tiptoed through the living room, careful not to disrupt any of her lacy things, and into the kitchen. She stood there, in front of the telephone, staring at it with a vacant look on her face.

"Ah, um, I found your flashlight."

She turned to him and while he watched, the veil seemed to

lift and her eyes cleared.

"My flashlight? Why do you have my flashlight?"

In an instant, Billy weighed his options. He could tell her he'd gone to look for it, that he'd checked in the barn, assuming she'd remember she'd accused him of sneaking in there and stealing more than just the flashlight. Or he could bet on her not remembering that she'd yelled at him about stealing it, that she'd forgotten her threats to call the police. Tell the truth or avoid the truth? It wasn't much of a decision.

"I found it in the grass by the side of the house. Thought maybe you were looking for it." Then he held his breath.

She cocked her head. "Oh, yes, I think I was. I needed it for something." She looked back at the phone, then shook her head and turned back to Billy. "Thank you."

She coughed a little, but just once. Nothing like the attack she'd had earlier. Billy wanted to tell her to learn a lesson from it and to stop yelling at him, but thought better of it.

"Sure. Well, gonna get back to the painting." He began inching from the kitchen.

"See that you do. At the rate you're going, you won't have it done by the end of the summer."

Billy spun on his heel. He stomped out of the kitchen and out of the house. As he continued his stomping across the porch and back to the ladders, he entertained himself with ways he could mess with the forgetful old witch.

Number One: Tell her he hadn't had lunch and see if she'd make him a second meal.

Number Two: Hide her glasses and see how long it takes until she asks for help finding them.

Number Three: Ask her if she has the ten bucks she owes him for the chicken feed he bought for her.

Number Four: Hide the paint cans in the barn and tell her he's out, see if she'll let him take the car into town.

Number Five: Tell her his name is Tommy, not Billy.

7

Billy would have gladly slept the morning away, but the library opened at nine and closed at noon on Saturdays. Sleeping wasn't an option.

After a bowl of cereal and a piece of toast, he hopped on his bike and started the three-mile ride. He'd made the trip so many times, he figured he'd made his own ruts on the edge of the bumpy gravel road. Ruts he wouldn't have to stare at if he were driving instead of riding a bike.

He looked up instead. Up and around. Sometimes it seemed as though the only colors in the world were the pale blue of the sky and the gold of the wheat fields. Billy wondered what it would be like to look around at something else for a change. Maybe those 'purple mountain majesties' that the song talked about, or the red Georgia clay he'd heard about in another song. Or maybe like the pictures of farms in South Dakota that he'd seen in the farming magazine that was still delivered to their house where it was nothing but sunflowers for miles. But he supposed he'd get tired of looking at yellow after a while too.

In town, it was the same old thing. The stores he rarely visited, the barber shop he needed to visit, the bakery with its fresh-baked smells filling the street, the churches and the clubs—just a fancy name for bars—facing off on opposite sides of the street. Nothing ever seemed to change.

When Billy threaded his bike tire through the rack at the library, he had his choice of slots. His friends weren't there, the parking lot was empty, and he found himself doing something he never dreamed he'd do…sitting in front of the library on a Saturday morning, waiting for it to open. His life was pathetic.

Joel was the first to arrive, bounding down the sidewalk, arms flailing, toward Billy.

"Thought I'd try that running thing," he said, panting, when he dropped next to Billy on the stone wall that ringed what lawn there was in front of the red brick building. "It's as stupid as I expected. All it did was make me sweat." Joel pinched the front of his T-shirt and pulled it away from his chest until it snapped back. He repeated the motion a few more times while he used his other arm to wipe the sweat from his face.

"Steve and John still coming?" Billy asked.

"Far as I know. John said he'll be here when he wakes up, and that it wouldn't be early, but I could tell he was kind of excited about the whole thing, just didn't want to let on."

"Maybe." If the tables were turned and one of them had been doomed to work for Old Lady Baxter for the summer, then asked for help searching for information on her—at nine o'clock on a Saturday morning and at the library—Billy didn't know how helpful he'd feel. He wouldn't blame his friends if they didn't show.

"I tried to ask my mom more about Old Lady Baxter," Joel said. "Didn't go well. She gave me the same old line about not spreading rumors and wouldn't tell me anything."

"Do you think she knows something?"

Joel shook his head. "Nah, I doubt it. She just gets weird about spreading rumors, you know?"

Billy didn't answer. He did know. Once people learned Joel's brother had died in Vietnam, rumors about him had spread like fire through a barn full of dried hay. Lies about him deserting, or about him shooting himself to get out of the army had circulated for weeks until there'd been a ceremony at city hall and the mayor had read the telegram Jeff's commanding officer had sent Joel's parents that detailed how Jeff had been trying to save a child who'd wandered into a dangerous area when he'd been shot by a sniper. That had shut up the gossipy town once and for all.

Billy recalled asking his dad why everyone was saying bad things about Jeff. His dad, in one of his better moments, had looked thirteen-year-old Billy in the eye and said, 'Sometimes people think they can get rid of their guilt by passin' it on to someone else. Those who fussed and cussed about this blasted war, right or wrong, are feelin' mighty guilty about that right now and are lookin' for a way to justify all the bad things they said. Tryin' to convince themselves one of our Munroe boys agreed with them enough to do somethin' stupid, well, they're thinkin' that would make them somehow right in all the stuff they said. Havin' to face the facts and admit that that boy died doin' the right thing? That's a bitter pill for some of them to swallow.'

Billy hadn't understood much of what his dad said that day, but over the years he'd thought about it and realized his dad made sense. And Joel's mom's feelings about gossiping made sense too.

"Hey, there's Steve!" Joel said as a car pulled into the parking lot.

"You drove?" Billy asked when Steve joined them. "Two blocks?"

Steve grinned. "It's my day to use the car. I wasn't going to leave it at home and let my sister get her hands on it."

A lady in a brown dress and ugly brown shoes marched up the sidewalk, her eyes never leaving Billy and his friends and, Billy thought, going out of her way to put as much distance between herself and them as possible. Billy watched as she fit a key into the lock, then gave them another glance over her shoulder before she disappeared inside.

"Guess that means it's open," Joel said.

"Guess so." Steve nodded toward the door. "She looked like she'll be more than happy to help us."

A blast of cool air met them when they entered the library. Billy inhaled and filled his lungs. Maybe there was something good about the library.

Joel made a beeline for the desk. The lady in the brown dress frowned at him.

"We're wondering if you have old newspapers we can look at."

The librarian sighed. "Old newspapers. What sort of newspapers and how old?"

"Munroe area newspapers." Joel scratched his head through his mop of red hair. "Maybe other Kansas newspapers too. About thirty or forty years old."

"I see. And what would you be looking for in these newspapers?"

Nerves jumped in Billy's stomach. He didn't think there were any rules against looking up old news stories about someone, but he was afraid the lady would get mad if she knew what they were after and would tell them to get lost.

"Just some local history, what it was like here during the depression, the start of World War II, stuff like that."

Billy was impressed with Joel's ability to feed her a line of bullshit.

"Hmm." One of her eyebrows rose above the rim of her cat-eye glasses and her lips pressed together in a hard line. "Getting a head start on schoolwork, are you?"

"Yep. Can't be too prepared." Joel grinned, and the lady rolled her eyes.

She stood and smoothed her skirt, then took her time looking each of them up and down, her scowl deepening the longer she looked. Just when Billy was sure she was going to come up with a reason they couldn't look at the newspapers, maybe why they couldn't even be in the library, she sighed and took a step out from behind her desk.

"Follow me."

Joel made a face at her back then followed her, mimicking her ramrod straight posture and quick footsteps. Steve and Billy, fighting to suppress their laughter, followed Joel.

They'd only gone a few feet when a voice rang out. "Hey, wait for me, you turkeys!"

Billy turned his head but kept walking. The librarian didn't. Billy almost walked right into her when her spine stiffened and she froze in place. Her face was red when she spun around.

"Keep your voice down!" Somehow, she managed to yell and whisper at the same time.

John's mouth twitched. "Sorry. Hope I didn't disturb all these people busy reading."

There wasn't a soul in the building besides the librarian and the four of them. From the choked laughs next to him, Joel and Steve found John's comment as funny as Billy did. The librarian did not.

"You will keep your voice down or you will leave."

"Fine. Sorry."

"I suppose you're going to tell me you're here to get a head start on your school work as well?"

John looked at Billy, Joel, and Steve and under his breath called his friends a string of names that would have gotten him banned from the library for life had the librarian heard him. Louder, he said, "Can't be too prepared."

"Hey, that's what I said!" Joel said too loudly and earned himself a steely glare.

"Perhaps you'd like to come back in a few months and show me your report cards. I have to assume you'll all earn top marks after working so hard over the summer."

She didn't wait for a response, just turned and resumed her brisk walk to the back of the library. It must be exhausting, Billy thought, to have to be so pissed off all day. He couldn't imagine a worse torture than to be doomed to spending his life talking about books and giving kids grief. What a stupid job.

When the grouch reached the back wall, she stopped in front of a machine and laid a protective hand on the top. A matching machine sat a few feet away.

"These are our microfilm machines. They are very expensive, and we are extremely fortunate to have them. Thanks to a generous benefactor, we were able to purchase them and be one of the first libraries in the county—in the state, even—to have them. I gather from your open-mouthed stares, you are not familiar with microfilm?"

"Microfilm?" Joel asked. "We wanted newspapers."

This time she closed her eyes when she sighed. If Billy wasn't mistaken, she also whispered something about God and patience.

"Our older newspapers are on microfilm. It's a storage and retrieval system that enables us to preserve countless documents in a very small amount of space."

"Film, you said? So the newspapers will be like a movie?" Billy was confused.

"In a matter of speaking. Every image, that's to say every article and picture and advertisement just as it appeared on the page of the newspaper, is copied onto the microfilm and can be viewed using this." She gave the machine a caress.

Before the librarian could stop him, Joel sat down at the chair in front of the machine and began poking at buttons, twisting dials. "How does it turn on?"

She swatted his hand away. "Do not touch until I've given you instructions. Listen very carefully. If you damage these machines in any way, I will contact your parents. As I told you, they are very expensive and I'm certain a phone call from me is not one your parents would enjoy."

"It's not one anyone would enjoy," John whispered and Billy had to turn away and bite his lips together.

"Get up," she told Joel. When he did, she took his place. "Now, watch closely and pay attention. If I don't think you're paying attention, you won't be viewing film today or any other day. Is that clear?"

"Yes," they all muttered.

She proceeded to instruct them on how to turn on the machine, how to feed a film into the viewer, how to advance and reverse the film, how to enlarge the image, how to rotate the image, and on the dozens of things they better not do with the machine. Even though her lecture was boring, and far too long, and she talked to them like they were five-year-olds, Billy was in awe of the whole thing. All those pages and pages of newspaper on a spool of film no bigger than his fist. It was amazing.

"Show me you've been listening. One of you, sit down and properly operate the machine."

Steve elbowed Joel aside. Good idea, Billy thought, as Steve was a lot more likely than Joel to have paid attention. And since Steve loved anything with moving parts, or with an engine, or with any kind of mechanics, he probably would have worked the machine just fine without ten minutes of instruction.

Without a word, Steve plucked a microfilm box from the file cabinet, eased the spool into his hand, then threaded it through the machine with one smooth motion. After just a few seconds, a headline about a blizzard filled the screen.

The librarian seemed more annoyed than pleased. She looked down her nose at Steve, then at the rest of them. "Very well, but I'll be keeping an eye on all of you. The other machine is identical to this one. I suppose you can use both of them. However, if someone else comes in today and wants to access microfilm, you will give up one of the machines immediately. Is that clear?" They nodded at her. "And, if yet another person comes, you will give up the second machine. We will discuss time limits if it becomes necessary. Are there any questions?"

When no one said anything, she gave them a tight nod. She started to walk away, but even though her feet were moving, she didn't seem to get any farther away. Joel didn't seem to care. He dropped down in front of the second machine and turned it on.

"Let's get started."

Once the librarian was finally back at her desk, Billy joined Joel at the table. "We need to have some idea of where to start looking. Like the dates when the kids disappeared. We can't just start looking through all this." Billy waved his arm in the direction of the file cabinet. It was enormous.

Joel pulled a piece of paper out of his pocket. "Here. I have some dates we can start with."

There were names and dates scrawled on the paper. Some dates had stars next to them.

"How do you know all this?"

"I've been writing stuff down for a long time. I told you, one day I'm going to figure it out."

"What do the stars mean?"

"Those are the dates I'm pretty sure about. If we start with those, there'll probably be stuff in the articles about the other kids so we won't have to do so much searching for the dates we're not as sure about."

Billy nodded. "That makes sense." He realized he'd come to the library with nothing but the goal of finding information on some missing kids. He wouldn't have had the faintest idea where to start if it weren't for Joel. "Cool," he added.

"We should start with papers from 1937. I'm almost sure of that date. We'll go from there."

Joel got up and after scanning the drawers on the cabinet, pulled one open. Steve and John were still looking through the film Steve had grabbed at random from the cabinet to prove he knew how to use the machine.

"Hey, guys, are you gonna look for stuff on Old Lady Baxter or keep drooling over 1950s swimsuit ads?" Billy asked them.

"Billy, my man, give us a little credit. If you look closely, you'll see it is, in fact, an ad about gaining weight. Apparently, being too skinny was a problem in the 1950s." John took his time studying Billy from head to toe. He shook his head sadly. "You're awfully thin. Perhaps you could benefit from one of these fine products."

"Funny. If you ever decide to help, Joel's got a list of dates you should check."

"We'll help," Steve said. He removed the film they'd been looking at and boxed it up. "Tell us where to start."

It was slow going. Billy sat with Joel and they took turns skimming through an endless sea of articles, the overwhelming majority of which had nothing whatsoever to do with Mrs. Baxter or missing kids. Billy found that if he stared at the blur on the screen for too long, he felt dizzy. What started out as fun, quickly became a chore.

"Here!" Joel said when Billy took a break to close his eyes in an attempt to stop the headache that was threatening. "The second kid. Thaddeus Miller. Disappeared April 27, 1937."

Billy glanced at the article while Joel picked out facts and recited them.

"Four years old, youngest of six kids. Last seen around seven o'clock in the morning. Mother said she thinks one of the other kids gave him something to eat, then they were all busy getting their garden ready for planting and she doesn't know when he disappeared."

"How do you not know if your kid is around?" Billy asked. He realized his dad had no idea when he was around. Then again, Billy wasn't four.

Joel shrugged and kept reading. "One of the older kids told the police Tad had wandered off before but always came back so they didn't think much of it. They went to bed..." Joel stopped and turned to Billy, eyes wide. "They went to bed? They didn't know where the kid was and they just went to bed? Without looking for him?"

"I don't know. Seems that way." He couldn't stop himself from wondering if his dad would have looked for him.

Joel shook his head and turned back to the article. His lips moved as he read it to himself. "Says the mother reported it to the police the next day. Over twenty-four hours after she last remembered seeing him." Joel looked sad. "If they'd been paying attention, if they'd noticed he was missing, maybe they would have found him. Maybe Old Lady Baxter wouldn't have gotten away with him."

Billy didn't know what to say to that, so focused on the information in the article. "Does it mention the kid's dad?"

"Just says the dad wasn't home, that he was out looking for work."

"Did he come back? Did he know his kid disappeared? Maybe he's the one who did it?"

"I don't know. We need to look at the next few papers."

Joel started buzzing through the film again and Billy had to look away. He'd seen in the article that the missing kid was a lot younger than his brothers and sisters, at least five years younger. Probably the family didn't have any money, maybe the dad didn't want another kid to raise. The others were older, they could go out on their own, could try to find work or could soon, but he'd be stuck with the young one. Maybe it seemed to the dad like he'd never be done raising kids. Maybe he'd had enough. Maybe...

"Here's another story. Two days later, no trace of the kid. And no sign of the dad. The mom said she wasn't surprised the dad wasn't home, that he'd said he was going to go as far as he had to until he found a job."

"Sounds to me like the mom is covering for the dad."

Joel frowned and his shoulders slumped. "Maybe. Then you think he did it?"

"Is there any mention of Old Lady Baxter?"

"Not yet, but I'll keep looking."

While Joel did that, Billy scooted his chair over to Steve and John. "You guys find anything?"

Steve nodded. "We tried starting with the fourth kid, but Joel didn't have much of an idea on a date and after we went through a bunch of papers without finding anything, we gave up and tried the third kid." Steve pointed at the screen. "Here. A girl, Jane Nichols, disappeared on the second of June, 1939. We got lucky. Joel's notes said 'summer, 1939.' We decided summer started with June, so that's where we started looking. Didn't have to look far. There's a lot about Old Lady Baxter in here."

Billy leaned closer. "What does it say?"

"That the girl was six, she was in first grade, Alma Baxter worked at the school and was questioned about the disappearance."

"Alma? Her name is Alma?"

"Seems so."

"June second. School was probably out, or just about out, by then. Did the girl disappear on a school day? She went to school in the morning and didn't come home that afternoon, or what?"

"School was already out, but the girl wandered off sometime that morning, according to her mother. It wasn't reported until evening, so at least eight hours had passed since Jane was last seen," John said.

"And what did Old Lady Baxter have to say?"

"Not much, I guess. Just that she knew the girl but had no idea where she was. She offered to help search, did help, but claimed to know nothing that would aid the investigation," Steve said.

"Okay, so there was a tie with her and this girl. We found information on the second kid and there didn't seem to be any tie between her and that kid. But, like this one, that kid wasn't reported missing until much later. A day later," Billy said.

John's eyebrows rose. "They waited a day? That's even worse than this family. Sure seems like parents would notice their kid is missing and would want to get any help they could get in finding that kid. Unless they didn't want to find the kid."

"You think the parents did it." It wasn't a question. Billy'd been thinking the same thing.

"I think it seems like a good possibility. What about the other kids? Same story?" John asked.

"I don't know. We haven't found anything yet."

"This article might be the first one to tie the disappearances together." Steve turned back to the screen and used his finger to scan the article. "It mentions a kid called Timmy Wagner who disappeared in February of 1936, and then Thaddeus Miller who disappeared in 1937."

"Yeah, Tad Miller. That's the kid we were reading about," Billy said.

"Seems like after this kid, after there were three, they started to suspect that the same person might be responsible for all three so the cops started looking for things that would link them. It says that Alma Baxter attended church with the Wagners, the first kid's family, so that's probably why she became a suspect," Steve said.

Billy nodded. Things were falling into place. "Now that we have a date for the first kid, we need to look back at those papers and see what they say, what the circumstances were. February 1936?" Billy asked.

"Yep," John said.

"Okay, I'll look for the film."

Billy went to the sea of drawers and searched for the correct drawer, then the correct box inside that drawer. The whole thing was turning into something that seemed far too much like school work, but Billy couldn't deny the fact that he was hooked. Not nuts like Joel, but curious enough to keep doing what amounted to school work in the middle of the summer. For someone who started in October counting the number of school days until summer vacation, it was saying something.

Billy found the box and dropped it into John's waiting hand.

"Move it, Steve. It's my turn to play with this thing," John said.

Billy left them to search and returned to Joel just as the librarian showed up. She stopped midway between the two viewers, and her eyes flitted from one to the other.

"Are you boys finding what you're looking for?"

Billy thought she didn't much sound like she cared, more like she just wanted to check that they weren't doing anything wrong with her precious machines.

"We are, thank you," Billy answered before John could make a stupid comment.

"Hmm." She peered over Joel's shoulder, but he'd advanced the film and the article displayed on the screen had to do with the tanking economy. Steve and John's machine was blank as they had taken out one film and hadn't yet threaded the new one through.

"Keep your voices down. It was getting a little loud over here," she said in a parting shot as she walked away.

"We'll keep our voices down if you keep your bitchy attitude down," John muttered at her back.

Billy held his breath, but the librarian didn't turn. "Anything new?" he asked Joel.

"Not much. I started taking notes so we can put everything together later." He hooked a thumb in Steve and John's direction. "They're reading about the first kid?"

"Yeah. The articles they read on the third kid, a girl, gave the date of the first one so they're checking on that."

"Okay, then we need to figure out the fourth one." Joel leaned back in his chair, let his head drop back, and closed his eyes. "This is harder than I expected."

"I'll look for a while."

Joel's notes on the fourth missing kid said only 'about a year later' so Billy started with June 1940. He skimmed until his eyes crossed, but he found nothing.

"We could ask the librarian for help," Joel said.

Billy quit staring at the screen and turned to look at Joel. He rubbed his eyes in an attempt to get rid of the dots of light that seemed to follow no matter where he looked.

"Do you think we should?"

Joel shrugged. "There's nothing wrong with looking at old newspaper articles. If it was against the law or something they wouldn't have them here."

"I guess." Billy chewed on his lip and considered. They may never find any more information without help. At least not without coming back another time and doing more searching. He didn't want to spend another day in the library. But if she knew what they were looking for, would she tell someone? Would it somehow get back to Old Lady Baxter? And if it did, what would that mean for him? Could his days at her house get even worse?

"So? Should we ask?"

Billy decided the pros outweighed the cons. "We should. Or, you should. Maybe tell her you found something that mentioned the missing kids, you remember hearing about it and thought there were four kids, and does she know any more about it? Make it seem like it wasn't what we came here looking for."

"Okay. She probably won't believe me, though." Joel pushed up from his chair and headed for the librarian's desk.

Probably not, Billy figured, but it was worth a try. Deciding it would be better if Steve and John didn't have stuff about the kids on their screen when Joel came back with the librarian, he told them to find something else to read, then headed to the restroom. In hopes of protecting himself in case the librarian got mad or decided to tell someone what they were researching, he selfishly decided it would be best if he wasn't around.

He gave it ten minutes before he inched out from a long row of books to sneak a look back at the microfilm machines. His friends were alone and focused on the screens, so he figured it was safe to go back.

"What did she say?" he asked when he took the seat next to Joel.

"She gave me four dates, the three we knew and one other one. She spit them out without thinking about it, like she was reciting the Pledge of Allegiance or something. Seems like we're not the first ones to ask."

Billy looked over his shoulder. "She's old enough that she might have been around when it happened."

"True. Anyway, I got the paper from August 9, 1940, and here's the first article that talks about the kid. I just started reading it."

"Okay. I'm gonna check with Steve and John and see what they're finding about the first kid. I'll make sure they're taking some notes."

Joel nodded, but was lost in the words splayed across the screen and Billy wasn't convinced Joel even heard him. John was still at the other screen. Steve was scrawling notes on a piece of the scratch paper that was stacked next to the machine and started spewing facts before Billy could ask.

"Timmy Wagner. Disappeared on February 18, 1936, during a snow storm. It says he wasn't reported missing for a few days because the parents couldn't get to town to tell the police until the storm let up and the roads were cleared. He was never found."

"And nothing about Old Lady Baxter?"

"Nothing. I don't think she was a suspect. Her name isn't in anything that we've read."

"That makes sense. Unless someone saw her around the kid, or maybe if she knew him, why would they suspect her? The first kid to disappear...no reason to suspect some lady who had no connection to him."

"We'll keep looking, but I don't think we'll find her name," Steve said.

"And keep taking notes," Billy said. "Joel wants everything written down so he can put it all together later."

"Joel's a dork," was John's contribution to the conversation. "You know he really believes he's going to prove she did it."

"You don't think she did?" Billy asked.

"Of course, I think she did it. I just don't think some sixteen-year-old who believes every rumor he's ever heard will be the one to prove it."

They stayed at the library until eleven-thirty when someone showed up who wanted to use the microfilm machine and they decided they'd done all they could anyway. A week ago, Billy would never have guessed he'd spend a perfect Saturday morning at the library, but on some level, it had been worth it. They'd made progress, and they knew a lot more than they had when they'd walked in the doors two-and-a-half hours earlier.

The librarian watched them, frowning over the top of her glasses as they joked and shoved and laughed their way out the library doors. The frown turned to a smile when Billy closed the door behind himself.

Once outside, John spread his arms wide and turned his face to the sun. "We need to go to the lake."

After the cool reprieve in the library, the heat sucker-punched Billy and nearly brought him to his knees. The lake sounded perfect.

"I'm in," Steve said. "Gotta go home and change, eat some lunch, then I'll head over. Who wants a ride?"

"I do!" Joel almost shouted. "Drop me at my house then pick me up?"

"Same here," John said.

"Sure," Steve said. "Billy?"

Something had been on Billy's mind all morning, but he hadn't figured out a way to do anything about it. He jumped at his chance.

"I've gotta talk to Mr. Thompson about my schedule," he lied. "I'll bike over to the store, grab something to eat, and you can pick me up there before you head to the lake as long as I can throw my bike in the trunk. I've got my swim trunks on my bike."

"That works. About quarter to one."

Steve, John, and Joel headed for the parking lot while Billy ambled toward his bike. He fussed around with the towel he had wrapped around his trunks and strapped to the back of his bike for a minute until his friends were out of sight. Then he turned back to the library.

8

Billy stood inside the doors of the library, his head turning in one direction, then the other. He had no idea where to start.

"Back so soon."

The librarian sounded less than pleased, but Billy didn't have time to care. He needed help, so he walked to her desk.

"Yeah. Um, I wonder if you can help me."

"More research?"

Her voice dripped with sarcasm. Holding his tongue and biting back his smart-ass reply proved almost impossible. Almost.

"Yes. I'm looking for a book or an article or something about...about..." He realized he didn't know what to call it.

"About?"

"Old people. Old people who forget stuff. But only sometimes. Like they're talking to you and then they forget what they're talking about, you know?"

All the meanness vanished from her face and her eyes turned sad. Her voice was hardly more than a whisper when she replied, "I do know."

"I don't know if it's normal or if there's something wrong with...with this person, but I wanted to maybe read a book about it, see if I could figure out how to deal with this person."

"This person. It's someone close to you?" She reached out her hand and put it on his arm. She looked like she was ready to hug him and Billy nearly gagged.

"It's someone I know," he managed.

"I see. Well, there are books that can help you. If you go to the card catalog and search senility or dementia it will point you in the right direction. Or try searching the stacks in the six hundreds, six-sixteen, to be precise."

She might as well have been speaking Swahili for as much as Billy understood. "Um…"

"You do know how to use the card catalog, don't you?"

"I'm not sure."

The eye roll was back, but there was still some kindness in her eyes. Billy held on to a bit of hope she'd help him.

"This way."

She marched across the library to a giant cupboard with dozens of little drawers. The card catalog. He knew that much. How to use it, however, was a mystery.

"Here." She pointed at the drawers. "You'll find books listed by title, by author, and by subject. If, for example, you're looking for Gone with the Wind, by Margaret Mitchell, a book set during the Civil War, you could search in this drawer," she pointed to a drawer with a tiny white card with the letters 'Gab-Go' typed on it, "to find the book by title, or this drawer," she pointed to another, "to find the book by author, or you could try searching for 'Civil War' in here." She pointed again.

Billy hoped she didn't expect him to show her he understood, because he didn't. "So, if I wanted a book about someone who forgets stuff…"

"Yes. Start with 'senile' or 'senility' and see where that takes you. Sometimes you start one place only to be led to another place."

It all sounded needlessly confusing to Billy, but he wasn't about to say so. He still needed her help.

"Senile? I should look for that word? And it's all in

alphabetical order?"

He thought she sighed, but she didn't turn and walk away. "Here, let me help you get started."

Billy watched as she pulled open a drawer and began flipping through cards so quickly, they weren't much more than a blur. He didn't have the first clue how she could possibly read them when they moved so fast, but she just kept flipping. When she finally stopped, she looked over her shoulder at him.

"Here." She nodded toward the open drawer and the card behind her finger. "The card shows you the title, a brief description of the book, and where to find it."

She grabbed a piece of paper, a stubby pencil, and scribbled some numbers that Billy assumed told her where the book was but meant nothing to him.

"Follow me."

Billy did, as she wound through bookshelves. She didn't so much as glance at the shelves, rather strode purposefully ahead at top speed. When she stopped, she pointed to a shelf full of thick, mind-numbingly dull-looking books.

"This is where you'll want to look." She pulled one from the shelf, one that was about four inches thick with a plain black cover, and Billy saw when she cracked it open, words so small he'd probably need a magnifying glass to read them. "This is the book we found in the card catalog. If you browse through the books nearby, you'll find others that deal with the same subject. Take a look, see which ones best fit your needs, and then check them out if you wish."

She stopped and looked at Billy. When she spoke, her sigh was back. "I don't suppose you have a library card?"

"Uh, no. Can I get one?"

She blinked a few times and her forehead creased as she studied him. It didn't take a genius to figure out he was about the last person she trusted with her books.

"Yes, I suppose you can." She answered like someone would answer the question, 'Would you like me to poke toothpicks under your fingernails?' "See me at the desk when you're ready." She lifted her arm and glanced at her watch. "We close in eighteen minutes."

With that, she handed Billy the book she'd taken from the shelf, then marched away. Billy was left holding a weighty book he didn't want to read, facing a shelf full of dozens of other books he didn't want to read, but resigning himself to the fact that if he wanted answers, he would have to try to make sense out of what a bunch of doctors wrote, probably for a bunch of other doctors and not for somebody like him.

Billy spent a few minutes looking at the titles on the shelf. Words like Geriatrics and Dementia appeared in many of the titles. Billy wasn't sure what either word meant, but when he pulled one off the shelf and looked at the table of contents, determined that they must have something to do with old people.

Sick of the whole morning, and with his eyes feeling like they were permanently crossed, he grabbed a couple of the books and went to try his luck at getting a library card.

He beat Steve to the sidewalk in front of Thompson's by less than a minute. He'd bought an apple, some potato chips, two hunks of jerky from the butcher counter, and a Coke, then had used the bag to cover the library books. Deciding it would be easier, and mean he could avoid answering questions, he'd stashed his bike behind the store, telling Mr. Thompson he'd be by to pick it up later.

"Hurry up, man." John hung out the passenger window and begged. "I'm dying in here."

It was hot, and getting hotter. The lake was going to be packed, but Billy didn't care. He hadn't been there all summer, and he hadn't seen Julie all summer. Of course, there was no guarantee Julie would be there, but he could hope. He knew she had a job babysitting a few days a week but thought that might mean her weekends were free. And John said she'd been at the lake whenever he'd been there.

"Where's your bike?" Steve interrupted Billy's day dream about Julie and her pink bikini.

"I decided to leave it here, back behind the store. It's easier that way, and a shorter ride home if you drop me here after the lake."

Steve shrugged. "No problem. Maybe if it's not too late, I can give you a ride home. It's too hot to be riding a bike."

They piled in the car and sweated through the short ride to the lake. In a state not known for its lakes, and in a town not known for much of anything, Munroe had one thing to brag about. Big Lake. One of only a few naturally occurring lakes in the state, Big Lake wasn't big at all, at least not compared to pictures Billy had seen of some actual big lakes, but it had water and that water's temperature was at least a few degrees below the current air temperature of ninety-eight, so Billy didn't care how stupid the name was, he just wanted to jump in.

Like usual, Joel forgot his shoes, so he hopped and twisted and swore his way across the fiery blacktop while Billy and the others tried to pretend Joel wasn't with them. The brown sand wasn't much cooler, but finally Joel made it to the wet sand and stopped yelling.

"Bring your damn shoes the next time." John shook his head and looked like he wanted to slug Joel.

Joel just grinned. "I will."

"No you won't," John said for all of them. Joel never remembered anything.

Billy had ducked into the bathroom at the store, so his trunks were on and he was ready to get in the water. He threw down his towel on an empty square of sand they found smack-dab in the middle of the crowded beach. His friends piled theirs alongside, and with only a glance and a grin, challenged each other to a race to the raft.

The four of them took off at a dead run, sidestepping sunbathers, hurtling over sand pails and even a few toddlers, and ignoring the shouts of those they sprayed with sand. Billy was a step behind as he'd taken a moment to scan the crowd hoping to spot a blonde ponytail and a pink bikini, but he was even with Steve by the time they hit the water. Stretching his arms out straight, Billy dove in and started paddling through the murky water.

The raft was nothing more than four barrels topped with shabby indoor-outdoor carpet stretched over some warped boards, but it provided endless entertainment when it came to challenging each other to cannonball contests, to shoving each other off when the lifeguard wasn't watching, and serving as the finish line for their races.

Billy came in second, passing Steve and John, but there was no catching Joel. The water was the one place Joel usually had bragging rights. The kid was like a fish, Billy thought, as he spotted Joel flipping over in a somersault while waiting for the rest of them to reach the raft. The awkwardness that seemed to follow Joel like a shadow disappeared in the water.

They were all panting as they hoisted themselves up and onto the raft. Billy had just stood up when a shove from John sent him right back into the water. Served him right, he figured, for fixing his eyes on the beach instead of on his friends. He didn't make the same mistake twice.

"Look at all the little kids," Steve said. "The place is crawling with crawlers." He laughed at his pun.

"It'll clear out in a while, always does. The kids get crabby, the parents get crabbier, and they argue their way back to their cars." John pointed. "There goes one now."

Billy watched as a clearly frustrated dad plucked a screaming kid from the water and held him like a football while the kid continued to kick and scream. The dad used his free hand to gather up a bunch of toys, whistled at a couple other kids who threw up their hands and yelled but trudged from the water, barked something at his wife who even from a distance looked pissed, and then stomped toward the parking lot. It seemed a lot easier to just stay home.

"Cannonball or diving contest?" Joel asked.

"I vote cannonball. I might stand a chance," Steve said.

"Okay, but then diving after that," Joel said. After just a few minutes in the sun, his freckles had already seemed to grow and spread. What skin showed was so pale, he looked like a giant, speckled marshmallow.

John went first. He got a running start and threw himself off the raft, landing partly on his back and sending up a respectable splash. They took turns, criticizing one another's form, lack of splash, and all-around crappiness. After five cannonballs and five struggles to climb back onto the raft, Billy was out of breath. With the exception of Joel, who seemed to spring from the water and onto the raft as if he'd bounced himself off a trampoline, the others were just as winded.

"I need a break," Billy said.

The raft was crowded, there'd be no sitting to take a break there, so they paddled back to the beach and to their towels they'd left in a heap. Some jostling on the part of Billy and his friends, some nasty looks on the part of their beach neighbors, but in the end, the boys staked claim to a six-foot square of prime beach property. Seated in a row, they leaned back on their elbows and surveyed the crowd.

"I see Randy's here. I didn't notice his car in the lot when we got here. Thought maybe we'd luck out and he wouldn't be here today," Billy said.

"Oh, didn't you hear?" Joel pushed up from his elbows and hovered over Billy. "He wrecked his car! Smashed the whole front end," Joel reported gleefully.

Billy, feeling the tugs of a grin at the corners of his mouth, swung his head to look at Steve and John. "Really? He wrecked the Firebird?"

John snorted out a laugh. "Thought you would have heard. Thought everyone had heard. Crashed it into a telephone pole, the dumbass. He's been driving his mom's car. Apparently his parents are as dumb as he is. It's only a matter of time until he wrecks the station wagon too."

Billy's grin grew and reached his eyes. It was almost too good to be true. "He's driving a station wagon?"

"Yep," Steve said. "A green woodie wagon. Ugly as sin."

Billy threw his head back and laughed. He didn't have much reason to, at least Randy had a car to drive instead of a bike, but the idea of the guy who couldn't quit talking about how great his Firebird was now driving a station wagon was too good to pass up.

"I think I'll go over there and tell him I'm thinking about getting a car so I'd like to take a look at his, see if I think a Firebird's right for me."

"He'll kick your ass," Steve warned.

"He'll try," Billy answered, but knew Steve was right. Randy was three inches taller and at least thirty pounds heavier, and when he wasn't driving up and down Main Street, he was lifting weights. He liked to make sure everyone knew how tough he was by crushing cans against his forehead.

Steve just shook his head. John, though, thought it was a fine idea. "Let's go over there."

He nodded toward the snack bar. Randy was leaning back, one knee bent and his foot pressed against the wall, his arms crossed over his chest, and stupid, round sunglasses on his square face. He looked like a fool.

Billy was ready to go tell him so when there was a soft voice behind him. "Hi, Billy."

His stomach flipped and his heart thudded wildly. He'd know that voice anywhere, he'd been hearing it in his dreams for two years. She was really talking to him? Billy swallowed over the lump that had taken up residence in his throat, then took a deep breath before he turned around.

"Hi, Julie."

His voice shook. He heard it, he knew his friends heard it, he prayed Julie didn't.

"How've you been? I haven't seen you all summer."

Julie was flanked by her friends Mandy and Kim. Kim, hands on her hips and eyes trained on John, made no attempt to hide the fact that she was studying him from head to toe. Mandy looked everywhere but at Billy and his friends.

"Um, fine. Been busy." Why couldn't he think of something clever to say?

Julie's eyes clouded. "Is it horrible working for her?"

Like everyone at school, Julie knew about the fire, knew about Billy's court appearance, and knew how he was spending his summer.

"It's not so bad." It was, of course, but that didn't seem like what Julie wanted to hear.

"That's good. Have you been coming to the lake? I'm not here every day, but it seems like we must be here on different days because I haven't seen you at all."

"I haven't been around much...I'm working at Thompson's too, so..."

Julie smiled. "Oh. I didn't know you were working there. That's nice." Her smiled dimmed a bit. "How do you have time?"

"It's just some nights, a few hours on the weekends."

"Oh."

An awkward silence followed. The sweat Billy felt trickling down his neck, under his arms, had nothing to do with the heat.

"You told Terrence you'd meet him for ice cream, Julie. Remember?" Mandy said. She didn't have any trouble looking Billy in the eye now.

Julie blushed and elbowed Mandy. Billy wondered if it meant she was embarrassed to be hanging out with Terrence, or if she didn't want Billy to know, or if she was just mad at Mandy. Girls were hard to figure out.

"Better go see *Terrence*," John said. "God, what an idiot," he added under his breath.

"It's just, well, I mean..." Julie stammered and her blush

deepened.

While the last thing Billy wanted was for Julie to talk to Terrence, he took pity on her. "I'll see you around. We were just heading back in the water. It's too hot on the beach."

"Okay. Well, bye."

Julie turned to go. Mandy couldn't get away fast enough, but Kim took her time, keeping her gaze on John. Billy had to give John credit. He cocked a hip and met her gaze without fidgeting.

After she'd taken a few steps, Julie turned back. "Terrence is having a party tonight. His parents are out of town. Do you think you'll be there?"

Billy had to swallow his laugh. He had about as much chance of being let into Terrence's house as he had of buying a Firebird.

"I have to work for Mr. Thompson tonight." It was a lie, but it was an easy way out.

"Oh. See you later, then."

She and her friends weren't more than ten feet away before the heckling started.

"Ooh, please come to Terrence's party, Billy," Joel said in a ridiculously high-pitched voice. His hands were on his hips, his chest pushed forward, and his shoulders rocking back and forth. When he started batting his eyes, Billy reached out to slug him. Joel skipped out of reach just in time.

"You should go," Steve said. "She wants to hang out with you."

"Yeah, right, like Terrence is gonna let me in his house."

"Maybe you could sneak in and find Julie. It would really piss off Terrence if he sees you with her in his own house." John grinned at the idea. "I'll go with you."

"You wanna see if Kim is there," Joel said. He puckered his lips and made kissing noises at John. When John swung at Joel, he didn't miss.

"Ow!" Joel rubbed his shoulder.

John ignored him. "What do you think?" John stared toward the snack bar. "Swim, or have some fun at the snack bar?"

Julie and her friends were talking to Terrence and Randy. All of them held ice cream cones. Billy watched as Julie licked the drips around the edge of her cone, the pink ice cream perfectly matching her pink bikini. He couldn't hear what she said, but when she smiled at Terrence, Billy relaxed and smiled too. The smile she gave Terrence was fake. Billy knew, because he'd seen her real smile a few minutes ago when she'd stood next to him.

"Let's swim. Maybe we'll talk to those jackasses later, but a diving contest sounds fun," Billy said.

Beside him, Joel jumped and clicked his heels, reminding Billy of the leprechaun on the Lucky Charms commercials. "Whoo hoo!" Joel shouted and darted off toward the water.

John shook his head. "That kid is so weird."

9

On Monday morning, as Billy pedaled his way toward Mrs. Baxter's house, he hummed to himself. After a minute, he started to mutter, "I know an old lady who swallowed a fly, I don't know why she swallowed a fly, I guess she'll die. I know an old lady..."

Maybe it was because he'd talked to Tracy for a few minutes the day before. Maybe it was because he'd looked at the books he'd checked out at the library. Whatever the reason, the song was stuck in his head.

Gradually, the house got closer and the words slowed, then died on his tongue. The library books were boring, at times impossible to understand, but he'd learned a few things. Old Lady Baxter forgetting stuff seemed to be normal for an old person, but the crazy outbursts, the anger, the accusations, seemed to indicate it was more than just being old.

Dementia was one of the words he'd come across over and over in what he'd read. Having to do with defects and problems with the mind, it wasn't a specific disease, more just a word to describe a bunch of different symptoms. Things like memory loss, forgetfulness, and poor judgement were signs that something was going wrong with a person's brain.

Alzheimer's though, a word he'd never before heard, was a

specific disease. From what he'd read, and from what he'd understood from what he read, the disease had been around for a long time, but doctors were learning more about it all the time. If he understood correctly, things go wrong in the brain, the brain stops working like it's supposed to, and a person starts having problems with memory, with doing normal, everyday things, and can have major changes in personality. There's no medicine to fix it and no recovery. It sure seemed like what was going on with Old Lady Baxter.

So the old lady really was going to die.

For as often as he'd wished for that, it still felt weird knowing it would happen. People could live for years with the disease, he'd read that, but they didn't get better. Ever. Alzheimer's didn't really kill the person, it was a fall, an infection, or something else that caused the person to die, but it was because the person had Alzheimer's.

Billy wondered if she knew.

The paint cans were on the porch, but so was a note telling him to start with the mowing. Billy groaned. He'd mowed his own lawn the day before and as much as he hated painting, he was starting to hate mowing more. His yard was big; hers was even bigger. And she insisted he use the lawn shears to trim around the fence and the garden. His hand would ache long before he finished. And then he'd have to hold a paint brush for the rest of the day.

Like almost every day he'd been there, it was hot, the sky was cloudless, and he was sweaty and tired and crabby before he started.

Things didn't improve as the day went on. He mowed, he trimmed, and he painted. And he passed the time replaying in his mind every word Julie had said to him Saturday at the lake. He tried to recall her tone of voice, her facial expressions.

At times, he convinced himself she was just being friendly. Maybe even curious. He knew she, along with everyone else from school, was dying to know what the real story was with Old Lady Baxter. Joel wasn't the only one with crazy ideas and theories. Once in a while, he let himself believe she might actually like him, but then he quickly came up with a long list of reasons why that couldn't be true and talked himself out of his fantasies.

What he didn't do was see Mrs. Baxter. His lunch showed up on the porch and he ate it greedily, but he left the empty plate and glass and went back to painting without so much as a glimpse of her. Not that he wanted to see her, exactly. If he spent the rest of the summer without laying eyes on her, it would be fine by him. But this week, he was going to have to talk to her.

Thursday was the Fourth of July. He didn't think he'd have to work for her that day, but he wasn't sure. It hadn't come up in the courtroom that he could recall. He'd asked his dad, because he'd actually seen his dad for a while over the weekend, but all he'd gotten was, 'Don't know. Probably should ask her.'

Lot of help that was.

His friends would be at the park for the parade, the carnival, and then the fireworks. He knew he could catch the fireworks even if he had to work, but he'd miss the parade and a good part of the carnival. The parade was stupid, a bunch of marching band idiots that couldn't play and walk at the same time so they kept bumping into each other, the same old fire trucks, the same old dumb clowns, and girls in sparkly dresses smiling, sitting on the backs of convertibles, and waving like they were robots or something. Not that the girls in sparkly dresses were all bad, but still. He hadn't looked forward to the parade since he was a kid and they used to go as a family.

He smiled just a little when he remembered his mom handing Tracy and him paper lunch sacks to use to collect candy. He could still see Tracy peeking around his mom's legs, afraid a clown would get too close but just as afraid she'd miss out on some candy. And he remembered how it felt to be hoisted up on his dad's shoulders, to tower over everyone, to know he had an important role to play being the first to spot and announce to the crowd what was coming next.

The parade hadn't changed, even though everything else had. He'd probably skip it even if he didn't have to work.

But he needed to know if he had to work.

The sun was getting lower in the sky and though he'd forgotten his watch, he figured it was quitting time. He climbed down, gathered the paint cans, brushes, and tools, and straightened up the work area. He took his time cleaning the brushes, something he didn't always do, but didn't want to give her a reason to be mad. She got mad enough for no reason.

Once he was done, and had lined up everything neatly on the porch, he lifted his hand to knock. But he held his hand a few inches from the door, paused, then turned and left. Why screw up a perfectly good day of not talking to her by choosing to talk to her? It would keep until the next day. Or the next.

He didn't ask the next day, but by Wednesday, couldn't avoid it. Deciding it was best to get it over with first thing in the morning, he dropped his bike on the lawn and strode to the porch, refusing to let his feet slow. He'd rehearsed his speech dozens of times over the past two days and felt confident he had a solid argument: No way even a crazy, mean old bat could refuse him a holiday.

His knock was answered so quickly, he wondered if she'd been watching for him. That worried him. If he'd done something wrong, if she was mad about something...he felt his chance of getting the day off slipping away.

But when she answered, she didn't look mad. In fact, she looked almost happy. There was a sort of smile on her face, she wore a bright blue dress with white flowers, and without an apron over it, and on her head was a white, floppy hat. A white purse hung from her arm.

"I'm glad you're on time. I have an appointment in town and I'd like you to drive."

She didn't give him time to respond, just marched out the door and down the porch steps. Billy pulled the door closed and followed. A morning away from painting sounded fine to him, even if it meant sitting in a car with her. Maybe they'd be going somewhere other than Munroe. Maybe he'd have a chance to drive on the highway.

His steps were light as he jogged after her, beating her to the garage and lifting the heavy door. He fleetingly wondered if she'd even be able to do that herself. When she held out the car keys, he took them with a smile.

He situated himself behind the wheel, checking the mirrors and the seat position. Alongside him, she struggled to get settled and strained to reach the door to pull it shut. Billy realized he probably should have helped her, but she didn't seem upset so he didn't let it bother him, just told himself he'd do it the next time.

"Where to?" he asked once she folded her hands over the purse in her lap and seemed comfortable.

"Into town. The Clyde Building."

The Clyde Building held some offices and businesses. A dentist, a realtor, a lawyer, he thought maybe a photographer, but she didn't offer any more details, so Billy quit wondering. A little disappointed he wasn't going to be able to drive farther, Billy backed out of the garage, jumped from the car to close the garage door, then climbed back in and set off for the short drive into town.

He squinted against the sun and told himself the next time he went by the drug store, he was going to look for a pair of sunglasses. Not ridiculous round ones like Randy's, but some cool ones like Clint Eastwood wore in Dirty Harry. Billy leaned back, shifted a bit sideways in his seat, then took his right hand off the steering wheel and flung it over the back of the seat. He pictured himself cruising by the drive-in. He'd look good, not stupid like Randy and Terrence, but cool. Julie would notice him, even if he didn't have a fancy new Camaro. It was more about the person driving than about the car. Or so he wanted to believe.

"Are you listening to me, boy?"

"Huh?"

Billy jerked and sat up straight, both hands back on the wheel.

"I told you to slow down. This isn't a racetrack."

The speedometer said sixty. The speed limit on the stretch of road was forty-five. As much as he wanted to tell her to shut up, Billy figured he should be grateful. That's all he'd need, for some bored cop to pull him over for speeding. He'd never get his damn license.

"Sorry," Billy mumbled and took his foot off the gas. "The Clyde Building, right?"

"Yes. I'll be an hour or so. Here." She reached into her purse and pulled out some money. "I need a pound of coffee and a half dozen oranges from Thompson's. Then go to the bakery and get me a loaf of white bread. It's too hot to bake." Billy glanced over and saw her thumbing through the bills she'd taken from her purse. She shoved a couple back inside, then snapped it shut. "You can take what's left and get a donut at the bakery if you'd like."

It was tempting to tell her he wasn't her errand boy, but he didn't really mind. He needed to talk to Mr. Thompson and if he walked from the store to the bakery, he'd pass the drug store. He could look for sunglasses and that way, he'd have them to wear to the carnival the next day. Assuming he could go.

"Ah, Mrs. Baxter, I—"

"I know, you're not expected to run my errands, but I'd appreciate it if you would just this one time. The stores will be closed tomorrow, it's getting harder for me to get into town, and, well, I'd be grateful."

"Oh, sure, no problem. I don't mind."

"Thank you."

He had his opening. "About tomorrow. It's the Fourth of July and I was wondering, if, um, if you'll be needing...if you'll be expecting..."

"If you have to work tomorrow?"

Billy dared a quick glance, then breathed easier when he saw she didn't look angry. "Um, yeah, I guess so."

"Of course not. It's a holiday, boy, and holidays are meant to be observed. Go to the parade, and watch the fireworks. I'll see you back on Monday."

"Thanks, Mrs. Baxter. That's..." Monday? Didn't she realize it was only Wednesday? Billy debated with himself but figured if he let it go, at some point she'd realize her mistake and be madder than hell when he didn't show up on Friday. "You mean Friday, right? Today's only Wednesday."

"I'm perfectly aware of what day it is. Do you want an extra day off or not?"

Billy didn't hesitate. "I do. Thank you. I'd love an extra day off. You're sure, though? Will it be okay with Judge O'Malley?" The name almost got caught in Billy's throat.

"Let me worry about that scrawny little nitwit. He hasn't checked up on you yet, but if he does, I'll remind him it's my house and it's up to me to decide whether I give you a day off. That idiot probably forgot about your sentence anyway."

Billy doubted that, but kept his mouth shut. He was trying to come to terms with the fact that Mrs. Baxter had called Judge O'Malley an idiot. When he turned to look at her, she grinned and Billy couldn't help but grin in return.

He bought the groceries, bought the loaf of bread—along with a chocolate donut for himself—and spent some time perusing the selection of sunglasses at the drug store, settling on a pair with black frames and lenses dark enough to hide his eyes. They not only looked cool, but the idea that he could watch someone without that person knowing made them worth the two dollars they cost him.

Since he still had fifteen minutes until he was due to meet Mrs. Baxter, and since Joel's house was close, Billy wandered that way. He was a few houses away when he heard Joel before he saw him.

"Stop that, Ronnie! If you pull Patty's hair one more time, you're not getting any cookies."

Billy caught up to the voice, then leaned against the fence that surrounded the yard next to Joel's house and watched Joel chase a towheaded kid in circles around a swing set. The kid snickered and taunted. Joel yelled and threatened.

"Seems like you should be able to catch a little kid."

Joel turned and stared, wild-eyed, at Billy. "Yeah? You think you can do any better, be my guest." He raked one hand through his hair and used the back of the other to swipe across his forehead. His face was red enough that his freckles seemed to disappear.

Billy laughed at him. "If I catch the kid, do I get cookies?"

"Shut the hell up," Joel said before he turned back to the kid whose mouth formed a wide O.

"You said a bad word. I'm telling my mom."

"Go ahead. I'll tell your mom how you wouldn't listen to a thing I said, and that you picked on Patty all morning. Then you won't be able to go to the parade tomorrow."

The kid's shoulders drooped, and he seemed to consider his options. Apparently the parade was too enticing to pass up because he came out from behind the swing set and mumbled a half-hearted apology to his sister.

"That's better," Joel said. "Now play nicely for a few minutes while I talk to my friend."

"Will it last?" Billy asked when Joel joined him at the fence.

"Hell no. Well, maybe for the rest of the morning cuz he really wants to go to the parade, but it will be the same thing next week. The kid's a pain in the ass."

"I thought you said you were going to have, and I quote, 'the easiest job in the world' this summer."

"Yeah, well it's not and I'm never doing it again. Twelve days. Twelve more days of summer school, their mom will be done teaching, and I'll be rid of these brats."

"You spend a few hours with them in the morning and you play in the yard. You could be painting Old Lady Baxter's house, so stop complaining."

Joel perked up. "Did you ask her? Did you ask if you get tomorrow off?"

"Yeah, and yeah, I do. And Friday."

"Two days! All right, man! We can go to the carnival and stuff tomorrow, then hang out at the lake on Friday. Steve has to work some on Friday, I think, but John's dad's office is closed Friday so he has the whole day off."

"I told Mr. Thompson I'd work for a few hours on Friday morning, he seemed desperate when I was in there earlier, and I have to get a haircut, but I'll have most of the afternoon free."

Joel sulked, but then shrugged. "Well, I guess that'll be okay. I have so much to tell you about Old Lady Baxter. I've been studying the notes we took at the library, and I went back there yesterday afternoon and read some more. You're not going to believe what I found."

"What?"

"I'll tell you tomorrow. It'll take some time, and that way, Steve and John can hear it at the same time."

Billy shrugged. He was curious, but figured Joel was exaggerating about what he'd learned. "I have to get going anyway. Have to pick up Old Lady Baxter."

"Ooh! Another date?" Joel giggled and jumped out of reach a second before Billy's punch could connect with his shoulder.

"Shut up." Billy turned to go but then shouted over his shoulder, "See you tomorrow."

Tomorrow, Billy thought as he headed back toward Main Street. The start of a four-day break from Old Lady Baxter. The carnival, the fireworks, heck, maybe even the parade, and all those chances to run into Julie.

As he walked, he came up with a list of things he could talk about with her if—no, when—he got the chance.

Number One: How she liked her summer job. He knew she was babysitting a few days a week and since he'd just watched Joel in action, figured he'd have a funny story to share.

Number Two: What he'd learned about Old Lady Baxter. If he could hold Julie's interest, he'd tell her anything.

Number Three: College. Julie's older sister was home after her first year of college and Billy was curious; curious what it was like, how hard it was, if you had to come home for the summer. Not that he thought he'd ever be able to go, but the idea of moving away, getting out of Munroe, was almost more appealing than buying a cool car.

Number Four: If Julie wanted to go to a movie or something some time. Billy kicked at a rock on the sidewalk. Yeah, like she'd ever say yes.

10

It was cloudy when Billy woke, leading him to swear as he threw open his window and stuck his head out as far as it would go. He stared up at the sky with a farmer's keen eye. The clouds were broken far to the west, a good sign, and there was no smell of rain in the air. A very good sign. If after all the blisteringly hot days without a cloud in sight it rained on the Fourth of July, he was going to be royally pissed.

But he felt reasonably optimistic as he headed to the kitchen, then more optimistic as he ate a couple pieces of toast and listened to the radio. The weather report promised clearing by late morning with temperatures in the low nineties. Hot, of course, but no rain. Good news, indeed.

Since he'd slept in, he was in the kitchen later than normal for a weekday. When his dad poked his head in, Billy wondered if that was his dad's normal routine, stay out of the kitchen until he was sure Billy was gone. Probably, as they rarely had anything to say to one another.

His dad looked like he wanted to duck back out, but stopped himself and walked to the coffee pot. It wasn't until the coffee was dripping that his dad spoke.

"So, you got the day off?"

"Yeah."

"Have to beg?"

"Nah. She was okay with it. Got tomorrow off too."

His dad's eyebrows rose a fraction. "Tomorrow? Why?"

"I dunno. She just said I could have it off. I didn't ask questions."

"Huh. Whatcha gonna do?"

"Gonna go to town, to the Fourth of July stuff. Be home after fireworks, I suppose. Maybe later," Billy added, mostly to see if his dad reacted.

"Okay."

As Billy had suspected, his dad didn't seem to much care when Billy showed up back home. But then his dad surprised him. His normally hard eyes went sort of soft and he rubbed a hand over his face.

"Remember the parades when you were a kid? Remember how much you liked chasin' after the candy? You'd always help Tracy since she was afraid of the clowns. Your mother would tell you not to eat all the candy at once, but then she'd look the other way knowin' very well that you'd eat it all before the day was out."

His dad paused then and looked out the window. He was quiet, hardly seeming to breathe, for a long time. Billy wondered what he was thinking, if the fact that he'd talked about Billy's mom for the first time in years made him happy or sad. Billy wanted—wanted so much—to ask questions, to have his dad tell him stories, to help him remember the things about his mom that he was starting to forget. He opened his mouth to ask, but before he could, his dad filled his coffee cup and walked from the kitchen.

The side streets were lined with cars and pickup trucks. Parents carried lawn chairs and blankets, coolers and bags, and corralled rowdy kids. Blasts and off-key squawks signaled the marching bands' practice, and the smells of cotton candy and popcorn floated on the breeze. Excitement crackled in the air like static on a dry winter's day. The town was ready to let loose.

So was Billy. He dodged cars, kids, and the occasional dog on his way to Joel's house. As he pedaled, he hoped he wouldn't be the first to arrive. If he was, Joel would probably want him to come inside, and Billy usually did whatever he could to avoid going inside Joel's house.

Ever since Joel's brother died, their house was like a shrine. Pictures of Jeff from the time he was a baby until just before he died hung on every wall. Framed artwork, if you could call a kid's scribbling and watercolor paintings art, decorated an entire hallway. Newspaper articles, also framed, told the story of Jeff's accomplishments on the football field and basketball court. The corner of the living room, though, was the worst. An American flag, folded tightly into a triangle and placed inside a case, sat on a table that was dusted and polished religiously. Alongside it were medals and commendations, also framed, and above was a huge picture of Jeff in his army uniform. While Billy understood, sort of, it was still creepy and he preferred to stay outside.

So it was a relief when he saw Joel, Steve, and John all in Joel's front yard. Joel tossed a frisbee in the air, catching it himself before it could fall to the ground. Billy figured this was after his several attempts to get Steve and John to play with him had been shot down. Joel could never sit still for long.

As if to prove Billy's point, Joel jumped up and down and waved when he caught sight of Billy.

"Hey! Hi, Billy!"

"Hi," Billy said as he parked his bike in Joel's driveway.

"Wanna play frisbee?"

"I just biked three miles. Give me a minute."

Billy dropped to the grass alongside John and Steve.

"Ready for the parade?" John asked. "Got your candy bag?" He snorted out a laugh.

"Based on the number of people I passed, we're not going to see much of the stupid parade unless we climb a tree. There are people everywhere."

"I don't think we'll get any candy if we're up in a tree." Worry clouded Joel's eyes. "I'm sure we can still find a spot on the side of the street if we hurry."

"If I want candy, I'll buy candy," Steve said. "I'm not going to push a bunch of little kids out of the way to get a Tootsie Roll."

"I am," John said. "I might give them the candy afterward, especially the crappy stuff, but half the fun is beating them to it and seeing their pathetic little faces when I grab it before they can get their fat, grubby paws on it."

Steve shook his head. "I hope you never have kids."

"So do I. What a pain in the ass that would be."

Joel was bouncing in place again. "Come on. We need to go."

"It doesn't start for over an hour," John complained.

"Billy just told you there are people everywhere. Let's go. It'll be fun." Without waiting for a reply, Joel bounded down his driveway and into the street.

Billy looked at Steve and John and shrugged. "We don't have anything better to do."

It had been a few years since Billy had watched the Fourth of July parade, but he could have scripted it to the minute.

The police cars came rolling down the street first, the cops waving from the windows, tossing candy, their eyes roaming over the crowd. Billy stared at the ground rather than risk making eye contact with one of them and refused to pick up a single piece of candy that came from a police car, even the pieces that landed right at his feet.

The color guard was next. They came on horseback, so it wasn't all bad. The grand marshall, waving from a car advertising the town's only car dealership, was next. Billy didn't recognize the grand marshall and missed the sign that would have clued him in, but figured it was probably the owner of the car dealership.

The Munroe High School marching band was next, playing the Star Spangled Banner as horribly as ever. The band director waved his arms like a maniac and looked ready to cry. The cheerleaders followed the band. Billy noticed their skirts were blue this year, a change from the yellow of the past few years.

The town's fire trucks, sirens blaring, inched down the street. A pack of cub scouts followed. They all wore their uniforms, they all held bags of candy they were supposed to be throwing, but most dropped only a stingy piece or two, probably figuring whatever was left over at the end of the parade was fair game.

The American Legion band followed the cub scouts. A bunch of overweight guys squeezed into their uniforms and blasting their horns with faces red enough to spontaneously combust. At least they could kind of carry a tune and *You're a Grand Old Flag* was recognizable.

The Shriners, in their ridiculous little cars and their stupid red hats, buzzed around in figure eights. This Billy watched attentively, certain a crash was imminent since they tried to steer and throw suckers at the same time. Billy waited until he spotted a grape one, grabbed it, and stuck it in his mouth just in time to focus his attention on the convertibles with the girls in sparkly dresses perched on the backs. They waved and giggled and Billy decided watching them wasn't as exciting as it used to be. Instead, he took a minute to scan the crowd, hoping to catch a glimpse of Julie.

The Rotary Club's float followed. Nothing more than a hay wagon piled with hay bales covered with white sheets, some red, white, and blue streamers, a few balloons, and all pulled by an old tractor. Given a half hour and a helium tank, Billy could have created a better float in his back yard.

Sweaty guys running for some office or another followed wearing T-shirts with their names, phony smiles, and foolish hats with little flags sticking out of them. The candidates' kids were roped into duty and followed along with the obligatory bags of candy, throwing handfuls to those they deemed worthy of their butterscotch drops and jaw breakers.

A few kids followed with their dogs decked out in red, white, and blue. The dogs paid no attention whatsoever to the commands from their owners, instead pulled like sled dogs, dragging the kids from one side of the street to the other and gobbling whatever candy was left lying unattended. It was the only new thing in the parade and mildly entertaining since by the time the kids and dogs reached the point where Billy and his friends were watching, most of the kids were so fed up and frustrated, they were crying or swearing.

Another Munroe Fourth of July parade in the books.

Gradually, the crowd filled the street behind the end of the parade, shouting and waving to those on the opposite side of the street as if they hadn't seen each other in decades. Billy and his friends strolled through the crowd, sucking and chomping on the candy Joel had filled his pockets with, and debating what to do next.

"The carnival starts now, but the rides won't be going for another hour or so. We could go get something to eat or play some games, I suppose," Steve said.

"Let's get some food then find a place to sit. I've got stuff to tell you about Old Lady Baxter." Joel beamed at them. "I figured some stuff out."

"Figured what out?" John's interest was piqued for the first time. "Figured out how to prove she did it?"

Joel looked over one shoulder, then the other. "I'll tell you when we're out of this crowd."

"Yeah, good idea. I'm sure everyone is secretly listening, waiting for you to tell your story."

John's sarcasm was lost on Joel who nodded, wide-eyed, at John as though they were co-conspirators.

They perused the long line of food booths. From popcorn to cotton candy, snow cones to funnel cakes, corn dogs to barbecued pork, sweet corn to watermelon, there was no shortage of choices. And no shortage of people waiting in lines. When they'd endured the lines and were all loaded down with what they wanted, they hiked away from the crowd and found a shady spot under a towering oak.

Billy started on his corn dog, washing it down with ice cold Coke. He kept his funnel cake safely on his lap and out of Joel's reach.

"All right, Joel, spit it out," Steve said.

Joel set down his popcorn, and unable to contain his excitement, rubbed his hands together. Billy kicked John in anticipation of the less-than-kind comment Billy knew John was preparing.

"Well," Joel began, "I read over all the notes from the library last Saturday, combined it with what I already had written down, things I've heard around town and things I learned from my grandma, and then I went back to the library on Tuesday. So I have a pretty detailed account of everything that was known about all four kids, about suspects, about evidence, and the excuses the police gave for never arresting anyone."

"You went back to the library?" John asked.

"Yeah. I wanted to read ahead for a few months after the fourth kid disappeared to see if anything new showed up, to see if the cops found any evidence to link Old Lady Baxter to the first couple kids. And I also looked at some other newspapers to see if there was anything interesting in them."

"Wow. That must have taken some time," Steve said.

Joel shrugged. "I only take care of the brats in the morning. I had all afternoon. Anyway, here's a rundown of what I know, starting with the first kid."

Joel pulled a few folded pieces of paper from his pocket and started reading. He recited facts Billy already knew. Timmy Wagner was the first kid to disappear, he wasn't reported missing for a few days because the family lived outside town and couldn't get through the snow storm. No trace of him was ever found. The second kid was Thaddeus Miller, a four-year-old and the youngest from a big family. Again, the mom didn't report him missing until the next day, claiming she hadn't realized he was gone. The dad was out of town when it happened, didn't return until a couple of weeks later. He was considered a suspect, but there was no evidence. A girl, Jane Nichols, was the third to disappear and after three, the town really started to take notice. She was six, had already started school, Old Lady Baxter worked at the school, so she was one of the people interviewed by the police, but more for information than as a suspect. This was also the first time there was talk of the disappearances being related. Finally, the fourth kid, Josiah Zimmerman, a four-year-old who lived with just his dad, his mom had died a year earlier. He disappeared on the one-year anniversary of his mom's death. His dad started drinking a few months after the mom died, neighbors reported he didn't take good care of the kid, and the day the kid disappeared, the anniversary of his mom's death, the dad was drunk by ten o'clock in the morning. The dad said he had no idea where the kid was or who, if anyone, had been looking after him.

When Joel finished reading, he grinned up at his friends.

"What are you grinning about? You didn't tell us anything we didn't already know," John said.

"Not yet. After the fourth kid disappeared, the police went back and looked for anything that tied them together. There wasn't much, but they learned a few things. All the kids seemed to come from homes where they weren't well cared for, where the parents rarely knew if the kids were even around, and certainly didn't take much interest in their well-being. The first, Timmy Wagner, had shown signs of physical abuse for most of his life. When the police dug a little deeper, people at the Wagner's church admitted to seeing the signs, even seeing the dad smacking the kid around during church sometimes. No one said anything, Timmy's mom never tried to protect him, and people suspected the dad was probably smacking her around too. But get this. One day, Old Lady Baxter told the dad to leave the kid alone. She confronted him after church, told him he was being too harsh with the kid, and that he needed to ease up or she'd report him. Now, things were different, parents knocked their kids around more than they do today, but this was a lot more, I guess. So that means there was a connection between Old Lady Baxter and the first kid."

"Did the police talk to her?" Billy asked.

"They did. They talked to several people from the church, got the same story from all of them, and actually it sounds like Old Lady Baxter wasn't the only one to say something to the dad, but still, it ties her to the first kid and there was already the school tie with the third kid."

"What's the story with the third kid? The girl. Anything else on her?" Steve asked.

"Again, it seems like she wasn't well taken care of. Her teacher reported she came to school dirty, hungry, and often crying saying she didn't want to go home."

"But Old Lady Baxter wasn't her teacher, was she?" John asked.

"No, she wasn't a teacher, she worked in the office or something, but that just means she probably knew all the kids, and knew a lot about their home life," Joel said.

"All I'm getting out of this is that all these kids came from crappy homes where the parents probably didn't care if the kids came home or not. Seems to me like the parents are the likeliest suspects," John said.

"You're right. And the cops claimed they checked out all the parents, then checked again. Their conclusion was that the parents didn't do it, but the fact that the parents weren't paying any attention to their kids made those kids easy targets for the person who snatched them. They weren't being watched, they were probably roaming around by themselves...easy pickings."

"So the police figured the same person did all of them? That there was a child killer in Munroe, that four kids disappeared in just over four years, but they could never find the guy? Or the lady? Not very good police work, if you ask me," Billy said.

"For sure," Joel agreed. "Crappy police work. The only real clue they ever found was a shoe that supposedly belonged to the fourth kid, Josiah Zimmerman, outside the entrance to the old mine. It was a couple months after he disappeared and some teenagers were out there, probably drinking, and they found a kid's shoe. They turned it in to the police and the dad said he was pretty sure it was his kid's. The police checked the mine as well as they could, at least that's what the stories said, but they never found any bodies or any other evidence. They admitted, after a lot of pressure, that it was possible all four bodies could be deep in there somewhere."

"That mine is huge, according to my dad," John said. "If a little kid was shoved way back somewhere, down one of the dozens of shafts, it's not surprising the kid was never found."

"Right," Steve said. "And this was the 1930s, 1940s. They probably didn't have the same equipment, or any decent equipment, to search a place like that. Maybe today they'd have more luck, but back then? Not surprising they couldn't find anything. I wonder if anyone's tried searching recently?"

"I don't know," Joel said. "I wouldn't know where to look for information on that. Five years ago? Ten years ago? It would be like looking for a needle in a haystack. It's more likely we'd remember hearing something about a search at the mine than it would be that I'd stumble across something in a newspaper."

"True," Steve said.

"I still don't see that there's any real connection to Old Lady Baxter," John said. "A couple times when she crossed paths with the kid or with the family, but this is a small town, she can't be the only one that would apply to."

"Okay, well get this," Joel said. "She'd already been mentioned in the girl's case, because she worked at the school, so after the next kid disappeared, they went to talk to her and *she wasn't home!*"

John threw his hands in the air. "Are you listening to yourself? If she wasn't home, how could she have anything to do with it?"

Joel just grinned. "She wasn't home the next day, the day after the kid disappeared and the cops started asking questions, but people reported seeing her around town the day before, the day of the actual disappearance. Doesn't it seem a little suspicious that she's gone right after the kid's gone?"

John put his hands on the ground behind him and leaned back, crossing his legs at the ankles and narrowing his eyes at Joel. "I guess. Maybe. What did the police think? What happened after she got back?"

"She got back a few days later and the police talked to her. It was summer vacation, she said she'd taken a few days to visit a relative since she had the time. The reports said the police followed up, the relative corroborated her story, but of course, a relative would do that. It's fishy, I tell you. I think the police must have thought so too because they talked to her a couple more times and that's, I think, when the real rumors started about her being the killer. Maybe they never proved it, but everyone knew she did it."

John dropped down on his back and threw an arm over his forehead to block the sun that filtered through the oak leaves. "I don't know. It's a lot of rumor, probably not a lot more than that. And there's not always a lot of truth behind rumors." John paused and lifted his head off the ground. He looked Joel in the eye. "You should know that."

Joel didn't answer, just dropped his head and flicked at his bag of popcorn. Billy glared at John, but it wasn't necessary. John had gone too far and he knew it.

"Hey, man, I'm sorry. I didn't mean anything…just talking, you know? It's just that I think we need a lot more evidence before we can be sure Old Lady Baxter really did it."

Joel sort of twisted back and forth for a minute, but then seemed to shake off John's comments. He looked at Billy. "Yeah, but that's where Billy comes in."

"Me? What do you think I'm going to do? I told you, I looked around her barn and I saw some stuff in the attic, but I can't exactly dig through her closets and dresser drawers." Billy shivered at the thought.

"No, but you can keep your eyes and your ears open. And you said yourself, she's forgetful. You need to ask her questions that don't really seem like questions. See if she'll start talking. Maybe she'll say something that she wouldn't have said a few years or even a few months ago. Maybe she'll screw up."

"Questions that don't really seem like questions? What's that supposed to mean?"

"You know, just word things differently. Don't come right out and say, 'Hey, did you kill those kids all those years ago?' Instead, say something like, 'I saw this little kid wandering around the park during the Fourth of July carnival. He was all dirty, looked like he had bruises, and there didn't seem to be anyone watching him. I was gonna tell the cops, but he disappeared.' See if she reacts or says anything."

Billy groaned. "Geez, Joel, I told you she's nuts. Who know's what kind of reaction I'll get."

"That's my point. You don't know unless you try." Joel looked at Billy through narrowed eyes, then giggled. "I think you're strong enough to take her if she goes crazy and attacks."

Billy fired an ice cube at Joel, hitting him on the head. "Maybe you should stop by and quiz her."

"I wish I could," Joel said.

"I wish I could go on some rides," Steve said. "Joel, you did a good job digging into all the history. Let's see if Billy can learn anything else this summer and take it from there."

Joel looked disappointed, but nodded.

"Good. Now let's go check out the Round Up. Did you see it yet? You stand in it and it spins in a circle, really fast, until you're plastered to the side by centripetal force and that force holds you in place while the ride tilts and turns. It looks far-out."

"Centri-what?" John asked.

"Centripetal force. You should have paid attention in physics."

"And you should have some fun once in a while." John sneered at Steve.

"Anyway, doesn't matter how it works, just that it looks really fun," Steve said.

"Didn't you hear? There was this kid who was on one of those, I think somewhere in Texas, and he flew right out of it. Killed him," Joel said.

"That didn't happen," Billy said.

"Did too," Joel shot back.

"Oh, for God's sake," John said. "If it killed someone, they wouldn't have it here. I'm riding on it. If you don't want to, then stand there and watch. I'm going on the Zipper too."

Joel gasped. "That one's *really* dangerous. The whole thing spins, then each car also spins. If you don't get hurt, you're at least gonna puke."

John pushed to his feet, walked a few feet to a garbage can and tossed in his wrappers. "No, I'm gonna ride it and I'm gonna see how many times I can make the car flip and it's gonna be a blast." He turned and headed for the midway.

"I'm riding," Steve said. "I'll take my chances." He followed John.

"What do you think, Joel? You should at least check out the rides. You always ride some of them," Billy said.

"Yeah, I guess. I'm not making any promises, though."

They rode Round Up, and the Zipper, and the Ferris wheel, and the Tilt-a-whirl, and then rode them all again. And again, until after their third ride on the Zipper, John threw up his corn dog and cotton candy.

While John sat in the shade sipping a 7-Up, Joel stood over him shaking his head. "I told you you were gonna puke."

John took another gulp of 7-Up, then wiped a shaky hand across his mouth. "It was worth it. Did you see how fast we got our car spinning?"

"You're lucky you waited to puke until we were out of the car," Steve said. "It's bad enough you spewed all over the ground underneath the ride," he looked at John's shoes, "and on your shoes, but if we'd still been inside, with the car twisting and spinning…" Steve looked down at his own shirt, shorts, and shoes. "Geez. I can't even stand to think about it." He turned a sickly shade of green.

John laughed. "Puke flying everywhere…it probably would have even gotten on those girls in the other car who screamed the entire ride. They deserved it."

"Gross," Billy said, feeling like he might puke himself. "Let's talk about something else."

"Did you see Julie?" Steve asked.

"Huh?" Billy whipped his head in one direction and then the other before catching himself. "Uh, no."

All three of his friends laughed at him. "I saw her from the top of the Zipper. She was walking around with Kim and Mandy and a couple other girls. Couldn't tell who they were," Steve said.

"Oh," was all Billy could think to say. He'd keep his eyes open watching for her, but he didn't need his friends knowing he was doing it. "What do you think, John, can you get up without puking?"

"Yeah, I'm fine." As if to prove it, he jumped to his feet, spread his arms out wide, and spun in a circle.

"Knock it off, you idiot! You're gonna get sick again," Billy told him.

"Let's go play some games and keep the idiot off the rides," Joel said. "I think this is my year to win one of those giant teddy bears."

"Right," Steve said, as they started their stroll to the long stretch of carnival games. "And this will be the year John aces science, and Billy finally asks Julie out. Hell, maybe I'll get drafted by the Chiefs."

"You just watch," Joel said.

They tried the dime toss first. Billy figured it was the hardest to rig, although the table was waxed to a gleam and a lot of their dimes slipped and skidded right off the table into the collection trough. Getting one to land completely within the red circle in the center, and winning one of the giant prizes, seemed highly unlikely. Billy earned himself a keychain with a whistle on the end. His friends didn't fare much better.

They walked right past the game where you had to try to pop balloons with darts. It seemed so simple, too simple, and they'd figured out years ago that with the dull darts and the under inflated balloons, their chances of popping enough to win a prize were close to zero.

The Hi Striker, though, was too enticing to pass up. They watched for a few minutes as others took turns. From a farmer in overalls and boots and with arms as big as tree trunks to a scrawny kid blowing giant pink bubbles, no one managed to ring the bell. The farmer seemed shocked when his strike rated only a 'Big Boy' and not the coveted ding of the bell.

Before they all dropped down their quarters to give it a try, Steve pulled them aside. "I think I've got it figured out. You need to hold the mallet at the very end of the handle, make sure it stays flat so the whole face of the mallet smacks the target instead of just an edge, and aim for the dead center of the target. And don't worry about heaving the mallet way back behind your head. Just lift it straight up, then swing it fast, and straight down."

"How do you know all that?" John asked.

"Again, pay attention in physics," Steve said. "Or, just watch these guys who are trying. They're all swinging like their life depends on it. Most of them are whacking only part of the target, and when they start with the mallet head behind their backs, they're losing momentum by the time it arcs back to the target. Trust me," Steve added when they all looked at him with blank stares.

So they did, and they tried to follow his instructions. John went first, and managed a 'He Man' rating, only one from the top.

"Not bad," Steve said. "But watch."

Steve stepped up, took a minute to run his hands along the handle of the mallet, to position his feet, and to give the mallet a couple of test swings. When he stepped up to the target, he pulled a Babe Ruth and pointed at the bell at the top of the shaft, then turned and grinned at his friends. A second later, the bell sounded to the surprise of all those watching, except his friends.

"And that, boys," he said as he passed the mallet to Billy, "is how it's done."

They all rang the bell at least once. It cost some of them a few quarters, but they were all bragging as they searched for the next game to conquer.

"Have some advice for that one?" John asked, pointing to Jacob's Ladder. "It's been kicking my ass since I've been old enough to climb up onto it."

Steve studied it. "Well, it's a matter of spreading out your weight evenly, I'd imagine. Keep your feet and hands spread out so they're at the edges of the rungs rather than in the middle." They all watched as a girl of about eight climbed on and immediately flipped and landed on her back on the mat below. "And every time you move one side of your body, make an equal move with the other side. Like if you move your right hand, move your left foot at the same time." Steve huffed out a laugh and shook his head. "And make sure the cheating carny doesn't tip it before you've had a chance to get moving."

"Think we should try it?" Joel asked. "If you kind of lie down on it, you only have to go up a few rungs to get to the top."

"Watch," Billy said. "No one is coming close."

"No one has Steve in their corner," Joel countered, and marched to the line.

He tried, four times, but even with Steve's advice, couldn't make it to the top.

"Damn thing," he said after his fourth attempt. "It's rigged, for sure."

"Of course, it's rigged. They're all rigged in one way or another," Steve said. "Sometimes you get past it, sometimes you can't. Anyone else want to give it a try?"

"Nah," John said, "it's a stupid little kid thing. If I want to climb a ladder, I'll climb a real ladder."

They challenged each other in the shooting gallery, threw a few rings at bottles, and tossed ping pong balls at fish bowls, all with limited success. Mostly, their prizes consisted of stupid plastic rings which they promptly threw away, super balls which they bounced sky-high until they lost them, and Chinese finger traps which amused all of them except John who got mad when he couldn't get his fingers free and finally chewed through the bamboo. They were starting to get bored with the games when Joel succeeded in landing a ping pong ball in a fish bowl.

"Whoo hoo!" Joel shouted. "I did it!" When the carny handed him a jar with a goldfish inside, Joel held it up to the sun and stared at it. "What the hell am I supposed to do with a fish? I want one of those big, stuffed dinosaurs."

"You win here, you win a fish," the carny answered.

"But–"

The carny turned, the sun glinting off his wide, bald head, his black eyes nothing more than slits as they bored into Joel. The hula girl and snake tattoos on the guy's arms danced when he flexed his muscles.

"Whatever," Joel mumbled and turned away. He took a few steps, stopped next to a little girl and her mom, and gave away the fish.

"Aw, aren't you just the big hero?" John said.

"Shut up. What do I want with a fish? Stupid thing will be dead before the day's out anyway."

"Enough games for a while?" Billy asked. "I need a snow cone or ice cream or something cold. I'm dying in this sun."

He turned to head back toward the food booths and came face to face with Julie. She was wearing cut-off jean shorts—very short, cut-off jean shorts—that were frayed around the seams, a white, sleeveless blouse she'd left unbuttoned at the top and knotted above her belly button, and she carried an enormous, stuffed pink dog.

"Billy. Hi," she said. She looked at the others. "Hi, guys."

"Hi. Nice dog." Nice dog? What a stupid thing to say. Billy wanted to kick himself, but he couldn't come up with anything better.

"I guess," Julie said. "Kind of big, though. It's hard to carry around."

"How'd you win it?" Billy asked. A little better, he thought.

"Oh, um, actually Terrence won it playing a basketball game, I think it was. I didn't see him win it, though, and I'm not sure he did."

Billy just grunted. He couldn't ever seem to get away from Terrence, or at least talk of Terrence.

"What I mean is, one of Terrence's friends made a comment about how much it cost, the dog, and made it seem like Terrence paid the guy running the game to just give him one after he'd spent something like twenty dollars trying to win one. Terrence got mad, told his friend to shut up, and acted like nothing had happened, just said he won it for me." Julie blushed a little and dropped her gaze to her feet.

Billy felt a smile tug at the corners of his mouth. Terrence really was the biggest jackass in the world. "Oh. We haven't won much of anything. Didn't really expect to."

"No, neither have we. Mandy won a fish. Her mom and her little sister are here, so she gave it to her mom to take home. She didn't know what to do with a fish all day."

"Yeah, Joel too. He gave his to a little girl."

Julie smiled that big smile of hers and Billy thought he might melt right into the sidewalk.

"It's kind of a strange prize to give someone at a carnival. I bet most of the fish die before people can get them home."

"Probably."

"Are you staying for the fireworks?"

"Yeah. We might do something else for a while, though. It already seems like we've been here for a long time."

"Have you been on the rides?"

"Yeah. Some of them. Have you?"

"Not yet. I think we're going to get something to eat and then head over there. Maybe I'll see you there?"

Billy tried to read her expression. Did she hope to see him there? Was she asking him to meet her there? Girls were so hard to figure out.

"Maybe. I was going to get a snow cone. I could um, I could get you one, or get you something else, you know, if you want."

"That would be nice."

It felt like the heavens opened and trumpets blasted from the sky. The sun shone down on him, only him, and wrapped him in blazing light. He was on fire, and nothing could stop him.

Then he heard the snickers behind him and remembered his friends. He jerked his head around and saw them, all of them, laughing and making embarrassing kissing sounds. Billy pleaded with his eyes, but they just laughed all the harder.

He was afraid to turn back around, but when he did, he was met with Julie's back and with her group of friends acting just as stupid as his.

They both needed new friends.

11

Billy bought Julie an ice cream cone, rode on the Ferris wheel with her, and wouldn't have cared if Judge O'Malley had shown up and sentenced him to another year of working for Old Lady Baxter. Nothing was going to ruin the day, easily the best day of his life.

Julie left after riding the Ferris wheel, telling Billy her mom had insisted she come home between the carnival and the fireworks to check in and to have something decent to eat. Billy's eyes had followed her as long as he could still make out a dot, afraid if he lost sight of her, he'd wake up and find it had all been a dream.

He didn't even care when his friends started up again with their vicious teasing. It didn't matter that John had ridden the Ferris wheel with Kim, or that Steve had spent most of the last hour talking only to Shelley, another of Julie's friends. It seemed to be 'Pick on Billy Day.' But if it meant he'd get to spend time with Julie, every day could be Pick on Billy Day.

"What now?" he said to try to shut them up. "We've still got hours until the fireworks start."

"The beer tent is open," John said.

The four of them were alone, sitting atop a little hill that overlooked the park, and where they could watch the crowds.

Sure enough, a line had formed outside the beer tent.

"They check IDs at the door," Billy said. "Always have."

"You need to think outside the box, my friend. Or, in this case, outside the tent." John pointed. "Look over there."

"What am I looking at?"

"That corner of the tent. The ties are loose on the stake. We can crawl under it."

The beer tent was the biggest in the park, and the only one with sides instead of just a canopy. The sides were mesh rather than canvas like the top, intended, Billy supposed, to keep some air flowing and to keep everyone inside from keeling over when the temperature soared. With the idea of keeping out those who were supposed to be kept out, the sides were all anchored to the ground, ropes dotted with little flags stretching from the stakes to the tent, but John was right, one corner was loose.

The only entrance was guarded by the priest from St. Luke's—the annual sponsor of the beer tent—on one side and a cop on the other. Both sat in lawn chairs, mostly chatting with each other, but occasionally glancing at an ID if the person trying to get in looked especially young.

"I could go for a beer," John said.

"Oh, okay, cool guy. *'I could go for a beer.'* You act like you have one every morning for breakfast." Billy scoffed at John, but a grin snuck through.

"Maybe I do. You ever try it on your cereal? Not bad, Billy, not bad."

"You're gonna get caught," Joel warned. "I heard these kids over in Wichita got caught sneaking into a beer tent and they got fined a thousand bucks and sent to jail."

John shook his head in disgust. "You say the dumbest shit."

"You won't think it's dumb when you're trying to come up with a thousand bucks and figuring out how to keep some four-hundred-pound guy from beating the crap out of you in jail," Joel said.

John didn't bother looking at Joel, just reached over and

shoved him, sending him toppling over.

"We could give it a try," Steve said. "They're not going to fine us or throw us in jail." He glanced at Joel and shook his head. "The worst that will happen is they kick us out of the carnival. They'll probably try to tell us we can't come back in the park, even feed us some bullshit about being banned from the carnival forever, which means we'd miss the fireworks, but how will they know? There'll be hundreds of people around. We're fine."

Billy's stomach knotted with nerves, the fear of getting caught doing something wrong again, and the fear of having to face Judge O'Malley again, never far from his mind, but he was sick of worrying about Judge O'Malley. He had a bonus day away from Old Lady Baxter, he was hanging out with his friends, and he wanted to feel like Billy Tupper again, not like a scared little kid. And he knew Joel's story was a bunch of crap. Joel's stories always were.

"We could give it a try." Billy echoed Steve's words.

"You told Julie you'd be watching the fireworks," Joel warned.

"I told you, we'll be able to watch the fireworks even if we get caught. There's no way one cop can guard the whole park, especially in the dark," Steve said.

Julie had said Terrence would be there, that their families usually hung out together during the fireworks. She hadn't seemed thrilled about it, but Billy worried he might have been seeing what he wanted to see. He wasn't sure he wanted to watch the fireworks with Julie if it meant he'd have to watch Julie and Terrence at the same time.

John stood up. "Come on, let's check it out."

"Let's." Billy stood and joined John. Steve followed, and after a moment and another round of dire warnings, Joel did too.

They wandered down the hill, past a few food stands, and to the back of the beer tent, being sure to stay out of sight of the guards stationed at the entrance. John looked around to make sure no one was watching, then bent over and lifted the corner of the tent. It easily lifted to waist-height.

"Look at that," John said, "plenty of room to get underneath."

"And when we get in?" Billy said. "Don't you think the guys pouring the beer will notice we're not twenty-one?"

"They don't have time to notice. Once you're inside, they assume you made it past the ID check. They won't pay any attention to us."

John seemed confident, but then he always did. Billy studied him like a stranger might. He couldn't decide if John's long, shaggy hair made him look older or younger than sixteen, but didn't have any doubt that John's body language and cocky expression made him appear older. John had more self-confidence than the rest of them combined. And, Billy guessed, what John said about the bartenders not paying any attention to who's grabbing a beer was probably true.

"I'm goin' in," John said, using his best attempt at a Southern drawl, "and don't try'n stop me." With a wink, he disappeared under the tent flap.

"It'll be fine. I don't think we can get in trouble just for being inside," Steve said. "Maybe we get a beer, maybe we don't, but it's worth a look."

Joel surprised Billy when he agreed. "All right, let's do it, but make sure no one's watching."

All three peered around. Their corner of the tent was at the edge of the park with no other carnival attractions behind it, so other than a few people taking a break in the shade and who all looked like they were sleeping, there was no one else around. Since they couldn't see much of the inside of the tent through the heavy mesh screen, it was unlikely anyone inside could see out well enough to be watching them.

Steve grinned, then ducked inside. Joel followed, almost on top of Steve. Billy took one last look around, then lifted the flap.

It was hot inside, the screen not doing much to keep any air moving. And it was crowded. People squeezed onto a few picnic tables or crowded around the tall, round tables that dotted the area, but most just found a spot to stand in small groups. The grass was already trampled and spilled beer had turned the ground to mud in front of the bar. It smelled like warm beer and sweat. Billy was having a hard time seeing the lure of it all, but those chugging beer from flimsy, paper cups seemed to be having a good time.

The four of them huddled together in the corner.

"Now what?" Joel asked.

John seemed a little less sure of himself now that they were inside. "I guess we head to the bar. Everyone still have money left?"

"Some," Joel said.

"Yeah, some," Billy echoed, and Steve nodded.

"All right, then." But John was rooted to his spot.

"Now you're chicken?" Billy asked.

That was enough to get John moving. "No," he said, and pushed his way past Billy and toward the bar.

Steve followed, but Billy stayed where he was. Joel hadn't moved either.

"Let's see what happens," Joel said. "Maybe it's better if just two of us go at a time. All four of us together might attract more attention."

"Maybe," Billy said. He kept his eyes on Steve and John as they waited in line. Inch by inch, they got closer, and from what Billy could tell, they didn't seem worried. John exchanged a few words with a guy wearing a St. Louis Cardinals ball cap. Knowing how seriously John took baseball, and how much he loved his Royals, Billy had a moment of panic thinking for sure John would start an argument, but both John and the other guy laughed then shook hands before the St. Louis fan exchanged his money for a half dozen cups which he proceeded to bunch together then fit his beefy hands around, trying to get all six safely through the crowd.

The guy behind the bar had a ring of grey hair on his otherwise bald head, a ring of sweat around the neck of his St. Luke's T-shirt, and a goofy smile that told Billy he'd likely been drinking as much as he sold. He didn't look twice at Steve and John, just whisked their money off the bar and handed them four cups. They each grabbed two, hustled away from the bar, and wound their way back to the safety of the corner.

"First round's on us," John said.

Billy took the cup John offered; Joel took one from Steve.

"Cheers!" Steve held his cup high, and they all tapped their cups together.

Billy chugged half his beer before stopping for a breath.

"Thirsty?" Steve asked.

The Munroe carnival might draw people from a dozen neighboring towns, but a good part of the crowd called Munroe home. And he may not know everyone in town, but he knew enough of them, and enough of them knew him, that it wasn't a stretch to think someone in the tent would recognize him.

"Don't want to get caught."

"Relax," John said. "While we were in line, I saw four people I know aren't legal. Remember Tupes? Graduated a year ago, so he's twenty, tops. He was with a girl I'm pretty sure was in his class, so also not legal. And look over there."

John pointed to the corner opposite them where a group of people stood with their backs to the crowd.

"Who is it?" Joel asked.

John took Joel by the shoulder and shifted him a few inches. Joel squinted, then laughed. "That's Terrence and Randy!"

Billy pivoted to get a better view.

"Sure is," John said. "I don't know who the other guys are, they might be old enough, but look at those two, hiding in the corner, sucking down Budweiser and trying to look cool."

"I'd say the security here leaves something to be desired," Steve said.

"All the better for us. Knowing those two idiots, it won't be long until one of them shoots off his mouth. If anyone gets busted, it will be them. Gentlemen, I'd say we don't have a thing to worry about," John said.

Billy relaxed a little, but still didn't waste any time finishing his beer and tossing the cup. He kept one eye on Randy and Terrence, worried if they noticed Billy and his friends, they'd do something stupid. As long as they stayed hidden in their corner and Billy and his group stayed hidden in theirs, Billy figured things would be okay.

John finished his beer, crushed his cup, and sent it sailing toward the garbage can. "Two points." He took a bow.

Steve shook his head at John over the rim of his cup. Joel sipped at his drink while his eyes darted from one side of the tent to the other.

"Hurry up," John told them, "I want another one."

"Are you going back up there?" Billy asked him. "I'll give you some money."

"It's your turn. Yours and Joel's."

It was the response Billy'd been afraid he'd get. "You got by the bartender once, you should do it again."

"How many do you plan on drinking?" Joel asked.

John shrugged. "Dunno. As many as I feel like, I guess."

"Well, how many do you think that will be?" Concern clouded Joel's eyes. "I don't want to haul your drunk ass out of here with you making a scene. We'll all end up in trouble."

John scowled at Joel. "It's gonna take more than a couple of these watered down beers before I'm drunk and making a scene."

"We got one. Maybe we should quit while we're ahead," Joel said.

"You didn't have any problem chugging down the whiskey Steve gave you a couple weeks ago. Stop being such a baby."

"I'm not being a baby, I'm just trying to stay out of jail," Joel mumbled into his cup.

"Give me some money." John held out his hand.

Not wanting any part of going to the bar, Billy happily slapped a few dollars in John's palm. Joel didn't look happy about it, but he did the same. John grabbed hold of Steve's sleeve and pulled him toward the bar.

There was no problem the second time Steve and John went to the bar, and no one paid them any attention as they stood in their corner and drank their second beers.

"Remember the first time we had a beer together?" Billy asked.

They'd barely been teenagers, and it had been on a dare. Steve's mom had a graduation party for Steve's sister, Carrie, and Carrie had talked their mom into getting a keg. No one was paying much attention to what Steve and his friends were doing, so it hadn't amounted to much of a dare, but Steve snuck to the keg, filled a pitcher, grabbed a few paper cups, and the four of them hid behind the garage and drank it. And then another, and, Billy thought, maybe another, but things got fuzzy after that.

None of them had liked it, though none of them would admit it. They tried to outdo the others, drinking as fast as they could, drinking while holding the cup between their teeth and tipping their heads back, and eventually spitting it between their teeth at each other. It was fun until Joel threw up. Then John, and then it had been his turn, Billy remembered. Steve still claimed he never got sick, but no one believed him, just figured by the time it was his turn to puke the rest of them weren't in any condition to care.

Somehow, they'd escaped notice by their parents. Billy's dad, of course, hadn't been around, so Billy hadn't needed to worry. Joel's parents stopped by for a few minutes, but the party wasn't that long after Jeff died and they rarely stayed anywhere or did anything for longer than a few minutes. John's parents drank enough that they wouldn't have noticed John was drunk if he'd stood right in front of them and sung the school fight song. Steve's mom was too busy with the party to pay much attention to anyone.

They'd all dragged themselves up to Steve's bedroom, flopped down on the floor, and slept off the worst of it.

In the years since, they'd snuck beer from Billy's dad a few times and had swiped half-full drinks at a party at John's house on occasion, but had never had a repeat of the graduation party.

"Not really," John said. "I remember the next morning, though. I was sure I was going to die."

"I was pretty sure my mom was going to figure out what we'd done and we were all going to die," Steve said. "Thank God people were slobs and she and Carrie had to spend the morning cleaning up the place."

They were reminiscing about some of their bolder, and some of their dumber, escapades over the years while debating whether to go back for a third round when a roar sounded from the opposite corner of the tent. Billy turned. As John had predicted, Terrence and Randy were in the middle of a scuffle that had ladies and the more sensible men jumping out of the way, and the decidedly less sensible men bullying their way into the mix.

Beer cups flew, some punches were thrown, and a shriek sounded from a lady wearing a white dress when that white dress was splattered with more than one beer, a streak of mud, and, it appeared, a spattering of blood.

John threw his head back and howled with laughter. "I *knew* coming in here was a good idea. Geez, have you ever seen two bigger idiots?"

It didn't take long until the cop that had been sitting outside the entrance pushed his way through the mob and started pulling people apart. It didn't appear anyone was truly mad at anyone else, so no one much minded when the fight was broken up. But once it was, the cop got a look at Randy and Terrence cowering in the corner and trying to make themselves invisible.

The cop grabbed each by the collar and pulled them toward the center of the tent. John laughed even harder, Steve joined in, and that's when Terrence noticed them. Billy couldn't hear what Terrence said, but he could see the finger point in their direction.

"Oh, shit," Billy said. The cop turned to look and Billy's heart thudded.

"I told you, I told you," Joel repeated over and over, making it sound like song lyrics.

The cop, who looked bigger and a lot more serious about his job than he had when he'd lounged outside the tent, glanced from Terrence and Randy to Billy and his friends, and then back. There was a crowd between them and maneuvering through it while hauling two beefy, and probably drunk, teenagers by the collar wouldn't be easy. Still, the cop seemed determined to try. Once he started shouting and elbowing his way past curious beer drinkers, the crowd shifted, and he had a clear path to Billy and his friends.

"We've gotta get out of here," Billy said.

They started pushing their way back toward the loose tent flap, but the corner was blocked.

"We're not gonna make it." Fear tickled Billy's spine and sent his stomach flipping. If he got caught, if Judge O'Malley found out he got in trouble again…

Billy felt a shove between his shoulder blades. "Run!" John hissed.

"But—"

"Just go!" John said. Then John, Steve, and Joel stood shoulder to shoulder and formed a wall in front of Billy, effectively blocking him from the cop's view.

He felt a twang of guilt at leaving his friends, but his overwhelming gratitude for their efforts far outweighed the guilt. With a twist and a duck, he got past the small group in the corner, darted under the tent flap, and in under ten seconds, was running as fast as his legs could carry him. He didn't stop running until he was over the hill and clear of the park.

An hour later, Billy couldn't sit and wonder any longer, so he ventured back in the direction of the carnival. It didn't take long until he found his friends sitting atop the same hill where they'd first hatched their plan to sneak into the beer tent.

"About time," Steve said. "We started to think you ran all the way home."

"Did you get in trouble?" Billy asked.

John shook his head. "Nah. The cop read us the riot act, told us he better not catch us in the beer tent again, but since he hadn't seen us drinking anything, there wasn't much else he could do. Now, Terrence and Randy, on the other hand..."

Billy's mood instantly improved. "What happened?"

"Not sure, but the cop hauled them out of the tent and to his car. We didn't want to get too close and have the cop spot us, but it looked like they were in plenty of trouble." Joel started to laugh and had trouble getting his next words out. "You should have seen them. I think Randy pissed his pants."

"Man, sorry I missed it. But thanks, you guys, for helping me get out of there."

"Hey, no problem. Can't have you thrown in jail, can we? Then we'll never get into Old Lady Baxter's barn." Joel winked at him.

"What do you think will happen to Randy and Terrence?" Billy asked.

"Probably depends on what kind of mood the cop's in. I suppose he could haul them in, arrest them for underage drinking, and cause them all sorts of grief. Or, he could decide it's not worth the trouble and just call their parents to come bail them out," Steve said. "That's what happened to my cousin. Got busted, cop told him it would go on his record or some other line of bullshit, and then called my uncle and told him to get my cousin's ass out of there. What he got at home was a lot worse than what he got from the cops."

"Then we have to hope the McMillans and the Bradys aren't very forgiving," Billy said, and leaned back on the grass to ponder Terrence and Randy's fate. After a minute, he found it felt good to do nothing but relax and look at the clouds.

The other three followed him, and for a while, they all were quiet, the rumble of the crowd, the carousel's organ music pumping out a waltz, and the clatter, screeches, and screams from the thrill rides joining together and floating on the gentle breeze to create a backdrop of sound that wanted to put Billy to sleep. He turned his head to the right and saw Joel with his eyes shut. To the left, John was already snoring. Billy decided a nap sounded like a good idea so closed his eyes and dreamt of Julie and her short shorts.

Billy wasn't sure he wanted to look for Julie when it was time for fireworks since he figured Terrence would be close by. There was no way Randy and Terrence would let it slide that Billy and his friends had managed to stay out of trouble when they hadn't. Since they already hated Billy just for existing, he was sure they were dreaming up new ways to make his life miserable. He didn't want to give them the opportunity to try out those ideas in front of Julie.

But John wouldn't take no for an answer. "Kim's gonna be there so I'm gonna be there."

"What's with you two?" Steve asked.

"Not sure, but it's looking good. She's always been kind of bitchy, but something changed over the summer, I guess, cuz she sure wasn't bitchy on the Ferris wheel. Pressed her thigh right up against mine. Did you get a look at that smooth, tan thigh? Yeah, we're gonna find them."

Something had changed with Julie too, but it wasn't just over the summer. Billy had known Julie since they'd started kindergarten together. With Julie's last name Tucker and Billy's Tupper, and since most of their teachers didn't have a lot of imagination, they'd been seated next to each other in most every class since they'd been five.

At first, Julie had bugged the hell out of Billy. Prancing around in her frilly little dresses, acting so prim and proper and looking down her nose at anyone who wasn't, always raising her hand and always knowing the answer, she'd driven Billy crazy. So that meant Billy had made it his sole purpose in life to drive her crazy. He'd yanked on her braids, he'd hidden a frog in her desk, he'd spilled his milk down her back, and he'd done his best to make her cry at least once a week. More often than not, he'd succeeded.

When they'd gotten a little older, Julie had stopped putting up with his shit and had fought back. And, while it had pissed him off at the time, Billy had to admit she'd held her own. There was the time she'd slipped a wad of chewing gum on his chair and he'd had to walk around with it stuck to his pants all day. He'd been furious since he'd been wearing his favorite pants, had even told the teacher, but that had backfired when he'd gotten in trouble for chewing gum in class. She'd also embarrassed the hell out of him when she'd drawn his name in the Christmas present exchange and had bought him a G.I. Joe doll which he'd unwrapped in front of the class. When he'd been ready to yell at her, his cheeks blazing red, she'd innocently explained that she'd seen him with one in the car just a few weeks ago and had assumed G.I. Joe was his favorite. He had been holding one, that he couldn't deny, but it was Tracy's because she'd decided her Barbie doll needed a new boyfriend after getting in a fight with Ken so had saved her allowance, bought G.I. Joe, and had asked Billy to open it for her. Billy had been doing so in the car outside the toy store when Julie walked by. Of course, there'd been no point in trying to explain himself. The whole class had been laughing too hard to listen.

While they'd never verbalized it, at some point, he and Julie had called a truce and had simply ignored one another. Until a few years ago when, all of a sudden, Julie didn't bug him quite so much any more. Then, after years of having plenty to say to her, he'd found himself hardly able to utter a word when she was around. Maybe it was because her long, blonde hair was no longer tied up in braids, or because he noticed just how blue her eyes were, or because…

"Billy!"

"Huh?"

"Geez, are you deaf, or what?" Joel asked.

"Sorry. What?"

"I asked if you're okay with finding them like John wants to do. Julie and her friends."

It had been thanks to John that he got away from the beer tent safely, so Billy figured he owed John one. Maybe if he didn't pay too much attention to Julie he could avoid Terrence's wrath, at least for one night.

"Yeah. Yeah, sure."

The girls weren't hard to find. They'd staked out a spot and had spread out scratchy, plaid blankets on the ground right where they said they'd be. Billy spotted Julie's parents a few yards away sitting with another couple, but not with Terrence's parents as he'd expected. That was promising. A closer scan of the area showed no signs of Terrence, or Randy, or any of their idiot friends.

Julie caught sight of Billy and stretched on her tiptoes to wave. "Hi, Billy!" she called over the crowd.

Sort of embarrassed, but mostly thrilled, Billy forgot all about Terrence as he threaded his way through the mass of people.

"We saved some spots," Julie said. "We were hoping you'd get here before the fireworks start."

"Oh, well, there are a lot of people, it took a while…"

"I just found out Terrence and Randy aren't going to be here. Did you hear they got into some kind of trouble? The Keatings told my parents that the Bradys won't be here because of something that happened with Terrence. Do you know what happened?"

Billy had to think fast. He didn't want to tell Julie that he knew because he'd been there to see it, but he didn't want to outright lie either. He knew she'd find out sooner or later, but with the fireworks ready to start, with a spot saved for him on her blanket, he decided later was better than sooner.

"I heard some kids talking about it. I think they got in trouble for drinking." True enough.

Julie's eyes rounded. "Really? Wow. Mr. Brady will go berserk if the football coach finds out and Terrence gets kicked off the team."

Billy bit hard on his lip to prevent himself from grinning as foolishly as the stupid clowns in the parade. Kicked off the football team? Hah! Not as bad, in Billy's mind, as a summer working for Old Lady Baxter, but for Terrence, it would be like a death sentence.

Julie was quiet and doubt started worming its way back in. Was she sad that Terrence wasn't there? Was she just being nice when she'd asked Billy to join them for fireworks? When she'd agreed to a ride on the Ferris wheel? Would she have done the same with anyone?

"Are you worried about him? Do you want to, I don't know, go find him or something?" Then unable to stop himself, he blurted, "Is he your boyfriend?"

For a moment, Julie looked shocked. Then, very slowly, she grinned before she started giggling. The giggling turned to laughter that had her doubling over at the waist. She didn't notice, but Billy did, that some of the conversation around them stopped and several sets of curious eyes watched her.

Finally, she caught her breath and shook her head. "You're serious? Boyfriend? No. Definitely, no. He's a friend, I guess, because we live just two houses away from each other, because our parents are friends, and because we've known each other since we were born, but no, he's not my boyfriend." She laughed again. "I don't really like him all that much, it's more that I'm used to him. I don't remember a time when we didn't play together, then hang out together. He doesn't think of me that way either, I'm sure."

It was Billy's turn to look shocked. He felt his eyebrows rise, his jaw drop, and heard the odd strangled sound come from his throat, but he couldn't seem to stop any of it. Was *she* serious? It appeared she was.

"Um, I think you're wrong about that," Billy finally managed. "Haven't you seen the way he looks at you? Haven't you noticed how he follows you around like a lost puppy? The way he buys you stuff, the way he—" Billy stopped himself when he noticed Julie's stricken face.

"But...I..." Julie stammered.

"Hey, I'm sorry, I just thought, I mean it's always seemed like you two were together, that you liked each other, you know, like-liked each other. I didn't mean to upset you."

"No, it's okay. I didn't know. I really didn't know. He's always just been there, you know? If I made him think..."

Julie put her hands over her face and turned away. She paced in a circle, twisted her hair in her hands, and twice opened her mouth as if to speak, only to close it again and resume her pacing. When she finally stopped, she stopped directly in front of Billy.

"Will you wait here for just a minute?"

"Sure."

She marched a few feet away, grabbed Kim—who was standing really close to John and appeared to be whispering to him—by the arm and yanked her away from John. Kim protested, but Julie didn't let go or stop her marching. The two went about twenty yards away into an area dotted with a few young trees and where no one was sitting, then stopped. It was getting dark, but Billy could make out their shapes as Julie leaned close to Kim, her arms flying up in the air as she appeared to yell. Kim stood without moving, waiting out the storm. It went on for a few minutes, Kim taking her turn yelling with her arms flying. Finally, they hugged and with their arms linked, headed back.

None of it made much sense to Billy, especially the hugging and the linking arms, but then he was realizing nothing about girls made much sense.

When they got back, Kim sidled up next to John as though nothing had happened. Julie sat on her blanket and smiled up at Billy, patting the spot on the blanket next to her. Not entirely sure it was safe, but deciding it was worth the risk, Billy sat.

"I'm sorry about that, but you caught me off guard. I guess I should have realized what was going on with Terrence, but like I said, I'm so used to him being there, being around all the time, that I didn't notice anything had changed. Kim agreed with you and said everyone but me knew it. I yelled at her for not telling me, she yelled at me for being dense. Anyway, Kim and I are fine but I'm going to have to talk to Terrence. Soon." She pulled a few blades of grass and twirled them between her fingers. "I don't imagine that will be pleasant."

Billy hoped it was incredibly unpleasant for Terrence, but didn't quite know what to say to Julie. She saved him from having to figure it out when she plucked a thick blade of grass.

"Hey, do you know how to do this?" She slipped the grass between her thumbs, squeezed it tight, and blew. A low whistle sounded.

Something in Billy's heart exploded. He selected his own blade of grass. "Yeah. I do."

12

It was such a good weekend, Billy was almost in a good mood when he headed to Old Lady Baxter's house on Monday morning. Almost. He pushed thoughts of the coming day and the coming week from his mind and filled the spot with all the memories, the laughs, and best of all, every second of the time he'd spent with Julie over the past four days.

After the fireworks, where he'd spent more time watching the smiles and oohs and aahs on Julie's face as the explosions bathed her in reds and golds than he'd spent watching the fireworks, they'd seen each other again on Friday afternoon at the lake, sort of planned after the fireworks, and then had run into one another again at the drive-in on Saturday, completely unplanned. So even though he'd spent his Sunday working for Mr. Thompson and then doing some cleaning at his own house and was now headed for a week of work underneath the blistering sun, he wasn't able to wipe the smile from his face.

He ambled toward the porch, still picturing Julie's smile and hearing her laughter when Joel had gotten in trouble for doing backflips off the raft at the lake and had talked the lifeguard into a swimming race to get out of his punishment.

On the porch, the paint cans were waiting. So was Mrs. Baxter. It was the first time she'd been standing on the porch when he arrived, and seeing her there caused his smile to slip. It couldn't possibly be good, he figured. More likely, she was mad about something, or had another ridiculous idea for a project. Then a terrible thought: What if she'd forgotten she'd told him to take Friday off and was pissed because he hadn't been there? Maybe she'd even reported it to Judge O'Malley.

Then again, maybe she wanted to go somewhere, and maybe he'd be able to drive.

"Hurry up, boy, I don't have all day."

Billy realized he'd barely been moving across the lawn, dragging his feet and pondering his fate. He studied her face as he got closer, trying to decide if she looked angry or just crazy. It was a toss-up.

"Did you have a pleasant weekend?"

"Huh?"

She frowned at him. "I asked if you had a pleasant weekend. 'Huh' isn't an answer."

"Uh, yeah, it was good. Thanks for the extra day off." Maybe that's what she wanted, another thank you for Friday.

"Good, because today, and this week, will be hard."

"They're all hard." He said it softly enough that she couldn't hear. Louder, he said, "Why is that?"

"It's hot today, going to get hotter, so it won't be easy going. Rain is forecast for this afternoon, so you'll have a shorter painting day, but I want as much as possible of that side of the house," she indicated with a nod of her head, "done before harvesting starts so you'll need to move quickly. Mr. Skelly will be out in the fields as soon as tomorrow if it's dry enough and you know what a storm of dust that will kick up. Can't have you painting in the middle of all that mess."

Billy hadn't considered the harvest and what that would mean for painting. He'd definitely lose a couple days while Skelly and the other farmers were out in their fields. Unless she wanted dust and bits of grain chaff stuck in her paint, he'd be doing something else.

"Okay, then I'll get started."

"I want the job done by the end of the summer. I know that seems like a long way off, but you've been at it a few weeks and there's a long way to go."

Billy felt his blood beginning to boil. "It takes a long time with all the scraping."

She stayed calm. "I know it takes a long time. From what I've seen you're doing a good enough job, I'm just reminding you that there is a deadline."

"I know."

"Good. Then get started. Keep an eye on the weather."

Billy grabbed a paint can, the rest of the gear, and as quickly as he could, put distance between himself and Old Lady Baxter. Maybe she should climb a ladder, maybe she should spend a day in the sun with dried paint flakes stuck in her hair and on her sweaty skin, maybe she should hold a brush in her hand, swipe it back and forth for eight hours, and see how fast she could get it done.

By the time he got to the ladders and the scaffolding, his mood was back to what he considered normal for a day at her house. He threw down the brushes, dropped the paint can, and kicked the ladder. After he grumbled for a minute, he hauled the paint can and tools up one ladder, situated himself on the board that stretched between the other two ladders, and plopped down to curse his fate. So many things could have gone differently.

If his bus driver wasn't such a jerk, making up new rules every day, expecting Billy to know them, and then blaming Billy for a fight that he hadn't even started and kicking him off the bus, Billy wouldn't have been riding his bike to school.

If it had rained last fall, at least a little, the grass wouldn't have been so dry, and a cigarette butt wouldn't have started a fire.

If Old Lady Baxter didn't have a stupid fence so close to the road, it wouldn't have burned. And if the fence hadn't burned, the fire wouldn't have spread to her yard and to part of Skelly's field.

If Judge O'Malley wasn't such a jerk, and didn't hate teenagers so much, he wouldn't have dreamed up such an asinine sentence.

If his dad had fought for him, if he'd told Judge O'Malley there'd be consequences at home, things may not have turned out so crappy, but his dad hadn't said a word while Judge O'Malley lectured and then handed down Billy's sentence.

If, if, if. No number of ifs was going to make his situation any more bearable. While Steve worked at the gas station, living out his dream of working on engines, while Joel argued with and bribed a couple of little kids and ate popsicles, while John played at some cushy job at his dad's office where he didn't do anything but deliver mail once in a while and get paid far too much for doing it, Billy painted. And put up with a senile child killer.

He needed to focus on that. He'd promised Joel he'd look around, even ask some questions, and see if he could learn anything that would help prove what Joel was now even more certain had to be the truth. At the moment, the last thing he wanted to do was talk to her, but he could look around. He knew he could get back into the barn, either by making up an excuse for why he needed to go in there or by just sneaking inside. She rarely came outside, rarely checked up on him, but it still might be better if he was in the barn for a reason. He'd think of something. Or, maybe if he wouldn't be painting for a few days, she'd either suggest he do some work in the barn or he could suggest it. Once the lawn was mowed and the garden work done, he didn't know what else there'd be for him to do outside. Since the chickens she'd mentioned earlier in the summer had yet to materialize, he figured the work he'd already done on the chicken coop would be the last.

Billy painted for hours. He'd remembered his watch so when it read twelve o'clock, decided to try his luck and see if he'd find lunch on the porch. He had a candy bar and some leftover peanuts from the bag he'd bought at the carnival back by his bike if he needed them. After stopping at the hose to gulp down some water, he wandered to the porch where, even from a distance, he could see a plate and a glass.

As much as he wanted the lunch, it kind of pissed him off that she was making it for him, mostly because it made it just a little bit harder to be pissed off at her. Whether she knew it or not, although he suspected she did, the food he got from her was the best, and the most, he ate all week.

He'd hardly seen his dad over the long weekend. One of Billy's fears, one that he hadn't been able to admit to his friends, was that his dad was going to show up in the beer tent at the carnival. Drunk already, of course. More than the fear of being caught, Billy'd dreaded having his friends see his dad stumbling around drunk and more likely than not, mouthing off to someone. Two years before, his dad had gotten in a fight with the priest from St. Luke's when Father Something-or-other tried to tell his dad he'd had enough to drink. But his dad hadn't shown up at the carnival while Billy was there, and he'd only shown up at home to sleep and to spend a few hours there on Sunday afternoon. Then, his dad had brought home hamburgers from the drive-in so they'd sat at the kitchen table and talked in awkward fits and starts over burgers and soggy fries until the conversation stalled and Billy had gone to his room only to hear his dad drive off a half an hour later. It was the first meal they'd eaten together in over two weeks.

When Billy got close enough, the lunch surprised him. Instead of the usual sandwich and lemonade, a plate of spaghetti, two pieces of toast, and a glass of milk sat on the table. Billy loved spaghetti. Except for the crap that came out of a can, and the stuff the school called spaghetti, he couldn't remember the last time he'd had it.

He didn't waste any time dropping into the chair and grabbing the fork. Since he'd never mastered twirling the noodles around his fork, he just shoveled them into his mouth. Then he sat back with a satisfied moan. It was good. It was really good. There were two big meatballs on top of the noodles. He cut into one and speared a piece of meat and then another after he'd gotten a taste.

Why did she have to be such a good cook? It was another thing that pissed him off about her. If she served him crappy tuna fish sandwiches or peanut butter and jelly, well, he'd still eat it, but it would be far easier to complain about. Hell, he could make peanut butter and jelly himself. There was no way, though, he could ever make spaghetti like he was eating.

The bread proved to be another surprise. It wasn't just toast, it was garlic toast, thick and full of butter. He used some to sop up a puddle of sauce, then washed it all down with milk that was still cold. All too soon, the plate was empty. Billy wanted to knock on the door and ask for more, but he couldn't bring himself to do it. He drained his glass of milk, let himself relax for a few minutes, then dragged himself back to the scaffolding.

Billy painted for three more hours before he noticed the sky had gotten dark. Too dark. Though no rain fell, with that sky, he knew it was only a matter of time. He climbed down, closed the paint can, cleaned the brush, and stacked all of it by the front door.

Since he didn't know if there was anything else she wanted him to do, and since he was afraid to leave early, he knocked on the door.

She answered sooner than he'd expected. "Have you finished for the day?"

"Looks like it's going to rain, so I quit painting, but if there's something else you want me to do, I still have time."

She looked at the sky. "Storms are coming. There's a tornado watch."

"There's always a tornado watch."

"True enough." She grinned and her wrinkles deepened. "Go on home. I don't want you riding your bike in a storm."

"You sure? It probably won't start for a while yet."

Mrs. Baxter cocked her head and studied him. "Well, I guess

you could hoe the garden and pick the tomatoes before the rain comes."

"Okay."

"The hoe's in the shed. When you finish, you can leave the tomatoes on the porch then head home. If you want some tomatoes, take them. I have more than I can use this summer."

Billy nodded, then went to get the hoe. While he attacked the weeds, he wondered if she'd be using all the tomatoes that hung heavy on the plants to make more of that spaghetti sauce. He'd rather have a bowl of sauce than a few tomatoes, but he knew how to fry bacon and make toast so he supposed he could use the tomatoes to make a sandwich for dinner. Could be worse.

The hoeing didn't take long, picking tomatoes and filling the basket he'd found in the shed took even less time, so he dumped the basket on the porch and was on his bike twenty minutes after talking to Old Lady Baxter.

It wasn't until he started pedaling that he noticed how still the air had become. Not a blade of grass stirred. When he looked up and to the west, his feet stopped pedaling. The sky was green, the kind of green he'd seen only a few times before. The kind of green that screamed tornado.

His mom had taught him to watch the sky, to know when to get out of the fields and into the house or into the cellar. Tornado watches didn't scare him—like he'd said to Old Lady Baxter, in Kansas there was a tornado watch as often as not—but a green sky did scare him. He'd never seen a tornado, but he'd seen the destruction one left behind.

His feet caught up with his brain, and he started pedaling as fast as his feet would move. He ate up a good chunk of gravel road before his feet slowed once again.

Old Lady Baxter. She'd never get her storm cellar door open. No way. He'd watched her struggle to carry boxes that weren't more than five pounds. She asked him to lift the heavy boxes, to haul the chicken feed, to carry paint cans. There was no way she was strong enough to open the door. He knew, because out of curiosity, he'd pulled on the cellar door when he'd been maneuvering his scaffolding over it and it had been a struggle. And maybe she'd have one of her episodes and wouldn't even realize there was a storm coming.

Billy's bike was turning around before he'd fully made the decision to go back. He tried to figure out why he was doing it, why he cared, but he didn't like the answer he came up with. He didn't want to care about someone who'd made his life miserable, but he heard his mother's voice telling him it was never okay to hurt someone or to stand by and choose not to help when you could help.

"Damn." Billy cursed his way back across her yard, back onto her porch, and while he pounded on her door. She didn't answer, so he pounded again. When he heard pounding in return, it confused him, wondering why she was pounding on the other side of the door, but then he turned.

Hail danced on the grass, bounced off the roof, and skittered along the driveway that was now barely visible from the porch. Billy banged on the door again, even harder. When there was still no response, he tried the door. It opened, so he stuck his head inside and yelled.

"Mrs. Baxter? Mrs. Baxter, where are you?"

He stepped inside and called again as he walked through the living room toward the kitchen and then down the hall. He found her struggling to get down the stairs. She was coughing, was pale, and looked terrified.

"The sky. Did you see the sky?"

"I know. You need to get in the cellar. Right now."

"I don't think I can." She stumbled, and Billy had to take her arm to steady her.

"You have to. I'll help you."

"I should get my purse, my papers…"

Billy heard a roar from outside and when he looked out the kitchen window, saw the enormous tree in the yard nearly bent in half.

"Shit," Billy said. "We have to hurry."

"But my purse is right there." She pointed to the kitchen counter. Billy spotted it so he grabbed it with one hand, grabbed Mrs. Baxter's arm with the other, and pulled her toward the door.

Billy pushed open the screen door and the wind took it, whipping it flat against the side of the house. Stepping out onto the porch, that wind almost pushed him against the side of the house. He wondered how he was going to get himself and Mrs. Baxter across the porch, around the corner, and into the storm cellar. It seemed impossible, and he was losing hope.

"Let's go," he pleaded with her.

She didn't talk, Billy wasn't sure she could have if she tried, she just bent her head and shuffled. Within seconds, they were soaked, and they were moving way too slowly. As much as he didn't want to, Billy put his arm around her and practically carried her across the porch. He kept his head down and fought the wind and the added weight.

Thankfully, the arrival of the rain drove away the hail, so when they left the porch, they weren't pelted with ice chunks. However, the rain was coming at them sideways and felt like needles, it hit so hard. Through it all, Billy felt a tugging on his shirt. He turned and squinted to see Mrs. Baxter trying to lift her arm and point. Following her hand, he saw the funnel.

"Holy shit!" It was terrifying and fascinating at the same time. It was huge; he tried to judge how huge, but that was difficult. A couple of hundred yards wide, maybe? Part of him wanted to watch, wanted to see what would happen when it touched down, but having been warned his entire life about the perils of a tornado, common sense took over and he dragged Mrs. Baxter toward the cellar door.

They were wet, and they were dirty. The ground was wet and slippery and the door handles were wet and slippery, and trying to open the door with one hand while holding up Mrs. Baxter with the other was practically impossible. The wind wanted to blow the door back down every time he managed to lift it a few inches. It was a battle, but one Billy was determined to win. He lifted; it slammed down. He pulled harder and moved his leg underneath so it couldn't shut all the way. That meant the door slammed into his leg, but at least it stayed open.

He'd heard a tornado described as sounding like a train bearing down on you. He had never believed that, but as the tornado roared and thundered toward them, he decided not even a train could sound that loud. Billy's heart pounded. It hurt, it thudded so hard, and had the tornado not been exploding in his ears, he bet he would have heard that thudding.

Finally, Billy had the door open enough that he could wedge himself underneath, holding it open with his back and pulling Mrs. Baxter down the steps. He tried to keep a hold on her arm as she tottered, afraid that after all his efforts it wouldn't be the tornado that would kill her but a fall down the steps. Somehow, she made it down a couple of steps and Billy was able to follow behind her, letting the door fall shut as he descended.

Then it was pitch black, even blacker than it had been outside, and Billy froze, unsure where to step.

"There's a lantern, and some matches."

"What? Where?" It was almost impossible to hear her over the roar.

"I don't know, they were, I think…"

The stuff was probably there forty years ago, Billy thought. The chances of it still being there, of there being any fuel, of there being any matches, were slim.

"On the crate. There was a crate with the lantern and matches. In the corner, in the back, I think."

Her voice was shaky, shaky like she was terrified. When she finished talking, she started coughing again.

Slowly, Billy's eyes adjusted to the dark, and he could make out some shapes. He shuffled and felt his way along the wall until his shin banged into something hard.

"Ouch!" He hopped on one foot, holding his other leg up and

clutching his throbbing shin. "Crap, crap, crap." It hurt like hell, but he put his foot down and reached for whatever it was he'd crashed into. Wood, he could tell, and a flat top, and then his hand touched something hard and smooth. The lantern. He let his hands roam until he found a small box. One shake told him he'd found the matches, and he breathed a little easier. Things never seemed as bad in the light.

Billy fumbled, lit a match, and took a quick scan of what he had to work with. There was a flashlight so he grabbed that first, but when he flipped the switch, nothing happened. Not surprised, but still a little disappointed, he lit another match and studied the lantern.

It was intact, from what he could tell. He lifted the glass chimney, raised the wick a bit. He didn't see a bottle of fuel, so hoped there was some in the lantern.

"Damn!" He dropped the match he was holding when it reached his fingers and singed them. He sucked on his fingers while he used his other hand to get a new match. Once it was lit, he held it to the wick and in a moment, a soft glow filled the small cellar.

Billy looked around. The floor was dirt, the walls cinder blocks, and aside from a few empty shelves on the walls and a couple of crates on the floor, the room was empty.

Mrs. Baxter still stood, stooped and shaking, where he'd left her at the bottom of the stairs.

"Here," he said, and reached for her arm.

She let him guide her to one of the crates and then help her sit. Billy wished he had a blanket or a jacket or something to give her to stop the shivering. It wasn't cold, rather it was hot and stuffy, but her shoulders shook and he worried she'd topple right off the crate. Maybe it was fear rather than cold? Or shock? Didn't people shiver when they went into shock? He didn't know, but the idea scared him. What in the hell would he do with her if she passed out or something?

He moved the crate with the lantern closer to her, hoping the light might help.

"Are you okay?"

"Oh, I...I don't know. Do you think the tornado will touch down? Hit my house? Will it? All my things, my...my memories..."

"I don't know, but it could miss us. It could skip right over your house. It'll probably be okay."

Her head jerked in an attempt at a nod, but she said nothing.

The noise hadn't let up any. Rain pelted the cellar door, and the wind howled and whistled through the sliver of a crack where the door fit into the doorframe. Every few minutes when something beat against the door, Billy wondered what the storm had found to pick up and drop.

"Do you think it's letting up?"

Letting up? Billy wanted to tell her it sounded louder and wilder than ever, but when he saw the hopeful look on her face, decided maybe lying would be the better option.

"Yeah, I think so. A little, anyway."

"I hope the house is okay."

"I hope the painting's okay."

Mrs. Baxter looked at him, confusion on her face. "The painting? Which painting?"

Billy didn't say anything, just raised his eyebrows and grinned.

Slowly, she smiled in return. Then she laughed. "Oh, the *painting*." Her chuckle turned into a cough. "Yes, I hope the painting's okay."

"It stinks, you know, all the painting."

"I do. I did it once."

Billy's eyes rounded. "You painted it? The house?"

She sat up a little straighter. "That I did. It was years ago, mind you, I was much younger, and I had some help, but yes, I painted it."

He studied her and tried to imagine her younger, up on a ladder, splattered with paint. He couldn't.

"Huh. How long did it take you?"

She chuckled again, but this time didn't cough. "A long time, but not the entire summer."

"But you said you had help," Billy countered.

"True. I hired the Trumble boys to help me. They were like monkeys, climbing to the highest spots like it was nothing. Of course, they weren't as clever as you and didn't think to rig up scaffolding, so they just hung on those ladders or sprawled on the roof and reached down. Crazy, those two."

Billy forgot for the moment how much he hated her, and his curiosity got the better of him. "How long have you lived in this house?"

"Oh, let me see. I moved here right after I got married, so that was 1918. Fifty-four years ago, that makes it."

She did the math quicker than he'd been able to do. "Wow, that's a long time."

She sighed and said, "Yes, it is."

"Why didn't you move? I mean, it's such a big house and you're alo—, I mean, the farm and everything..." He didn't know how to finish.

"Alone? Is that what you were going to say. I'm alone, yes, I've been here alone for almost forty years."

She blinked hard, then looked at the floor. Billy thought she was crying, and the thought sent him into a panic. He hated it when people cried. Not that he'd seen people cry often, but one time had been enough.

His mom had been sick for a while. Billy knew she was sick because she stayed in bed, sometimes for the entire day, but as young as he was, he didn't fully understand. Until one day. It was a Monday. Billy knew that, because he'd gone to school and come home expecting to find his mom in the kitchen doing the ironing like she always did on Mondays, but she wasn't there. His dad was. And his dad was crying.

Billy had never seen his dad cry before, he didn't even know dads cried, but there he was, his clothes clean which they never were when Billy got home because his dad would have spent the day somewhere on the farm, and he was crying. Billy could still remember the feeling he'd had standing there, before his dad knew he was there, and watching his dad stare out the kitchen window with tears streaking his face. His dad's shoulders rose and fell with his silent sobs. Billy had been scared, a kind of scared he'd never known before. If his dad was crying, who was going to make everyone else better?

Soon after that, his dad had sat Billy down and tried to explain cancer. Five years later, Billy wasn't sure he understood cancer any better than he had that day. What he was sure of, though, was that when he saw someone cry it made him want to run from everything that was wrong, everything that was bad, everything that hurt.

To Billy's relief, Mrs. Baxter lifted her head after a minute. Her eyes were dry, and she seemed to have tucked away whatever had upset her.

"Right or wrong, sometimes we just keep doing what's familiar," she said. "Maybe I should have left years ago, but it's my home." She lifted one shoulder and let it drop. "I hired people to run the farm for years until I decided it was easier to let Bud Skelly lease the land. I didn't want the worry, the decision-making, any longer."

"Why didn't you sell him the land? He bought our land. I heard him tell my dad he wanted to buy yours too."

"Because it's mine. It's been mine for a long time and as long as I'm living here, I'd like to look out the window and know that it's still mine. Once I'm gone, well, then it won't matter, will it? I don't have any family to take over, so if Bud buys it, I'll know it's in good hands. If someone else does?" She shrugged again. "It won't matter."

"I think it would matter." The words were out before Billy could stop them. "I mean…"

She reached across the space between them and put her hand over his. Billy's brain told him to pull his hand away, but he didn't. She seemed to need to do it, and somehow, he seemed to be okay with it.

"I know what you mean," she said, "and it's very kind of you." Then she winked. "Although, maybe you just meant it would be hard to think of the place as anything but Old Lady Baxter's."

Billy was glad for the low light because he was sure his face turned fire engine red.

"You think I don't know what you call me?"

"We don't... I don't..."

"Yes, you do, but I don't mind all that much. I'm old. I'm a lady. My name is Baxter. It's accurate."

Was she setting him up? Billy wasn't sure. "Accurate, maybe, but not respectful."

"Sticks and stones." She waved her hand. "They're just words."

Billy wasn't so sure.

"Is your dad working?"

"Huh?"

"You like saying that. Huh. I don't care for it. It makes you sound unintelligent."

She was having one of her episodes again, that had to be it. Ten seconds ago, they'd been talking about her house, about her farm, then she asks about his dad, and then she tells him he sounds dumb. Geez, she really was crazy.

"What?"

"Not great, but better than, 'huh.' I asked about your father. Is he working?"

"No. Not that I know."

"Do you have what you need?"

"What I need?"

"Does he buy you food, clothes, see that you get to the dentist, to the doctor, that you're ready for school?"

"I'm fine."

"I didn't ask if you're fine, I asked if your father is behaving like a father should behave."

Billy felt that all-too-familiar rage build inside him. His life was none of her business. He may have to spend his days with her, but that didn't give her the right to pry into his life.

"He's fine."

"No, he's not fine. I've seen enough of him to know he's not fine. I'm sorry for that, but I'm more concerned that he's putting food on the table and clothes on your back. You may not like to hear it, Billy, but you're still a child and he's still responsible for you."

She'd called him Billy, not boy. He was pretty sure it was the first time. Billy inhaled, then on his exhale said, "He'll get a job. The manager at the elevator will hire him any day, if he hasn't already. It's harvest time. They need him. Dad may be a screw-up, but there aren't many better when it comes to dealing with farmers at harvest, and they know they won't get through it without Dad. He'll work for a while, earn some money, until they get sick of his sh—, his attitude, and fire him. Again."

Billy didn't know why he told her, or why it felt somehow right telling her. A little part of his brain knew it was because it was the first time in a long time someone had asked if he was okay. The first time someone had cared enough to ask. He wanted to shut up that little part of his brain, to crawl back into that space where no one could find him and no one would know what he was thinking, but he realized it felt kind of good to come out from that space. Just a little way, though.

"Did you notice it's quiet?"

Billy didn't know how long he'd been lost in his thoughts, but apparently in his head, his thoughts had been loud enough that he hadn't noticed it had grown quiet outside.

"The storm's over?"

"It sounds that way."

"I'll look. Stay where you are until I make sure it's safe." What he didn't say, but what he thought, was that he wanted her to stay until he knew if her house was still standing.

He climbed up the steps and pushed tentatively on the cellar door. After the bangs and the thuds, he half expected to find the door blocked, but it creaked open.

Sunlight met his eyes and made him squint. How the sun could be shining such a short time after the chaos of a half an hour ago was a mystery. Billy pushed the door open and let it fall back to the ground. He felt like an owl as he turned his head as far as it would go in one direction, then the other.

The house was standing, so was the barn. He couldn't see the shed or the garage, but from where he was, things didn't look too bad. There were a few branches from her giant tree down and scattered around the yard, something was on the ground a few yards away, he thought it was a shutter, and it looked like maybe a few shingles here and there, but otherwise things were just wet.

"Billy? Is it bad?"

Later he'd have to think about why he felt so happy to be able to tell her things looked undamaged, but for the moment, Billy just answered, "No, it's not bad at all."

Without the storm battering and thundering, it was eerily quiet, so quiet that he heard her breathe out a prayer of thanks.

Billy went back down the steps, extinguished the lantern, and helped Mrs. Baxter up from the crate. She struggled up the steps, but Billy held her arm and together they walked into the wet, sun-drenched yard.

"Oh, the house looks okay." She kept her hand on his arm as she turned in a circle. "The barn."

They walked around the side of the house to the porch. Her flower pots were overturned, the spilled soil turned into rivers of mud, but the garage was intact, as was the shed.

"I was lucky," Mrs. Baxter said. "I was afraid there'd be nothing left."

"So was I. It's kind of a mess, though. I'll clean up what I can today, fix what I know how to fix."

"No, you need to go home and check on your house. Make

sure things are okay, make sure your dad, if he's there, is okay."

Billy nodded. "Yeah, I suppose, but let me walk around the rest of the house before I leave, make sure there's no more damage."

Billy helped her inside first, watched that she made it up the stairs to her room to change, then went back outside. He picked up branches as he walked. It wasn't all that bad considering what he'd seen in the sky. Mrs. Baxter would have been okay inside her house, but he realized he felt good about his decision to go back and help her. She wouldn't have been hurt, but she would have been scared. She had been scared, even in the cellar. For some reason, he felt kind of responsible for her. He wasn't sure he liked it.

Billy stopped in his tracks when he rounded the corner and saw his scaffolding. Or rather, what had been his scaffolding. The ladders were on the ground, the boards that had been suspended between them flung far out into the yard. The first ladder he picked up was broken, one leg snapped off half way down with the bottom rungs hanging worthlessly. He didn't see any practical way to fix it so it would function as a ladder again, but figured he could rig up something so it would still serve as a support for the cross boards.

The other two ladders were undamaged. Billy tracked down the boards and dragged them back to the side of the house. Only one broken ladder, so other than a mess, nothing too serious. He picked up the broken ladder again and tried to figure out how best to fix it. His conclusion had a lot less to do with the ladder and a lot more to do with the fact that he'd just gotten his free pass back into the barn.

On his way home, with a bowl of spaghetti sauce tucked under his arm, Billy surveyed the damage and listed off the things he hoped were flattened by the tornado.

Number One: Munroe High School, because how cool would that be? Cleanup and repair would mean school would have to start late. The idea of a shortened school year had him smiling.

Number Two: Judge O'Malley's house because he deserved it.

Number Three: Terrence's house. His family would have to move, and Billy couldn't think of too many things better than having Terrence move far away from Julie.

Number Four: His house. Maybe his dad would move away and Billy could live with one of his friends. And for as much as Mrs. Baxter had worried about the tornado robbing her of her memories, Billy thought having a tornado wipe out some of his might not be such a bad thing.

13

It turned out some houses in town were flattened. Word spread, even his dad heard the reports, and he relayed the details to Billy the evening after the tornado when he rushed into the house. Billy hadn't seen him move that fast in years. Once his dad had assured himself the house was undamaged, and, Billy wanted to believe, assured himself Billy was undamaged, he gave Billy a run-down of what he'd heard.

"Don't know any of those people who lost their homes," his dad said, "but do know a few who have some pretty serious damage."

"Anyone I know?"

"The Kuehns lost part of their roof. The Youngs' shed ended up in the neighbor's yard. There are others. Lots of swing sets and picnic tables picked up and dropped blocks away. Cops have most of the streets in town closed. Trees down all over. It's a mess."

"We don't have any power," Billy reported.

"Figured as much. You're okay, though? You're sure? Where were you?"

"At Mrs. Baxter's. Started home, but the sky turned that green color, so I went back." Billy turned away, embarrassed to tell his dad he'd gone back to make sure Mrs. Baxter was okay.

"Went back?"

Billy kept his back to his dad and looked out the window. "Yeah, you know, I figured she couldn't get herself to the cellar."

"Well, I reckon that was the right thing to do. Her place okay?"

"Yeah. Some mess, but no damage."

"Good. Way I see it, we were lucky. Haven't heard of any serious injuries, any deaths. Stuff that's broken can be fixed. Can't fix a life."

Billy turned back to look at his dad. It was the first emotion he'd heard from his dad in a long time.

"Where were you?" he asked his dad.

"Workin'. At the elevator."

Now his dad looked embarrassed. He moved his toe along the floor, tracing a design.

"Yeah? That's good."

"They're short-handed, what with the harvest. Figured I'd help 'em out."

"That's good," Billy repeated. "You hungry?"

Billy took a good look at his dad and noted how skinny the man was. His jeans hung low on his hips, his shoulders drooped, making his shirt look at least a size too big, and his face was hollow.

"Hungry? You cookin'?" Billy's dad grinned crookedly at him.

"Could. Got some spaghetti sauce. Figure I can boil some noodles."

Billy's dad cocked one eyebrow. "Where'd you get spaghetti sauce?"

"Mrs. Baxter. She sent it home with me."

"Huh. That so? Guess I could eat some spaghetti. Good thing we still got that old gas stove."

So Billy set a pot of water on the stove to boil and filled another with the spaghetti sauce, then lit the flame to heat both. His dad paced around the kitchen picking up a plate, a box of matches, setting them back down again and moving on to the next item, anything to keep his hands busy. He went to the refrigerator and opened it.

"Hope the power's not out too long, stuff'll spoil."

Billy watched as his dad glanced back over his shoulder at Billy, then stuck his hand in the refrigerator and pulled out a beer.

"Didn't know beer spoiled," Billy muttered under his breath. His dad didn't react, just used the bottle opener attached to the refrigerator to pop the top, then closed his eyes and took his first long pull from the bottle.

"Thought I'd check the barn for some tools and a board so I can fix it," Billy said to Mrs. Baxter the next day. She was outside with him, looking at the mess that was the scaffolding.

"If you think you can. Or, I can buy a new one if you need it."

"No, it'll be fine. It just has to hold the boards. I can rig up something."

"Try, but if it's too difficult, we'll go to town as soon as we can. Roads are still blocked today."

"I'll clean up the yard and then get started."

"Thank you, Billy, and thank you again for yesterday. I want you to know I appreciate you coming back and helping out an old lady. You didn't have to do that."

Billy felt his cheeks heat. He was getting really sick of being put in awkward spots where that kept happening. Not meeting her eyes, he nodded.

"My garden took a hit yesterday. A lot of the tomatoes were knocked from the vines, more damaged by hail. Again, it could have been worse."

Billy was grateful for the change of subject. "I'll see what I can do in the garden. Maybe I can tie up some of the plants."

"You're a good boy, Billy. That's been a pleasant surprise."

She turned and walked away, leaving Billy staring after her.

He cleaned up the yard, he picked up fruit and vegetables

knocked to the ground by the storm. Some of the tomato plants were beyond help, snapped off near the ground, but for others, he used sticks and twine to offer some support to the battered plants. Flower petals littered the corner of the garden where she had rows of some kind of flower Billy didn't know the name of but that were full of hundreds of big, colorful blooms. Some stems were broken and bent and some leaves had holes clean through where the hail had struck.

Billy straightened and looked at the house with its dozens of windows. A couple of shutters were missing, one was hanging by a thread, but all the glass was somehow intact.

They'd been lucky, indeed.

Once the yard was in shape, the garden tended as well as he knew how, Billy went back into the barn. Mrs. Baxter had given him a flashlight this time, so along with the light from the double doors which he'd propped wide open, he could see far better than he had on his previous trips inside.

With the layout now familiar, Billy didn't waste any time heading to the back corner that housed the car and the mystery barrels. He'd decided the night before the barrels would be the first thing he investigated.

With the aid of the flashlight, he was able to find labels on a couple of them as he crept around and wound his way between them. Motor oil. That's what he'd figured. Most of the writing was long faded, but the logos were visible. More than likely, the barrels had been there since Mrs. Baxter's husband was farming, or at least since she'd been hiring people to farm the land for her.

But that didn't mean the barrels still held oil. Wouldn't they have used it? Six barrels was a lot of oil. It made sense that they'd used up at least most of it and hung on to the empty barrels to use for storage, for burning. That meant if they all sounded full, chances were they were full of something other than oil.

Billy knocked on each barrel again, starting at the bottom and tapping his way to the top. Dull thuds sounded everywhere he knocked. He stood, pulled off his ball cap, and raked his hand through his hair, letting his eyes roam over the tops of the barrels. A ring and gasket held each dusty lid in place. He'd need a wrench to open them but with as rusty as they looked, wasn't sure he'd be able to get them open at all.

They were probably just full of oil, he decided as he gave the closest barrel another half-hearted knock. No way she'd stuck dead kids in some barrels and kept them in her barn, regardless of what Joel believed.

Far more interesting than some rusty barrels was the old car next to them. Billy forgot about the barrels and uncovered the car. With the extra light, he could study it more closely, and he was more intrigued than ever.

He'd never seen a car like it close-up before. It looked new, and to Billy, that was the most fascinating part. Underneath the tarps, protected from the dust and grime and years, the black paint still gleamed. How was that even possible? He didn't hesitate this time to open the door and climb inside. He ran his hands over the smooth dash, the even smoother seats, and around the steering wheel. What he wouldn't give to start it up, drive into Munroe, and slide into a spot at the drive-in. Terrence and Randy would have to pick up their stupid jaws from the ground.

Billy checked the glove compartment again, crouched to look under the seats, even wedged his hands between the seats and their backs to see if he could find anything tucked away... intentionally, or not. He came up empty. The car was as clean, if not cleaner, than her house.

Another thing missing, he realized, was the key. He wondered if Mrs. Baxter still had it, and if she did, if she had any idea where it was. Maybe the better question was whether she remembered she had the *car*. He wasn't sure what, exactly, was involved with starting a car that old, he didn't think they had ignitions like modern cars, but there was a spot for a key. Since he didn't have a key, it didn't much matter.

He wanted to get a better look underneath the car. When he'd looked before, he hadn't spotted anything unusual, but maybe with the flashlight, he'd find something. Billy got down on his stomach, next to the running board, pointed the flashlight, and squinted. It was still dark, and he wasn't able to see anything but dirt and bits of hay. Squeezing himself under as far as he could, he ran his hand over the ground. He wasn't sure what he expected, or hoped, to find. Joel's voice sounded in his head, telling him to look for signs of a trapdoor. Even though it seemed ridiculous, he felt for cracks, for some kind of latch, for anything that might indicate a door. There was nothing.

But the barn was big, and there were hundreds of places to search. He lifted lids, shoved aside rusty farm equipment, opened boxes, stood on top of a wagon to see on top of a stack of boxes, and found nothing but old, dirty junk. There were some tools that looked ancient and held his interest for a while, but there was nothing suspicious. The whole thing, the whole idea that Mrs. Baxter had ever done anything wrong, seemed less and less likely, and searching every nook and cranny seemed more and more stupid.

Just so he could tell Joel he'd done it, he climbed back to the hayloft and poked around. The only thing he found worth anything was another ladder. Back in a corner, buried under a pile of loose hay, he found it when he used his foot to scatter the hay with the idea that something might be hidden underneath. He supposed the ladder hadn't been intentionally hidden, but it was covered enough that he'd missed it on his first visit.

Cheered that he wouldn't have to fix the broken one, he threw the ladder over his shoulder and hauled it to the opening. Billy sneezed his way back down to the ground floor, kept sneezing while he carried the ladder outside, and decided he'd had enough of dusty hay for a while. He hardly even dreaded a day of painting.

Lunch showed up on schedule. When Billy finished, he decided he could stop being a slob and return the dishes to the kitchen. He knocked, and when Mrs. Baxter called for him to come in, he did.

She was in the kitchen, sitting at the table and eating her own lunch. She looked tired.

"Did you find what you needed in the barn?"

"I found another ladder so I don't have to fix the broken one unless you want me to."

She waved her hand. "I don't need four ladders."

Billy nodded. "The garden was pretty messed up. I did what I could with the tomatoes, but some of the plants were wrecked."

"I figured as much. That's okay, I have too many. I can't keep up with canning like I used to."

When Billy put his dishes in the sink, he spotted a bottle of medicine next to a half glass of water. He felt a little surge of excitement. Knowing someone was going to die was a creepy feeling, no matter who the person was. Maybe there was some kind of new medicine for Alzheimer's. Maybe the books he'd read were outdated. The books made it seem like lots of doctors were working on it, so maybe something changed.

"As long as you're there, would you please bring me my medicine? And a glass of water? It's supposed to help this cough that I can't seem to get rid of."

The feeling disappeared just as fast as it had appeared.

"Oh, sure."

Billy brought the medicine and the glass of water to the table. Mrs. Baxter's face puckered when she swallowed a spoonful of the liquid.

"Ach. I'll never get used to that taste." She took a sip of water. "That foolish doctor I've been seeing told me not to eat or drink for thirty minutes after taking this garbage. I told him, 'You take some and tell me how long you can wait before taking a drink of water,' but he didn't much like that. Treats me like I'm a child, that one does."

"Last doctor I saw called me a whippersnapper. I was fourteen. I thought about slugging him."

Mrs. Baxter slapped her hand on the table and laughed. "Maybe it's the same doctor."

Billy couldn't help but laugh with her. "Maybe."

"Did you have enough to eat?"

"Yeah, thanks."

"If you'd like, you could join me in the kitchen. You don't have to sit on the porch."

It seemed like they were getting too friendly, but the summer was already half over, he wouldn't be seeing her after the end of August, so what could it hurt?

"I guess. Okay."

She smiled. "Noon, then."

Billy nodded. "I'll get started on the painting, get as much done as I can before Skelly heads out into the fields."

Billy started out of the kitchen, but then stopped and turned. "You have a car in the barn. A really old car. Why?"

Mrs. Baxter drew in a sharp breath and Billy thought she was going to yell at him, but instead, she put her elbow on the table, dropped her head into her hand, and looked away. "I rarely think about that car these days."

"Why is it just sitting in the barn? It must be valuable."

"Valuable? I suppose it is. It's the first car we owned, you know. A Cadillac, top of the line in its day. My husband insisted."

"Why? I mean, what did you need such a fancy car for out here on a farm?"

"Believe me, that's what I asked. My husband was a...well, he had his ideas. His grandfather was a very wealthy man. He owned textile mills in New York. Jasper, my husband, hated his grandfather. As a child, Jasper lived with his grandparents for a number of years. He never spoke much about it except to tell me his grandfather was a hard, demanding man. He expected his eldest grandson to want to learn the business, to be interested, to follow him to work every day, that sort of thing. Jasper didn't want any of it, just wanted to go back home to his parents and the farm. His grandfather looked at it as giving Jasper every opportunity. Jasper looked at it as a punishment. Anyway, Jasper was eventually sent home, started farming, and never gave New York and his grandfather another thought.

"His grandfather outlived all of his children and when he died, he left a pile of money to Jasper. This was during the depression, no one had much of anything, and here we were with more money than we'd ever dreamed of. Jasper wanted to refuse it, he was that stubborn, but in the end he took it and the first thing he did was buy the most expensive car he could find. Ridiculous. Granted, he used some to replace farm equipment that badly needed replacing, and having a little extra helped during the years when we could have otherwise lost the farm, but buying that car was purely out of spite. As if his grandfather would somehow know Jasper had more or less thrown away the money."

"So he never drove it?"

"No. Not once. He bought it, had it delivered and parked in the barn, threw some tarps over it, and never looked at it again."

Billy couldn't believe it. What a waste! "So for forty years, it's just been sitting in the barn?"

"No, not entirely." She winked at him. "I didn't say it's never been driven, I said Jasper never drove it."

Billy put a hand on his hip and leaned back a little. He narrowed his eyes at her. "You?"

"Ha! You better believe it. One of the first things I did after Jasper was gone was get behind the wheel of that car and drive it through town."

Her face took on a determined—angry, even—expression. For just a second, the years seemed to slip away and Billy sensed he got a glimpse of the person she'd been long ago. Alone, widowed, but strong, determined to keep her farm, getting a job at the school when she'd probably never worked before, and driving a big, fancy car through Munroe when most people didn't even have a car.

"It looks brand new."

She blinked a few times and was back to herself. "Yes, well I drove it some, but a few years later the war started, gasoline was rationed, and I parked it in the barn. After the war, when I decided I'd like to drive again, I bought something more reasonable. I've had other cars since, but I've hung on to the Cadillac. I don't think of it often, but I like knowing it's there."

"Will you sell it?"

She lifted one of her hands and let it drop. "Oh, I don't know. One day, I suppose."

"You could get a lot of money for it."

"Why do I need money? What could I possibly buy? I have what I need, plenty that I don't."

"But, well, it just seems like it shouldn't be hidden away in a barn."

"You may be right. I'll do something with it one day and someone else will have a chance to appreciate it."

Billy left then, rebuilt his scaffolding, and got a few hours of painting done. It hardly bothered him, the endless back and forth, because he fantasized about what he'd do if someone left him a pile of money.

Number One: Move out. So what if he was only sixteen? If he had enough money, he could live anywhere he wanted.

Number Two: Take a trip. Billy had never been outside Kansas. Since he'd been a little kid, he'd had to endure stories from other kids in school about the trips they'd taken. California, New York, Florida, some had even been to Canada. He'd visit all fifty states, even Hawaii.

Number Three: Buy some new clothes. He was sick of wearing his old, cheap crap that barely fit.

Number Four: Buy some decent food. Corn flakes and candy bars were getting old.

Number Five: Buy Mrs. Baxter's Cadillac.

14

That evening, Billy decided to bike into town. He wanted to see for himself how the tornado cleanup was coming. Since the spaghetti dinner with his dad, he hadn't gotten any more information on where things stood. And he hadn't talked to any of his friends. He'd tried calling a few times, but the phone just made a weird sound and never rang. Billy supposed it was screwed up by the storm too.

At least the power was on again.

All along the road to town were signs of the storm. Trees were down, one of Skelly's barns was missing part of its roof, and his house had boards over the windows on the west side. When Billy got into town, it was worse. Splintered tree boughs littered yards and streets. Debris was stacked haphazardly at the ends of most driveways. Billy spotted everything from toys to upholstered furniture, all of it twisted and battered. Men worked together to remove the bigger trees, sawing them into pieces and hauling them away.

Then he turned the corner onto Maple Street and found the houses flattened. Gone. Nothing but broken wood and glass, furniture and clothes tossed around like a child might toss the contents of a dollhouse. Adults and children alike, expressionless and moving almost as if they were sleepwalking, sifted through the rubble, picking up and discarding broken parts of their lives. It was depressing and more than a little frightening, like a scene from a horror movie. How easily it could have been him sorting through the broken pieces of his life.

Billy pedaled faster, putting distance between himself and the worst of the carnage. Steve's street looked a little better. The houses were still standing, many with some degree of damage, but still standing. Steve's house looked okay. A tree had fallen in the neighbor's yard, half of it landing in Steve's yard, and no one seemed to be doing anything about it, but Billy figured there were far more urgent matters to see to than a tree.

He hadn't planned on stopping, but decided he'd knock on the door and see if Steve's family needed some help. Since Steve's dad died, and since Steve had gotten old enough, most of the responsibility for repairs, work around the house, that sort of thing, fell to him. Steve didn't complain, but Billy knew it was sometimes hard for him.

"Billy," Steve's mom said with a sigh of relief when she opened the door. "I'm so happy to see you. You're okay? Your house?"

"We're fine. The house is fine." Billy looked around. "It's not like this."

Tears welled in Steve's mom's eyes. Tears, Billy sensed, had been coming easily in the past two days. "We're safe. That's what matters," she said, and rubbed her hand up and down Billy's arm as if needing reassurance he was really there, was really okay.

"Steve's over on Maple Street helping with the...the cleanup. He's been working so hard." She swiped at her eyes. "Such a help to those who need so much help."

Increasingly uncomfortable, Billy shifted his feet. "Uh, do you need anything? Any help?"

She shook her head. "No, no, don't worry about us. I'll tell Steve you stopped by. I'm going to insist he take a break this weekend. Maybe you can get together then." She smiled at him with tired, watery eyes.

"Okay, thanks, Mrs. Casper."

"Bye, Billy. I'm so glad you're safe."

Billy biked on, the scope of the damage, physical and emotional, starting to sink in. There was more to it, he was realizing, than just picking up and rebuilding a house. These people would have to rebuild their lives, with some parts gone forever. Starting over, though nothing would ever really be the same again.

Billy sort of knew how they felt.

Joel was home. His house looked like it always did. If there'd been any damage, any mess, they'd already taken care of it. Joel bounded out his front door before Billy could knock.

"Hey, Billy! You're here!"

"Yeah. You guys okay?"

"Yep. Had some branches and stuff to pick up, but that's about it. Weird how a couple of streets away the houses are gone and here, we're mostly untouched."

"Steve's mom said he's over on Maple helping with the cleanup."

"Steve's hardly stopped moving. He's been working his shifts at the gas station, cleaning up at his own house, and then helping anywhere it looks like they need help."

"You too?"

"Some. Summer school was called off for the rest of the week so Mrs. Gripp's home and I don't have to watch her kids. I helped my dad clean up our yard, then helped out the Fergusons. They got it pretty bad."

"School's called off? Did the tornado hit the school?" For the first time since he'd gotten into town, Billy felt something other than sadness and pity.

"Nah, the school's fine. Kinda hoped it wouldn't be."

Billy nodded. "Me too."

"Is your house okay?"

Billy nodded again. "It's fine. Just some mess. Have some repair work to do at Mrs. Baxter's, but her place is mostly okay too." Billy watched Joel. "I was back in her barn yesterday."

Joel's eyes lit up. "Yeah? Did you find our proof?"

"I didn't find anything. At least not anything that has to do with those kids."

Joel's face fell. "Did you have enough time? Did you look everywhere?"

Did he look everywhere? No, that would have taken forever, but he wasn't about to tell Joel that. "Yeah, I had enough time. There's nothing there, man."

"I don't think that's right. Did you open up those barrels?"

"The barrels are sealed with what looks to be the original seals. They're full of oil, nothing else."

Joel was shaking his head before Billy finished. "You don't know that for sure."

"I'm pretty sure. The seals were unbroken. The rings, the bolts, they were all rusted and looked like they'd never been opened. Motor oil, Joel, that's all that's inside."

Joel shrugged. "Maybe. That just means the evidence is in her house. You'll have to get back in the attic. What about talking to her? Did you get anywhere with that?"

He'd talked to her, more than he ever had before, but not about the things Joel wanted to hear about. Had he tried? Billy tried to recall their conversation in the cellar, but couldn't remember if he'd asked any of the kinds of questions Joel had told him to ask. It hadn't been the right time, he assured himself. Mrs. Baxter had been scared, worried about her house. Bringing up crap about the missing kids would have been nothing but mean.

"I've started, but I have to go about it slowly. Jumping right in would have pissed her off."

"And you're afraid of pissing her off? Since when? Isn't she always pissed off?"

Now *Billy* was pissed off. "Geez, man, I'm the one who has to deal with her every day. Let me do it my way."

"Okay, just so your way is to do something before summer's over and your chance disappears."

"Yeah, yeah."

Billy felt his anger growing, but he looked around him, took in the scope of the damage and the mess, and decided getting into a fight with his best friend in the middle of all the destruction and devastation seemed really stupid.

"I did talk to her about her car."

"Yeah?" Joel's grin told Billy that Joel was also willing to let go of whatever argument they were on their way toward. "What'd she say?"

Billy told him what he'd learned about Mrs. Baxter's husband buying the car, about it sitting unused for years, and about her driving it after he died.

"She drove it? Old Lady Baxter drove that car?" He shook his head and squinted his eyes. "I can't see it."

Billy huffed out a laugh. "No, I can't either, but it was a long time ago. Even she was young once."

"I don't know. She seems like she was born old. Why does she still have it?"

Billy shrugged. "I don't know. She said it's been sitting there for so long, she kind of forgets about it. I told her it's got to be worth a lot of money, but that didn't seem to matter to her. I think she must have a lot of money."

"Yeah, that's what people say."

"Next time she wants me to drive her to town, I should tell her I wanna drive the Cadillac."

"Wow! Do you think she'd let you? Will you call me so I can watch for you?"

Billy rolled his eyes. "No, you moron. She's not going to let me drive it."

Joel frowned. "You never know. You could ask," he mumbled. "Apparently, you're friends now."

Billy reached out and shoved Joel. "Shut up. We're not friends, you jackass."

"Sure. You just hang out together and tell secrets in the storm cellar."

This time, Joel was smart enough to jump out of the way before Billy's fist could connect with his shoulder.

Billy and Joel joined the cleanup efforts on Maple Street and spent the next few hours hauling and stacking the remains of what just two days ago had been homes. It was weird to pick up part of a wall, shattered and splintered, but with posters of Shaun Cassidy and Donny Osmond still pinned to them. Dolls and stuffed animals, soaked and battered, were set aside for the family to keep or discard. Billy had to look away when he picked up a picture frame, the family smiling at him from behind spider-webbed glass.

It was hard, dirty work. Billy had scrapes and cuts on his arms, splinters in his hands, bruises on his legs, and from head to toe, more bug bites than he could count. But with every new cut, every new bruise, he worked harder, because the guilt that he'd wished this fate on anyone, even Judge O'Malley, ate away at him.

When it got too dark to continue, Billy, Joel, and Steve sat on the curb to eat sandwiches and drink a Coke provided by one of the ladies who walked up and down the street pulling wagons loaded with food and drinks.

"Has John been around?" Billy asked after he'd satisfied his growling stomach and quenched his brutal thirst.

"Didn't you hear?" Joel said. "His dad's office was hit hard. The place is a mess. His dad's been over there almost nonstop since the tornado. John too. He's actually working, if you can believe that."

It had to be serious. John usually wormed his way out of anything resembling hard work.

"Is the whole building flattened?"

"No, but a bunch of the windows blew out, so the inside is

destroyed. Desks, papers and crap everywhere," Joel said. "And everything's soaking wet. Some cars in the parking lot were picked up and tossed around like Matchbox cars. Crazy stuff. And…some news people from Kansas City were over there with cameras interviewing people. John was determined to get his face on TV."

John's willingness to work made more sense.

They sat for a while, watching people say their goodbyes, hug one another while fighting tears, and gradually head home. It almost seemed like a dream, Billy thought, like he'd landed in the middle of The Wizard of Oz movie, like he'd wake up any minute and find out the town hadn't been destroyed.

But it was all too real, and people would be picking up the pieces for a long time.

Billy stretched his arms over his head and yawned. "I should get home."

"I'll give you a ride," Steve said. "My mom's been crying all the time, she does whatever she can think of to make Carrie and me happy. She'll let me use the car."

"Sounds good. I'm beat."

Billy and Joel pedaled their bikes with Steve on the back of Billy's, to Steve's house. Steve's mom came outside before they got off their bikes.

"Is everyone okay? No one got hurt? Are you hungry? I could warm up chicken and potatoes, it will only take a few minutes."

"Mom, we're fine." Steve's voice was slow, soothing. He stood next to his mom and put his arm around her shoulders. "We had a sandwich over on Maple. You stand still too long and those ladies are pushing food down your throat."

Steve's mom smiled up at him, then leaned her head against his shoulder. "You're a good boy, Steven."

"Billy needs to get home. Do you mind if I take the car so he doesn't have to ride his bike?"

"Of course, you'll give him a ride. Billy, you've worked too hard and for too long to bike all that way. Go. But be careful.

Some of the roads are still covered with debris. Please be careful."

"We'll be careful, Mom."

"Thanks, Mrs. Casper. We'll be careful," Billy said.

Joel left, heading home on his bike. Billy loaded his bike in Steve's trunk, and they headed out of town. More destruction, more mess, everywhere Billy looked. They took a detour past the building that held John's dad's office. Most of the windows on the side facing the street were gone, only shards left, and jutting up like a shark's teeth, looking ready to attack.

"I can't believe no one died," Billy said.

"There's a little girl in the hospital. She got hit on the head by a window that blew in, but that's all I've heard about."

"I had to drag Mrs. Baxter into the storm cellar."

Billy didn't need to see Steve's eyes to feel them on him. "What do you mean by drag? She didn't want to go or she couldn't make it?"

"I was on my way home when I saw the sky turn green. There was no way she was gonna get that storm cellar door open. Didn't want to show up the next day and find her dead in her kitchen, so I went back and got her down in the cellar. Were you outside? It was so damn windy she could hardly walk."

"Hmm. How was that?"

Billy told him some, told him they'd talked, and unlike with Joel, told him he was starting to believe she didn't have anything to do with the kids.

"You think she's innocent? Have you told Joel?"

"I think she might be, and no. Joel will lose his mind."

"Probably. He's been talking about it since I've known him. If that dream is dashed, I don't know what he'll devote all his energy to."

"I don't plan on telling him any time soon. He keeps bugging me to get information on her, to find the evidence that will prove she did it, but I don't think there's anything to find."

"Have you looked? What about in the storm cellar? You know,

Joel may be nuts, but he's not the only one who's convinced she did it."

"Ive looked." Some, Billy said to himself. "There's nothing to see in the storm cellar, it's just an empty room. But guess what! I got another look at the car in her barn."

"Yeah?"

"Yeah."

Talk about the car got them all the way to Billy's house.

15

The next day when Billy woke, Skelly was already in the field. Billy watched out the kitchen window as the combine made a pass, the dust billowing and bits of chaff swirling. There'd be no painting for a couple of days.

His dad was up too. So far, so good, it seemed as far as the job went. His dad ate some toast, drank a cup of coffee, then filled his thermos with more, and left for work. Billy didn't know how long it would last, probably not long, but he was going to enjoy it while it did.

When he got to Mrs. Baxter's, he knocked on the door. The lawn needed mowing, he supposed that would be a good place to start, but from there, he didn't know what he was supposed to do.

"Come in, Billy."

"Morning, Mrs. Baxter."

"Harvesting's started, so you'll get a break from painting for a while," she said as she walked from the kitchen drying her hands on her apron.

Billy couldn't help himself. He took a deep breath. "It smells really good in here."

Her eyes crinkled with her smile. "I'm baking. I don't do much in the summer, it's too hot, but I felt like cookies today.

We'll have them with lunch."

Billy'd forgotten about their lunch plans. "Okay. Um, I thought I could start with the mowing today, then do whatever else you need done."

"Thank you, Billy. Maybe after you mow, you could look at those shutters that blew off the other day. If you think you can fix them, please do. Otherwise, I'll have to see if I can buy something to match or have some made."

"I'll take a look."

Billy mowed, and didn't mind it. He counted how many rows he mowed before Skelly turned the combine and made another pass. Then he'd see if he could get more done before the combine turned next.

It had been years, but Billy remembered the feeling of sitting up high with his dad and watching rows of wheat get chewed up by the cutter, then disappear into the auger. He'd liked to watch the front for a while, seeing the endless, golden field, then turn and look behind to see the field reduced to stubble.

It was a powerful feeling, and a satisfying feeling, knowing that they'd planted the seeds, grown the wheat, then cut and harvested it, that it would end up at the elevator, dumped from their trailer over the grate in the ground to be hauled up the silos. He remembered pointing and asking his mom if their wheat was in the bread or the cereal on the shelf at the grocery store.

Billy'd always loved the days when he got to go to the elevator with his dad. He'd listen as the farmers talked about their harvests, their yields, the moisture content, the price that year. His dad, at least to Billy's ears, had always sounded the smartest. He'd explain to the other farmers about why it had been a good year, or why the price was going to be lower, or why they should dry their crop longer. And the others would listen.

If his mom hadn't died, if his dad hadn't started drinking, if things hadn't gotten so crappy, Billy would probably be driving in his field that morning instead of mowing. At sixteen, he'd be old enough to do it. He and his dad might have been able to purchase Mrs. Baxter's land. His dad used to be able to talk anyone into anything, and he probably would have managed to convince Mrs. Baxter to sell. The Tupper farm would have more than doubled in size, they'd have new equipment, and Billy would know what his future held.

Instead, he didn't know from one day to the next if his dad would be able to keep the house, if he'd stay in Munroe, or if one day he'd just disappear. And Billy's future was nothing but a big question mark.

When he finished the mowing and the trimming, Billy was ready to examine the downed shutters. Four had been ripped from the house. He'd piled them next to the porch so after stopping for a drink from the hose, he spread them out on the lawn and stood back to take stock of the damage.

They were black, matching the doors and the trim on the house. If he ever finished painting the house yellow, he'd have to start on the trim that Mrs. Baxter wanted white. He realized it would make sense to paint the shutters before rehanging them or he'd be taking them down again before long. Billy looked up at the house, counted windows and shutters, and sighed. The trim was going to take as long as the house.

He crouched down next to the shutters. One was barely more than half a shutter, the other half still hanging forlornly from the house. Two were intact, the hinges still attached, so just needed to be reattached to the window casing. The last one was cracked, but Billy thought he could fix it. Mrs. Baxter would have to get one new shutter and he'd have to find some glue and some clamps, but it didn't seem like too big a project.

Most of the hand tools were in the shed rather than the barn, so Billy started there. He found some clamps, but the wood glue he found was long dried and was nothing more than flakes and crumbles that rattled when he shook the bottle. There were some cans full of nails and screws, a drill, a hammer, everything he'd need.

The half shutter hung from a second-story window so Billy moved a ladder, then armed with the screwdriver and hammer, he climbed up to see about taking down the fragments. Mrs. Baxter's house had shutters that could be closed over the windows, so they were connected with hinges on the side of the window frame. Screws were still in place on the hinges that remained. It took some doing, but Billy loosened the screws. The hinges stayed in place, though, so Billy used the claw end of the hammer to pry them away from the house.

When he finally freed all of it, he let the pieces fall, then climbed down and put his ladder back in place by the scaffolding. Two of the attic windows were missing their shutters. He'd have to get a better look to see if there was damage to the window casing where the hinges had come loose or if it would be a matter of simply reattaching the hinges. He debated moving his scaffolding underneath the attic windows, but decided first he'd head up to the attic to see if it might be easier to do the work from inside. Maybe he could sit on the windowsill and reach outside.

But after lunch. He was starving and with the sun high in the sky, figured it must be noon.

Mrs. Baxter had ham, potato salad, rolls, watermelon, and a plate overflowing with chocolate chip cookies on the checkered tablecloth that covered her kitchen table. It looked like a picnic, like the picnics Billy's mom used to have at their house where she'd invite their friends and neighbors and his dad would lay sheets of plywood over saw horses making giant tables to hold all the food people would bring. His mom had a bunch of huge, checkered tablecloths and she'd throw them over the boards. All day long, the kids would run and play tag, hide and seek, capture the flag, until they flopped on the ground, exhausted. The adults would sit and talk, laugh and reminisce, and usually everyone would stick around until it got dark. Reinvigorated, the kids would plead with their parents to stay just a little bit longer so they could play ghost in the graveyard. He knew Mrs.

Baxter had been at some of those picnics because his mom invited everyone who lived near them, and he wondered if Mrs. Baxter remembered.

Billy didn't realize he was standing in the doorway to the kitchen, staring, until Mrs. Baxter got his attention.

"Billy? I asked if you're okay. Did you get too warm outside?"

"Ah, no, I'm fine."

To buy himself some time, he walked to the sink and carefully washed his hands. With his back to her, he took a few deep breaths and pushed the memories to the back of his mind.

"I hope you're hungry." She laughed a little. "I seem to have a lot of food."

"I'm hungry."

Billy sat down and she passed him a platter stacked high with thick slices of ham. He took two. They passed the food back and forth until Billy's plate was loaded. This time he remembered to wait for her to say grace. Once she was finished, he dug in.

"I went into town last night," he said after he'd quieted the worst of his hunger. "It's a mess."

"Yes, it is. I went to the store and saw some of the destruction along the way. Horrible, isn't it? Your friends...are they well? Their homes undamaged?"

She drove? A feeling of dread came over him. She could have gotten in an accident, or forgotten where she was going, or forgotten how to get home.

"Billy?"

He shook his head and tried to get the images out of his mind.

"Yeah. Their homes are mostly undamaged. No one's hurt, but there's some mess. A couple streets away from my friend Steve's house, a bunch of the houses are gone. Flattened. There's a lot of work to do cleaning it all up."

"We've had bad storms here before, but never a direct hit from a tornado." She looked away and her forehead creased. "There was one, a long time ago, I think. I remember I couldn't get down into the cellar and the boy who worked here at the time helped me. I don't remember where Jasper was, maybe he was in New York. No, that's not right. I don't remember, I…I…I think, maybe…"

Her hands moved without stopping. She rubbed them over her hair, she wiped them on her apron, she wrung them together. She started to cough and her eyes seemed to plead with Billy for help, help he didn't know how to offer.

At first, he was going to explain to her that he'd been the one to help her into the cellar, that the tornado was only two days ago not fifty years ago, but something told him to change the subject.

"The rolls are really good, Mrs. Baxter. Did you make them?"

"Rolls?"

Billy took another from the bowl and held it up. "Yes. They're very good. Will you pass the butter, please?"

"Of course." She smiled and passed the butter dish. Her eyes still seemed a bit far away, a bit clouded, but her hands calmed, the coughing slowed, and her breathing regulated.

"I couldn't sleep. I was up early and baked before it got too hot. Cookies, too. You should have some cookies."

"I will." He smiled and reached for the plate. "Mmm. They're great."

"You've always liked your cookies, Tommy. I'll never forget when you had your very first one. You got the biggest smile on your face and tried to put the entire thing in your mouth at once. You…"

Billy ignored the wrong name, the confusion. "Your cookies are really good."

"Thank you. Eat as many as you want."

They were quiet for a few minutes. Billy watched her carefully for either signs of recognition, or for signs she was slipping further away. She ordered the plates and bowls on the table, she swept some crumbs into her hand and stood to drop them into the sink. She brought over a pitcher of lemonade and filled his glass.

"If you think you'd be of more help in town for a few days, you should go. There won't be any painting happening here and from the little I saw last night, those poor people need all the help they can get."

"You mean go to town and help with cleanup instead of working here?"

"Yes. You've worked hard here, my yard is cleaned up, there's nothing on the house that can't wait, so go help where your help is needed."

Billy thought about it. It was depressing work, sorting through the rubble of what had been a family's home, a person's life, but he could lift, he could carry, he could clean. He could help.

"Okay. I'll finish up here today and then tomorrow, go to town. I was thinking...there are four shutters down, two just need to be reattached. They go on the attic windows and if it's all right with you, I thought I'd go up to the attic and see if I could do it from the inside. Since it's so high, it might be easier doing it from the attic than from a ladder."

She nodded. "That's fine, but be careful. Watch where you walk. There are a lot of boxes, old furniture, breakable things. I don't want you to hurt yourself."

"I'll be careful. One shutter is cracked. I think I can fix it with some wood glue, but I couldn't find any in the shed. If you don't have any, I could stop at the hardware store and get some."

She nodded. "I'll give you some money before you leave today."

"The last one is in pieces. It needs to be replaced. I'll check at the hardware store and see if there's anything that will match and if not, ask Mr. Peters if he can get one."

"Thank you, Billy." She nodded at him. "You continue to surprise me."

Billy got the two shutters from the yard and carried them up to the attic, figuring even if he wasn't going to reattach them until they were painted, he'd want them to determine if the hinges were damaged. The stairs gave him a moment of concern when they creaked and groaned under his weight, but they held. He found the string for the light and pulled. With the light bulb and the sunlight coming through the windows, he could see much more clearly than he'd been able to on the rainy day a few weeks ago.

He set down the shutters and looked around. Bathed in sunlight, it didn't look so much like a haunted house. The old furniture was actually kind of cool, and the old coat and hat he spotted hanging on a coat rack interesting enough to make him take a closer look.

The coat was dark grey, long, with a double row of buttons, and fur around the collar. Billy ran his hand along the fur. It was dusty, but silky, and slid like water between his fingers. The hat was also dark grey with a shiny, satiny, black band around it. Billy dropped it on his head, cocked it sideways, and turned to look at himself in the cracked mirror.

He could be a gangster in an old black and white movie, he thought. Turning his back to the mirror, he held his arms out straight, clasping his hands and extending his index fingers to make a gun. Pivoting, he whipped back to the mirror and fired, his hands jerking with the imaginary kick from the gun. He grinned and looked down at his victim. "That'll teach you to mess with Billy Tupper," he snarled.

Somewhat reluctantly, he put the hat back on the rack. Stepping over bags and around boxes, he picked his way to the window. There was a latch at the top which he turned and then tried to raise the window. It stuck and held firm. Billy pushed and pulled. He banged on the edge. He wiggled it and swore at it. Finally, he leaned back and blew out his breath.

He crossed his arms over his chest, tapped his foot, and glared at the window. After muttering another curse at it, he tried the next window. Again, he banged and pushed and rocked it, but this time, he felt it give. He struggled and grunted, putting his shoulder under the top rail on the window and heaving until it rose.

There was no screen, so he was able to stick his head outside. To the right, the shutter was still in place, but to the left, holes dotted the window casing where the screws had pulled loose. He'd have to fill the holes. After a battering by the wind, they were gaping and far too big to hold the screws. He remembered his dad showing him a trick once to make a screw fit in a hole that was too big. His dad had used toothpicks and glue. Billy thought he could probably do it, but he'd need that wood glue.

There was still the matter of the other window. Maybe if he found a knife or something thin to wedge between the window and the casing, he could loosen it. He turned in a circle, looking for a likely hiding place for such a tool. Clues were hard to come by. Other than the furniture and junk that didn't need to be packaged, most everything else was in some kind of box, bag, suitcase, or can. He could either go back to the shed and look for a tool or he could open a few boxes and try his luck.

While he'd more or less convinced himself Mrs. Baxter didn't have anything to do with any missing kids, he couldn't quite get Joel's voice out of his head telling him to keep looking. He could open some bags and boxes, maybe find a tool, and at the same time, satisfy Joel.

A pile of fabric bags, Billy thought maybe they were pillow cases, were on top of the giant table. He started there. The bags were loosely twisted closed. Lifting the first one, he found it heavier than he'd expected. Maybe because he had the pillow case idea in his head, he'd expected it to feel like a pillow when he picked it up. Untwisting and unrolling the top, he found nothing but more material. It could be folded up sheets, it could be fabric she'd planned on using for sewing something, but Billy didn't really care. It wasn't anything that would help him open the window or anything that interested him.

Taking a quick glance in the rest of the bags, he found more of the same. Either she never threw away old sheets, or she'd planned on doing a lot of sewing.

Underneath the table were a few big boxes. Billy reached to pull one closer. The contents rattled and clanked. It wasn't taped, so Billy had to only lift the flaps to see stacks of old pots and pans. Not for the first time, he wondered how a person could possibly accumulate so much crap.

He kept searching, finding clothes, shoes, books, pillows, more of the lace things she had all over the house, a bunch of fake flowers and fruit, and in an impossibly heavy box, an old sewing machine which made sense considering the ridiculous amount of fabric.

Bundles of newspaper were piled around the room. There were old phone books, paint cans that were so light the paint had to be dried up, and photo albums. They held his interest for a while and he flipped through pages of black and white photos of what he figured was a much younger Mrs. Baxter, the man who must have been her husband, and a young boy. The pictures were grainy, many of them cracked, so it was hard to make out details.

The boy intrigued Billy, so he searched for photos with him. In some, he was hardly more than a baby; in others, he looked to be about six. Under one, written in small, precise script, he found what he was looking for. 'Tommy's fifth birthday.'

So Tommy was her son. That'd been his guess. When she was confused, when she was having a bad day or a bad spell, she'd called him Tommy more than once.

He flipped through, but didn't find any pictures of the boy where he looked to be more than six or seven years old. Billy knew the boy had died. Had he died that young? Billy wondered why, if he'd been sick, if it had been a farm accident, or some other kind of accident.

He looked a little longer and found more household stuff, more books, and then finally opened a box that held some old silverware. He grabbed a knife and went back to the window. Not entirely sure what to try first, he slid the knife around the edge of the window, trying to fit it between the window and the casing, then shifting it back and forth. After squeezing it through in a few different spots, he tried the window again.

It gave, just a little. Encouraged, he attacked it again, forcing the knife in farther and trying to twist it more to enlarge the gap. When he finished, he set down the knife, wiped his palms on his shorts, then grasped the top rail and pushed. It moved a couple of inches and got stuck again. Billy wiggled it and pushed, determined to not be defeated. When it was finally open wide, he gave it a slap. "Take that!"

As with the other window, the screw holes were too big to hold the screws that fit the shutter and would need to be plugged. He checked the shutter that was still on the house and found it tightly secured, but missing the hook used to keep it in place, either open or closed. He'd found that to be the case on a few of the other shutters he'd moved closed when he'd painted around them. The hook could have come off during the storm, but it could just as well have been missing for years. Another thing to look for at the hardware store.

Billy rested his hands on the windowsill and leaned outside. Skelly was still in the field. Billy wondered if he'd taken a break for lunch or just eaten a sandwich while he worked. Probably the latter. There wasn't any time to spare when it came to harvest. Billy ran his hand over the peeling paint on the window frame. There wasn't any time to spare when it came to painting, either.

Billy pulled his head back inside and fought with the windows until he got them closed. There wasn't much more he could do at Mrs. Baxter's before a trip to the hardware store, but the more he thought about it, the more he realized there might not be much of anything left at the hardware store. He wouldn't be the only one looking to repair what had been damaged during the storm. Biking over there, checking to see what was left, and talking to Mr. Peters to see how long it would be until he expected to get more stock seemed like the best use of his time that afternoon.

Billy picked up the shutters and made his way through the maze back to the stairs. When he pulled on the string to turn out the light it snapped, and he was left holding it as it dangled around his arm.

Billy groaned. Was everything just waiting to break until he was there? Setting down the shutters, he reached for a box he remembered being full of books. He'd need something heavy and sturdy to support his weight. He shoved it a few feet to the spot directly beneath the lightbulb, then climbed on top. Thankfully, the string had broken a few inches from the light fixture so it was only a matter of tying the two ends together. When he had a knot tied, he gave it a tug to test it and the light turned off.

"Finally something easy," Billy mumbled as he jumped down from the box. He pushed it to move it back against the wall, but the bottom caught on an uneven floor board and the box tipped, sending a few books spilling out. "Never mind," he said, "nothing's easy."

He righted the box and stacked the books inside. A bunch of cookbooks, one about handicapped children, stuff about homemaking, some catalogs, but nothing interesting. Billy threw them in haphazardly, only to find he had to start over if he hoped to close the box. He pulled a few out again and began rearranging, starting with the thickest cookbook. He tried fitting it in sideways but when he turned it, the pages cascaded out and fluttered over the box and the floor.

"Oh, for God's sake!"

When he gathered the pages into a pile, he realized they weren't pages from the book, but handwritten pages full of what he guessed were family recipes. Chocolate cake, rhubarb jam, cucumber salad. He stopped reading and started shoving the pages inside the cover. When they were all inside, at least sort of inside, he started to close the cover of the book, but his hand stilled, his heart thudded, and his eyes saw nothing but a name.

Timmy Wagner.

* * *

Ten hours later, Billy stared at his bedroom ceiling, unable to sleep, as he'd been unable to eat, unable to remember why he'd gone to the hardware store, and unable to answer the phone when it had rung three different times that evening.

Instead, he'd tried to come up with a reason, an explanation, something that would keep him from losing his mind. But he couldn't. So he stared, wishing he could see something other than the small, precise script spelling out Timmy Wagner.

And Thaddeus Miller.

And Jane Nichols.

And Josiah Zimmerman.

Minutes and hours ticked by with things becoming no clearer. Finally, in the purple of the predawn, Billy made a list of the reasons Mrs. Baxter would have a paper with the missing kids' names, telling himself that like always, he needed to come up with at least four.

Number One: No idea.

Number Two: No idea.

Number Three: No idea.

Number Four: Because she killed them.

16

Hauling garbage and cutting up downed branches was exhausting, but Billy welcomed the work. He sweated through an interminable day of back-breaking labor, pausing only when someone insisted he sit down for a few minutes and have something to eat and drink.

The cleanup effort was much more organized than the last time Billy had been there to help. This time when Billy'd biked into town, a lady with a clipboard had met him and directed him to an area she'd shown him on her map of the town. The worst-hit areas were marked in red and most of the efforts were focused there. When he'd arrived at his assigned spot, he'd checked in with another lady who recorded his name, phone number, and the time he arrived, explaining that they wanted to be sure all the volunteers were accounted for at the end of the day. Billy had been tempted to ask if that was for the safety of the volunteers or to be sure those volunteers weren't stealing stuff.

He recognized only a few people working on the crew with him. After a couple hours, and after listening to snatches of conversation, Billy realized that many of the volunteers had come from neighboring towns. He heard talk of the football team from Kansas State being there to help, but he hadn't yet spotted anyone that looked like a college football player.

Billy had been smarter when he'd left home that morning. Though he was operating on no sleep, his brain had functioned enough to tell him to grab a pair of gloves and to wear jeans instead of shorts so he'd avoided some of the cuts, scrapes, and splinters that had plagued him the last time. When he hauled armloads of fiberglass insulation, he was thankful for his long sleeves. He may be hot and sweaty, but it was better than the burning and itching he knew would have come from rubbing against the insulation.

It seemed many of the people who'd suffered the worst of the damage were gradually moving past the initial shock and heartache. There weren't as many tears and hopeless faces. What Billy saw was determination and the beginnings of something like acceptance.

Still, there were more than enough difficult moments. Billy watched a grown man fall to his knees and weep when he lifted a section of wall to find a flattened crib underneath. And he saw a girl he recognized as being a few years ahead of him in school collapse into the arms of a man when she picked up a muddy and tattered wedding dress.

Through it all, Billy did his best to keep his head down and avoid talking with anyone while he let his mind chew up and spit out facts and ideas. He couldn't get the image of the sheet of paper with the names of those kids out of his mind. At times, he was convinced Mrs. Baxter was a murderer. Other times, he was convinced she'd only been curious, maybe even trying to solve the mystery. Most of the time, he didn't know what to think, except that he had to get back into the attic.

When he'd found the paper, and he'd seen the names, he'd been too shocked to do much more than stare. He wished he had taken the time to dig through the box looking for other papers, or notes, or newspaper articles, or anything that would have provided a clue as to what it all meant. But he'd been shocked stupid, Mrs. Baxter had called up the stairs to check on him, and he'd shoved everything back inside the box and run from it all.

Thankfully, he had a few days away from her. Sure, he wanted to get back into the attic, but he wanted to do it when he had things worked out in his mind and that didn't seem like it would happen any time soon.

And thankfully, he hadn't run into any of his friends. He was afraid he'd have trouble keeping the information from them and he wasn't ready to share it. He had to figure it out himself before he told anyone else. Especially Joel, because Joel would grab Billy and drag him to the police station.

The number of volunteers dwindled as it drew near supper time. Another round of sandwiches was being distributed and when Billy paused to straighten his back and stretch, he saw a line forming in front of a folding table about a half block away. Those who made it to the front of the line walked away with a bowl between their hands and a smile on their face. Some sort of casserole, Billy guessed, and decided to keep working.

"Darlin', you've simply got to take a break before you work yourself to death."

Billy turned in the direction of the voice. A lady wearing bright pink pants, a tight yellow top, and giant white sunglasses, and with blonde hair curled and piled up so high on her head, Billy wondered how she managed to keep her balance, stood smiling at him.

"I'm not tired," Billy said, but he stopped long enough to wipe the sweat from his forehead using it as an excuse to get a better look at the lady.

She was older than he'd first thought. Based on her outfit, he'd expected twenties, but the wrinkles starting to form around her mouth and on her neck told Billy she was probably twice that. He knew he'd never seen her before—someone like her would stand out in a town like Munroe—so assumed she'd come from a neighboring town.

"Oh, darlin', tired or not, you need to take a break. Those are the orders I was given." She straightened her arms, slapping her hands against her thighs, and stood ramrod straight, her eyes staring ahead. Her voice dropped several octaves. "*See that everyone sits down for a while and has something to eat.*" She giggled, then relaxed.

"Join those folks over there." She pointed with a finger tipped with a long nail that matched the color of her pants, toward the group at the table. "I don't know what they're serving, but it smells good."

"Maybe in a little while."

"In a little while, it may be gone."

Billy blew out a breath. "Look, if I get hungry, I'll get something to eat. Until then, can't I just work?"

The lady raised her hands, palms up, to her shoulders. "I'm just the messenger, darlin', and you know what they say about shooting the messenger." She winked at him. "You're not supposed to do it."

"Yeah," Billy muttered and dropped his head to continue sifting through the rubble of what had been someone's kitchen.

"Listen, I understand it's tough losing your home, your things. I do. I've been through it. I'm not going to tell you what to do or how to feel, I'm just going to tell you that if you push yourself too hard, you'll wind up being more of a burden than a help. Take care of yourself. Eat. Rest. The mess will still be here."

Billy kept his head down. "I didn't, I mean, it's not my—"

"You don't need to explain, darlin'. I see some kids over there in the food line that look to be about your age. Maybe they're your friends? Go talk to them. Find something to laugh about. Maybe you even know my niece? She must go to school with you. Julie Tucker? She and her boyfriend have been working a couple of streets over, but I think they're headed this way to get something to eat."

The lady kept talking, but Billy stopped listening. Julie and her boyfriend? Her *boyfriend*? The word sounded in Billy's head, over and over, louder and louder. Was she with Terrence? Had she lied about being just friends with him?

Could his life get any worse?

Billy dropped the pile of splintered wood he'd been ready to haul to the curb, then peeled off his gloves, turned his back on the lady who was still chattering, and walked away.

Billy didn't hear the man who yelled after him until the man caught up with him and put a hand on Billy's shoulder.

"Son," the man panted. "Son, you need to give me your name before you leave."

It was an old guy, his face flushed, wearing a pair of grease-stained coveralls and a faded John Deere trucker hat. He sucked air through tobacco-stained teeth that held a toothpick he moved from side to side.

"Need to get you checked off."

"Tupper. Billy Tupper."

"Billy. Let's see…" The man ran his finger down a sheet of paper. "Billy. Don't see you on here."

Who the hell cares? Billy wanted to shout. "I checked in with some lady this morning."

"Yeah. Supposed to have all the names here." The guy lifted a shoulder and squinted at Billy. "System ain't perfect."

"Yeah. Well, I gotta go," Billy said.

"Sure. Thanks for your help, son. Tupper, right?" he called after Billy.

Billy didn't answer, just nodded once as he kept walking. He figured the guy probably didn't see the nod, but didn't care. He was going to be far away before Julie and her *boyfriend* showed up.

His bike was leaning against the tree where he'd left it. Billy barely slowed as he grabbed the handlebars with his left hand, pulled the bike upright, positioned his left foot on the pedal, put his weight on that foot and pushed off with his right. What remained of the houses on the street blurred as he sailed past.

He didn't stop pedaling until he got home, and by then, he was starving. His dad wasn't around, but Billy held onto some hope that things were running late at the elevator and that his dad was there and still working instead of sitting at the club while the rest of the town struggled and sweated through the cleanup effort.

Crossing his fingers, Billy opened the freezer. It was empty except for a half-full tray of ice cubes and what he'd hoped to find, a few TV dinners. Billy grabbed one, threw it on the table, then started the oven. He'd probably starve to death waiting for the chicken and potatoes to get hot, but at least he wouldn't have to try to cook something himself.

Billy peered out the window and down the road. He didn't know if he hoped to see his dad's truck or not. It would be a relief, he supposed, to know where his dad was for a change, but if his dad came home, there was the chance they'd have to talk, and Billy didn't feel like talking. Not to his dad, not to anyone. So many questions swirled and churned in his over-tired brain, it was like a mini tornado, complete with the roaring, happening right in his head.

He needed to figure out what to do about Julie, and he needed to figure out what to do about the list of names he'd found in Mrs. Baxter's stuff. Since it hurt too much to think about Julie and her *boyfriend*, he'd hold off on that for the time being.

As maddening as it was, he decided he also needed to hold off on doing anything about his Mrs. Baxter problem. There were times when he'd been hauling garbage that he'd been ready to ditch the cleanup crew and go straight back to her house and up to the attic. No way could he wait four days to get some answers. But he'd talked himself out of it every time because when he thought about what he might find, his stomach knotted, and that bugged him. And confused him.

For most of his life, at least since he'd started hearing stories from kids at school, he'd been convinced he lived down the road from a child killer. He'd spent the months since Judge O'Malley had sentenced him to work for her willing the stories to be true. But now, there was a part of him, a part that seemed to grow bigger every day, that hoped the stories weren't true.

And if that wasn't enough to piss off and confuse a guy, then he didn't know what was.

The smells of cooking chicken began wafting from the oven and Billy's stomach rumbled. Unable to wait another fifteen minutes to quiet the rumble, he went to his room and dug in the back of his closet for one of the candy bars he'd stashed there. Tearing off the wrapper and taking a bite that filled his cheeks, he dropped to his bed. He sat for only a second before popping back up and, holding the candy bar between his teeth, lifted the bottom corner of his mattress.

The notebook had a red cover and was the fourth notebook with a red cover he'd kept tucked under his mattress. Billy opened it and leafed through the pages. Some were neat, his lists precisely organized and numbered. Others were hardly more than scribbles that now, months after writing them, Billy had to squint at to read. When he got to the first list he'd made after starting work at Mrs. Baxter's house, he slowed and carefully read it and each one that followed.

The first few were filled with anger, a sort of anger Billy had a hard time remembering just six weeks later. Mostly he frowned at the stuff he'd written: People he hated; Ways to mess with forgetful Mrs. Baxter. He started to smile when he saw the list of things to talk to Julie about, but then he remembered Julie's boyfriend, and the smile turned to a grimace.

After he'd read all the lists from all of his days at Mrs. Baxter's house, he paged back to the beginning and read them all again. The oven timer dinged before he finished, so he carried the notebook to the kitchen. Once he'd pulled the aluminum tray from the oven and peeled back the foil covering his fried chicken, mashed potatoes, mixed vegetables, and apple crisp, he sat down with the tray, a fork, and his notebook.

Starting a couple of weeks ago, his lists had become a little less angry, a little less hate-filled. Lists like: What he'd do with a bunch of money, or Things to talk to Julie about, were a little more…Billy didn't really know what. Hopeful, maybe? Like there might be something good to look forward to? Even the list about why Mrs. Baxter had a piece of paper with the missing kids' names wasn't nearly as mean as it would have been if he'd written it a few weeks ago.

While he scraped the last of the potatoes from the tray, Billy had to admit to himself that at some point, he'd stopped hating Mrs. Baxter. He wasn't sure when, and he really wasn't sure why, but it had happened.

Just because he didn't hate her didn't mean he liked her, he reassured himself. She was still nuts. Although, he knew her disease was to blame for that. And she was still mean. But not all the time, and mood swings were also part of the disease.

"Shit."

Billy stared at the square filled with mixed vegetables, all that remained of his dinner. The change in his attitude, in his opinion of her, was unexpected, there was no doubt about that. Very unexpected. And for as much as it was unexpected, it was just as much unwelcome. More.

Billy flicked the peas and carrots around the tray with his fork. He may still be hungry, and he may not have tasted much of what he'd already eaten, but he couldn't stomach the mushy vegetables. He tossed the tray in the garbage and then opened his notebook to a blank page. He needed to think, and to figure things out, and he hoped the notebook he'd once thought the stupidest thing ever would help him do that.

Deciding he didn't want to face his dad, assuming his dad decided to come home, Billy grabbed a pencil and headed to his bedroom. He flopped down on his bed and, like the night before, stared at the ceiling. Also like the night before, there were no answers. After ten minutes, Billy raised his legs then flung them downward, using the momentum to sit up. He turned and hung his legs off the bed, resting the notebook in his lap.

Then he stared at the notebook. He tapped the eraser on the blank page and tried to not get frustrated. The words of the doctor he'd been forced to see five years ago sounded in his head.

'Sometimes, you may find the words come faster than you can write them. Other times, it may seem like the words will never come. Be patient. Write whatever comes into your mind.'

Billy had hated that doctor. After his mom died, some of his mom's friends had convinced Billy's dad that Billy should see a doctor to talk about his feelings. Billy may have been only eleven, but he'd been old enough to know the doctor was full of shit.

Sure, Billy was sad. Who wouldn't be? Sure, sometimes he got mad. Who wouldn't? And sure, sometimes he refused to talk to anyone, refused to eat, refused to go to school. If your mom died, you'd do those things too, Billy had told the doctor. Okay, maybe he'd yelled, but the doctor hadn't been listening.

And that yelling had earned Billy his first notebook.

He'd refused to write in it for a while, but had eventually figured out filling it with a bunch of crap seemed to make the doctor happy so he'd started making up stuff to fill the pages. Stuff about how he wished he could die so he could be with his mom, and stuff about how much he hated it when his dad drank. Bullshit stuff, but the doctor told him how good he was doing and reported to his dad on his progress, so he'd kept writing.

And he'd kept writing ever since. No one looked at his notebooks now, no one even knew about them, but sometimes, even though he'd swear to anyone that asked that the whole thing was stupid, sometimes it helped sort out his feelings. And sometimes, to even find answers.

He needed some answers now, but no matter how long he stared at his notebook, the answers didn't come.

17

What did come, and all too soon, was Monday. Billy had worked the weekend away, helping with cleanup, working his two scheduled shifts at Mr. Thompson's plus an extra shift on Sunday, and when he wasn't in town, working at home. Sitting still, doing nothing, had been impossible.

But keeping his body busy for four days straight hadn't freed up his mind to come up with an explanation the way he'd hoped. When he knocked on Mrs. Baxter's door, he had no idea what he was going to say or do.

His knock went unanswered. So did his second, as well as his shout through the partially opened window.

"Mrs. Baxter!" He knew he sounded pissed off, but he didn't care, because he was. "Answer the damn door," he added under his breath.

When she didn't, he tried the door and found it locked. Maybe she wasn't home. It seemed unlikely, but he'd stopped trying to make any sense out of her actions.

"Fine," Billy muttered. "You leave, I do what I want."

But he knew he needed to paint. He'd lost almost a week with the tornado, with helping in town, and with Skelly's harvesting. He'd never finish if he didn't get busy.

The paint cans and tools weren't on the porch, but since he

hadn't been there in a few days, he figured she must have moved stuff to the shed or the garage. He tried the shed first and found nothing. The garage door was shut, but unlocked, so he heaved it open. He swore and kicked at the dirt when he spotted her car parked and with a coat of dust as if it hadn't been moved for a while, at least not since Skelly had been out in his fields.

That meant she must be inside. That niggle of worry was back, no matter how hard he tried to fight it. He supposed she could be taking a bath—he shuddered at that thought—or on the phone or something else that meant she hadn't heard the door. But he knew just as likely, or more likely, was that she wasn't able to answer.

He stopped at the shed, grabbed a knife, and headed back to the front door. It took him less than a minute to wiggle the knife between the door and door frame and pop the lock.

"Mrs. Baxter!"

That niggle of worry became tidal waves that swamped and threaten to drown him. What if he found her dead? What if she'd been dead for days? What if…

He couldn't help it, he gagged and had to swallow back the burning, bitter taste in his throat.

Calling for her as he made his way through the house, it took more and more effort for Billy to lift his feet and force them forward when he got no response. She wasn't in the living room, the kitchen, or anywhere on the first level. Climbing the steps to the second level and her bedroom with still no response left Billy out of breath and sweating.

Her bedroom was his first stop. The door was open and from the hallway, he could see a corner of her bed and could tell it was unmade. For as neat as she kept her house, it was an ominous sign. He poked his head inside the door and there she was, part way under the covers, unmoving, her eyes closed, and skin looking sort of grey.

Fear warred with nerves and with a sadness that wanted to claw its way in as he stared, this time unable to convince his feet to move, no matter how slowly.

"Mrs. Baxter?" With his throat dry and raw, his words were barely more than a whisper. "Mrs. Baxter, are you okay?"

There was no reply, no movement under the blankets. Billy lifted one foot, then the other, and with slow, plodding steps, moved alongside her bed. He watched the blankets, hoping to see them move even just a little to indicate she was breathing, but nothing moved, not the blankets, not Mrs. Baxter.

"Oh, man." Billy reached a tentative hand toward her, pausing to feel for breath, then bracing himself and placing the hand on her cheek.

It wasn't cold, like he'd expected, but hot. Really hot. Like she had a high fever. When he looked closer, he spotted tiny beads of sweat on her forehead. She couldn't be dead and be sweating, could she? He was pretty sure the answer was no, but she didn't respond to his shouts or to the shakes he gave her shoulder, so he figured she was probably close.

She needed a doctor, Billy knew that, but what he didn't know was how to get her to one. She probably needed an ambulance and Billy didn't know how to call one except maybe to try calling the operator. The only other idea he had was his dad. They hadn't talked that morning, but his dad had been home when Billy'd left and Billy figured that couldn't have been more than a half hour ago. Maybe he was still there, maybe he'd know what to do. And maybe he'd be willing to do it.

Billy's feet touched only two of the steps as he flew to the kitchen. He grabbed the phone, dialed his number, and tapped his foot while he listened to it ring. He was just ready to hang up and try the operator when he heard his dad, out of breath and out of patience.

"Yeah?"

"Dad," Billy breathed into the phone.

"Billy? Billy, what're you callin' for? You better not be in trouble."

Part of Billy wanted to be angry that his dad assumed the

worst, but there wasn't time.

"Dad, it's Mrs. Baxter. She's sick. Real sick. She's not waking up. I think she needs an ambulance."

"Slow down there, son. You're at her house?"

"Yeah, I'm at her house. I came to work, she didn't answer, I went inside and found her. She's unconscious, I think. And she feels hot, like her temperature's really high."

Billy thought he heard a sigh, but his dad surprised him. "Okay, stay calm. I'll call for an ambulance then be right over. Stay with her. Get a cold washcloth and put it on her head. If her fever's that high, it needs to come down."

"Uh, okay. Thanks, Dad."

Billy didn't wait for a response, just slammed down the phone and started yanking open drawers until he found a cloth. He ran it under the water until it was cold, then squeezed it out and started back for the stairs. Before he got out of the kitchen, though, he had an idea and sprinted back, grabbed a bowl from the counter, filled it with some ice cubes and water, and carried everything back upstairs.

He did what he could, wiping her face with the cool cloth, and trying not to panic while he waited for what seemed like hours. She was breathing, he determined, but barely. Finally, he heard the door and his dad's voice.

"Upstairs!" Billy yelled.

He hadn't been so happy to see his dad in years. Most of the time, Billy did what he could to avoid his dad, but today, his dad's eyes were clear and focused, he was dressed neatly for a job he was, for the time being, managing to keep, and he looked ready to take charge. Billy was happy to let him.

"Has she been awake at all? Said anything?"

"No."

Billy's dad eased the covers back, something Billy hadn't thought to do. Mrs. Baxter's thin nightgown was soaked in sweat.

"The ambulance should be here shortly, but we've got to do

what we can to bring her temperature down. This is good," he nodded at the cloth, "but we need more. Find a few more rags and get more cold water. Prop the front door open, if you can, so the doctors can get in without any trouble."

Billy felt his jaw drop and once again his feet wouldn't move. He didn't know if he'd ever seen his dad so calm, so controlled, so commanding. Maybe years ago, when his mom was still alive, but not since, he was certain.

"Billy. Go."

Billy blinked and nodded. Then he ran.

They did what they could, adding more cold cloths under her arms and somewhere under her nightgown. Billy didn't know where, and didn't want to know where. He turned and looked out the window as soon as his dad reached for the hem of her nightgown and Billy realized what he was going to do.

Billy's foot wouldn't stop tapping. He waited for his dad to say something, to complain, to tell him to knock it off, but his dad stayed focused on Mrs. Baxter, replacing the cloths and talking, without stopping, in a low, soothing voice. Billy didn't know his dad had a voice like that.

"County Ambulance. Can you hear me?"

Billy jumped to his feet. He hadn't heard a siren, and he'd been listening. "Upstairs," he shouted as he sprinted for the stairs.

Two men in uniform, each with one hand clutching a bag and the other holding one side of a long board, were already on their way up.

"In there." Billy hopped out of their way and pointed.

They brushed past him and into Mrs. Baxter's room. Billy stayed in the hallway, leaning to watch some of what was going on, but afraid of what he'd see. He heard his dad talk to the doctors, to tell them what he knew and what he'd done, then his dad joined him in the hallway.

"There's not much more we can do now, son. It's best we stay out of their way."

"Is she going to be okay? Did they say?"

Billy felt his dad's hand on his shoulder and he stiffened at the contact. When he looked at his dad, he thought he saw a flash of something, sadness, maybe? Regret? Whatever it was, it disappeared as fast as it appeared, and his dad's serious expression was back in place.

"They'll do everything they can for her. I think she must have been sick for a while and it got worse. Might be pneumonia, that's why her breathin' was so shallow and she looked sorta grey. They're givin' her oxygen, that'll help, and they'll take her to the hospital where they can better tend to her."

"But will she be okay?"

"I hope so, son, I hope so."

Once the ambulance was gone and his dad left for work, Billy stood in Mrs. Baxter's yard without the faintest idea of what he was supposed to do. His dad had seen that the house was locked up, then had tucked the keys in Mrs. Baxter's purse and sent it along with her. The doctors driving the ambulance hadn't said much except to tell Billy's dad that he could call later to check on her. Once the commotion was over, his dad hadn't said much either, had just patted Billy once more on the back, then had gotten in his truck and left for work. But no one had told Billy what to do.

He still had the painting, but was he supposed to carry on like nothing had happened? That didn't seem right, but then neither did leaving and doing nothing.

He figured his sentence from Judge O'Malley didn't end just because Mrs. Baxter was in the hospital. He also figured he sort of owed it to her to try to get the house finished. She'd get better, she'd be back home before long, and she'd appreciate—and be surprised, he supposed—if the house was sunny yellow with white trim instead of a mess of yellow and faded, greying white and peeling black trim.

So he got to work and painted. Lunch time came and went,

but Billy never noticed. He worked on autopilot, focusing on the brush strokes and blocking out everything else. His progress was good, but the amount of work left to do had him frustrated. For as many hours as he'd logged, it seemed like there was precious little to show.

Long past his normal quitting time, he finally set down his brush when his growling stomach demanded it. While he cleaned brushes and returned the paint cans to the garage, he let himself wonder about Mrs. Baxter. Was she okay? Better? Worse? Would his dad call the hospital and check? What would happen to her house if she never came back?

As Billy pedaled for home, he brainstormed ideas for finishing the painting. It didn't take long to determine he'd need help. Working by himself, along with taking care of the lawn, the garden, repairing the storm damage, and whatever else might come up while Mrs. Baxter was gone, he'd be lucky to finish even if he worked long days every day. Where to get help, though, was the question.

His friends.

Joel's job watching the neighbor kids would be ending before long. He'd have time. Steve worked a lot at the gas station, but some of his shifts were nights and weekends so he'd have some free time during the week. John...well, John barely worked, but that's how he liked it. He'd be harder to convince.

And how to convince them? Billy listed ideas in his head.

Number One: Offer to pay them. Yeah, right, like he could afford to pay them.

Number Two: Threaten them. He knew stuff about all of them that he could let slip, but, no, Billy knew he'd never do that.

Number Three: Beg. They were friends, after all, so shouldn't they help each other out? Besides, painting always sounded like fun until you actually started doing it.

Number Four: Billy smiled when he got to number four. During their junior and senior years of high school, as part of their graduation requirement, they were expected to log fifty hours of community service. Billy had heard some of the things kids in the past had called community service and they'd been laughable. But, the fact remained, they had to do something. Billy knew he wouldn't be able to count his hours at Mrs. Baxter's because, duh, he had to be there, but the others didn't. With Mrs. Baxter sick and in the hospital and with her house only partway finished, it was the perfect opportunity to get some hours completed. Billy knew Mrs. Baxter would sign off on their hours, that wouldn't be a problem. And even if his friends claimed they were getting enough hours helping with the tornado cleanup, he'd remind them of the rule that said not all their hours could come from the same activity.

And if that didn't work:

Number Five: Promise them they could snoop around in the barn.

Perfect.

It wasn't until he was home and digging in the freezer for something to eat that Billy realized he'd never gotten a chance to look around in Mrs. Baxter's attic.

It was late, at least Billy figured it was because it was dark in his room when the knocking on his door woke him.

"Yeah?"

The door opened a crack, and Billy's dad stuck his head inside.

"Billy. Sorry to wake you."

"Dad? What's wrong?"

There had to be something wrong for his dad to wake him. They'd stopped checking in with one another years ago, and Billy liked it that way. He didn't want to know when his dad came home drunk.

"Nothin's wrong. Can I come in?"

His dad didn't sound drunk. Billy squinted at his clock. 10:34, so not that late, but late for his dad to be getting home unless he'd been out drinking.

"Yeah."

Billy sat up. He was still wearing his clothes and was on top of his bed, so he swung his legs over the side, clicked on the lamp, and squinted again, this time at his dad.

"You just getting home?"

"Yeah. Long day at the elevator. Everyone's tryin' to get their crop in and we had a malfunction, slowed things down." His dad rubbed his hands over his face. "Anyway, I called the hospital earlier. Mrs. Baxter is awake and doin' much better."

Billy took a deep breath and let it hiss out. The vise around his heart, one he hadn't even realized was there, eased.

"That's good. She coming home?"

"Not just yet. They didn't give me much information, just that she's okay and they're treatin' her for pneumonia."

Billy blinked at his dad. "That's what you thought, what you said was wrong with her."

"It was just a guess."

Billy's dad lifted one shoulder in a shrug as if it were no big deal. Billy thought it was kind of a big deal. He never would have known it was pneumonia and he wouldn't have known to try to bring down the fever with cool cloths.

"There's somethin' else."

The vise tightened again. "Something else? What?" Billy tried to read his dad's face. Was he angry? Worried? Was the something else good or bad? Billy couldn't tell.

"I had a visit at work today from that judge. O'Malley."

Billy sucked in a sharp breath. Bad. It had to be bad.

"A strange man, that one. Seemed nervous the whole time he was at the elevator and kept lookin' around at the guys like he was afraid of somethin'." Billy's dad shook his head. "Guess I gave them the address at the elevator as my work address back when....when we were at the courthouse."

Billy couldn't speak. There were words spinning around in his head, as fast as if he were back on that stupid ride at the carnival, but they wouldn't come. He could only stare at his dad through huge, rounded eyes, and brace himself for the worst.

"Anyway, it was a strange conversation with a strange man, but the gist of it is you have an appointment tomorrow mornin' at nine o'clock to take your driver's test and so long as you pass, you'll have your license."

"Muh...my license? Tomorrow?"

One corner of his dad's mouth inched up in a grin. "Yup. Told them at work I'll be a little late again tomorrow mornin'. Figure I can stay late to make up for it."

"To-tomorrow morning? But...but why?"

"That judge didn't make much sense but from what I gathered, Mrs. Baxter called him last week and told him he needed to let you get your license. Told him you've been doin' what you're supposed to be doin' and doin' it well, and you've earned it. Not sure why Mrs. Baxter calls the shots with that one, but..." His dad shrugged.

"So tomorrow I can take my driving test? And you...you'll take me into town to do it?"

"That's what I said. You okay, Billy? You look funny and you're stutterin' almost as much as that judge."

Billy jumped to his feet. "I'm fine. I'm great. I'm getting my license!"

"You gotta pass first. You think you're ready?"

"I'll pass. Hell, dad, I've been ready for three years."

His dad grinned at him. "I reckon you have."

Billy's excitement waned just a bit. "You'll remember? Tomorrow morning? You'll be here and you'll take me?"

"I said I would, so I will." The look Billy had seen earlier at Mrs. Baxter's house flashed back on his dad's face. Regret, this time Billy was certain, and something that looked a lot like sadness. "Tomorrow mornin', eight-thirty." He turned and left, closing the door behind him.

Billy would worry about his dad and what the look on his face meant later. At the moment, he had bigger things to think about. The next morning, he'd have his driver's license.

18

It was amazing how life could go from totally crappy to kind of good in a matter of a day. Billy looked around him, at Joel whistling while he slopped yellow paint on the lower part of the house, at Steve who was handling the higher parts, and then at the slip of paper he'd kept in his pocket since the cop handed it to him that morning.

He had his friends helping him, and he had his driver's license. Yeah, life wasn't so crappy after all.

It was late afternoon and Billy had been painting since his dad dropped him off after the driving test. Once Joel had finished his morning of watching the neighbor kids, he and Steve had joined him and the progress was already noticeable. When they'd arrived, Joel immediately climbed the scaffolding and immediately fell off when he'd started jumping around like an idiot. He wasn't hurt, at least Billy didn't think so, but Billy had made a rule that Joel wasn't allowed to paint any higher than he could reach.

The weather wasn't quite as hot as it had been, so the afternoon was tolerable. They took turns chugging water from the hose and spraying each other with it when they got sweaty, and Billy shared the Coke and potato chips he'd bought at Thompson's when his dad let him stop there on the way home from town.

"Do you really think John will show up tomorrow?" Joel asked.

"I don't know. He said he would, but he says a lot of stuff. If something better comes along, he'll jump at it," Billy answered.

"He really does have to help at his dad's office today," Steve said. "The new windows are in and they're trying to put the inside back together. They need John for some of the heavy lifting. There's supposed to be carpet installed tomorrow so there won't be as much need for him to be there. He might show."

"We'll see," Billy said. "Thank you guys again for helping. I know it's not any fun."

"It's going to be fun poking around in the barn," Joel said. "Remember, you promised."

"I know," Billy said. "When we're done for the day."

"I can't wait to get a look at that car," Steve said, his voice dreamy. "Just think if we could start it, drive it. She'd probably never know."

Billy stood up straight. "We're not driving it. That wasn't part of the deal. Even if you can figure out how to start it, we can't risk taking it out. I mean, what if—"

"Geez, calm down. I know we can't take it out. Allow me my fantasy." Steve frowned at Billy. "Wait a minute...*Even if I can figure out how to start it?* Give me some credit, man."

"I do, and that's why I'm worried. I'm sure you'd be able to get it started, but I'm also sure we'd never be able to afford the cost of the repairs if we damaged it."

"I just want to get a good look at it," Steve said, "and then mourn the fact that it's locked away in an old barn."

"Well, I want to find evidence," Joel said. "It's in there, I know it is. Buried, or behind a fake wall, or shoved inside some old container. You know, those oil drums are the most likely place..."

"I told you, we can't open them," Billy said with a sigh. "They have the original seals. There's nothing but oil inside them."

"If they've been sitting there for all these years without being used, Old Lady Baxter isn't going to decide next week she all of a sudden needs a few hundred gallons of oil. She'd never know," Joel argued.

Billy was shaking his head before Joel finished. "Doesn't matter. You can look around, but you can't make it obvious. Remember, this isn't some stupid summer job for me. It's a sentence from that stupid judge. I can't afford to screw up."

"Seems like he's easing up. You got your license. Maybe he's ready to let the whole thing go," Joel said.

The idea had crossed Billy's mind, but he'd quickly discarded it. No way would Judge O'Malley let him off the hook. Billy still didn't fully understand why he'd been able to get his license, but he wasn't going to ask questions and he wasn't going to push for more.

"I don't think so."

Joel shrugged. "Well, you never know."

Though they painted in silence for a while, Billy's mind was anything but silent. He hadn't told his friends about the paper he'd found in Mrs. Baxter's attic. Part of him felt guilty about it, but part of him didn't want to say anything until he somehow figured out the truth for himself. The house was locked now, and he didn't know when, or if, he'd have a chance to get back inside. He still needed to fix and replace shutters, but he could do that from the outside if he had to. If Mrs. Baxter didn't come home before the end of the summer, or if she didn't come home at all, he'd never get the chance to look more closely at the paper and at the rest of the stuff in the box.

Maybe it was for the best. Billy didn't know what there was to be gained by solving the mystery. It happened so many years ago and none of the families involved lived nearby any longer. With Mrs. Baxter as sick as she was, even if she did it, what then? Put an old, sick lady in jail?

His hand stilled, and a chill stole over him. What if she got the death penalty? They'd talked about that in school, about how it was legal in Kansas but hadn't been used for several years. Billy tried to remember what else the teacher had said, but the details were fuzzy. He knew they used to hang people but didn't think they did that anymore. And what about a lady? Would they do that to a lady? Billy didn't know, but the idea of that happening to anyone made him feel sick.

Billy swiped the back of his hand across his forehead. He needed water, and he needed to stop picturing Mrs. Baxter hanging from the end of a rope.

They painted for another hour, then Billy let Steve and Joel loose in the barn.

Joel didn't find anything—nothing buried, nothing behind a fake wall, and nothing crammed inside a box or can—but he was as determined as ever when they finally called it a day. As for Steve, he went over every inch of the car, oohing and aahing and almost kissing it. When he was done, he pronounced it the coolest thing he'd ever seen.

And Billy kept the list of names to himself.

Later that evening, Billy paced around his kitchen. His dad wasn't home and for the first time in a long time, that bugged Billy. Maybe his dad was working late again, he'd said he'd probably have to after taking Billy for his driving test that morning, but how late? The last couple of days, things had seemed like they might turn around for the two of them. His dad had surprised him with how he handled the situation with Mrs. Baxter, and he'd surprised him again by being willing to take Billy for his test. They'd talked more than they had in months, years maybe, and about stuff that actually mattered.

But now, it was nearly eight o'clock and there was no sign of his dad. Billy had eaten, had straightened up the house, and had looked out the window more often than he'd admit. It pissed him off that he was worried, pissed him off that he'd let himself start to care enough that he'd worry. It'd probably be best for both of them if they let things go back to the way they were. That had worked for them for years.

When the phone rang, Billy jolted. Their phone almost never rang, so Billy eyed it with skepticism. He supposed it could be his dad, he supposed it could be John with an excuse for the next day. He doubted it was Tracy since they weren't scheduled to talk for another twelve days, but the idea that it could be her had him reaching for the phone.

"Hello?"

"Billy? Is that you, Billy?"

The voice was rough, scratchy, hard to hear, but familiar.

"Mrs. Baxter?"

A sigh. "Yes, Billy. I'm sorry to bother you at home, but I want to thank you. I understand if it weren't for you, I might not be making a phone call right now."

Even though he was alone in the kitchen, Billy shifted uncomfortably. "That's probably not true, you would have...I mean..."

"Thank you, Billy. And please thank your father for me. The doctors filled me in on what the two of you did. I'm grateful."

She coughed, but it didn't sound quite as bad as it had, and she got it under control quickly.

"Are you feeling better?"

"I am, though they don't want to let me go home just yet. Pneumonia, they say. Nonsense, I say, but does anyone listen to me? No."

"It's probably best you stay there until you're better."

Billy didn't know what else to say. It was weird talking to her on the phone, and he wanted the conversation to be over.

"Did you take your driving test today?"

And that was really weird, her knowing about what he was doing, knowing about his life.

"Yeah."

"Well? Did you pass?"

"Yeah, I passed." As weird as it was, he couldn't stop the feeling of pride at being able to tell her he passed.

"I knew you would. Now, that leads me to another question, but before I ask, I want you to know that you can say no. You don't have to do anything but work the hours you're supposed to work at my house."

She wasn't making much sense, and he started to wonder if she was going to go crazy on him again.

"Um, okay," he said.

"I need a few things from my house. The hospital said it's possible to arrange for someone to go get them, but I don't much trust some stranger alone in my house, around my things. Would you be willing to pick up a few things and bring them to me? I'll give you a list, tell you where to find everything, and you'd use my car, of course."

Billy had been coming up with excuses as to why he couldn't do what she asked, but then he heard 'use my car' and everything changed.

"Uh, sure, I can do that. Oh, wait, I don't have a key for your house. My dad locked it up and sent the key in your purse." He didn't think telling her how easily he could break in was a good idea.

"There's a house key hidden in the garage. An extra set of car keys too. You're sure you don't mind? Of course, I'll count the time you spend as the time you're supposed to work for me."

"You don't have to do that, I don't mind."

"Nonsense. It counts. Now, if you're sure, here's what I need."

Billy dug through the drawer for a pencil and a piece of paper, but his mind was only half on the instructions he got from Mrs. Baxter. He was going to drive, by himself, and farther than just into town.

His sunglasses in place, his arm slung over the back of the seat, and the radio cranked, Billy cruised out of Munroe and onto the highway. He'd never driven on the highway, but how different could it be? He'd driven as fast as if he were on the highway. That had to count for something. Anyway, at nine-thirty on a

Wednesday morning, traffic was light. With the windows down and the wind blowing in his hair, Billy soaked it all in.

It was how he should have spent the summer. The whole summer. Driving where he wanted, when he wanted, his friends —or maybe even Julie—in the car with him. He ignored the fact that he didn't have a car, that his dad would likely have refused to let him use the truck, at least most of the time, and the fact that he still needed to figure out if Julie had a boyfriend, and instead focused on the feeling of freedom.

Mrs. Baxter's car moved pretty well. It wasn't what he would have chosen, the brown Oldsmobile was boring to look at, but it roared to life when Billy floored the gas pedal. He eased off when the speedometer inched up toward seventy. The last thing he needed was a ticket.

He covered the twenty miles to the hospital, and all too soon, was gliding off the highway and into the hospital parking lot. The drive had been a snap. Billy was congratulating himself on being a natural-born driver as he opened the car door, grabbed Mrs. Baxter's bag, and then felt his muscles lock and his stomach drop.

The ugly, brown brick, the tiny, sad windows, the rows of sickly shrubs, it was all the same. Paralyzed by a sense of dread he hadn't expected and that he certainly didn't know how to deal with, Billy couldn't move; not his legs, not his arms, and not his eyes which, unblinking, stared at the building and at the memories.

It hadn't crossed his mind, not for a fleeting moment, what it would feel like to be back, to see the building, to have to go inside and walk the halls, smell the smells, hear the noises. It had been over five years, but it could have been yesterday.

He could feel his dad's hand, rough and sweaty, grasping his and guiding him toward the entrance. Billy had wanted to see his mom, of course he had, but not here. Every time his dad brought him, it got worse. Sometimes his mom didn't even wake up to talk to him. Sometimes she seemed awake, but she hardly spoke, rarely smiled. It wasn't really his mom, he'd told himself. His mom had hair with smooth curls, not a frizzy, sticking-up-all-over-the-place mess. His mom had happy eyes, not cloudy eyes that didn't recognize her own son. And his mom would hug him and he'd like it, not like the hugs his dad made him give his mom where she barely lifted her arm over his back and groaned when she did so. No, she'd really be his mom again when she came home. He'd told himself that for over a month until the morning when he'd been eating Frosted Flakes with Tracy and Aunt Cindy and his dad had come in to tell him his mom wouldn't ever come home.

When he finally managed to move, he dropped back inside the car and leaned his head on the steering wheel. One deep breath after another, in, out, in, out, until he stopped feeling like he was going to throw up. He could turn around and go home, telling Mrs. Baxter the car wouldn't start, and never have to see the inside of the hospital again.

Or he could stop acting like a baby. He wasn't the eleven-year-old kid who'd cried so hard he *had* thrown up that morning in the kitchen. He was a man with a job and a driver's license, and if he was afraid to walk inside a building, he didn't deserve either of those things.

After a few more deep breaths and slaps on his cheeks, arms, and legs in an effort to feel like the blood was actually still flowing instead of frozen in his veins, Billy got out of the car for a second time. He kept his eyes down as he walked toward the wide, double doors. They whooshed open as he approached and a rush of cool air seemed to suck him inside.

A lady with tight, grey curls, a wrinkled face, and dark red lips stretched in a wide smile greeted Billy.

"Good morning, young man. May I help you?"

"I'm here to see someone. Mrs. Baxter. Alma Baxter."

The lady bent over a book and ran her finger down a list of names. "Baxter. Room 312. If you take the elevator to the third floor then turn right, you'll find it. Or check in with the nurses on three. I hope you have a nice visit."

"Yeah. Thanks."

It smelled just like he remembered, like someone had taken every cleaning product ever made, dumped them all together, then added flowers and sprayed the whole mess all over the place where it mixed with the stench of death. He pulled his shirt over his mouth and nose and fought the urge to gag.

When he got to the third floor, it sounded like he remembered too. Phones ringing, call bells dinging, rubber-soled shoes slapping against the shiny floors, the wheels on the beds and wheelchairs the nurses pushed up and down the hallways squeaking, low, mumbled conversations from every room and every desk, and as he walked down the hall, moans and gasps that he did his best to ignore.

No one paid any attention to him, so he scanned the numbers alongside the doors until he found 312. He paused a moment, bracing himself for what he might see when he came face to face with Mrs. Baxter. His mom hadn't looked anything like herself, so he figured Mrs. Baxter wouldn't either. He tapped on the door.

"Mrs. Baxter?"

"Yes. Billy?"

Her voice still sounded rough and scratchy, but she sounded sort of happy. He took a deep breath, the antiseptic smell tickling his nose, then inched the door open.

"Hi."

She didn't look that bad, he decided. Much better, actually, than she had the last time he'd seen her when he'd thought she was dead. Her face wasn't as grey and though there was some kind of tube strapped to her face and stuck in her nose, he didn't see any other weird machines buzzing and whirring like the ones his mom had been hooked to.

"Thank you for coming. Come on inside."

Billy moved closer, his eyes darting from one side of the room to the other and trying to take in everything at once so there'd be no surprises later.

"How are you feeling?"

"Better. Tired, but better. You can set my bag over there." She pointed to a dresser against the wall. "Thank you. Did you find everything?"

"Yeah. Everything was where you said it would be."

Billy had to grasp his arms to keep from shuddering when he remembered going through her dresser, touching her nightgowns and underwear. He'd done that as fast as possible and had held his breath the entire time. And if he never had to think about it again, he'd be thrilled.

"Good. How was the drive?"

She winked at him, and her eyes had a spark.

Billy grinned. "It was good."

"I'll bet. Sit."

Billy pulled the chair from the corner closer to her bed. It wasn't as scary, or as gross, as he'd expected being in the room with her. Except for the fact she was lying down, she seemed almost like she usually did.

"Did you thank your father for me?"

Billy had, but not until morning, because he didn't see his dad until morning. "Yeah. He says you're welcome."

"How is he, your father? Working?"

Billy nodded. "Back at the elevator."

"Like you said. And it's going well?"

"From what I can tell. He's working late. They're busy."

Mrs. Baxter looked like she wanted to say more, but let it drop.

"If you hand me my purse, I'll give you some money in case you need to buy more paint or any other supplies. I'm not sure when I'll get out of here."

Billy did as she asked. Mrs. Baxter opened her wallet and handed him seventy dollars. He tried to keep his jaw from dropping.

"I don't think I'll need this much."

"You have the key to the house. Put the money in the drawer underneath the phone. If you need it, use it. If not, it will be there when I get home."

Billy shrugged. "Okay."

He'd debated when to tell her about his friends helping with the painting. First, he'd thought he'd wait. That way, if she got mad, a good chunk of the work would be done before he had to tell them they couldn't help any longer. But in the end, he'd decided it wasn't fair to his friends if she refused to sign the forms stating they'd put in hours working for her. And, he figured, it wasn't fair to her, either.

"Um, I got some help with the painting. I hope that's okay with you."

"Help? What sort of help?" Her eyes got the faraway look they sometimes did. "Is it the Trumble boys? I hired them, but they haven't been around yet. Did they finally show up?"

"It's a few of my friends."

Billy waited to see how she'd react, what she'd do. Sometimes, she'd snap out of her episode right away. Other times, she'd get more and more lost in her twisted memories.

"Your friends. What are their names?"

"Joel, Steve, and John. I don't think you know them. They go to school with me."

"Munroe High School?" Then she shook her head. "Of course, it's Munroe High School. Billy." She looked him in the eye and repeated herself. "Billy. Billy Tupper. I'm glad you're doing the painting. Those Trumble boys scare the daylights out of me."

"Well, with my friends helping me, it should get done a lot quicker. There's one more thing. I wonder if you'd be willing to sign a form saying that they worked for you? For free, that is. At school, at Munroe High School, we all have to work community service hours for graduation. Um, if it's okay, I thought this would count. For them, not for me."

Mrs. Baxter blinked a few times before she answered. "Community service. I qualify as community service?" Then she chuckled. "I suppose I do. Of course, I'll sign their forms. I'm glad you have help, Billy, it's a big job. Did I tell you I once painted that house?"

"You did."

She nodded. "It's a big job. I had help. You should have help."

"I should probably go and get back to the painting. A couple of my friends are planning on coming over this afternoon to help, so I suppose I should be there."

She smiled at him. "I suppose you should be. Before you go... about the car."

"I'll put it away in the garage and put the keys back where I found them."

"If you want, but what I was going to say is you're free to use it as long as I'm cooped up in here. I don't have much use for it, do I? Besides, I was hardly using it anyway."

"Oh, I don't know. I don't think I could do that."

"Why not? You're a good driver, aren't you?"

"I guess so, but—"

"Then it's settled. You're free to use it as often as you like. You'll need to pay for the gas and I'd ask that you be careful, but drive it when you need to. Or want to."

Billy felt the smile stretch across his face. "Gee, thanks, Mrs. Baxter. Thanks a lot!"

On the way home from the hospital, while Billy drove a little more cautiously than he had on the way there, he made a list of the places he'd go with Mrs. Baxter's car.

Number One: Work. How nice would it be to drive into town when he had a shift at Thompson's? He was plenty tired of riding his bike home in the dark.

Number Two: The drive-in. But then again, maybe not. Those idiots Randy and Terrence would probably be there and they'd ask questions. Billy didn't think he wanted everyone to know he was cruising around Munroe in Mrs. Baxter's car.

Number Three: On a date with Julie. He decided he'd talk to her, find out the truth about Terrence, and if she didn't have a boyfriend, ask her out on a date. His stomach clenched at the thought.

Number Four: Far away from Munroe. It didn't even have to be to see the red clay or the purple mountains. Just far away.

Number Five: Back to the hospital to visit Mrs. Baxter. Because it seemed like the right thing to do.

19

Since he had a key to her house, and since he had to take care of the shutters, Billy convinced himself a trip back up to the attic was more out of necessity than curiosity. He had to keep telling himself that as he rifled through the box where he'd found the list of names.

It was there, shoved in the book, and in the middle of a bunch of recipes. He studied it, but his memory had served him and there was nothing on the sheet of paper but four names. No additional names, no notes, nothing. Billy sorted through every other piece of paper in the box and came up empty-handed.

Leaning back on his heels, he looked around at the piles and piles of stuff that cluttered the attic. He could open every box, every bag, every drawer, shake the pages of every book, empty the pockets of every coat, and likely still wind up with nothing. On the outside chance Mrs. Baxter had been the one who killed the kids, she wasn't dumb enough to leave something like a notebook full of details on what she'd done with them lying around waiting to be found.

No, even with her mind less sharp than it used to be, she was too smart for that. He repacked the box, with more care this time, folded the flaps, and pushed it back where he'd found it. But he kept the sheet of paper, folded tightly and tucked in his pocket next to his driver's license.

John showed up that afternoon and together with Joel, the three of them painted. The progress was slower than the day before, John not putting in the effort Steve had, but providing more laughs with stories of the cleanup at his dad's office and of his moment of fame when he was interviewed by Candi Newton, the new, young, and according to John, sexy, TV reporter out of Kansas City.

"Yeah, she tried to play it cool, but she was checking me out."

"You're sixteen, John. If she'd been checking you out, she'd be on her way to jail," Joel said.

"She didn't know I was sixteen." John stood straight and flexed his muscles. "I could be eighteen or nineteen. Nothing illegal about that."

Joel's eyes rolled so far back, Billy thought they might stay there. "I saw you on the news. She barely looked at you."

"She couldn't make it obvious on TV, you idiot." John shook his head. "She gave me her phone number before she left."

"No way." Billy didn't believe much of what John said, and this was no exception.

"Yes way. Gave me a card with her picture, her name, and her phone number."

"She gave you her business card, just like she gave to everyone else she talked to that day," Joel said.

"Does it have her picture? Does it have her phone number? Yes, it does," John said. "I'll probably give her a call one of these days."

"You will not," Joel said.

"What kind of stuff did she ask you?" Billy asked.

"You mean you didn't watch me? I'm hurt, man, hurt." John put his hand over his heart.

"Do you want to tell me, or not?"

"Yeah, yeah. She asked about the damage, whether my house was hit, what I was doing to help with the cleanup, that sort of thing. I told her how I'd been working in the office building when the tornado hit and how I got everyone off the upper floors in time so no one was hurt. She was impressed."

"And the only reason you were even a little bit responsible is because you were hiding in the supply room listening to the radio and heard the tornado warning," Joel said. "Don't bother denying it."

"I may have been in the supply room, the radio may have been playing, but I was there...getting supplies. Doing my job. And anyway, it's a good thing, or it may have been too late by the time someone noticed the tornado coming. A bunch of people might be dead now if it weren't for me."

"You're a real hero, John," Joel said.

John's story may be mostly stupid and mostly made up, but Billy could hear the jealousy leaking through in Joel's voice. Joel wanted the spotlight. Just once, Joel wanted the attention on him and not on the memory of his brother.

"I know. A hero who was on TV," John said.

"Hey, hero, watch what you're doing," Billy said. "You're dripping paint on the window."

John pulled a rag from his pocket and wiped the drip. He looked up and then around. "There are so many damn windows. All that trim has to be painted?"

"Afraid so. On the bright side, the house is almost finished."

And it was. For as much as Billy had feared the job would never be done, there was finally a light at the end of the tunnel. Only part of one side of the house remained, then it was on to the trim. What was left of the black needed to be scraped, and like John said, there was a lot of trim, but Billy could see that light, however dim, and it lifted his spirits.

"Help me get this side of the house done this afternoon, and I'll treat you guys to a burger at the Pine City drive-in tonight." He waited a beat. "I'll even pick you up."

"Pick us up? Your dad's letting you use the truck?" John asked. "He'd have to be home...I mean...if he's..."

"Not the truck." Billy stopped painting to look at his friends.

They stopped too and waited, foreheads creased and eyes squinting at him.

"You didn't steal a car, did you?" John asked.

"No, I didn't steal a car. Mrs. Baxter's letting me use hers."

"What?" Joel threw his hands, including the one holding the paint brush, up in the air. Paint dripped and landed on his nose. He swiped at it, succeeding in smearing it across his face.

"She's letting me use her car while she's in the hospital."

"You asked her if you could use her car? I didn't realize you two were on such good terms," John said.

"Shut up. She asked me to bring her some stuff she needed in the hospital, told me I could use her car to get there since I have my license now, and then when I was there, she told me I might as well use the car as long as she's not here to use it."

"So now you're her errand boy?" John smirked at him.

"I'm not her errand boy, you jackass. I did her a favor. Turns out it was worth it, don't you think? I can use her car. Whenever I want."

"I guess that's not such a bad deal," John said. "But why Pine City?"

"Because I don't feel like running into Randy and Terrence and getting the third degree about where I got a car."

"Makes sense," Joel said. "I'm in. Steve's done working at five. He'd probably go along."

"So you have a car as long as she's in the hospital? Can you bribe the nurses to slip her something to keep her there longer? On second thought, I should probably be the one to talk to the nurses. The ladies like me, you know."

Billy balled up his rag and fired it at John.

Billy was painting the trim, a job he'd discovered was worse than the endless stretches of siding, when he heard a car door slam. He climbed down from the scaffolding, and wiping his hands on his rag, walked toward an unfamiliar car and an unfamiliar man in Mrs. Baxter's driveway.

"Morning. I'm looking for Alma Baxter."

"She's not here."

"And are you her grandson?"

"No."

The man put his hand over his eyes and turned to look around the yard and the fields. "Is there anyone here I can speak with?"

"I suppose you can speak with me."

The man breathed out a sigh. "I have some papers for her. I told her I'd drop them off when they were finished. She told me she's usually home."

"She usually is." Billy looked the man up and down. In his dark suit, his shiny shoes, and with skin that looked like it hadn't seen the sun in years, he couldn't look more out of place. "Today she's not."

Billy watched the man fight another sigh. "Do you know when she will be home?"

"No."

The man's curiosity, and suspicion, seemed piqued. "Then why are you here?"

"I work here."

"Do you have a name?"

Before Billy could give him another smart-ass retort, the man held up a hand. "And would you give me your name?"

"Billy. Billy Tupper."

The man's eyebrows rose and for some reason, it made Billy uncomfortable.

"I see," he said. "Well, Billy Tupper, do you have any idea how I might be able to reach Mrs. Baxter if she's not home?"

Billy was growing tired of the conversation and decided the man seemed annoying, but harmless. "She's in the hospital. I suppose you could try to call her there. Otherwise, you'll have to wait until she gets home and I don't know when that will be."

"In the hospital? Oh. I hope she's okay." He looked like he didn't really care one way or the other.

Billy nodded. He didn't feel like sharing any more information with the stranger.

The man tapped a large envelope on his open palm. "I need to get these papers to her. Which hospital?"

"Meadowview. I'm going there tomorrow. I could take them, if you want."

The words surprised Billy even as he was uttering them. He'd sort of been thinking about maybe going back to see her, but he hadn't decided anything for sure. Until now, he corrected himself. It appeared as though now he had decided.

The man looked annoyed. "I can't leave them without the okay from my client. From Mrs. Baxter." The tapping picked up speed and his scowl deepened. "I'll tell you what. I'll go back to my office, I'll try to reach her in the hospital, and if she gives me the okay, I guess I'll drive all the way back out here and give them to you. You'll still be here around noon?"

"I'll be here." Then softer, "I hope that three-mile drive isn't too much for you."

"What's that?" the man snapped.

"I said, I'll watch for you."

"Uh huh. Fine, then, I'll see you later."

The man spun on his shiny heel and stomped back to his car, which was even shinier than his shoes.

"Jackass," Billy said to the back of the car as it sped away in a cloud of dust.

Since he didn't have to work at Thompson's until afternoon, Billy biked over to Mrs. Baxter's on Saturday morning, something he never would have believed he'd do. But he had the papers, and he had access to her car, and since he didn't think there was anyone else to visit her, figured it was the least he could do.

The drive cleared his head and this time when he arrived at the hospital, he got out of the car and marched to the door. He kept his eyes down, not wanting to see the brown color of the brick, the only place he'd ever seen that particular color, or the narrow windows that made him think of a prison.

He didn't stop at the information desk this time, just headed for the elevator, for the third floor, and for room 312. When he tapped on the door at room 312, she answered right away.

"Well, hello, Billy." She smiled when he walked in.

"Hi. How are you doing today?"

"Better, but the doctor doesn't seem to believe me. Worse than the doctor in Munroe for as much as he listens. Seems like if they're going to ask you questions every few hours, the least they can do is listen to the answers."

"Seems so."

Billy tried to decide if she looked better than when he'd last visited. The tube was still under her nose, and she still looked pale, but her voice was stronger. He figured that must mean she wasn't coughing as much.

"Here. This is what that guy dropped off for you. He called you, right?"

Billy held out the envelope and she took it, but set it down on the table next to her bed without looking at it.

"Yes, he called. Thank you for telling him how to reach me and for bringing the papers to me. What did you think of him?"

"Who? The guy with the papers?"

She nodded.

"Kind of a jerk. Why?"

Mrs. Baxter threw her head back and laughed. "You sure don't mince words, do you Billy Tupper? But you're right, he is kind of a jerk."

"Who is he?"

"Blaine Atterbury. A lawyer. I needed some papers drawn up and he's the only lawyer in town. I used to work with Stan Paulson, I've known him since he was a boy, but he retired and that left me with Blaine. The kind-of-a-jerk."

Billy pulled up a chair and looked around the room. It was depressing. White walls, white sheets, a tiny window that looked at another wall of tiny windows, a little table with a scatter of old magazines, and a TV that Billy guessed might pull in a staticky channel or two on a clear day. Some of the rooms he'd passed had the doors open, and he'd seen flowers and cards. There was nothing in Mrs. Baxter's room and that left him feeling a little sad and a lot guilty. He could have cut some flowers from her garden. She always had them in her house.

"How is the painting coming? Are your friends helping?"

Billy had wondered if she'd remember. "Yeah, when they can. They have jobs so they have to work around those schedules, but we're making progress. We've started on the trim."

Her face lit up. "You have? My, you have made progress. How does it look, the yellow with the white trim?"

Billy tilted his head and thought. "It looks happy," he said, and then was embarrassed. "I mean, it looks—"

"Happy." She smiled at him. "That's what I had hoped. The house hasn't looked happy in a lot of years."

"Well, it looks good. There's still a lot of trim left, but it's coming along. And I mowed, and I've tried to keep up with the garden. I hope it's okay, but you had so many tomatoes, I let one of my friends take a few home. His mom doesn't have time for a garden, she works a lot, but she loves to cook so they'll make her happy."

"I'm glad. Take whatever you want, give your friends whatever they want. Much better than letting things rot and go to waste. Thank you again, Billy. You're doing so much more than you have to do."

"It's all right. I don't mind."

"Well, I appreciate it. You bring me those forms you were talking about, for school, for your friends' service hours, and I'll sign them. And you keep track of anything you do outside of your scheduled day and I'll sign one for you too."

"I don't know, I have to be there, I'm not sure it would count."

"You have to be there during the week from nine to five. Any time other than that is extra and should count since you're helping an old lady who's in the hospital. Bring me the forms."

Billy wondered where his was. They'd had an assembly with all the sophomores at the end of the school year and the principal had explained the expectations, the rules, and how he'd seen every kind of cheating anyone could come up with, so not to bother trying. Then they'd been given forms for an adult to sign when they completed any service hours. It was somewhere in his room, he supposed, probably where he'd dropped the junk he'd hauled home from school on the last day. He hadn't looked at that pile since that last day of tenth grade and hadn't planned on looking at it until the first day of eleventh grade.

"Okay." Billy wondered, if he did find it, if she'd remember this conversation.

They talked for a while about school, about what classes he'd be taking for his junior year.

"You don't sound as though you're looking forward to it. Don't you like school?"

"Like school? No. Who likes school?"

"I did. When I went to school and when I worked at the school."

"Well, I don't."

"Why not?"

"Just because. Because it's school."

"That's not a reason. Is it too hard?"

"No."

"Do you do the work that's assigned?"

"Sometimes."

"Why not all the time?"

"Geez! What do you care?" He was ashamed before he finished speaking.

"I care because I think you sell yourself short, Billy. I've watched you this summer. You're smart, you're articulate when you want to be, and deep down, you have a good heart. Those are qualities that will take you far, if you let them. School is the first step."

Billy frowned and didn't answer.

"What about after high school? What are your plans?"

"I don't have any."

"Then what are your dreams? If you could do anything, what would it be?"

Billy had never told a soul, mostly because there was no one to tell, but he had dreams of going to college. He didn't really hate school, and the work wasn't really very hard. He thought maybe, just maybe, he could handle college, he could get a job away from Munroe, and he could start his life over.

"I don't know."

"Yes, you do. I can see it in your eyes. Tell me."

Billy blew out a frustrated breath and pulled at a loose thread on his T-shirt. His eyes stayed focused on the thread when he finally answered.

"I guess I'd sort of like to go to college." His eyes cut a glance at Mrs. Baxter. "But I know that's not going to happen."

"Why isn't it going to happen?"

"It's expensive and you have to have top grades to get in."

"Those things are easily overcome with some effort. Study, do your work, and your grades will improve. There are grants, loans, different ways to pay for college."

"Hah! That stuff's easy? I don't think so."

"I said easy with some effort. Things you have to work for mean more than those that are handed to you."

"Hard to compare when nothing's ever handed to you," Billy mumbled.

"It's been hard since your mother died, I know that, and I'm sorry. I would never have wished that fate on you, I'd never wish it on anyone, but if there's a silver lining, it's that you're going to come through strong, and resilient, and smart. Does that make up for losing your mother? Of course not. But she'd be proud of you, Billy, she'd be so proud."

"Proud? Of what? Proud that I got kicked off the school bus, that I smoke cigarettes, that I drink when I get the chance, that I skip school, that I had to go to court, for God's sake? I'd argue there's not much there to be proud of."

A hand blue with a complicated web of veins reached from the bed to Billy's chair. Mrs. Baxter calmly, gently, put that hand over Billy's.

"She'd be proud. Don't let yourself believe otherwise for even a minute. Kids make mistakes, all kids, that doesn't mean a parent stops being proud. Or that a parent stops loving." She was quiet and Billy felt her hand tremble on his. "I had a son. I was proud of him, no matter what happened, and I loved him, no matter what happened."

Billy didn't know whether to respond or just be quiet and wait and see if she said any more about her son. She'd never mentioned him before and other than the few photographs he'd found, Billy knew nothing about him. When she stayed quiet, gazing out the window, Billy was afraid she'd slip away into that fog that seemed to envelop her more and more often.

"Tommy?" he prompted.

"Tommy. My Tommy. He was such a sweet boy."

"What happened to him?" His voice wasn't much above a whisper, Billy figuring if she wanted to ignore the question, if she didn't want to talk about her son, he'd make it easy for her.

Billy looked at her while he waited and spotted the tear in the corner of her eye. He wanted to run, but her hand gripped his tighter and she spoke before he could get away.

"An accident. It was an accident. He didn't mean to do it, he was only trying to help, trying to show his father that he could do it. All by himself. And it was only one egg." She shook her head and turned to Billy. "He didn't start the fire. I know he didn't. Tommy was there, it was easy to blame him, and I wanted to help him. Billy needed my help, and it was the only way I knew to help him. Tommy, you won't tell Billy, will you? I don't think he'd understand."

Tommy? Billy? Eggs? The *fire*? Billy's head was spinning. She no longer knew who she was talking to, that much was clear, but the rest? It didn't make any sense, but he couldn't get past the fire. She knew he didn't do it? There may have been a fire, that may have been what killed her son, but the idea that she had her stories mixed up and was referring to the fire last fall was too hard to ignore. She knew he didn't start it? He, Billy, didn't start it? And she knew?

Good Lord, none of it made sense.

"What fire?"

He had to try, but her eyes were closing. She coughed a little, then her head fell toward her shoulder. Billy took her hand and put it back on the bed, then stood and with a last look, slipped from the room. He had to get to Thompson's, but he'd be back to figure out what in the hell she was talking about.

20

Billy had told Mr. Thompson he'd spend part of Sunday doing some cleaning at the store, moving stock, stuff that was hard to do when customers were there, but the rest of his Sunday was free.

Since he couldn't get Mrs. Baxter's comments out of his mind, and since he didn't have anything better to do, he biked to her house, cut some flowers from her garden and stuck them in the vase he'd grabbed from his kitchen—out of the high cupboard over the refrigerator no one ever opened any more—then got in her car and headed for the hospital. Driving was starting to seem normal and the idea that he'd have to give up her car before long was something he preferred not to think about.

She was sitting in a chair when he got there, wearing the blue robe he'd brought, and with a blanket thrown over her lap. It was hot outside but always seemed a little chilly in the hospital, so Billy convinced himself the blanket wasn't a sign she was getting worse.

"Billy. Flowers?"

"Hi, Mrs. Baxter. Yeah, they're from your garden. I hope that's okay. I know you always cut some and kept them in the house so I thought you might like to have some here."

"I'd love to have some here. Oh, my, but don't they make the room brighter?"

"Yeah, I guess they do."

"Thank you."

"Sure."

"I didn't expect you today," Mrs. Baxter said as she fussed with the flowers Billy had placed on the table next to her chair.

"I have your mail." Billy'd come up with the excuse the night before and held up the bag containing everything he'd pulled from her mailbox. "I thought there might be some important stuff and I'm not sure when I can get back here during the week."

"Well, then, thank you again."

She turned from the flowers and smiled at him. Billy noticed a little more color in her cheeks, her eyes looked a little brighter, and without the tube under her nose, she looked a lot less sick.

"Did you have to fight the doctor to get out of bed?"

Mrs. Baxter laughed. "No, believe it or not, it was his idea. Suddenly, lying around isn't good for me." She shook her head. "First, they tell me I can't get up, that I need to rest, then they tell me I have to get up and that I have to walk up and down the hallway. I wish they'd make up their minds."

"You walked up and down the hallway?"

She nodded. "Had to push a cart with an oxygen tank, but I guess I did well enough that they took that ridiculous thing out of my nose."

"Do you think you'll go home soon?"

"I don't know. They won't give me any answers when I ask."

Billy didn't know if they'd give him any information, but he decided he'd ask on his way out in case they'd told her and she'd forgotten. He realized there could be a lot of things the doctor had told her that she'd forgotten. While she was in the hospital, the doctors and the nurses would see to it she took her medication, that she got up and walked, but when they sent her home, who was going to make sure those things happened?

It was a problem for another time. Right now, it was time to see if he could get some answers.

"I was wondering if after I finish with the trim on the house, you'd like me to paint the new fence. Seems like it would look good white like the trim."

Mrs. Baxter tilted her head, then nodded. "I think you're right. A white fence would be nice, but only if you have time."

"I think with my friends helping, I'll have time." He paused a moment and mimicked Mrs. Baxter's head tilt. "Was it painted before? Before it burned?" He dropped his head. "Before I burned it?"

"It was white, but that was a long time ago. It had faded, much like the house. It looked like old, weathered wood before Fred started the fire."

Billy sucked in his breath. Fred? The only Fred he knew around Munroe was Fred Hyland who lived on a run-down farm a few miles from Billy.

Billy was afraid to push, but risked a question. "Fred?"

"Fred, um, Fred...what's his name. Oh, for heaven's sake. I can't remember."

"Fred Hyland?"

"Hyland. Of course. He's always driving that old truck of his, always dragging a chain behind since more often than not, he's hauling another old junker out to his place. Says he's fixing them, but I don't think he does anything with them but let them sit. I've seen that chain spark when it knocks against the rocks, and I've told him he's going to start a fire, but does he listen? Of course not. Too stubborn, or more likely too stupid, to take a few seconds to secure the chain. He started the fire, I'm sure of it."

Billy's heart banged in his chest and he knew if they connected him to one of those blood pressure machines he'd blow the thing up. Fred Hyland started the fire? She knew that? And she let him take the blame?

Billy jumped to his feet and stomped toward the door but before he yanked it open, whirled to face her.

"What the hell? If you knew Fred started the fire, why did you tell the cops I did it? Why did you let me sit in that courtroom with that jackass O'Malley and let him sentence me to the worst summer possible? Why?"

Any color that had returned to Mrs. Baxter's face drained while Billy yelled. The hands that rested on the arms of the chair shook. Her mouth opened and her jaw moved up and down, but she didn't speak.

"Shit." Billy stormed into the hallway and was halfway to the elevator before it registered that someone was calling him.

"Young man!" He slowed and turned toward the voice. "Hold it right there."

Even if Billy had wanted to move, he didn't think he would have been able. A nurse who looked to be almost six feet tall with grey curls tight to her scalp, a stare that put the fear of God into him, and an expression that dared him to take another step stood with her hands fisted on her hips. "You stomp across my floor like that, you tell me why."

"Just leaving."

"When a person's *just leaving*, he walks, he doesn't stomp so hard it causes my cart to rattle. You were in 312."

"Yeah, so?"

"So that means you were visiting Mrs. Baxter." He thought her voice softened just a little, but he wasn't taking any chances.

"I was, now I'm leaving." He took a backward step toward the elevator.

"Just hold on. Before you leave, I want to have a word with you."

Billy didn't think he had to do what she said, if he ran he could probably get away from her and if he never came back, what trouble could he get in? But she looked like she meant business and since he didn't know how to get downstairs except with the elevator, figured his chances of the elevator opening, of him getting on, and it closing before she got to him were nonexistent. He gave in.

"About what?"

"Come and sit down."

She gestured to a few chairs grouped together near the nurses' area. Billy kept his eyes on her, but did as she asked and headed for the chairs. He dropped into one with a grunt.

"Nan, will you please see to 312? I'll be just a few minutes."

A younger nurse nodded and got up. Billy guessed the giant nurse must be the boss.

She settled into the chair next to his and for a moment, just leaned her head back, stretched out her legs, and sighed.

"Mmm, sometimes there's nothing better than just sitting."

She wore a white uniform, white shoes, and white pantyhose on her legs. Billy wondered why everything in a hospital had to be white. So the blood showed up better? Seemed pretty gross, like it would be better if they wore red and had red sheets. Who wants to see a bunch of bloodstained stuff? His stomach started to protest, and he put a hand over it.

"I've seen you here before. Are you a relative of Mrs. Baxter?"

"No."

"A friend?"

"No." Not any more, that's for sure.

"Then why are you here?"

"I work for her. I had some stuff to bring her."

"I see."

She studied him and Billy had to grip the armrests to keep from squirming.

"You seemed angry when you left her room. Did your visit not end well?"

"You could say that."

Billy focused on the rhythm as she drummed her fingers on the armrest of her chair. Tap-tap-tap, tap-tap-tap, tap-tap-tap, until he thought he'd go crazy. She pulled her bottom lip between her teeth and her eyes narrowed as she continued to study him. Billy told himself he wouldn't let her get to him, he wouldn't volunteer any information, but that only lasted another minute until the combination of the incessant tapping and her apparent willingness to wait all day had him shouting.

"She's crazy, you know."

The nurse's fingers stopped and she leaned back, nodding, nodding, nodding like she'd never stop. It reminded Billy of the stupid toy dogs people liked to put in their cars, the ones with the heads that never quit bobbing up and down.

"How much do you know about what's wrong with Mrs. Baxter?"

"I know she's nuts. That's all I need to know."

Billy started to stand, but the nurse lifted one finger and he dropped back into his chair with a huff.

"She's not nuts, and I think you know that. She's sick. Very sick. If she said something, did something that seemed odd, or cruel, or out of character, know that she likely won't remember doing it." The nurse stared at him again with those eyes he swore saw right through him. "But I think you know that too."

"Alzheimer's, right?"

For the first time, the nurse looked surprised, but again, she took her time speaking.

"There are nurses, doctors even, who aren't familiar with that term. How do you know about it?"

Billy kind of liked the fact that he'd surprised someone who he figured wasn't often surprised. "I went to the library, read some books."

The nodding started again. "I see. You must care about Mrs. Baxter if you were willing to research her disease at the library."

"I don't care about her, she's—"

"I'll ask you not to shout. We have sick people here and I'd prefer not to upset them."

"Sorry," Billy muttered. "But I don't care about her."

"You did. I can tell. If you let one incident change that, that's too bad, especially given the fact that you understand her disease."

"But I don't understand it, not really." Billy lifted his arms and let them fall. "She acts normal and then she has these…these episodes where she seems like she doesn't know where she is, or what she's doing, or who I am, or anything. She talks to me like I'm someone else, she yells at me for stuff I didn't do, she tells me the same thing she told me fifteen minutes before. How can she be okay one minute and then act crazy the next? And how do I know what to believe when she tells me stuff?"

Billy fell back, let his head drop, and closed his eyes. His breath was coming so fast it made his chest hurt. He hadn't meant to say all that stuff. More than ever, he wanted to run. Run fast and far.

"It's hard, I know. It's hard to understand, and it's hard to watch her struggle, suffer. You're Billy, is that right?"

Billy opened one eye to look at the nurse. She lifted a shoulder.

"She mentioned a Billy, I figured it must be you. I know it's difficult, but the best thing you can do for Mrs. Baxter is to be patient with her, to try to guide her back to your conversation if she falters, but don't push. Sometimes, her mind will wander, will take her places she doesn't understand herself. It's difficult for us to know what's happening in her mind, but it's not difficult to see it's just as frustrating for her as it is for us. She didn't choose this, and she's not doing it on purpose. You've likely noticed some days are better than others, some hours are better than others. It can be stress that triggers an episode, as you called it, it can be any number of things, or it can be nothing at all. I wish I could tell you she'll get better, but I think you already know she won't."

Billy opened both eyes. The scary nurse was gone and in her place was someone Billy would want taking care of him if he ever needed to be in a place like Meadowview.

"Yeah. I know."

"Whatever happened today, I hope you don't let it change your feelings for Mrs. Baxter. If you care about her, and I sense that you do, try to remember that she didn't mean to hurt you."

"She didn't hurt me, she..." Billy didn't know how to

continue. Had she hurt him? Made him mad? "She told me something, something that affects me. A lot. How do I know if it's true?"

"Hmm. That's a good question. You probably can't know. Not for sure, anyway, if it's only her word you have to go on. I've had patients who make up elaborate stories and are convinced they're the God's truth. I've had patients who get their memories so twisted, they don't know any more what's true. Sometimes, a person will sense they're losing track of what they're saying and just continue weaving a tale so it seems like nothing's wrong. That's the hardest to watch, I think. A part of them knows what's happening to their mind and they try to fight it but don't know how because there isn't any way to fight it. It's a cruel, cruel disease, Billy."

"So what do I do?"

"That's up to you. If you're willing, I'd say keep visiting, keep talking to her, keep treating her the way you've always treated her, but watch for signs she's not doing well. In that case, let her talk without correcting and then let her rest when she needs it."

How he'd always treated her. Billy felt a stab of guilt at that. For most of his life, he'd either talked about her like she was some kind of witch, had ignored her, or had plotted ways to torment her. He didn't think he wanted to tell the nurse that.

"Okay. Is she going to get to go home?"

"The doctor is working on that. Her pneumonia is better, but he's worried about her being on her own. He's looking into arranging for a nurse to visit her at home, at least a few times a week. We'll see what happens."

Since he'd calmed down some, he nodded.

"Okay, thanks."

Billy stood. When the nurse did the same, he noticed her name tag for the first time. His throat tightened, and it was a struggle to keep standing.

Dolores.

His mom's name.

* * *

By Tuesday, Billy knew it was time to get back to the hospital. He'd spent over twelve hours at Mrs. Baxter's house the day before, some of it with his friends, a lot of it alone, and the progress was noticeable. More than that, though, was the fact that he'd let go of whatever anger he'd been holding onto since his last visit to the hospital.

Maybe she knew what she was talking about, maybe she didn't, but either way, he may never know the truth. He'd have to live with that.

Even though the trim wasn't done, Billy had spent part of Monday painting the fence. Steve and Joel had questioned him about it, Joel concerned it meant they'd have to paint the barn and the garage and everything else that didn't move, but Billy had told them the fence had been part of the deal from the start. What they didn't know wouldn't hurt them.

Before he left for Mrs. Baxter's house, Billy pulled out his notebook and reviewed what he'd written since his last visit with her. Questions he had for her if he caught her with her wits about her.

Number One: Who started the fire? And was she sure?

Number Two: If it was Fred, why didn't she accuse him?

Number Three: What happened to Tommy?

Number Four: Did she really think he could go to college?

He'd drawn a line through that question because how should she know?

Number Five: Why did she have those kids' names on a piece of paper tucked away in the attic?

Billy heard his dad in the kitchen, then heard him grab his keys. He wanted to talk to his dad for a minute, so he tucked his notebook under his mattress and jogged to the kitchen.

"Hey, Dad, I've been meaning to tell you something."

"Don't know that I like the sounds of that. Somethin' bad?"

"No. At least I don't think so. Mrs. Baxter told me I could use her car while she's in the hospital."

Billy's dad leaned back against the kitchen counter, crossed one boot over the other, and sipped his coffee under raised brows.

"She needed some things from her house the other day and asked me if I'd mind bringing them to her. She told me to use the car and then said I could use it for other things too, if I wanted. I've been careful, and I've been back to the hospital to bring her some papers a lawyer dropped off for her, bring her the mail, that sort of thing. I guess I just thought you should know."

"Huh. That's quite a drive for someone just startin' out. You doin' okay on the highway? We never practiced that."

"I'm doing fine." Billy shrugged. "There's not much traffic."

"You take the car anywhere besides the hospital?"

"I drove to Pine City the other night with Joel and John and Steve. We were back early."

"Don't know as it's right to treat the car like it's your own. Usin' it to go to the hospital's one thing, drivin' all over tarnation is another."

"One trip to Pine City, and into town for my shifts at Thompson's. That's not exactly *all over tarnation*."

Billy's dad sipped and eyed him. "When's she comin' home?"

"Don't know. The doctor hasn't told her yet, far as I know."

"Huh. I guess if she said it's okay, it's okay, but you get in an accident, well, you'll be figurin' out how to pay for the repairs."

"I won't get in an accident."

"Some day I'd like to meet the guy who says he's goin' to get in an accident. That'd be an interestin' conversation, now wouldn't it? Be careful, son, and don't do anything dumb. And don't take advantage of Mrs. Baxter."

Billy nodded as his dad left the house. The truck roared to life and his dad was off for another day at work. As far as Billy knew, his dad had been at work every day since being hired back. How long it would last was anyone's guess, but for now, it wasn't quite as horrible living in the same house with him.

* * *

He brought more flowers, just because they were there, in the garden, with no one looking at them. Mrs. Baxter plucked out a few wilting ones from those in the vase, then added the fresh ones.

"One more week in the hospital. That's what the doctor told me this morning. A week? When I'm feeling fine? Seems foolish, but he argued since there's no one at home to see to my recovery, it's best I stay here for a while longer." She flicked her wrist at the metal bars that ran the length of her bed.

"A week isn't that long."

"Not that long? Hmpf. You lie here with nothing to do and tell me how quickly a week passes."

"I brought your mail again." Billy pointed at the bag he'd set on the dresser. "There's a magazine in there. That's something to do."

"I suppose. One of the nurses brought me some puzzle books. I've never done puzzles, but she swears they're fun. I'm skeptical."

Billy wondered if it was Dolores. In one of the library books he'd read, it said doing things like crossword puzzles was good exercise for the brain. Giving Mrs. Baxter puzzle books seemed like something Dolores might do.

"Billy, the last time you were here…"

The tone of her voice sent prickles dancing over Billy's skin.

"Did we discuss the fire? You'll have to forgive me, but I don't always remember the details."

"A little."

"I see. And you left rather abruptly. I assume I told you I believe Fred Hyland started the fire."

Billy tried to judge if she was angry, if she was afraid of having the conversation, if she was testing him, but her face was blank of any telltale emotion. Her eyes, however, were clear and focused. He took that as a good sign.

"You mentioned him."

She sighed and gazed out the window. "That left you with

questions."

"A few."

"Billy..."

"Why? If Fred started the fire, if you knew that, why did you tell the cops I did it?"

"I was trying to help you."

"Trying to help me? Or trying to help yourself? Getting your yard work done, getting your house painted, getting everything done that you didn't want to do?"

"Trying to help you. Billy, I've been trying to help you for five years."

"What are you talking about? Five years? What's that supposed to mean?"

Billy paced the tiny room but worked to keep his voice down. He hadn't seen Dolores on his way in, but didn't want to risk her wrath.

"Will you sit down? I can't talk to you when you're bouncing around like a jumping bean."

Billy glared at her, but dropped into the hard, straight-backed chair in the corner, glad there was some distance between the two of them.

"It broke my heart when your mother passed away. She was a friend when I didn't have many of those. I don't know if it meant much to her at the time, but during my last visit with her, shortly before she had to go back into the hospital for what turned out to be the last time, I told her I'd do what I could to look out for you and Tracy."

"So you got me arrested?"

"What I tried to do was take care of you for the summer. Give you a place to be where you'd stay out of trouble, feed you a decent lunch, teach you the importance of being on time and doing what you've been hired to do."

"Wha—, what?" Any attempt to keep his voice at a reasonable volume was futile. "How is it any of your business what I do with my time? If I get into trouble, that's my problem! And teach me to be on time? To do my job? It's not a job! It's a sentence! Who do you think you are—"

"Billy." She said it so calmly, so softly, it got his attention far better than if she'd yelled right back at him.

He threw himself back in the chair. "What?"

"Even if it wasn't your cigarette butt that started the fire, it could have been. How many times did I stand outside when you rode your bike through the fields and tell you to keep those cigarettes away from all the dried grass?"

Tell? Billy wanted to laugh. More like hollered and shook her fist at him. Still, he had to admit, she was right. He'd tossed a butt into the grass just about every day he'd ridden through her property, something he wasn't supposed to be doing in the first place. He'd been told to stay to the road, but the half mile he could cut off his ride by cutting through was too hard to pass up. If he hadn't started the fire, if Fred had, it was only dumb luck that had kept Billy innocent.

Still, he wasn't ready to admit it.

"I understand why you're angry. It seems very unfair. When I talked to Judge O'Malley, when I told him what I wanted, he was reluctant. He wanted to fine you, sentence you to community service, and wash his hands of the entire matter. It took some talking on my part, reminding him he wasn't always the model teenager, before he agreed. In the end, I convinced him you'd be better served by working for me and learning a thing or two over the summer."

Billy sat up and leaned forward in his chair, resting his elbows on his knees. He clasped his hands together and squeezed them tight.

"You decided my sentence?" Each word was slow and clipped. He watched her for any sign that she was drifting away, but her eyes stayed alert.

"I did. And before you ask, the hold on your driver's license was part of my deal."

Billy threw himself back so hard the chair banged against the wall. He dropped his hands over his face and scrubbed.

"Unbelievable."

"As I said, it seems very unfair, I'm sure, but I had your best interests at heart. You were headed down a dangerous path, and I saw no signs of your father doing anything to set you on the correct one."

He kept his head back and stared at the ceiling. "I'm not sure how my father is any of your business either."

"I told you, I made a promise to your mother. I've tried over the years...food, clothes, school supplies, toiletries, sometimes money, but it wasn't enough. It helped, maybe, to feed you or clothe you, but it didn't help with what really mattered. This summer was my attempt to do something that did."

Food? Clothes? Money? He didn't have the foggiest idea what she was talking about. There'd been the stuff from the church...

"Wait." He kicked his legs and sat back up. "You left the stuff at our house? The stuff my dad said was from the church?"

"There may have been some things from the church, I don't know, but I did leave some. Yes."

Billy thought about it. He'd often wondered why the church kept bringing stuff when he and his dad never went to church. There hadn't been as much lately, not as much as at first, so maybe they had doubled up for a while, the church and Mrs. Baxter, and maybe more recently it had been just Mrs. Baxter. It was too much to think about.

"Did my dad know?"

"I don't think so. He never said anything, but I preferred it that way. I wasn't looking for thanks."

Billy fisted his hands in his hair and scratched at his head. Trying to make some sense out of it all made his head hurt.

"I don't know what I'm supposed to say. You may think you did the right thing, but I was supposed to work all summer for Mr. Thompson. I was supposed to earn money, money that I need."

"Oh, you'll be paid. I've always planned on paying you."

That was it, she was headed for one of her episodes. Pay him? Right.

"You don't believe that."

"Believe that you were going to pay me? No. I had to be there. You didn't hire me, Judge O'Malley sentenced me. That's a lot different than having a job."

"But that was my point. To teach you what it's like to have a job, a job you have to show up on time for, where you have to do the work you're told to do no matter how much you dislike that work, and a job where you have to show some respect to your employer. I'd like to think we succeeded on all fronts."

"But...but I was going to work for Mr. Thompson. I would have done a good job there. I would have been on time, I would have..."

He stopped speaking because he knew it wasn't true. Having to bike to town and back for every shift would have quickly gotten old. Having to work when his friends were free to go to the lake, to go to a party, to do whatever they wanted...he knew he would have made up excuses to skip out on a shift when there was something more fun to do instead. And he would have learned how to get out of a shift, how to lie to his boss, how to feel okay with lying to his boss.

Damn. She was right. Again.

"I suppose," Billy mumbled.

"And I meant it when I said I planned on paying you. If you work the entire summer, that's five days a week for twelve weeks. Is Mr. Thompson paying you minimum wage?"

"Yeah."

She picked up the puzzle book and a pencil. After a minute she looked up at Billy.

"You work the rest of the summer, that's seven hundred and sixty-eight dollars you'll have earned. I'll pay you at the end of August."

Billy gulped so hard it hurt. "Seven hundred and sixty-eight dollars? You're serious?"

"Of course, I'm serious. I'll write myself a note, but you still may need to remind me. My memory doesn't always fire at a hundred percent."

She winked at him and Billy cracked his first smile of the day.

"Thank you," he said. "For all the other stuff too. The food, the clothes, that was nice of you. We didn't always have much at home. My dad, he'd forget to shop, and didn't always notice when I needed new clothes. I'll be able to buy some stuff for myself now."

"It wasn't much, but I tried. If things had worked out as I'd hoped, back in the beginning with Tracy, then—"

There was a tap on the door and a nurse came in pushing a cart. "Oh, you have a visitor, Mrs. Baxter. That's nice. I'll only be a minute, but we have to take care of a few things." She turned to Billy. "Would you mind waiting in the hall?"

Tracy? What about Tracy?

"Uh, sure."

Billy left and wandered the hall for a few minutes, wondering what in the world Mrs. Baxter had meant about things working out with Tracy. Had she been sending things to Tracy too? Billy didn't think Tracy needed anything, Aunt Cindy and Uncle Dan were rich, but maybe he was wrong. Maybe there were things he didn't know.

Like a determined mouse gnawing its way through a wall, worry gnawed at Billy's mind. Even dreaming about what he'd do with all the money Mrs. Baxter had promised to pay him didn't distract him from the one thing that never failed to cause him to worry. The one person who could always cause him to worry. If he could talk to Tracy more often, if he could spend more time with her, maybe the worry would ease, but somehow he doubted it. He was the one who should be looking out for her, making sure no one was picking on her at school, comforting her after she had one of the nightmares he knew still plagued her, seeing that she did her homework, that she was happy. Instead, he had to rely on far-too-occasional reports from Aunt Cindy, reports he now wasn't sure he could believe.

The nurse who'd gone into Mrs. Baxter's room came back out and waved to get Billy's attention.

"She's getting tired. You might notice a change when you go back in to talk with her."

Billy nodded before heading back to try to get more information from Mrs. Baxter.

"Tommy, is that you?"

"Hi, Mrs. Baxter. It's Billy."

"Where's Tommy? Tommy was just here, before that nurse made him leave. Well, he'll be back soon, I'm sure."

"Um, Mrs. Baxter…"

But she'd closed her eyes with a smile on her face, and Billy was certain she was already asleep. Maybe they'd given her some medicine that made her tired because she hadn't seemed ready to fall asleep before the nurse came.

Knowing he shouldn't wake her, and figuring even if he did, it was unlikely he'd be able to pick up the conversation where they'd left off, Billy mumbled, "See you later," and pushed through the door back into the hall.

He spotted Dolores while he was waiting for the elevator. She smiled and lifted her finger in what Billy took as a request to wait, so he let the elevator come and go.

"Billy. I'm pleased to see you back here."

"Yeah, I had some mail for Mrs. Baxter."

"Um hmm. Well, whatever your reason, visitors are good for her, so thank you."

"Yeah, um, I sorta wanted to thank you too. I mean, thanks for explaining more about what's wrong with her. I read those books, but they didn't always make sense."

"I don't have all the answers, far from it, but if you have any more questions, feel free to ask."

"Okay. Thanks."

"Did you have a nice visit today?"

"I don't know if it was nice, exactly. Mrs. Baxter's been telling me stuff that I don't think she'd be telling me if she always knew what she was saying. Do you know what I mean?"

"I think I do. You're feeling guilty, maybe, that you're learning things she might rather keep secret? Things that you think she wouldn't have told you if she wasn't ill?"

"Yeah, that's about right, I guess."

"Hmm. That's tricky. I stand by what I said that it's good for her to have visitors, but I also agree that she might tell you things that you don't want to hear. There may be times you struggle with what to do with those things you hear. My advice is to listen, to know that some of what you hear may not be entirely accurate, and to remember that if she says something that bothers you, there are times when she's not in control of what she's saying. She's not trying to be cruel, and I don't believe that she's saying what she truly believes, like the disease has loosened her inhibitions, almost like being drunk, and has allowed her to speak the truth for the first time."

Dolores took a deep breath and shook her head. "No, I don't believe that. Mrs. Baxter's brain is changing, deteriorating, and there are times, there will be more times, when she's confused and she struggles for what to say. It might not always come out the way she intended."

She patted Billy on the shoulder. "When it's one of those times, don't argue with her, don't force an issue even if you know you're right, just try to be patient and perhaps try to change the subject to something less upsetting."

"Okay." Billy would have to think about what kind of questions he could ask her and figure out whether he'd be okay with the answers. "I was talking to her and a different nurse came to do something with her and when I went back in her room, just a few minutes later, she thought I was someone else and then she fell asleep."

"That's not unusual. It can be the littlest things, or nothing at all. We can't always know what will trigger a change."

"Do you think she'll be okay back at her house?"

"Her doctor has arranged for a nurse to visit a few times a week. Mrs. Baxter insisted she wanted to go home, the disease hasn't progressed so much that her doctor feels it would be unsafe, so they're going to give it a try. The nurse will report back on how Mrs. Baxter is doing. If there is a change, or if the nurse spots problems, then the doctor will reevaluate."

Billy nodded. "She said in a week."

"That's correct. Billy, do you know of anyone else we should contact about Mrs. Baxter? Maybe someone who can check up on her? She has no family listed on any of her medical records and when we've asked, she says there's no one. The only name we found was on a form from several years ago and we haven't been able to reach her. Dolores Tupper."

Billy turned away. He had to. "I don't think Mrs. Baxter has any family. And Dolores Tupper died. Five years, three months, and six days ago."

Billy didn't turn back, just walked down the hall. He'd find the stairs somewhere. He heard Dolores call after him, but he just kept walking.

21

Determined to have the house finished by the time Mrs. Baxter came home, Billy worked long, sweaty hours and convinced his friends to do the same. It was miserable, the heat cranking up again as if to remind everyone summer was far from over, but they did it, and on Friday afternoon Billy packed away the paint cans, brushes, and ladders for the last time. When he stood in the driveway and surveyed the house, he was proud. Sure, he'd had some help, but he'd done it. When he'd first lifted the scraper, only to be told by Mrs. Baxter he was doing it all wrong, he'd have bet every cent he had or he'd ever have that the job would never be finished, but she'd been right, he'd learned a thing or two about responsibility, and the house looked great. Happy, even.

With his long days, he'd been to the hospital just twice, and just for short visits. The jerk lawyer had been back and had dropped off another envelope, so Billy had driven over after he'd finished for the day on Wednesday. It hadn't seemed like the right time to ask Mrs. Baxter what she'd meant about helping Tracy, but Mrs. Baxter had quizzed him more about his plans after high school and it had led to him thinking more about what the future might hold.

As for the immediate future, he'd worked up the nerve to call

Julie. It may have taken him four times dialing her number and hanging up before he'd let it ring, but he'd managed on his fifth try. The conversation hadn't been too awkward, she'd assured him Terrence wasn't her boyfriend, and later that evening, he'd be taking her to a movie.

If he didn't throw up or pass out or something else equally embarrassing.

When Billy got home from the final day of painting at Mrs. Baxter's, his dad was there. Unable to remember the last time his dad had been home on a Friday evening, Billy couldn't help but worry.

"Billy," his dad said when Billy walked into the kitchen. "I made us some supper."

"You made supper? Why?"

"Because I was hungry and because we need to eat."

Billy sniffed, and unless he was imagining things, smelled something cooking on the grill. He knew his dad hadn't grilled since his mom died. Billy didn't know they even still had a grill.

"What did you make?"

"Got some steaks on the grill, couple potatoes. Made some lemonade but that came out of a packet so I don't suppose I can take much credit for that."

"Steak? Are you kidding?"

His dad looked a little hurt. "No. Thought I'd surprise you."

"You did. I mean, we haven't had steak in a long time. We haven't had much of anything in a long time."

His dad's head dropped and he turned toward the sink, his back to Billy. "I know. I'm sorry about that, I really am. I'm gonna try to do better."

He washed his hands, dried them, then fussed with the towel, pulling it through the handle on the refrigerator and making sure the ends were even. With his back still to Billy, he said, "They offered me a manager job at the elevator. Thinkin' about takin' them up on it."

That was a bigger surprise than the steak.

"They've offered before. You've turned them down. What's changed?"

Billy's dad turned. "You, I guess. You've changed, and that's made me wake up and realize I need to, too. I'm proud of you, Billy, proud of the way you've accepted what happened in court and proud of what you've done since. I drive by Mrs. Baxter's place, I see how it looks, and it looks good. Real good." His dad nodded. "I'm darn proud of you, and I figure a dad needs to give his son somethin' to be proud of."

That was more than Billy'd bargained for. "Oh," was all he could think to say.

Billy watched his dad shift his weight from foot to foot and twitch his fingers. "I know I haven't been much of a father these last years. Your mom would be so disappointed in me." One of his hands jerked to his face, and he swiped it under his nose as he sniffed. "I know that, I've always known that, but I haven't seemed able to do much about it. You're almost grown now. There's not much time left for me to show you I can be a decent father. I owe it to you, and I owe it to your mother. I'm sorry, Billy Boy."

It was a lot to process. For years, Billy had listened to Joel talk about his parents, about all the times they'd told him they were sorry for the way things had been since Joel's brother died, that they knew it wasn't fair to Joel, and that they'd try to make things better. But things never really changed.

He'd also heard John's stories about how his parents apologized for embarrassing him after they'd had too much to drink. Again and again. They, too, made lots of promises about cutting back on the booze, promises they never kept.

So Billy had plenty of reason to be skeptical. And he was, but part of him wanted to believe that in his case, things were a little different. Billy's dad had never apologized or made any promises. Whether that meant now that he had, he was serious, Billy didn't know, but he supposed his dad deserved a chance. Billy wasn't a little kid any more. If it turned out his dad didn't keep his promise, no big deal. Billy would handle it the same way he'd been handling everything else for the last five years.

"Okay. I know you can be a decent dad. You used to be." Billy paused, then added, "Is part of being a decent dad knocking off all the drinking?"

Billy feared he'd pushed too far, that his dad was going to yell, but his dad just looked sad.

"It means I'll try, but I want you to know I wasn't always drinkin' when I wasn't around. I wasn't always at the club."

It was expecting a lot if his dad expected him to believe that. "Then where were you?"

His dad looked away, but Billy swore he'd caught the hint of red tinging his dad's cheeks.

"Visitin' your mom," his dad whispered.

"Visiting...you mean at the cemetery?" Not once had his dad ever mentioned going to the cemetery. Not once had he offered to take Billy there.

"Yeah. Sometimes I need to talk to her. She always knew what to say, you know? Sometimes I need to feel like I'm close to her. Sounds stupid, I suppose." His dad stole a quick glance at Billy, but turned away again. "Sometimes I spend the night."

Billy didn't think it sounded stupid, just sad. He wished his dad had told him, had talked to him. Sure, he'd been just a kid at first, but he wasn't a kid any longer.

"It's not stupid. I know I'm not Mom, but maybe you can talk to me sometimes."

His dad blew out his breath as if he'd been holding it. "Yeah. I think I can." He patted Billy on the shoulder. "I'm gonna go check those steaks."

Billy watched his dad through the kitchen window. When he got to the grill, he bent forward and rested his hands on his thighs, letting his head drop, almost like he was ready to throw up. But he stayed that way for only a moment before straightening and looking up to the sky. His lips moved, but it was too far away for Billy to know whether his dad said anything aloud.

Deciding he should let his dad have his moment, Billy moved away from the window and set the table. He found some napkins printed with yellow and green flowers instead of the flimsy white ones he usually used, the ones that came shoved inside the to-go bags from the drive-in. The steak knives were pushed back in the drawer and looked dusty, so Billy rinsed them before setting them alongside the plates.

K-n-i-f-e, he spelled to himself, and grinned. He could picture his mom standing in the kitchen handing him silverware, one piece at a time, and reminding him on which side of the plate to put everything.

'F-o-r-k, l-e-f-t. K-n-i-f-e, s-p-o-o-n, r-i-g-h-t.'

His mom had made a song out of it, bopping around the kitchen and singing while Billy and Tracy spelled out fork, spoon, and knife. Four letters, left side because 'left' has four letters. Five letters, right side, because 'right' has five letters. Somehow, it had made sense. And somehow, thinking of it now didn't make him sad. When he reached for the salt and pepper shakers and caught a glimpse of his reflection in the toaster, he had to look twice because he hardly recognized the person smiling back at him.

By the time his dad came in with the steaks and potatoes piled on a platter, Billy had the table set and the lemonade poured.

"It looks like an actual meal's about to happen in here." His dad grinned one of his lopsided grins that had Billy realizing how much he'd missed his dad's grin.

"Looks like," Billy answered. "Smells good. Did you keep 'em rare?"

"Only way to eat a steak."

They sat down and after an awkward moment where it seemed like maybe one of them should say grace, or at least say something, they both dug in.

"Wow, Dad, this is incredible."

"It is, isn't it? Wasn't sure I remembered how to cook on the grill."

"I'm glad you did." Billy shoveled the steak in as fast as he could. "Maybe you can do it again before summer's over."

They talked, in fits and starts at first, but it became easier with each passing minute and before he realized he was doing it, Billy was telling his dad about Mrs. Baxter.

"It's called Alzheimer's disease, and it means her brain doesn't work right any longer. She forgets stuff, she gets mad or sad for no reason, and she's not going to get better."

"How do you know all this?"

"I read a little about it when I started noticing her acting strange. Then I talked to one of the nurses at the hospital and she told me more about it."

"And there's no cure? No medicine to help?"

Billy shook his head. "Sometimes she's fine, but other times she says stuff that either doesn't make sense or that seems like something she wouldn't normally say."

"Hmm. That's tough. Has she talked about the disease with you? Does she understand what's happenin'?"

"Not really. A few times she's made a comment about not remembering or her mind not working like it should, but she's never mentioned Alzheimer's or the fact that she won't get better."

"Then I'll say it again, Billy. I'm proud of you. You've worked your tail off this summer at her house and now visitin' her, well, it takes a special sort of person to do that."

Billy shrugged. "I don't know that there's anything so special about it, it just seemed like the right thing to do."

"That right there is why it's special. Not every sixteen-year-old would realize it's the right thing to do."

"And I had some help at her house. I talked Joel, John, and Steve into helping me paint."

Billy's dad set down his fork and knife and leaned back in his chair. "How in the world did you do that?"

Billy didn't answer right away. He wasn't sure what he should and shouldn't tell his dad. Letting his friends into her barn to snoop around didn't seem like a particularly admirable thing to do, and he was suddenly very much aware of the fact that he cared what his dad thought of him.

"I told them I'd ask Mrs. Baxter to sign off on their time as some of their required service hours. She agreed, and they didn't mind the painting so much when they only had to do it for short periods."

Maybe it was his tone of voice, maybe his expression gave him away, but whatever it was, his dad eyed him.

"They're still makin' you do that, huh? Workin' off some of their hours seems like a good deal, but is that all? Seems like maybe you're holdin' somethin' back."

He wanted to lie, he almost did, but if they were going to make a fresh start, it needed to be an honest one.

"I sorta let them into her barn to look around. She's got a lot of old stuff in there and the guys were curious."

His dad stayed silent, barely moving, just staring into Billy's eyes.

Billy sighed. "They think she killed those kids all those years ago. They, mostly Joel, wanted to search for evidence that she's guilty. I let them."

Billy didn't think anyone could nod so slowly, but his dad seemed to have some special skill.

"I see. So they snooped and poked around in her barn, her private property, property she's trusted you to look after, and you thought that was okay?"

His dad's voice didn't get louder, or faster, his face didn't get red, he didn't throw his hands around, he just sat and asked his question. It was far worse than if he'd done all the other things at the same time.

"I don't know. Not really. I made sure they were careful, and that they didn't break anything." His dad's eyebrows rose a fraction of an inch. "But, no. It wasn't okay. I don't think she did it," Billy added, as if it would make what he'd done somehow less wrong.

His dad nodded once, then broke eye contact and looked away. "Your mother never thought so either. She was one of the few who thought that way. Your mother was always a good judge of character, so I figure if she thought Mrs. Baxter was innocent, then she must be."

"We never talk about her, you know. Mom. We've never talked about what happened, not since the morning you told me she died."

His dad's shoulder jerked, but he kept his eyes averted and didn't speak.

"I miss her, Dad. I miss her so much."

The whoosh of breath from his dad startled Billy. So did his dad's shimmering eyes when they turned to lock on his.

"Geez, Billy. So do I. So do I. Every single day. It's been five years and I still feel like I'm nothin' without her, like I don't know how to act, don't know what to do, or why I should bother tryin'."

"Maybe we have to try because it's what she would have wanted. Trying is harder than not trying, but sometimes I think about what Mom would say if she could see us, see what's happened to us."

"Your mom would be plenty disappointed in us. Family was the most important thing to her and, well, I've let this family fall apart. That's my doin', I know that. I told myself I tried, for a while, but I didn't try hard enough. I let that grief eat away at me and I let it be an excuse for all the mistakes I've made. It's the coward's way, I know that too, but when you do somethin' for so long, it's hard to change."

"I didn't try either. Once Tracy was gone, I didn't see much reason to try."

This time, Billy's dad dropped his head so his chin nearly touched his chest. "I messed up with your sister. I messed up bad. That's the worst, I think, the thing that's just about killed me. I let your aunt take away my baby girl, and I didn't so much as put up a fight."

A tear leaked from his dad's eye and Billy felt like he was eleven years old again; helpless, scared, and wanting nothing more than to run and never look back.

But the tiniest glimmer of hope made him realize he wasn't helpless any longer.

"We could get her back, Dad. You've got a job, you said you're going to try to turn things around, we could tell Aunt Cindy that Tracy needs to come home."

Billy's heart swelled at the thought. To have Tracy home, to have things back the way they should be, would be just what they all needed. They'd be a family again. A different kind of family, for certain, but a family nonetheless.

His dad, though, was shaking his head.

"Billy, I don't think we can do that. Tracy was a little girl when she left here. It's been five years. She's not a little girl any longer, she's got a life, friends, a school, her dance classes. Everything she knows is there with your aunt and uncle. No, I don't think we'd be doin' what's best for her if we brought her back here."

Billy jumped to his feet. His temper had the heat rising up his neck and to his cheeks. "But you just said you want to try! Was that just bullshit? Again? How can you say you're going to try to make things better if you don't bring Tracy home?"

Billy shoved his chair and it toppled, crashing to the floor. His hands shook so badly, he didn't think he could right it if he wanted to.

"You can be mad, but it's not gonna change things. She's better off where she is, Billy."

"How can you say that? How in the hell can she possibly be better off there than here, with us?"

"I know you don't want to think about it, but she's not the same little girl who left here five years ago. If you care about her, and I know you do, you'll know it's best for her to be where she is. A girl needs a mother, and if she doesn't have one of those, then she needs another woman who cares about her, who loves her. Aunt Cindy does. She treats her like she's her own."

"So then you don't care about your own daughter? You don't love your own daughter?"

For the first time, Billy saw anger flare in his dad's eyes. In a strange way, Billy was glad of it, and it gave him hope. If his dad didn't care, the anger wouldn't be there.

"That's not fair, and I'd like to think the two of us can fight fair. Tracy needs things I can't give her. I don't have to like it, but what I have to do is do what's best for her. I owe her that."

"But—"

"Hold on. I promise you this. We will visit her. As often as we can. And we'll see that she comes here more often. We've gone too long between visits, and that's not right. Like I said before, I will try."

Billy leaned against the counter and without realizing it, crossed one foot over the other, mirroring his dad's stance and body language.

Calmed enough to think, Billy didn't like his conclusion, but there was still a glimmer of hope. As much as he hated to admit it, his dad was right about Tracy. Uprooting her just like that would hurt her more than help her. But, if his dad meant what he said and they all spent more time together, Tracy coming home for visits, there was the chance that Tracy would decide on her own that she wanted to come home for good. Billy would hold on to that hope.

"Yeah. Okay. I guess you're right about her being settled and everything. It wouldn't be fair to pull her away from the life she has now."

His dad looked surprised, but relieved. "Yeah. Come on and finish your supper."

Apparently his dad was willing to let the argument, or more accurately Billy's outburst, go. Seemed to Billy like maybe a dad should have something to say about his kid yelling and swearing at him. One step at a time, Billy told himself. With his dad, with Tracy, with everything. He picked up his chair and sat down.

They ate in silence for a few minutes. When his dad spoke, it was as if nothing had happened.

"I was thinkin' maybe we could do somethin' this weekend if you've got time. I think it's for the best that I stay busy. Maybe we take a look at that tractor that hasn't run for a few years. Don't know that we need it, but if we get it runnin' we could see about sellin' it."

"Yeah, sure, we could do that, but not tonight. Got a date."

He hadn't planned on telling his dad, but it sort of slipped out.

His dad set down his silverware again. "Whoa ho. A date? Is that so?"

One side of Billy's mouth turned up in a grin, a lopsided grin uncannily like his dad's.

"Anyone I know?"

"Probably not. Her name's Julie."

Some of the lightheartedness slipped from his dad's face. "I reckon I should know the answer, but is this your first date with Julie? Your first date with any girl?"

Yeah, his dad probably should know the answer. To be fair though, for as often as his dad hadn't asked, Billy hadn't offered.

"Yep. First with Julie, first with anyone."

The smile returned. "Nervous?"

"A little."

"I remember my first date with your mother. I was so nervous, I nearly made myself sick. Your grandfather didn't much help matters. The look he gave me when he opened the door just about had me runnin' for the hills. But your mother..." His dad's face softened and his eyes got a faraway look to them. "Well, she was the prettiest thing I'd ever laid eyes on. By the time we'd walked from her house to school for the dance, I knew I was gonna marry her."

His dad was quiet, lost in his memories, but then he turned and faced Billy, waving a finger in his direction.

"Don't you go gettin' any ideas 'bout gettin' married. You've got a lot of livin' to do before that happens."

Billy gave his dad an embarrassed sort of half-grin. "Don't worry, Dad. I won't be getting married anytime soon." But even as he said the words, his mind drifted to thoughts of Julie in a white dress.

22

It wasn't so bad, going to Mrs. Baxter's house. The painting was done, and that was part of it, but he still had the mowing, the gardening, and the cleaning—because he'd started helping with that when Mrs. Baxter came home from the hospital—and still, it wasn't so bad.

They were sitting on the porch, out of the relentless sun, chatting and sipping the lemonade she always seemed to have cold and ready to serve, and stretching out Billy's lunch break longer and longer.

"That nurse will be here soon," Mrs. Baxter said. "She's starting to get on my nerves."

"She's not that bad. It's better than being in the hospital."

"That part's true, the hospital stay was horrible, but this Corrine is horrible in her own way. Poking at me, telling me to do this and do that, asking me the same ridiculous questions a half dozen times. The pneumonia is gone. I don't know why she has to keep coming here."

Whenever she talked about her time in the hospital, Mrs. Baxter talked about pneumonia. She never mentioned her other diagnosis, so Billy wasn't sure she understood it. Or if maybe she was ignoring it.

She hadn't had one of her episodes, at least not a bad one, in the two weeks she'd been home from the hospital. At least not that he'd witnessed. Billy wasn't sure, but his best guess was that the familiarity of her home combined with the fact that she'd hated being in the hospital meant she was more at ease, more relaxed, and less prone to the stress and upset that sometimes seemed to trigger the episodes. That meant they'd spent a great deal of time talking about a wide range of topics from school which would be starting soon, to the year's crop and the coming fall planting, to Billy's date with Julie, to the continuing tornado cleanup. Nothing except her disease seemed off limits.

And the piece of paper with the names.

Every day, Billy told himself he was going to work it into the conversation and every day he went home without having done so. There was never a good opening, never a way of easing into it that wouldn't upset her and bring on an episode. Because once he lost her, once her mind started to wander and she stopped making sense, he was afraid of what he'd hear.

"Corrine's not that bad. A little bossy, but not mean."

"No, she's not mean, and I've seen enough mean in my life to recognize it."

Hoping she wasn't referring to the kids, himself included, who'd enjoyed nothing more than snooping around her property and spreading rumors, Billy asked, "Who was mean to you?"

She was quiet, looking out over her bare fields, with a sad smile on her face.

"How much have I told you about Tommy?"

Worry had him on high alert. She had only mentioned Tommy when she was either headed for, or in the middle of, one of her scary episodes.

"Your son?"

"Yes. My son. I've been thinking about him a lot lately. You know, I always thought I'd have a houseful of children, but that wasn't to be. Tommy, though, was such a joy, always smiling, always ready with a hug, always trying to please. I knew early on something wasn't quite right, that Tommy had problems. The first time I saw him, right after he was born, there was something about his eyes, about the shape of his face. He looked…different. As the weeks and months passed, I knew for certain. I read what books I could find. Mongoloid, they used to call children like him. Today, they like to use the term Down Syndrome, but the name doesn't matter as much as what it means for a family."

Billy let her talk. She seemed to need to. He thought he knew what she meant. He remembered a girl, years ago, who went to their church. Billy's mom had used those terms.

"It will tear a family apart, if you let it. I wasn't going to let it. Tommy was perfect the way he was, but his father saw things differently."

She paused and exhaled a long shaky breath.

"Jasper wouldn't admit there was anything wrong with Tommy. He insisted there was no reason to treat Tommy differently than he'd treat any child, but Tommy needed patience, not a belt or the back of a hand. When he couldn't get his words out fast enough, when he couldn't remember which feed was for the chickens and which for the goats, when he couldn't get to the toilet in time, he got a slap to the head or a belt to the backside. Back then, people said children needed discipline, but Tommy needed understanding. He never got that from his father.

"I don't think Tommy ever understood why he got in trouble as often as he did. I think to him, that's just how life was. I tried to give him a good life, I tried to protect him, but ultimately I failed him. And so did the rest of this town. No one said anything, not a single word, when Tommy showed up at church with a black eye and bruises. And no one batted an eye when Jasper swatted him right during the service."

Billy's skin prickled. Timmy Wagner. The first kid who disappeared and the kid who went to the same church as Mrs. Baxter. There'd been that connection. Joel had told them there'd been times Mrs. Baxter hadn't stayed quiet when she saw the signs of abuse on Timmy. Her speaking up and confronting Timmy's father made a lot more sense.

Mrs. Baxter seemed to have forgotten Billy was there. She stared, unblinking, while she rocked in slow rhythm with her words.

"One egg." The chair went back and forth. "When he fell off the tractor, when he hit his head so hard he never woke up, it was because he was already dizzy, not quite stable, after the beating his father had given him earlier that morning. One egg." The chair rocked. "Tommy dropped one egg. He was trying to help, trying to show his dad that he could collect the eggs all by himself, but he dropped one. Just one. I lost my baby because of one egg."

Billy didn't know when it had started. As uncomfortable as her words made him, he'd been looking everywhere but at Mrs. Baxter, but when she stopped talking and when he turned toward her, her face was wet with tears. The urge to run was strong. Billy fought it. He told himself his days of running from everything difficult had to be over.

"I'm sorry," he whispered. "How old was he?"

"Seven. I had only seven years with my Tommy. Jasper called it an accident, Tommy falling off the tractor, but it was no accident. It was Jasper's fault Tommy fell. Jasper killed my baby."

Billy didn't know what to say. He waited, expecting Mrs. Baxter to burst into a rage or to slip into sorrow, but neither happened.

"But he got his due, Jasper did."

She used the handkerchief she always carried in her apron pocket to dry her face. She continued staring, as if into the past, but what she saw must have changed because her face did. Her jaw set in a hard line and her eyes narrowed.

"His due?"

She still didn't acknowledge him, just stared.

"That same tractor, another accident...this time, Jasper was dead. And this time, I was at least somewhat responsible."

Billy stiffened. Reflexes sent him jerking back in his chair, away from Mrs. Baxter. She killed him? She must have. And if she killed him…

"Responsible?" The word wasn't much more than a squeak.

"I was right there at that window." She tipped her head toward the kitchen window, but she kept her unblinking gaze straight ahead. "He drove too close to the ditch, he'd done it before and I'd warned him, but that day, the tractor rolled. It was a horrible sight, his leg pinned underneath that giant tractor tire. I was close enough that I could see the blood." Billy spotted the tremor in Mrs. Baxter's hands, the trembling in her jaw. "So much blood. I couldn't move, I couldn't scream, I couldn't do anything but stand and watch. Jasper yelled, I'm almost certain he did. Whether it was to call for help or simply to curse his fate, I don't know, but still, I stood, frozen.

"And I waited. Instead of going for help, instead of trying to free him or at least being there at his side, I waited, because all I could see at that point was my Tommy lying alongside that tractor, his breathing so shallow, his eyes closed as if he were asleep, but knowing he wasn't asleep. Knowing the angels were coming to get my baby."

She turned now to face Billy whose face had gone white and whose fingers clutched the chair so tightly they too were white.

"I didn't move until there was no chance Jasper was still alive. You must think I'm awful. I suppose I am. He wouldn't have survived, regardless of what I might have done, that was obvious from the amount of blood, but I suppose that doesn't much matter to someone hearing the gruesome details. I'm sorry, Billy. I'm sorry if that changes your opinion of me. Or maybe it just solidifies your opinion."

Did it? Did it change his opinion? Maybe, but not in the way she probably thought it did. If anything, Billy had a little more respect for her and figured he better understood her. She'd been through unbearable tragedy and heartache, and she hadn't let it break her. While he didn't know what it was like to lose a kid, he knew what it was like to lose a mom when you were just a kid. It was probably kind of the same. It was hard not to let it break you.

"I've never told anyone that. I guess when a person's facing the end, she needs to get a few things off her chest. I'm sorry you had to be the one to hear it, but if these last few weeks have taught me anything, it's that life's too short to wait for the perfect time, the perfect opportunity. You grab what you can, while you can."

Whether it was a reference to her diagnosis or just to the fact that she was getting old, Billy wasn't sure. He had so many questions, he didn't know where to start. Questions about her husband, her son, what she knew about her disease, how she felt about what her future held. And about Timmy Wagner. The similarities were impossible to ignore.

"That's okay. You telling me stuff, I mean. My dad told me when he was a kid my grandpa rolled his tractor. Grandpa only just got out of the way or he would have been pinned underneath it. Farm accidents happen all the time, even when a person's careful."

She nodded, but said nothing.

"I'm sure your son was happy, even if his dad was a jerk sometimes. He had you. He had his mom."

"Oh, Billy, I'm sorry. I know it's been hard with your father, without your mother. I didn't mean to upset you."

"I'm not upset. My dad's been better. I told you he's working and he's been around more. He's making an effort. It'll be okay."

"I hope it's more than okay. I hope it's good. I hope that he turns things around and starts to make up for all the years when things were far from good."

Billy shrugged. "One day at a time."

The sound of car tires crunching over gravel drifted to the porch. Mrs. Baxter's head whipped toward the driveway and in an instant, her demeanor changed. She sat up straight in the chair and fisted her hands in her lap. Her lips moved, but Billy couldn't hear what she said. She turned back with frantic, pleading eyes.

"I thought I'd get you out of there. I thought I'd save you both from what your father was becoming. I never meant to split up the two of you. I couldn't help Tommy and I couldn't help you. I'm sorry. I tried. Please believe me."

Her voice broke and she choked on a sob.

"Hello Mrs. Baxter, Billy. How's everyone today? It's another hot one."

Corrine bounded up the porch steps in a flurry of white. She moved so fast, and seemed to never stop moving, she reminded Billy of a swirling snowstorm.

"Um..." Billy wasn't sure what to say. Mrs. Baxter looked ready to break, but since Corrine was fussing with her bags and the big bouquet of flowers she carried, she hadn't yet noticed.

"I cut these from my garden this morning. I know you have a garden full, but I hadn't spotted any dahlias. They're just so pretty this year, I had to share. I'll pop them inside before we get started."

When Corrine rushed inside the house, Billy jumped at his chance.

"What do you mean, split us up? Me and Tracy? What did you do?"

"You and Tracy?"

She was drifting in and out, Billy could tell. He'd learned to recognize the signs. Her eyes darted from side to side, her hands twisted and untwisted, and her breathing became fast and shaky.

"You said you didn't mean to split us up and that you wanted to help me."

"I did want to help you. I still do. I will. It's all arranged."

"But what did you do after my mom died? How did you try to help?"

"It was like those other kids. It was a bad home. Kids don't deserve to be mistreated by a parent. Parents are supposed to love and protect, not frighten and endanger. Just like the others. You were just like the others, Billy, but you were too old."

"Those flowers look positively lovely on your kitchen table, Mrs. Baxter."

Billy wanted to strangle Corrine. He'd never get a straight answer out of Mrs. Baxter now.

"Is everything okay?" Corrine looked from Mrs. Baxter to Billy, then turned so her back was to Mrs. Baxter. She kept her voice low. "Is she having a rough day?"

Billy used both hands to rub viciously up and down on his face. The whole thing was more than he could take.

"Just started. She's been fine until now."

Corrine nodded. She turned and held out a hand to Mrs. Baxter.

"Should we head inside? You said you'd show me your recipe for apple pie."

"My mother's recipe." Mrs. Baxter smiled. "Best apple pie you've ever tasted."

"I'm sure you're right. Mine always seems to be a runny mess."

Mrs. Baxter nodded. "You're using the wrong apples and you're cutting the pieces too small, I'll bet. I'll set you straight." She took Corrine's hand and they disappeared into the house.

Billy flopped back in his chair and fought not to scream.

Since he'd mowed earlier in the week and since the garden was winding down for the season, there wasn't much work to do outside. Corrine always kept Mrs. Baxter in the living room or the kitchen and since he'd told Mrs. Baxter he'd vacuum the upstairs, he decided he might as well get that done even though he preferred to be outside when the nurse paid her visits.

As frustrated and angry as he was that it seemed he'd never get a straight answer from Mrs. Baxter about anything, he still found himself chuckling when he pulled the vacuum from the broom closet and hauled it upstairs. If, when Judge O'Malley had handed down Billy's sentence he'd mentioned house cleaning was part of the deal, Billy figured he would have asked for jail time instead. Now, vacuuming, dusting, and scrubbing floors didn't seem like such a big deal. In fact, he was already worrying about who was going to do that cleaning, and all the other things, once school started. Because in just a few days, Billy would have his sentence fulfilled.

Three months ago, the countdown would have been cause for celebration. It still was, but not the ticker tape parade-worthy event he'd expected. Mixed in with the excitement was nervousness about leaving Mrs. Baxter alone and even a little sadness thinking about an end to their daily visits. Weird. He'd never admit that to his friends, of course, he could already hear their merciless heckling, but he knew it was true.

Billy vacuumed, dusted, and cleaned up the bathroom. That was the worst, cleaning someone else's bathroom, but like most of Mrs. Baxter's house, even after a week, it looked barely used. After a week at his house, the sink was full of toothpaste globs and whiskers, the bathtub had a ring around it, and the mirror was so full of splatters, he could barely see his reflection.

Once the cleaning was done, Billy reluctantly went back downstairs. He heard Mrs. Baxter and Corrine in the living room and based on Mrs. Baxter's tone of voice, Billy guessed Corrine had been asking her some of those same questions Mrs. Baxter claimed she asked over and over again.

"The same as last time. April eighth. And my middle name is still Elizabeth, it's still nineteen hundred and seventy-two, and I still live in Munroe, Kansas. And you're still bugging me."

Billy grinned. He kind of liked it when Mrs. Baxter got feisty with the nurse. It helped him believe that she wasn't as bad off as she sometimes seemed.

Billy stayed in the kitchen, wiping the already spotless counters and table, then getting himself a glass of water and sitting at the table to wait until Corrine finished. In addition to the questions Mrs. Baxter hated was a whole slew of tests that included taking her temperature and blood pressure and listening to her heart and lungs. A couple of times Corrine had taken a blood sample. Billy wanted to be sure he was far away in case that was on the schedule for the day.

When he heard Corrine say her goodbyes, he ventured into the living room. The week before, Corrine had called him aside before she'd left and asked him to be especially mindful of any coughing or labored breathing on Mrs. Baxter's part since the doctor was still concerned about the pneumonia returning. Corrine wanted another set of eyes watching for any signs it may be happening.

This time, she edged closer and asked Billy if he'd noticed anything but didn't give him any additional instructions. Once she was out the door, Mrs. Baxter leaned back in her chair and closed her eyes.

"She can be exhausting, that one."

"She's just doing her job."

"I suppose. She appears to be a decent cook. That's something. I gave her my recipe for apple pie and in return she put together a chicken casserole and left it in the refrigerator. All I have to do is put it in the oven when I get hungry. I'll have leftovers to last me the rest of the week."

"Just before you went inside with Corrine to give her that recipe, you started to tell me something about Tracy. About me and Tracy. About trying to help. Was it something you'd promised my mom?"

Mrs. Baxter's forehead creased, and she tipped her head as she studied him. It seemed to Billy she was trying to decide whether she wanted to answer. When she did, she seemed remarkably clear-headed.

"Billy, I'm afraid you're not going to like what you hear, but I think it's only fair I tell you. As I said earlier when I told you about Tommy and Jasper, I think it's time."

Billy didn't like the ominous tone to her words and if it was any indication, he figured he really wouldn't like what came next. He braced himself.

"It wasn't something I specifically promised your mother. I did promise her I'd do what I could to look after you and your sister. How I went about that was all my doing. You have to understand I did what I thought would be best, but things didn't work out as I hoped." She looked him straight in the eye. "I was the one who contacted your Aunt Cindy and told her what life was like with your father."

Billy felt like he was cemented to his chair. He couldn't have moved at that point to save his life. His mouth also appeared to be cemented shut as he wasn't able to utter a sound. All he could do was sit, and stare, and wait.

"I saw what was happening at your house. I saw your father's truck outside the club at dinnertime when he should have been home getting dinner on the table for you and your sister. I saw him hanging around town, or going into the club, in the middle of the day which told me he wasn't working. I saw you hustling your sister onto the school bus, no sign of your father anywhere. That was no life for an eleven-year-old boy who needed someone to be taking care of him instead of that boy trying to take care of himself and his six-year-old sister. I called your aunt, I told her what was going on, and I pleaded with her to take you away from there. Both of you. Your aunt, she came right away. I took that as a good sign, but then, she took your sister. Only your sister. She split up the two of you, and I've never forgiven myself for that. I'm sorry, Billy, I'm so very sorry."

Billy was surprised when he didn't yell, didn't pick up the pink candy dish from the table next to him and hurl it across the room, didn't storm out, slam the door, and vow to never lay eyes on Mrs. Baxter again. He was more surprised that all he wanted to do was close his eyes and try to make sense out of something that should have sent him into a rage, but instead just made him tired. Exhausted, actually. Mentally exhausted, sure, because it was a lot to take in, but his whole body suddenly felt tired, as though he'd put in his hardest day of the summer.

Out of all the scenarios he'd imagined, this wasn't one of them. Mrs. Baxter was responsible for Tracy leaving home. Had she not contacted Aunt Cindy, it was very likely his aunt would have never had an inkling of what was going on in their home. And what wasn't going on.

Billy had been just a kid back then, but he knew his dad wasn't doing the kinds of things a dad was supposed to do, let alone the things a mom would do and that were now also his job. Billy remembered trying to help Tracy get dressed in the morning, trying to help her brush her curly hair, and even trying to get those stretchy, rubber band things with the balls on the end to hold her pigtails in place without them snapping against his fingers and leading him to utter some of his first swear words. Billy had been more of a dad to Tracy then their dad had been.

"I guess you did what you thought was best. Anyway, it's more my dad's fault for letting Tracy go with Aunt Cindy. And Aunt Cindy's fault for taking only Tracy."

With that, he leaned back in the chair and let his eyes close. Did he like what he'd heard? No. Was he angry? Not really. It didn't matter any longer. He couldn't change the past, so there wasn't much point in being angry about it. He'd focus on the future, because in that, he still had some say.

"Billy Tupper, you've gone and surprised me again."

She'd been quiet so long, and he'd had his eyes closed for so long, he'd almost forgotten where he was and that she was sitting across from him. Billy opened one eye and looked at her.

"Three months ago, you would have reacted much differently. I doubt my candy dish would still be in one piece."

Billy, both eyes closed again, grinned at that. "It almost wasn't."

"You've changed, you've grown up, and I'm confident you have a bright future in front of you. I'm proud of you, Billy. Why, you didn't even swear."

Billy opened his eyes and pushed himself upright.

"Trying not to do so much of that anymore." He gave her a crooked grin. "Don't always succeed."

"Keep on trying." She paused a beat, then asked, "You're not angry with me?"

"Nah. No point. It was five years ago, and you did what you thought was best. I get it that you were trying to look out for us. You did that for my mom. Even though it didn't turn out the way you wanted, it turned out good for Tracy. That's what's most important."

"I repeat, I'm very proud of you."

Billy glanced at the clock ticking loudly on the mantle. It was well past his quitting time.

"I suppose I should head home," Billy said, pushing to his feet.

"You're right. It's late."

"There's nothing else you need before I go?"

"There's one thing, but it can wait until tomorrow."

"No, that's fine. What is it?"

"There's a box up in the attic with a bunch of cookbooks and handwritten recipes. I was telling Corrine about how I used to make tomato aspic, but I couldn't find the recipe in the kitchen. It's been so long since I've made it, I figure it must be packed away. If you don't mind getting the box, I can dig through it tonight and see if I can find it."

It must be the box he'd tipped over. The one with the list of names. He had his opening.

"I'll go get it."

Before she could say any more, he turned and hurried from the room. Halfway up the stairs, he realized he should have asked which box because how would he know which one out of the dozens was the box with her cookbooks? He decided he'd just waste a few minutes up there as if he were looking around before coming back downstairs.

Five minutes later, he was back in the living room, the box in his arms.

"When I was up there working on the shutters, I tripped over a box with a bunch of books so I looked for it. I think this is the one. It has some cookbooks in it."

"Let's take a look."

Billy opened the flaps and pulled out a couple of books, setting them on the coffee table. Mrs. Baxter nodded.

"Yes, I think this is right. There should be note cards and papers tucked inside with recipes I've scribbled over the years. I'll sort through and see what's in there. Maybe I'll find something interesting."

Billy knew exactly which book had held the paper with the names. It was a Betty Crocker cookbook, the same one his mom had used and that was probably still somewhere in their house. He picked it up and held it out toward Mrs. Baxter.

"Do you think I could take this one home with me? My mom used to have one just like it, and I remember she always used it when she made gingerbread cookies. I'd like to try to make them. They were always my favorite."

"I'd be happy to make you some gingerbread cookies. I'll have them ready for you tomorrow."

"No, I mean thanks, but I think I'd like to try. I remember how my mom used to let us help her decorate the cookies. I'd like to know how to make them."

It was true, even though he had an ulterior motive. Mrs. Baxter smiled kindly at him.

"Of course, you can take it. Keep it as long as you'd like."

Billy pulled out the loose papers that were stuck inside the book and handed them to Mrs. Baxter.

"Thank you. I'll see you tomorrow."

Later that evening, Billy sat on his bed, the cookbook in one hand and the paper with the names in the other. He folded the paper into a small square and tucked it deep inside the book. Then he picked up his notebook and reread a summer's worth of thoughts.

23

Billy rode his bike and hummed to himself.

I know an old lady who swallowed a fly
I don't know why she swallowed a fly
I guess she'll die.

He was down to two days. It was strange that as he pedaled, he was more nervous than he'd been on his very first day. Then, he'd been more pissed off than anything, determined he'd either avoid Mrs. Baxter or make her as miserable as he knew he'd be. Now, it was just plain nerves.

Working on little sleep made matters worse. He had stayed up late into the night reading and writing in his notebook and trying to decide what he'd do if he learned what he was afraid he might learn about Mrs. Baxter. In an attempt to wake himself up, Billy had started his morning with a cup of the coffee his dad swore by. A caffeinated, jittery stomach didn't help those nerves.

I know an old lady who swallowed a fly
I wish she hadn't swallowed that fly
I don't want her to die.

Mrs. Baxter seemed in good spirits when she answered Billy's knock. She was dressed nicely, which wasn't always the case, and her hair was smoothed into her favored bun instead of being the mess of flyaway strands it was some days.

Billy smelled gingerbread as soon as he walked inside.

"I know you said you wanted to try the recipe yourself, but you got me thinking about gingerbread cookies, and I couldn't resist. Did you bake some too?"

"No, I didn't get around to it. Maybe over the weekend. I found the recipe, though."

"Good, but today, you can try some of mine. I don't expect them to be as good as your mother's, but I do hope you enjoy them."

"Um, okay, thanks."

Mrs. Baxter headed for the kitchen and Billy followed.

"Only two more days. It hardly seems possible. The summer went by so quickly. Oh, I suppose it doesn't seem that way to you, what with working here, but it does to me. Maybe it was being away in the hospital that made it seem so short, or maybe it's just that I'm an old lady and time seems to move so much faster than it did years ago. Did I ever tell you—"

"Mrs. Baxter? Can I ask you a question?" Now or never, he told himself.

"Of course."

Billy pulled the sheet of paper from his pocket and fumbled with it, finally opening it and using his palm to flatten it on the kitchen table.

"I found this inside the cookbook I took home."

"Is it another recipe? Something that sounds good?"

"No. It's a...it's a list. A list of names."

"A list of names? Whose names? I'm afraid that's likely been in there for years and there's a good chance I don't remember much about what I wrote. There was a time when I kept track of people I knew from—"

"It's four names. The names of those four kids who disappeared from Munroe a long time ago."

The room was silent. The kind of silent that seems really loud. Billy waited and watched as a dozen emotions came and went on Mrs. Baxter's face.

"Did you know them? Know the families?"

Billy knew he wasn't playing fair. After the research at the library and all the information Joel had added, Billy knew far more than he was letting on. It felt like setting her up and he felt kind of guilty.

She didn't answer right away, instead walked to the stove and turned on the flame under her tea kettle. She fussed with her jar of tea bags, took two cups from the cupboard, set them on the table, and finally sat down.

"Not well. Some of them, not at all."

"But you had all their names written down."

"I thought yesterday was the day for confessions. I should have known we weren't done. What happened with Jasper, my part in Tracy going to live with your aunt, I'm afraid those will pale in comparison."

The tea kettle whistled, sending screeching shock waves through the room and through Billy. While Mrs. Baxter got up to fetch the kettle, her words replayed over and over in his head, faster and faster as if he'd played one of his records at the wrong speed on his record player.

'Pale in comparison' had to mean something bad was coming. Something really bad. He watched her shuffle to the stove, her steps slower than they'd been since he'd seen her in the hospital.

She sat and poured two cups of tea, pushing one toward Billy. Her face was pale, paler than usual, and her hands shook, sending the tea pot clattering on the rooster-shaped trivet.

"It seemed like getting things off my chest was a good idea, but now I'm not so sure."

For the first time in a long time, Billy's gut told him Mrs. Baxter killed the kids. He was sitting across the table from a murderer. His stomach churned and burned and he regretted choosing that day to decide he should become a coffee drinker.

"If you don't want to talk about it, that's okay."

Her short laugh sounded sad, not really like a laugh at all.

"At this point, I don't think not talking about it is an option. I have to say, though, I fully expected to die without ever having talked about it." Her eyes travelled to the yellowed sheet of paper. "May I see that?"

Billy slid it across the table.

"Funny, I don't remember writing the names down. I wonder why I did it?" She shrugged with one shoulder. "Doesn't matter now, I suppose."

Billy felt sick to his stomach. He had to know.

"Did you kill those kids?"

Five measly words, but they echoed in the kitchen like a cannon blast.

"Are you hoping to hear that I did? It's what everyone in town has believed for over thirty years."

Billy put his hands in his lap and squeezed them together until his knuckles cracked.

"Did you?"

"No, I did not."

Billy felt his body go lax, almost melt into the chair, as a sense of utter relief washed over him.

"But I'm not innocent."

"What does that mean? You know who did it?"

"No one killed those children. Someone took them. Me. I took them in order to help them. Think what you will, but I don't regret my actions."

Billy sat up straight in his chair and laid his arms on the table, palms up, as if pleading.

"What do you mean, you took them? What did you do with them? And how can you think that was okay?"

"I took them because they were being mistreated. Very, very badly mistreated. I watched that sort of abuse cost my Tommy his life. I wasn't going to stand by and watch it take more lives, not when I could do something about it."

Mrs. Baxter sat up straighter and taller in her chair, as if ready for a fight. Her hands were steady now, her eyes clear and focused, and some of the years seemed to slip away from her wrinkled face. Before Billy could ask another question, she began reciting, in a clear, even voice, a long list of details, some of which Billy knew, many he didn't.

"Timmy Wagner. February eighteenth, 1936. I knew of Timmy and his family from church. I saw them there most Sundays. Timmy was a sweet little boy. He was about three when I first spotted the bruises. Ugly, purple bruises on his arms, his legs, even his face. He wasn't much older when he had such a sprained and swollen knee he could barely limp into church. I watched his father swat him during the service, again outside after the service, and I saw Timmy cower, scared to death of his father. When I heard Timmy's father shout at him, all I could hear was 'Tommy' in place of 'Timmy'. It could have been Jasper shouting at Tommy."

She drew in a shaky breath. "Timmy's mother was no help. She cowered nearly as often as her son, and though she did her best to hide them, she had bruises of her own. She was terrified of her husband, so was no help to her son. I tried speaking to her first, but she wouldn't make eye contact, let alone listen to reason. Later, I tried talking to Timmy's father, but he scoffed and told me to mind my own business.

"I knew where they lived, about six miles outside town, and I would drive by occasionally. I don't know what I expected to find, or to do, but the urge to be closer, to try to help, was too strong to ignore. One day I spotted Timmy wandering on the road, alone, limping, dirty, and crying. I stopped, I tried talking to him, but he was too afraid to answer. In the end, I put him in the car and drove home.

"My intention was to tend to him, clean him up, determine if he needed to see a doctor, then go to the police instead of returning that poor boy home for more of the same. Then something came over me. I saw his future play out like Tommy's short life and I knew I could never let Timmy's father get his hands on that boy again. I put Timmy back in the car and started to drive. I ended up in Kansas City at my sister's house.

Originally, I thought Betty would take in the boy and raise him since she and her husband had never had children of their own. Betty, though, talked some sense into me and said if the police should ever start looking, it would be simple for them to track Timmy to her. She was right, but I couldn't take Timmy back. In the end, Betty kept him and found him a home. Timmy was the first of four."

Billy was shocked into silence. Questions tumbled around in his head, but he couldn't get them out.

"Thaddeus Miller. April twenty-seventh, 1937. Tad was just a baby, hardly more than four. I knew the family, they had several children, all of whom showed up at school, however sporadically. I first laid eyes on Tad when I went to the family home to deliver some paperwork citing truancy violations for most of the children after repeated attempts to mail the paperwork proved to be a waste of a stamp. The house was in disarray, not uncommon during the depression, but this was beyond what was acceptable. Filth, squalor…those children were being raised in a dangerous environment. The littlest, Tad, hovered in a corner during my brief visit. I left unsure if he could speak, let alone walk, he was so thin and gaunt looking.

"I went back a couple more times, trying to get the parents to take responsibility for their children, without success. At some point the police made a stop, and the mother claimed the children were too ill to attend school. Again, I was asked to visit the home, this time with books and homework assignments to try to keep the children on track. The mother didn't let me inside this time, she simply grabbed the books from me and closed the door in my face. On my way back to town I came across Tad over a half mile away from his home. It was a bitterly cold spring morning. He was shoeless and barely clothed. His ribs showed through the tear in his threadbare shirt. It was a pitiful sight, I tell you.

"I swear it was never my plan, but I grabbed that little boy, put him in the car, and drove to my sister's house. It took over twenty-four hours until the mother reported the boy missing. That says a lot, I think."

"So—" Billy coughed, his voice hoarse from sitting and listening, his attention so riveted on Mrs. Baxter's story. "So your sister found Tad a home too? How?"

"Times were different. It's hard, impossible maybe, for someone who didn't live through the depression to understand what it was like. Men lost their jobs, families lost their homes, people were desperate. It wasn't uncommon for parents to send their children to live with relatives who could afford to care for them. In a city the size of Kansas City, most people knew at least one family in such a situation. Betty and her husband were well-off, they knew others who were well-off, and who wanted children. She placed both the boys with people she felt would care for them and love them. I never asked for the details, I didn't want to know, but I'm confident Betty did right by those children."

"No one asked questions when a kid just showed up one day?"

She shook her head. "Like I said, most people were focused on surviving and didn't have time to worry about what might be going on with their neighbors. Law enforcement, the courts, same thing. A child who was being fed, clothed, and cared for wasn't cause for concern when there were countless others who weren't."

Billy let the information churn in his mind. It seemed like she'd done something wrong, but he couldn't deny that at the same time, she'd probably done something right.

"And the kids? Weren't you afraid they'd ask for their parents or say something to give away the fact that they were…were kidnapped?"

Mrs. Baxter smiled that sad smile Billy had seen earlier. "Jane Nichols. June second, 1939. Jane was older, six-years-old, already in school, and I did worry about her more than the others. She was such a sad little girl. Mistreated by her mother. That's

301

different than most abuse cases. Jane's mother felt it was her duty to give her husband sons so, I learned, from the time Jane was born, her mother more or less ignored her. The poor girl came to school without breakfast, and more often than not she was in dire need of a bath. She was supposed to walk home with the neighbor kids, but Jane would hide until the kids eventually left without her. She didn't want to go home.

"As much as I wanted to help, I feared Jane was too old. Then one day, the first day of summer vacation, Jane showed up at school, same as if it were a school day. I explained to her that there was no school, that there wouldn't be for three months, and sent her back home, but it continued. My job went through the first week of vacation, so every morning I had to send that little girl back home to a mother who didn't care enough to look for her six-year-old who left the house every morning. By Friday, it was clear the child was afraid of her mother and wanted no part of going back home, so I took a chance. I took her home with me, fed her and cleaned her up, then took her to my sister. Same as the others."

"And it worked? Jane never said anything? No one knew?"

"I have to assume it worked. I told you, I never asked where any of the children were so in case the day ever came, I wouldn't have any information to give the police. For as badly as I wanted to know, it was better I didn't.

"Then there was Josiah Zimmerman. August eighth, 1940. Josiah was an only child, and after his mother died, he lived alone with his father. His father did okay for a while, but then he started drinking. Kansas hadn't yet repealed prohibition, but it was no secret there were farmers with stills and it wasn't hard to get booze if you wanted it. Josiah, like the others, was often left alone. He was only four. There were rumors he was alone overnight at times. Josiah's father lost his job, what money he had he was squandering on illegal booze, and Josiah was paying the price. August eighth, 1940, was exactly one year after his mother died, and was an especially bad day for his father. I saw the man stumbling down Main Street at ten o'clock in the morning when I went to pick up a few groceries. A half an hour later, on my way out of town, I saw his father being arrested. There was no sign of the child in town, there was no sign of him when I rode my bike past their house. That evening, I biked into town again and on my way, found the child sitting outside his house crying. I can't explain why the police didn't find him or why no one else did, except to say I was meant to be the one to find him. As with the others, I got him to my sister and I have to believe he's had a far better life than he would have if I hadn't acted."

That was four. Four kids, four stories, and the last one eerily familiar. Mrs. Baxter's words from the day before sounded in his head. 'Like those other kids...a bad home, you were just like the others, Billy, but you were too old.'

"Is that why you wanted to get me and Tracy away from my dad? Why you tried to help us?"

"I told myself after Josiah that I couldn't risk any more children. I spotted one or two over the years, but..." She shrugged. "Then your mother passed away, I saw what was happening with your father, and I couldn't sit by and do nothing. You were too old, it wouldn't be the same as with the others, but I knew I had to get you away from your father. I failed. Like I said, things didn't go the way I'd planned."

To give himself something to do, Billy reached for the teacup and took a sip. Cold. And disgusting. He didn't spit it out, but wanted to. He nudged the cup away and stood to pace around the kitchen.

What was he supposed to do with the information? A decades-old mystery solved. He didn't have to think hard to know he wasn't going to do anything with it. What would be the point? Put an old lady in jail, start an all-out search to find the kids who were no longer kids and shatter the lives they'd built for themselves? Much like he realized Tracy was better off where she was, he knew those four people were better off with whatever memories they had of what had hopefully been happy childhoods. As young as some of them had been, it was likely they knew only the family that raised them. It would do more harm than good to dredge up an old story, no matter what sort of glory might come from being the one to finally have the answers.

He figured he must have been pacing for a while because Mrs. Baxter sounded tense when she interrupted his thoughts with a single word.

"So?"

"So, that's quite a story. I'm glad the kids weren't killed like everyone always said. I never considered they were taken and given something better than what they were taken from."

"I'm glad you believe it was better."

"Of course, it was better. I mean, those parents didn't deserve to have kids. It's one thing when a kid's old enough to take care of himself, but when he's just four or five, well that's—"

Billy felt his cheeks heat and turned toward the window.

"I know, Billy, but regardless of a child's age, a child shouldn't have to take care of himself. He's still a child."

Billy kept his back to her and nodded.

"I know what I did was a crime and I won't ask you to keep what I told you to yourself. If you choose to go to the police, I'll understand and I won't think any less of you. I've come to know you're a good boy and going to the police would be the right thing to do."

Billy whirled around.

"You think I'm going to tell the cops?"

"I know you've been curious since you started working here, curious about whether I was the monster most people believe me to be. Going to the police would be the normal response to what you've learned."

Billy snorted. "Well, I'm not going to do that. First, because I can't see voluntarily walking into the police station." He thought back to the Fourth of July incident and shook his head. "Second, because I don't think you did anything so wrong. What's the point in telling some cops who probably weren't even born when it happened? Seems stupid. Third, we talked about the statute of limitations at school and since it's been so long, they might not be able to arrest you anyway."

Mrs. Baxter smiled. "I don't know about the statute of limitations, but you think about it. I don't want you doing something, or not doing something, that makes you uncomfortable."

A knock on the porch door sounded before Billy could reply. Mrs. Baxter gave Billy a confused look.

"Was that the door?"

"Sounded like it. Want me to see who it is?"

"My door? At my house?"

Her hands started trembling like they did when she got upset. Billy knew she was slipping into one of her episodes.

"I'll go check. You stay here."

"The police don't know I'm here, do they? I don't want them to find me. Don't let them find me."

"I won't. You stay in the kitchen. It will be okay."

Billy left her clutching the back of the chair, her eyes wide and full of fear. He hated watching her slide into that place where she didn't seem to know where she was and where he couldn't reach her.

Corrine was at the door.

"Hello, Billy. I know I wasn't scheduled to stop by today, but Dr. Fuller was concerned about one of Mrs. Baxter's tests and wants me to check on her. I didn't call because I was afraid it would either confuse or upset her. How is she today?"

"She had a good morning, but when she heard the door, she got confused. She's in the kitchen."

"Oh, dear. It can be the littlest things."

Billy wanted to laugh. If Corrine only knew.

24

Billy's seventeenth birthday fell on a Saturday. A warm, but not hot, sunny Saturday in late October. Tiny, green wheat sprouts were poking through the fields where Skelly had planted a couple of weeks ago. According to Billy's dad, the perfect October weather meant the crop was off to an optimal start.

As he'd done every Saturday morning since school started, Billy biked to Mrs. Baxter's house to mow and to do whatever other chores she may need done. He could have driven, since he was the owner of a ten-year-old partly rusted Ford Falcon that he loved as much as if it were a shiny, new Corvette. Well, maybe not quite as much, but it was his, he'd bought it with some of the money Mrs. Baxter had paid him on his last day of work, and he loved the car he'd nicknamed Rosie after listening to Neil Diamond's *Cracklin' Rosie* over and over on one of the two eight-track cassettes he'd bought after he'd used a little more of that money to install an eight-track player in his car.

In less than two months since that last day, he'd noticed a steep decline in Mrs. Baxter. There were days she didn't recognize him when he knocked on the door and it took him a few minutes to explain who he was and why he was there. Even then, he wasn't always convinced she really knew. Other days, she was fine, and they had lengthy conversations if Billy didn't have to get to work at Thompson's.

He stopped by after school some days too, and he knew his dad stopped by sometimes on his way to or from work. Corrine was checking on Mrs. Baxter every day now, and had insisted Mrs. Baxter go back into the hospital for a few days in early October when her coughing seemed to get worse again, but the stay hadn't been as long as the one over the summer.

Billy hadn't told a soul what he'd learned about Mrs. Baxter, and he and Mrs. Baxter had never discussed it again. Billy was okay with that. He knew what he needed to know and if there were any other details she hadn't shared, he figured they were her business.

On the morning of his birthday, Mrs. Baxter greeted him with a smile and a chocolate birthday cake. He knew she hadn't been doing much cooking or baking the past few weeks and figured Corrine had played a part in having the cake ready for him, but seeing as it was the first birthday cake he'd had in five years, he wouldn't have cared if the school lunch ladies had baked it.

"Happy birthday, Billy."

"Gee, thanks, Mrs. Baxter. I love chocolate cake."

"You'll have a piece now. Any rules about cake in the morning go out the window on your birthday."

"I wouldn't say no."

Billy gobbled his while Mrs. Baxter picked at her tiny slice. Her appetite was nearly gone, and he knew some days Corrine had to force her to eat.

"I'm glad you stopped by, but I don't expect you to do any work here on your birthday. Go enjoy the day."

"I have the day off from Thompson's so I'll have plenty time to enjoy my birthday. The mowing won't take long. Shouldn't be too many more times to mow this year. Did you see the wheat's coming up?"

"Is it? That's good. That Mr. Skelly works hard."

"He does."

Billy scraped his plate clean and eyed the rest of the cake.

"You can have another piece now or take it home and eat it later. Your choice."

"I think now. Just a small one."

Billy winked and cut a thick slice. It was really good and the blue lettering that spelled out *Happy Birthday Billy* in squiggly lines made him smile. It was just like his mom used to do.

"How was that science test?"

Sometimes she remembered the smallest details, and sometimes she couldn't remember that she didn't have to go to work in the school office the next morning.

"Good. Think I got 'em all right."

"That's a good boy. Did you ever talk to Julie's sister about college?"

He had, and he'd told her about it a few times already, but he repeated the story as if telling it for the first time.

"I did. She told me she loves it, some of the classes are really hard but some aren't all that much harder than high school classes. She loves the dorm, except for the food, but she was ready to come home for the summer."

"And have you given more thought to what you'd like to study?"

That they hadn't discussed. Actually, Billy had never discussed that with anyone, being purposely vague if anyone ever asked. Today, he decided he'd bounce his ideas off someone.

"I like farming. I understand farming. But I don't want to farm. Since I've been a kid and my dad took me to the elevator with him, I've wondered about what happens with all that wheat once it's loaded onto the train cars. I mean, I know it goes to a mill and it's made into all kinds of stuff, but how? It has to be cleaned, and ground, and all sorts of things have to happen before it becomes flour for someone to use to bake a birthday cake. That's what I want to study. That's what I want to do. I want to take that wheat and turn it into food."

Mrs. Baxter's eyes were wide with wonder.

"My, isn't that an interesting plan? I think it's wonderful."

Regardless of whether she understood, Billy appreciated the vote of confidence. Maybe one day he'd have the nerve to tell someone else.

He ended up not mowing that morning. The grass didn't really need cutting, and Mrs. Baxter seemed to need the company, so he spent a few hours with her talking and sneaking peeks when he could to make sure things seemed in order around the house.

He was thinking about how he'd fix Mrs. Baxter's vacuum cleaner handle as his house came into view. His feet slowed on the pedals. There were cars in his driveway. Several cars.

His first feeling was one of panic. Something happened to his dad. Just when things started to get better, something had gone wrong. That didn't seem likely, though, because his dad's truck was there and for some reason, that gave Billy a sense of security.

His next thought was Tracy. Something happened, his aunt and uncle had come to tell them the horrible news, and his dad had called other people. Who, he didn't know, but that didn't ease his worry.

When he got close enough, he realized he recognized Steve's car, and John's car, and even Julie's car. For a moment, he let himself believe that maybe it wasn't bad news, maybe they were there because it was his birthday, but then he noticed a shiny, black Lincoln he knew belonged to his uncle, and his heart nearly stopped. It had to be bad. Really bad.

Every fiber of his being wanted to turn his bike around and pedal in the opposite direction, never turning back, until he finally collapsed in some far-away place. There'd been too much bad in his life. He couldn't take any more.

But he forced his bike to stay pointed toward home, and though he pedaled slowly, he kept pedaling.

No one was outside waiting for him with bad news. When he listened at the door, he didn't hear anyone crying. When he finally worked up the nerve to open the door, all he heard was,

'Surprise!'

Billy stood rooted to his spot. The only part of him capable of movement seemed to be his eyes. Steve was there, a Coke in his hand and a stupid grin on his face. John was there, looking a little bored, but Billy would know John's fake bored expression anywhere. Joel was there, wearing a stupid hat and blowing into a paper noisemaker. What a dope. And Julie was there, in a pair of jeans and a pink blouse, her blonde hair curling over her shoulders, her lips smiling, and painted pink to match her top.

His dad looked nervous. "Are you surprised, Billy? I know you had to have spotted the cars, we didn't have anywhere to hide them, but are you surprised everyone's here? Did I give it away?"

"No, I mean yes. I mean, no, you didn't give it away, and yes, I'm surprised."

He was. A birthday party? A surprise birthday party? It was a little dorky, but it warmed him all the way through.

"Thanks, Dad, this is really cool." He looked at his friends. "Thanks, you guys. Thanks for coming." He smiled at Julie who returned the smile, her eyes dancing.

Then he remembered. "But I saw Uncle Dan and Aunt Cindy's car—"

"Happy birthday, Billy."

The voice was soft, so unlike the shouts that had greeted him moments earlier. Tracy peeked out from behind the door to the kitchen. She was taller, a couple of inches, her hair was longer, her eyes a brighter blue, and she seemed a little hesitant. For only a moment, though, because the next thing Billy knew, she was launching herself at him. She wrapped her arms around his neck and held on. Just held on like she'd never let go.

"I missed you, Billy. I missed you so much."

Billy couldn't speak. He breathed in the apple scent of her shampoo, the trace of something that smelled like baby powder but he guessed was perfume, and he held her right back.

"I missed you too. I'm so glad you're here. You have no idea how glad I am that you're here."

"Tell me everything. We can talk all night because we get to sleep over. We'll have so much more time than we do on the phone. You can show me your car! Dad wouldn't let me go look because he was afraid you'd come home and see me before we could surprise you."

It seemed once she started talking, she couldn't stop. Billy stopped hearing the words, just listened to her voice, so happy, so carefree, and still like a little girl, though he spotted the signs she wouldn't be one for much longer.

"And I like your girlfriend."

Billy heard the teasing in her voice, but he didn't care. Tracy could tease him forever if it meant she'd stay, but he realized he had a houseful of people there because of him. He'd have to give them some time too.

He pulled away from Tracy, but kept her close by his side.

"Thanks Uncle Dan, Aunt Cindy. I appreciate you coming all this way."

"You're welcome, Billy," Aunt Cindy said. "It's not everyday you turn seventeen. I'm glad your father called us." Aunt Cindy wiped at a tear. "And, well, just look at you. You know, you have your mother's eyes."

Billy nodded, but didn't know what to say. His dad seemed to sense his discomfort.

"How about I fire up that grill? I've got burgers and hotdogs, chips, there's a cooler full of Coke and 7-Up, Julie brought some potato salad, and Cindy brought a cake that looks almost too pretty to eat."

It broke the ice, and conversations started around the room. Billy caught up with his dad as he was heading for the back yard.

"Thanks, Dad. I meant it when I said this is really cool."

"You're welcome, Billy. I reckon it's about time we do some fun stuff around here."

"Thanks for getting Tracy here."

"Wasn't sure your aunt and uncle would agree to makin' the drive, but they seemed pleased I asked." His dad scratched his head. "I've missed my little girl. It's mighty good to see her, isn't it?"

"It is. It's mighty good."

Billy had the best birthday he'd had since his mom died. His friends goofed off, played frisbee, told jokes, and surprised him with stupid presents. Steve gave him a can of shaving cream because Billy had mentioned the week before he expected he'd have to start shaving every day.

Billy'd been bluffing and Steve knew it.

John gave him a keychain in the shape of a four-leaf clover and told Billy he was going to need all the luck he could get when he and Rosie raced Terrence.

Billy had no intention of racing Terrence. In fact, Billy intended to avoid Terrence as much as possible. Since Terrence and Randy had gotten in trouble on the Fourth of July, and especially since Billy and Julie had started dating, Terrence practically growled every time he came within five yards of Billy. Instead of rubbing it all in Terrence's face, Billy found more satisfaction in simply ignoring Terrence as it seemed to bug Terrence to no end that Billy wouldn't rise to the bait. Laughing behind Terrence's back was more fun than getting pounded in the face.

Joel gave him a Donny Osmond record, because Joel was a dork.

It got a good laugh from everyone, but Billy noticed Tracy's eyes go round. She didn't laugh. *Puppy Love* would be going home with Tracy.

Julie found something to talk about with everyone there, a skill Billy knew he'd never master. The few times he'd tried to talk to her parents, he'd mumbled and stuttered like an idiot.

Late in the afternoon, after Billy had been assured Tracy got to spend the night, he ducked into his room. He'd give Tracy his bed, he'd sleep on the floor, and like Tracy said, they'd talk all night. Since he wasn't sure when he'd last changed his sheets, he was armed with a clean set. When he pulled the old ones off, his notebook fell out from between the mattresses. He glanced at it for a moment, admitting to himself that it had helped him and that maybe that doctor hadn't been such an idiot after all. He gave it a shove out of his way while he wrestled the clean sheets into place.

"Billy?"

He heard Julie call from the kitchen.

"Be right there!"

He scooped up the dirty sheets, dumped them in the hamper in the hallway, and found Julie in the kitchen holding a brightly wrapped box.

"I got you something. I didn't want to give it to you in front of everyone."

"You didn't have to do that," Billy stammered.

"I wanted to. Open it."

Billy was nervous. He'd never gotten a gift from a girl before. What if he didn't like it? He was smart enough to know he needed to act like he did, but what if it was something embarrassing and she expected him to use it, or wear it, or show it to other people? For one wild moment, he pictured a GI Joe doll, and he started to laugh before he caught himself and turned it into a cough.

It was a picture frame. He could see that when he tore off the paper, but he could only see the back. When he flipped it, he found a picture of himself and Julie.

"Remember, my dad took it before the Homecoming dance? Do you like it?"

Billy thought he looked kind of stupid dressed in brown pants, a yellow and brown striped shirt, and a brown tie. The guy at the store had assured him it was the most popular style, but looking at himself, Billy wasn't so sure. Julie, though, looked like an angel. She wore a light blue dress with puffy sleeves and a lacy collar. Some of her hair was pulled back, but the rest curled and bounced on her shoulders.

"I love it. Thank you."

"I know it's kind of silly, but it's the first picture of us. I have a copy in my room…"

"I'll put in on my dresser. Thank you."

Billy smiled and leaned over to kiss Julie lightly on the lips. She blushed and Billy thought it was about the cutest thing he'd ever seen.

He'd only kissed her a couple of times before and he didn't think he was very good at it, but she hadn't complained. He hoped he'd get to keep practicing.

Later, when Aunt Cindy brought out the cake, complete with seventeen candles and told Billy to make a wish and blow them out, he realized he had nothing to wish for because everything he wanted was right in front of him. Still, he puffed up his cheeks and extinguished the candles in one breath.

Billy was eating his third piece of cake that day when he heard Joel yell.

"Oh, sh—, crap! Ouch!"

Billy turned to see Joel jumping around and swatting his stomach.

"What are you yelling about?" Billy asked, but before Joel could respond, Billy had his answer. Joel held a birthday candle in one hand and the hem of what was left of his T-shirt in the other.

John was shaking his head. "He lit a candle and tried to stick it in his mouth to put it out. Must have been a little hotter than he expected, because he dropped it on his shirt."

"Geez, Joel," Billy said.

"Sorry. I saw a guy do that once. Didn't look that hard. Maybe he knew a trick."

"Yeah, maybe," Billy said.

"You okay, son?" Billy's dad asked.

"Yeah, fine. I don't suppose you have a shirt I could borrow, do you, Billy?"

Billy sighed. "In my dresser. Bottom drawer."

"Thanks, man."

Joel skipped away, leaving a sea of head shakes and eye rolls in his wake.

When ten minutes passed and Joel didn't return, Billy went to find him, figuring he'd forgotten what Billy had said and was rummaging around the room in search of a shirt.

What Billy found was a whole lot worse.

Joel sat on Billy's bed, Billy's notebook open on his lap, and Joel's face a shade of purple Billy didn't think he'd ever seen before. After staring at Joel for a moment, speechless, Billy figured his face probably looked the same.

"What do you think you're doing?"

Joel slapped the notebook shut. He had the look of someone caught red-handed, but not one of regret.

"A little reading."

"A little reading?" Billy's voice roared. "That's mine. You had no business snooping in there!"

"And you had no business keeping this from me!" Joel's voice matched Billy's.

"I had every right. It's my business."

Joel got to his feet, shaking his head. His eyes were wild. "No, it's not. It's everyone's business. She did it, Billy! She took those kids, you knew it, and you didn't tell me? You didn't tell anyone? What the hell? We had a deal. At the very least, I thought you were my friend."

"And I thought you were mine! What kind of friend digs through another guy's private stuff?"

"It was open, right there on the floor next to the dresser." Joel pointed. "Bottom drawer, you said. I had to crouch down. It was hard to miss."

The sheets, he'd kicked the notebook out of the way, Julie had called him. Damn. He'd left it lying there, open.

"Still. It's pretty obvious what it is. You didn't need to read it."

"I saw her name. What do you expect? I've been waiting all summer, all my life, for this and you kept it from me."

"This isn't about you! Don't you get that? She's old, she's sick, and she doesn't deserve whatever would happen to her."

"She doesn't deserve it?"

Joel's voice rose so high, Billy expected the mirror to crack.

"How much did you read?"

"Enough."

"How much? Do you know what happened? She didn't kill those kids, she helped them."

Since Billy's entries in his notebook were typically lists, maybe Joel hadn't figured out that part. Billy held onto some hope Joel would understand.

"Helped them? Kidnapping them was helping them? What did she do to you, Billy? She really is a witch."

"Oh, for God's sake, she's not a witch," Billy hissed at Joel. "She took those kids from horrible situations and gave them a chance. She very well could have saved their lives."

"Or, she could be a crazy old freak who thinks it's up to her to decide what happens to kids in Munroe. I read about you and Tracy."

Billy turned away. He was so angry, he felt ready to explode. He knew he could beat the crap out of Joel, but he also knew that wouldn't solve anything.

"You have to let it go, man. There's nothing to be gained by turning her in."

Joel's eyes were as round as dinner plates. "Let it go? Nothing to be gained? You've got to be kidding."

Billy hollered, "Damn it, Joel, your parents aren't going to like you any better if you turn an old lady over to the police!"

Joel's body went rigid. Billy watched the color drain from Joel's face until his friend was a sickly white. Billy braced himself for Joel to holler right back, but Joel threw the notebook on the bed, pushed his way past Billy, and disappeared down the hall.

"Joel, wait! I'm sorry. I didn't mean that."

Billy yanked the notebook from his bed and tucked it under the mattress, then ran after Joel, but the gravel was already spitting from behind the tires of Joel's car.

That night, Billy tried calling Joel, but Joel's mom said he wasn't feeling well and couldn't come to the phone. Billy wanted to go to Joel's house, to apologize and to try to convince him to forget about what he'd read, but Tracy was there and he couldn't disappoint his sister.

He and Tracy talked well into the night. For stretches, Billy managed to put the mess with Joel out of his mind but at the first lull in the conversation, it all came thundering back. Billy laughed at Tracy's stories of her teacher who had different sized bells to ring depending on how badly the class was behaving. And he worried Joel was at the police station right then. He plotted with Tracy on how to get their dad to go to Aunt Cindy and Uncle Dan's for Christmas. And he imagined the police knocking at Mrs. Baxter's door. He assured Tracy she could come visit him at college. And he pictured himself visiting Mrs. Baxter in jail.

Hours later, as the crickets quieted and night edged toward day, Tracy fell silent and he drifted into an uneasy sleep.

Tracy left after breakfast, Uncle Dan saying he wanted to beat the traffic. Billy wanted to ask, 'What traffic?' but didn't want to give his uncle any reason to get angry.

As soon as they drove away, Billy hopped on his bike and raced to Mrs. Baxter's house. Sometime during the night, he'd concluded he needed to warn her. Maybe she could go away before the police came looking for her, because he'd also concluded there was no way Joel would keep the information to himself.

Billy lifted his fist to pound on the door, to shout at her to hurry, but caught himself just in time. He didn't want to frighten her or it was likely he wouldn't be able to have a meaningful conversation with her. Instead, he knocked and waited. When two minutes passed and she hadn't opened the door, he pounded harder and called her name. After another two minutes, he ran for the key hidden in the garage.

The day last summer replayed in his head as he called and went through the living room, the kitchen, and up the stairs with no sign of Mrs. Baxter.

Like last summer, she was in her room, but unlike last summer, she was sprawled on the floor, her leg underneath her at an awkward angle. Billy rushed to her side.

"Mrs. Baxter? Can you hear me? Are you okay?"

She didn't respond. She was warm, not burning hot like last summer, but she didn't wake up when Billy gently shook her shoulder and tapped her cheek.

He felt sick. She could have been there for almost twenty-four hours. Hurt, alone, scared, and no one to hear her or to help her.

Maybe the police had come. Maybe they'd talked to her, scared her, and she'd been so upset, she'd fallen.

It was all Joel's fault.

Billy yanked a blanket from the bed, tossed it over her, then ran for the phone.

Ten days later, Billy was dressed in his brown pants, his brown and yellow shirt, and his brown tie. This time instead of dancing with Julie, he listened to a preacher read from the Bible and talk about Mrs. Baxter being free from her terrible pain.

How did he know what kind of pain she'd been in? He'd barely known her.

Billy had visited once in the hospital, but Mrs. Baxter had never opened her eyes, and the visit had been one of the hardest things he'd ever done. She was in a different room and on a different floor than her other stays, but Dolores had poked her head in the room when Billy had been there and had told Billy he should talk to Mrs. Baxter.

'We don't know for sure, but there's a good chance she can hear you even if she can't respond. Talk to her. It will do her good to hear a familiar voice.'

So even though he'd felt stupid at first, he'd talked to her. He told her about his birthday party and about his surprise visit from Tracy. He talked about school, told her the same story about college, and he told her he'd take care of everything at her house until she came home. Deep down, he knew she'd never be coming home, but he wasn't ready to admit it.

Mrs. Baxter died later that night.

There weren't many people at the funeral, just Billy and his dad and a couple of people who said they knew her from church, and that lawyer who'd been by over the summer.

Billy blinked hard against the tears that burned the backs of his eyes as the preacher finished his remarks. After a few words to Billy and his dad, the preacher wandered away, and it was just the two of them left standing by the grave. Men with shovels hovered near the tree line like ghouls outside a haunted house. Billy looked away.

"You can stay as long as you'd like, Billy. I'll be over by the truck."

"I'm ready to go."

When Billy and his dad began walking, the lawyer popped out of his car and caught up with them.

"Billy? Can I talk to you for a minute?"

Billy stopped and turned.

"You must be Mr. Tupper." The lawyer held out his hand. "Blaine Atterbury. Mrs. Baxter's lawyer."

Billy's dad shook the man's hand. "What is it you want to talk to my son about?"

"How old are you, Billy?"

Billy felt his dad tense, but answered before his dad could give the lawyer a dose of Tupper attitude. "Seventeen."

"Yes. Well then, seeing as you're a minor, I need to talk with the both of you."

"You ever gonna tell us what you want to talk about?"

The lawyer looked annoyed, but kept his voice level. "Of course. Billy, over the last several months, Mrs. Baxter made some changes to her will. As you know, she owned her house and a substantial amount of land. In addition, she had quite a number of investments. She's left it all to you, Billy. With a couple of stipulations."

Billy blinked. Then blinked again. He was certain he'd heard wrong, but when he looked at his dad, his dad wasn't doing anything but blinking either.

"Huh?" Billy heard Mrs. Baxter telling him it made him sound unintelligent when he uttered 'Huh?' so he corrected himself. "Pardon me?"

"With the exception of a few donations to charities, everything she had is yours with the understanding that you will attend college and graduate from college. You will receive money to pay for your schooling and for your expenses while you're in school, then upon graduation, the rest of her estate will be yours. I'd say you're a lucky young man, Billy Tupper. A lucky young man, indeed."

Billy didn't know how someone dying made someone else lucky and he kind of wanted to tell the stupid lawyer just that, but he held his tongue and took a deep breath.

"Thank you, Mr. Atterbury. Is there anything I need to do right now?"

"No. Mrs. Baxter wanted her house sold. During our conversations, she said she didn't think you'd want the house so that will be handled within the next few months. The land is to be offered for sale to a Bud Skelly. If he chooses to purchase it, it's his, otherwise the land will be put up for sale as well. An auction company will handle the sale of her personal belongings, but she wanted me to tell you you're free to go through the house and take whatever you want before that happens."

"This is a lot to take in, Mr. Atterbury," said Billy's dad as he rubbed his hand on the back of his neck. "Do you have a copy of that will or some other paperwork I can take a look at? I want to make sure you're not steerin' my son wrong."

"Of course. I don't have it with me, but I'll get you a copy by tomorrow. For now, like I said, there's nothing you need to do but go through her house if you so choose." The lawyer nodded. "Billy. Mr. Tupper. I'm sorry we're meeting under such difficult circumstances. You may find you have additional questions. Please don't hesitate to call me."

He handed Billy's dad a card, then turned and walked away. Both Billy and his dad stared after him until his car was out of sight.

"Well, I'll be," Billy's dad finally said. "Did you have any idea?"

"No. No idea. Is it okay, Dad? Is it okay for me to take all her money? It seems weird, or wrong, or something. She didn't know me for that long. Don't you think there's someone else she should have given it all to? Maybe she wasn't thinking clearly when she made those decisions."

Billy's dad rubbed his chin. "You know, sometimes things happen that we're not prepared for. Sometimes those things are good, sometimes those things are bad, and sometimes I think they can be a little of both. I reckon this is one of those times.

"I'm certain that lawyer fellow would have known if she wasn't up to makin' that sort of decision, so I'm just as certain that Mrs. Baxter wanted you to have what was hers. You were good to her, son, and she knew that. You helped her, she wanted to help you. Seems this is her way of doing that."

Mrs. Baxter's words came back, words she spoke when she'd told him she was responsible for Tracy leaving.

'I did want to help you. I still do. I will. It's all arranged.'

Was this what she'd meant? He figured it probably was.

An overwhelming sadness swamped him and left him lightheaded. "Okay, Dad, thanks."

Slowly, they headed for the truck.

"Do you think you'll want to go through her stuff? You don't have to if you don't want to. I'd imagine there's a lot there."

"There is, but I think I owe it to her to sort through things. I don't know that I'll take any—"

Billy stopped in his tracks. The car. The old car. It was his. As horrible as the past ten days had been, as horrible has it had been to stand in the cemetery and stare at a box holding Mrs. Baxter like he'd done five-and-a-half years ago, staring at a box holding his mother, as horrible as the whole situation with Joel had been, the tiniest of smiles tickled Billy's lips.

"What is it, Billy?"

"Dad, you have to come check out her barn. You're not going to believe it."

He didn't say more, just walked the rest of the way to the truck in silence, thinking.

Billy's dad had just put the truck in gear when there was a tap on Billy's window. Sucking in a sharp breath, Billy jumped and whipped his head around. He hated the cemetery. Sudden noises made him hate it more.

Joel stood outside the window. The two hadn't spoken since the birthday party. Billy considered, but then cranked the window open part way.

"Do you have a minute, Billy?"

"Ah…"

"Please? Just a minute?"

Billy looked at his dad. "Go ahead. I'll wait," his dad said.

"Or I can give you a ride home if you want," Joel said.

Billy looked from his dad, to Joel, and back again. His dad was taking time off work and Billy knew he needed to get back. Billy was taking the whole day off school, so he had time.

"Dad, I'll catch a ride with Joel. Thanks for being here today."

His dad reached across the seat and clamped his hand on Billy's shoulder. "I'll see you later, son." Then he nodded in Joel's direction. Once Billy climbed out, his dad put the truck in gear and inched away. Billy watched as the truck made a right instead of the left that would have taken his dad toward the road. Billy knew exactly where his dad was headed.

"How'd it go?" Joel asked.

"It was a funeral. It wasn't great."

"I suppose not."

Billy looked at Joel bouncing nervously from one foot to the other, and Billy realized there was no anger left inside him. "Listen, Joel, I'm sorry for what I said that night in my room, but you didn't need to go to the police. I wish you had talked to me first. Maybe we could have figured something out, maybe we could have...maybe Mrs. Baxter..." Billy's throat tightened and he had to look away.

"I didn't. Honest, Billy, I didn't go to the police. I've been trying to tell you that, but you haven't been in school much and when you have, well, we haven't been hanging out."

The doctors at the hospital told Billy Mrs. Baxter had fallen and broken her hip as well as hit her head. They'd talked about bleeding and swelling around her brain. They used a lot of words, said a lot of stuff, but mostly it boiled down to the fact that without some kind of miracle, Mrs. Baxter wasn't going to wake up. Billy had convinced himself the police had frightened her and she'd been so upset, she'd fallen. He'd seen a police car at her house a couple of times since. It only made sense they'd been looking for evidence.

Billy turned back to Joel, unsure whether to believe his friend. "You didn't?"

"No. I wanted to, but I knew you were right. Nothing good would come of it."

"Then why did I see cop cars at her house?"

"Because she died. They had to look around to make sure it was an accident, not that someone broke in and hurt her. Besides, my dad said the cops always make sure things are okay when they find out a person died and there's no one else living at a house."

Billy digested Joel's words. It made sense. Billy had been so angry, and so sad, that he'd refused to listen to any of the talk at school during the little time he'd been there. He'd also refused his dad's offers to talk about any of it until just a day or two ago.

"So you haven't told anyone? Not even John or Steve."

"No one."

For Joel to keep something that big to himself was almost too much to believe, but Joel looked sincere and Billy believed him.

"Well, thanks for that."

Joel nodded. "I won't tell anyone ever, I promise."

"I think that's for the best."

"But it's kind of cool knowing something that no one else, except you, knows."

"Yeah, Joel, it's kind of cool."

They walked toward Joel's car.

"Are we okay?" Joel asked after a minute. He sounded afraid to hear the answer.

"Yeah, we're okay."

Billy heard Joel exhale.

They got in Joel's car and started to drive.

"How come you're not at school?" Billy asked.

"Told my mom I had diarrhea. She can't take my temperature to check for that."

"Man, you are so weird."

Joel laughed. "Do you think you wanna hang out this weekend? I heard about this kid over by Pine City who found a gold coin. I betcha anything it's part of the Dalton Gang's treasure. We should go look for it. I've been doing some reading, and I think I've narrowed it down to just a few spots where they could've hidden it. John and Steve said they'd go. Will you? Just think, we could find a real buried treasure! How cool would that be?"

Billy leaned his head back and closed his eyes. "Sure, that'd be cool," he murmured.

Joel was quiet as they left the cemetery and headed toward Billy's house. When Joel turned into Billy's driveway he asked, "Hey, who was that guy talking to you and your dad after the funeral?"

They were okay, he and Joel, but there were a few things Billy wasn't ready to talk about.

"Just someone who knew Mrs. Baxter."

25

Ten Years Later

Billy held tight to one of Julie's hands. Her other hand rested on her swollen belly. It was warm for April and when Billy looked at Julie, he saw sweat beading on her forehead.

"Why don't you go wait in the shade. I'll only be a minute."

Julie stretched to her toes and kissed Billy on the cheek. "Take your time."

Billy watched his wife walk away. Waddle, she'd say, as these last few weeks before the baby was due had her convinced she looked like an overstuffed penguin, but to Billy, she'd never been more beautiful.

He turned back and stared at the letters and numbers etched in the granite headstone.

Alma Elizabeth Baxter
Loving Mother, Brave Friend
April 8, 1900 - October 22, 1972

Billy and his dad had ordered the headstone shortly after Mrs. Baxter's funeral. The cemetery had placed a small marker on her grave, but Billy felt it wasn't enough.

"Hi, Mrs. Baxter. It's Billy. Happy birthday." Billy took a deep, shaky breath. "The last time we talked it was my birthday. My seventeenth birthday, and I ate about a half a chocolate cake.

"Anyway, I...um, I've been meaning to stop by, to talk to you, but, well... I guess it took me a while to get here, didn't it? There are some things I've been wanting to tell you. Things about me, about how you helped me. I went to college, like we talked about, graduated with a degree in something called Grain Sciences, and have a really good job at a mill in Mission. I like it. It's what I thought I wanted to do back when I was trying to figure things out. You were the first person I ever told about that. Whether you knew it or not, you made me believe I could do it.

"My dad's doing well. He's still working at the elevator in Munroe, running things, and keeping the farmers in line. I'm proud of him. He said he was going to try to turn things around and he did. Oh, the Skellys bought your land, and Little Skelly bought your house. He and his dad run the farm together. Little Skelly got married and has four kids, so your house is full like you always wanted. You'd like how they're taking care of the house and the land. The house just got a fresh coat of yellow paint.

"Tracy will be finishing up school this spring. My little sister is going to be a nurse. I know she's smart enough, but sometimes it's hard not to still think of her as a little kid. She has a serious boyfriend, so I suppose one of these days I'm going to have to get used to that little kid getting married.

"Speaking of getting married, Julie and I got married. It was four years ago on a sweltering hot day in July. We drove away from the church in your old Cadillac. I've had offers from collectors over the years, but I can't let it go.

"In just a few weeks, Julie and I are going to have a baby. Some days, I still can't believe that. We've decided if we have a boy, we're going to name him Thomas William. We'll call him Tommy. If it's a girl, Elizabeth Dolores. Julie keeps asking me if I'm hoping for a boy or a girl. I don't have an answer for her. I don't think it matters. Julie will be an incredible mother. I hope I can be a good father."

Billy shook his head. So much had happened in ten years. So much had changed, but a few things hadn't changed at all. Billy stuck his hand in his pocket and slid his finger over the piece of paper pushed deep down inside.

"You helped me, Mrs. Baxter, more than you'll ever know, and in ways that had nothing to do with the money you left me. You helped make me who I am today. I know I'd never be married to Julie, I'd never have gone to college, I'd never have the sort of job I have now if it hadn't been for that summer working for you. You taught me so much more than how to paint a house and how to trim around a fence. You taught me how to be the kind of person I didn't know I wanted to be. So, thank you.

"I know there are four other people who'd thank you if they could, so I'm going to thank you for them too. Thank you for taking Timmy, and Thaddeus, and Jane, and Josiah out of horrible situations and giving them a chance. The mystery of what happened to those kids is still unsolved. It always will be, but I hope you'd like the fact that a donation is made every year in your name to an organization that helps find homes for children who are taken out of abusive situations."

Billy pulled the paper from his pocket, unfolded it, and stared at it for a moment.

"That summer I worked for you, I had this thing I'd do. It started years earlier, but I did a lot of it over that summer. I had a notebook and I'd write things in it; things about my day, things about how I was feeling, things I was angry about. Usually, I wrote those things in lists. It sounds weird, I know, but doing it helped me figure things out and helped me work through some really bad times. Those lists weren't always very nice; in fact, most of them were downright mean. I still make lists sometimes, but now they're more like lists of goals, and hopes, and dreams. I've kept the old notebooks, though, and once in a while I look at them. They help me remember where I came from and who helped me along the way. This morning, I made a list with the same heading as the first one I made after working for you that summer."

Billy placed the sheet of paper on the ground in front of the headstone.

"I guess I wanted you to have it because without you, I'm afraid the list I made this morning would have been very different."

Billy sucked in a deep breath through his nose, then blew it out slowly through pursed lips.

"Goodbye, Mrs. Baxter, and thank you. Thank you for everything."

Billy turned, swiped at the tear that threatened to slip down his cheek, and walked toward Julie who was standing next to the car and smiling at him.

Billy hugged her, tucked her in the car, then circled around to the driver's side and made his way out of the cemetery.

"What did you put on the ground?" Julie asked.

Billy put his hand over Julie's and squeezed. "Oh, nothing. Nothing important."

And he was right. Partly. Because on that sheet of paper titled 'People I Hate' was nothing.

But he was also wrong, because it was important.

It was very important.

If you enjoyed reading *I Know an Old Lady*, please help other readers find and enjoy it by leaving a review on Amazon or Goodreads or wherever you review books. Just a few words will do and will be very much appreciated.

Thank you!

Also by Margaret Standafer:
Misty Lake
The Inn at Misty Lake
Misty Lake in Focus
Anchored in Misty Lake
Sunset Over Misty Lake

Praise for the Misty Lake series:

"Wow. The Inn at Misty Lake was just amazing and I know I won't be able to say enough good things about it. The dialogue and progression of the story are flawless and made everything easy to imagine. The characters, including the dogs, are entertaining, funny, and realistic." - *Shanon Winings, Readers' Favorites*

"The writing was well-crafted and the dialogue had a natural flow to it...The description of this small Minnesota lake town was beautiful and charming, a town you'd want to live in. It was a sweet and thrilling read that kept me turning pages...The characters are an interesting and fun cast." - *Charlie Anderson, Girl of 1000 Wonders Blog*

"Margaret Standafer is quickly establishing herself in the "clean" romance genre with her captivating "Misty Lake" series. I enjoyed the Misty Lake setting, and the characters were well-developed. The prose was superb, and the story never bogged down. Five stars and a job well done." - *J.W. George, Amazon Reviewer*

"Anchored in Misty Lake is a well-written story that took me on a beautiful and heart-warming journey that left me begging for more time in Misty Lake.The characters are well-developed, the descriptions are vivid, the dialogue is on point and the setting is well-done. An absolute must-read!" - *Lorraine M.L.M.*

Margaret Standafer lives and writes in the Minneapolis area with the support of her amazing husband and children and in spite of the lack of support from her ever-demanding, but lovable, Golden Retriever. It is her sincere hope that you enjoy her work.

To learn more about Margaret and her books, please visit www.margaretstandafer.com

Made in the USA
Columbia, SC
16 April 2024

34474915R00202